MORE

THAN

WE

CAN

TELL

BOOKS BY BRIGID KEMMERER

Letters to the Lost
More Than We Can Tell
Call It What You Want

• • •

A Curse So Dark and Lonely

A CURSE SO DARK AND LONELY

A *New York Times* Bestseller
An Indie Next List Pick

"Has everything you'd want in a retelling of a classic fairy tale: a finely-drawn fantasy world, a heroine rarely seen in fiction, and a tortured hero with a secret." —Jodi Picoult, *New York Times* bestselling author of *A Spark of Light* and *Small Great Things*

"Absolutely spellbinding. . . . Full of fierce new characters, wicked magic, and wondrous amounts of heart." —Stephanie Garber, #1 *New York Times* bestselling author of *Caraval* and *Legendary*

"Heartwarming, thoughtful, and romantic." —Jodi Meadows, *New York Times* bestselling coauthor of *My Lady Jane* and *My Plain Jane*

"I couldn't get this creative, suspenseful take on 'Beauty and the Beast' out of my head." —Sara Holland, *New York Times* bestselling author of *Everless*

"Slow-burning, big-hearted, magical fun!" —Wendy Higgins, *New York Times* bestselling author

"Beautifully dark, filled with wild adventure." —Alexandra Christo, author of *To Kill a Kingdom*

★ "A fast-paced, richly detailed feminist epic." —*Kirkus Reviews*, starred review

★ "This enthralling modern fable champions altruism while illustrating intimacy's relationship with honesty, respect, trust, and consent." —*Publishers Weekly*, starred review

★ "A complex, creative, and compelling reimagining of *Beauty and the Beast*." —*School Library Connection*, starred review

★ "Fans of Cassandra Clare, Marissa Meyer, or Alex Flynn . . . will want to read this book." —*VOYA*, starred review

BRIGID KEMMERER

BLOOMSBURY

NEW YORK LONDON OXFORD NEW DELHI SYDNEY

BLOOMSBURY YA
Bloomsbury Publishing Inc., part of Bloomsbury Publishing Plc
1385 Broadway, New York, NY 10018

BLOOMSBURY and the Diana logo are trademarks of Bloomsbury Publishing Plc

First published in the United States of America in March 2018
by Bloomsbury Children's Books
Paperback edition published in June 2019
by Bloomsbury YA

Bloomsbury books may be purchased for business or promotional use. For information on bulk
purchases please contact Macmillan Corporate and Premium Sales Department at
specialmarkets@macmillan.com

ISBN 978-1-68119-991-7 (paperback)

The Library of Congress has cataloged the hardcover edition as follows:
Names: Kemmerer, Brigid, author.
Title: More than we can tell / by Brigid Kemmerer.
Description: New York : Bloomsbury, 2018.
Summary: When Rev Fletcher and Emma Blue meet, they both long to share
secrets, his of being abused by his birth father, hers of her parents'
failing marriage and an online troll who truly frightens her.
Identifiers: LCCN 2017025086 (print) • LCCN 2017039055 (e-book)
ISBN 978-1-68119-014-3 (hardcover) • ISBN 978-1-68119-015-0 (e-book)
Subjects: | CYAC: Secrets—Fiction. | Family problems—Fiction. | Online trolling—Fiction. |
Computer games—Fiction. | Role playing—Fiction. | Adoption—Fiction. |
Foster home care—Fiction. | Child abuse—Fiction.
Classification: LCC PZ7.K3052 Mor 2018 (print) | LCC PZ7.K3052 (e-book) |
DDC [Fic]—dc23
LC record available at https://lccn.loc.gov/2017025086

Book design by Colleen Andrews and Jeanette Levy
Typeset by Westchester Publishing Services
Printed and bound in the U.S.A. by Berryville Graphics Inc., Berryville, Virginia
2 4 6 8 10 9 7 5 3 1

All papers used by Bloomsbury Publishing Plc are natural, recyclable products
made from wood grown in well-managed forests. The manufacturing processes
conform to the environmental regulations of the country of origin.

To find out more about our authors and books visit www.bloomsbury.com
and sign up for our newsletters.

For my mother,
who raised me to be strong,
but also, and more importantly, who raised me to be kind

ONE

Emma

OtherLANDS Player Dashboard
USER NAME: Emma Blue (PRIVATE)
USER LEVEL: Admin/Developer
PLAYER NAME: Azure M
NEW MESSAGE
Thursday, March 15   5:26 p.m.
From: N1ghtmare
To: Azure M

You suck.

And that's what I'm going to say when I find you and shove it in your mouth hole.

Gross. At least this guy didn't include a dick pic.

My finger hovers over the Ban Player button.

I should do it. I know I should.

Nightmare is pissed because I booted him from a team for harassing another player. It was right at the end of the mission, and me booting him meant he lost any XP he'd earned. Two hours of gaming, down the drain.

But OtherLANDS doesn't have the biggest fan base. Maybe two hundred players on a good day. I only created the game as part of a school project. I uploaded a link on the county school's 5Core forum because I needed a few players to test it. I never thought anyone would actually *play*.

But they did. And now . . . I *do* have players. I've created a community. And one idiot trolling me on 5Core could be enough to chase the rest of them away.

I can see his post now.

Azure M got mad about a little trash talk and she banned me. This is why girls are ruining gaming.

Because trust me, it's a *him*. Find me a female who'd say "shove it in your mouth hole."

I sigh and delete his message.

Then I click over to iMessage and send a text to Cait Cameron.

Emma: Some guy just sent me a message that he's going to "shove it in my mouth hole."
Cait: Mouth hole? Isn't that kind of redundant?

Emma: Right?

Cait: Some days I'm so glad that the worst I get are people telling me I'm ugly.

Cait does makeup tutorials on YouTube.

She's not ugly. Not even close.

But her makeup gets a little out there. She's into cosplay and character re-creations, and my geekery doesn't extend quite that far. Her real talent lies in the designs she creates herself. The other day she showed up at school with tiny glittered mermaid scales across her cheeks. Once she made her face look like she was unzipping her skin, but a teacher made her wash it off.

I'm not big on makeup, but I let her do mine last month after she begged and pleaded and told me she'd thought of something perfect. She put this translucent circuitry along my temples and down my jaw, very faint, then lined my eyes with dark liner and silver shadow. I thought it looked pretty cool—until the douchebags at school started asking me if I was programmed for pleasure.

I washed it off in the bathroom midway through first period. Cait hasn't mentioned it. I haven't either.

I send another message.

Emma: I'm about to get online. Want to play?

Cait: I can't. I just set up to try a new winged eyeliner look on my mom.

Ugh. Of course she is.

The instant I have the thought I feel like a real bitch. Cait and I used to be connected at the hip, but somewhere around the beginning of the school year, we began to drift apart. I don't know if it's the gaming or the makeup or what, but more and more, it seems like one of us is always doing something *else*.

I wish I knew how to fix it. But if the solution is fish scales and translucent circuitry, it's not happening.

I sigh and switch back to OtherLANDS and log in as a player instead of an admin.

Immediately, I get a team request from Ethan_717.

I smile and slide my gaming headset over my ears. Maybe the afternoon isn't going to be *total* crap.

I have no idea who Ethan is in real life. He's in high school, because his 5Core profile says he goes to Old Mill, but that doesn't exactly thin the crowd. Ethan could be a fake name, but Ethan_717 isn't really a "character" name, so it might be real. In-game, he's built like a warrior, clad in black armor and a red cape. A mask covers the lower half of his face, and he carries two electrified swords. Blue electricity sizzles along the steel when he draws them in battle—some of my best design work.

He barely knows anything about me, though he's one of the few people I've told that I created OtherLANDS. To everyone else in-game and on 5Core, I'm just Azure M, another random gamer. And no one on here can connect Azure M to Emma Blue.

Once we're teamed together, we can speak through the headsets.

"Hey, M," Ethan says. His avatar waves.

"Hey, E." I smile wider. He's got a nice voice. A little lower than you'd expect, with the tiniest rasp. It's kind of sexy.

Okay, yes, I might have a little crush on Ethan. Animated bluebirds aren't circling my head or anything, but still.

Which is ridiculous. Old Mill is forty-five minutes away from here. I have no idea what he really looks like. He could be a freshman, for god's sake.

"I was going to grab a few more people," he says. "Feel like running a mission?"

This is the other thing keeping the animated birds at bay: though he's funny and friendly, he only ever talks about the game.

Sigh.

"Sure," I say.

"I've been meaning to tell you; you've got a gap in the graphics in the elven woodlands. I'll send you a screenshot on Five-Core when we're done so you can fix it."

"Sweet. Thanks."

Like I said. Only gaming. Only tech.

Which is okay. I suppose I should be grateful that Ethan hasn't asked for my bra size.

After a moment, another player name appears in the team list. GundarWez. His avatar joins the team on the screen. He's huge and dressed entirely in black—which is a complete waste of all the customizations I spent so much time building in. I've never played with him before.

"Hi, Gundar," I say into my mic.

"Hey," says Ethan.

"Hi, Azure. Hi, Ethan."

I stifle a giggle. After the huge avatar, I expected a deep voice. Gundar sounds like he's nine.

Another player joins. The name appears on the team list, and the smile drops off my face.

N1ghtmare. Mr. Mouth Hole himself.

His avatar is female, because of course it is. Breasts as large as my coding will allow—which thankfully isn't too obscene. Tiny waist. Wide hips. He's customized the costume and skin color to be uniformly beige, so his avatar looks naked. It makes me want to remove the color from my coding.

I'm frozen in a mental space somewhere between disgust and irritation. This feels purposeful, but I can't figure out how. He wouldn't have known I was on the team until Ethan added him.

Maybe this will be okay. I know a lot of people will say things in a private message that they won't say over a microphone.

"Sorry," he says, and his voice is rough and gravelly. For half a second, I think he's actually *apologizing*, but then he says, "I thought this was a real team."

"It is," says Ethan. "We've got four. Want to run the mission through—"

"No. Not until you boot the bitch."

Apparently, some people will say things over a microphone that should never be said out loud. Disgust shifts into anger—and humiliation.

"Go ahead." My voice is even, though my heart gallops in my chest. "Boot yourself, Nightmare."

"No way. I'm here to play. I just don't want to play with some chick on the rag."

"Well, I don't want to play with a douchebag," I snap.

"Guys," says Ethan. He sighs. "There's a kid on this team."

"I'm not a kid!" says Gundar.

I wince. I forgot about him.

"Dude," says Nightmare. "Would you boot her? She can't game. She's going to drag the whole mission down."

"Dude," says Ethan, his tone full of dry mockery, "she built the game."

I wince. I try not to tell anyone that.

"Is that why it sucks so hard?"

"What is your problem?" I demand.

"You're my problem," says Nightmare. "Stupid whiny bitches who think they know how to game because they took a few coding classes, but really, they just *suck*. Now shut your mouth hole or I'll keep my promise to shove something in there—"

I slam my laptop shut. I yank the headset off. My heart pounds away. My eyes are suddenly hot.

It's nothing new. I shouldn't be upset.

I'm good at this. I built this game. I know what I'm doing.

You've got a gap in the graphics in the elven woodlands.

Okay, so it's not perfect. But I can *fix* it. What does that Nightmare guy have? A chip on his shoulder? An exhausted right hand?

Ugh. I can't believe I just thought that.

Nails scratch at my bedroom door. Before I can get up to

open it, Texas, my yellow Lab, shoves the door open with her muzzle. She's full of wags and a snuffling nose that keeps pressing at my hands.

It sounds adorable, but really this is her way of telling me she needs a walk.

Good. I need a distraction. I lock the computer, shove my phone in my pocket, and hurry down the stairs.

All the lights are on, but no one is around. Texas hops up and down on her front paws, looking eagerly at the back door.

I grab her collar and peer out into the darkness. Mom stands on the patio, a glass of wine in her hand. She's wearing dark jeans and a trim jacket, and her hair is in a ponytail bun. No makeup. She thinks it's a waste of time. She's a pediatric cardiologist, so you'd think she'd be oozing with empathy and compassion, but maybe she uses it all up at work. Around here, she's buttoned up and critical.

Compared to her, Dad looks like a stoner. He hasn't shaved in days, and he's wearing a zip-up sweatshirt and jeans. He's sprawled in one of the Adirondack chairs, a laptop balanced on his knees. A bottle of beer sits open on the pavement beside him.

Light from the fire pit reflects off both of them. I can't hear what they're saying, but considering their irritated expressions, I would bet money that Mom is lecturing him about *something*.

I catch the tail end of a sentence. ". . . don't like the influence it has on Emma."

Gaming. She's whining about gaming. As usual.

She spots me, and her face shifts to exasperation. "This is a private conversation," she calls.

These are the first words my mother has spoken to me all day. I slide the door open a few inches. "The dog needs a walk."

"Take her, then." As if I wasn't about to do that. She takes a sip of wine. "You need to get out of your room once in a while. Spend some time in the real world."

That's a dig at my father. He spends his life attached to a computer, living in otherworldly realms. He's a game designer.

Apple, tree. Yeah, yeah, I get it.

You can imagine how much this pleases my doctor mother, who I'm sure envisioned me running Johns Hopkins by the time I turn twenty-five. She'd have no problem if I were holed up in my room with a biology textbook.

Dad sighs and runs a hand down his face. "Leave her alone, Catharine."

"I would appreciate it if you would back me up on this, Tom." A lethal pause. "Unless you're too busy with your game."

I slide the door closed. I don't need to hear the rest of this argument. I could practically write the dialogue.

No one in this house would ever say "mouth hole," but the vitriol is the same.

With a sigh, I grab the dog's leash and turn for the front hall.

TWO

Rev

Happy birthday, son.

I hope you'll make me proud.

Robert.Ellis@speedmail.com

The note was in the mailbox. The envelope is addressed to me.

Not to me *now*. He'd never call me Rev Fletcher. He might not even know that's my name.

It's addressed to who I was ten years ago. There's no return address, but the postmark reads *Annapolis*.

I can't breathe. I feel exposed, like a sniper rifle is trained on me. I'm waiting for a bullet to hit me in the back of the head.

Ridiculous. I'm standing on the sidewalk in the middle of suburbia. It's March. A chill hangs in the air, the sun setting in the distance. Two elementary-school-age girls are riding bikes in the street, singing a song and laughing.

My father doesn't need a bullet. This letter is enough.

He didn't need a bullet ten years ago, either.

Sometimes I wish he'd had a gun. A bullet would have been quick.

He knows my address. Is he here? Could he be here? The streetlights blink to life, and I sweep my eyes over the street again.

No one is here. Just me and those girls, who are riding lazy figure eights now.

When I was first taken away from my father, I couldn't sleep for months. I would lie in bed and wait for him to snatch me out of the darkness. For him to shake me or hit me or burn me and blame me. When I could sleep, I'd dream of it happening.

I feel like I'm having a nightmare right now. Or a panic attack. The rest of the mail is a crumpled mess in my hands.

I need this letter gone.

Before I know it, I'm in the backyard. Flame eats up a small pile of sticks and leaves in one of Mom's Pyrex bowls. Smoke curls into the air, carrying a rich, sweet smell that reminds me of fall. I hold the envelope over the bowl, and the tongue of fire stretches for it.

The paper feels like it's been folded and unfolded a hundred times, in thirds and then in half. The creases are so worn the paper might fall apart if I'm not careful. Like he wrote it ages ago, but he waited until now to mail it.

Happy birthday, Son.

I turned eighteen three weeks ago.

There's a familiar scent to the paper, some whiff of cologne or aftershave that pokes at old memories and buries a knife of tension right between my shoulder blades.

I hope you'll make me proud.

The words are familiar, too, like ten years doesn't separate me from the last time I heard him speak them out loud.

I want to thrust my entire hand into this bowl of fire.

Then I think of what my father used to do to me, and I realize thrusting my hand into a bowl of fire probably *would* make him proud.

My brain keeps flashing the e-mail address, like a malfunctioning neon sign.

Robert.Ellis@speedmail.com

Robert.

Ellis.

Robert Ellis.

The flame grabs hold. The paper begins to vanish and flake away.

A choked sound escapes my throat.

The paper is on the ground before I realize I've thrown it, and my foot stomps out the flame. Only the corner burned. The rest is intact.

I shove back the hood of my sweatshirt and run my hands through my hair. The strands catch and tangle on my shaking fingers. My chest aches. I'm breathing like I've run a mile.

I hope you'll make me proud.

I hate that there's a part of me that wants to. Needs to. I

haven't seen him in ten years, and one little note has me craving his approval.

"Rev?"

My heart nearly explodes. Luckily, I have razor-keen reflexes. I upend the bowl with one foot, stepping square over the letter with the other.

"What?"

The word comes out more of a warning than a question. I sound possessed.

Geoff Fletcher, my dad—not my father—stands at the back door, peering out at me. "What are you doing?"

"School project." I'm lying, obviously. I've been forced into a lie by one little letter.

He surveys me with obvious concern and steps out onto the porch. "Are you okay?"

"Yeah. Fine."

I don't sound fine, and he's not an idiot. He comes to the edge of the porch and looks down at me. He's wearing a salmon-pink polo shirt and crisply pressed khakis—his teaching clothes. He turned fifty last year, but you wouldn't know it to look at him. He stays in shape, and he's well over six feet. When I was seven, when a social worker first brought me here, I found him terrifying.

"Hey." His dark eyes are full of concern now. "What's going on?"

My thoughts are a tangled mess.

I should step off the letter, pick it up, and hand it to him. He could make it go away.

I think about my father. *I hope you'll make me proud.*

I'm almost shaking from the inner conflict. I don't want Geoff to know about it.

Geoff. Not *Dad.* My father already has a hold on me, and I've had this letter in my possession for fifteen minutes. Now that I've lied, I have to keep lying.

I do not like this feeling.

I can't look at Geoff. "I said I'm fine."

"You don't look fine."

"I'm fine." My voice is rough, almost a growl. "Okay?"

"Did something happen?"

"No." My fingernails dig into my palms, and my heart races like it needs to outrun something.

"Rev—"

I finally snap my head up. "Would you just *leave it*?"

He waits a beat, and my anger hangs in the air between us for the longest moment. "Why don't you come inside and talk to me?" His voice is low and mellow. Geoff is the master of chill. It makes him a good foster parent. It makes him a good dad. "It's getting late. I was going to start dinner so we can eat when Mom gets home."

"I'm going to Declan's."

I expect him to tell me no. I don't realize how badly I *want* him to tell me no until he says, "All right."

It's not a rejection, but somehow it feels like one. All of a sudden I want to beg for forgiveness. For the lying, for the anger, for doing something that protects my father.

But I can't. I pull up my hood and let hair fall across my face. My voice is penitent. "I'll clean this up first."

He's silent for a long moment, and I fish the bowl off the ground, scooping the burned pieces into it, keeping my foot over the letter. My movements are tight and jerky. I still can't look at him.

"Thanks," he says. "Not too late, okay?"

"Yeah." I fidget with the bowl and keep my eyes on the edge of it. A breeze teases at the hood of my sweatshirt, but it keeps me hidden. "I'm sorry."

He doesn't answer, and a nervous tension settles across my shoulders. I chance a glance up. He's not on the porch.

Then I hear the sliding glass door. He didn't even hear me. He's gone back inside, leaving me out here with the mess.

• • •

My best friend isn't home.

I've been waiting in the shadows like a criminal, sitting on the blacktop at the back corner of Declan's driveway. The chill in the air wasn't bad before, but it's soaked into my bones now, freezing me in place.

Light shines through his kitchen windows, and I can see his mother and stepfather moving around inside. They'd invite me in if they knew I was out here, but my brain is too heavy with panic and indecision. I fish out my phone to send him a text.

Rev: Are you working?
Dec: No. Movies with J. What's up?

"J" is Juliet, his girlfriend. I stare at my phone and focus on breathing. I hadn't realized how much I was counting on Declan being here until he *wasn't*.

I uncurl from the shadows and start walking. I can't go home, but I can't stay here unless I want to freeze to death. I should go to the gym, but they teach beginners on Thursdays, and if I rolled with someone tonight, they might not walk away from it.

I must be silent too long, because Declan sends another message.

Dec: Are you OK?

My fingers hesitate over the face of the phone. I'd been ready to tell him about the letter, but now . . . it doesn't feel right.

I force my fingers to work.

Rev: All OK. Have fun. Hi to J.

My phone rings almost immediately. It's him.

"What's going on?" he says in a rushed whisper. I wonder if he's actually calling me from inside the movie theater.

"It's nothing. I'm fine." My voice is rough and low.

He's quiet for a long moment. Declan knows every secret I have. It's not like me to be reticent.

"Do you need me to come home?" he says quietly.

His tone reminds me of Geoff. Like I need to be handled. Maybe I do, but I don't like the reminder.

I force my voice to be easy. I get halfway there. "Yeah, will you pick me up a pint of chocolate ice cream, too? Dude. No. You're at a movie."

"Rev."

"It's nothing, Dec."

"Something happened."

"Nothing happened. I'll talk to you later, okay?" I push the button to end the call.

Something is definitely wrong with me.

My cell phone buzzes almost immediately.

Dec: What is up with you?

My father sent me a letter and I don't know what to do.

I can't write that. Even thinking it feels weak and immature. I have a purple belt in Brazilian jiu-jitsu, but I can't deal with three lines of chicken-scratch on a piece of paper that showed up in the mailbox.

Rev: It's nothing. I'm fine. Sorry to bother you.

He doesn't write back. Maybe he's pissed. Or maybe I am.

Good. I don't even know why that makes me happy.

I lift my phone again. I start a new e-mail. Add my father's e-mail address.

I type *Leave me alone* in the subject line.

I don't type a message.

I just press Send.

And then I walk, letting the darkness swallow me up.

THREE

Emma

The night air is crisp, just a hair too cold to be perfect. If we're lucky, spring is around the corner. Texas trots along beside me, tail gently wagging. We've been walking forever. I should be enjoying the peace and quiet and fresh air, but instead, I'm replaying the interaction with Nightmare.

I'll keep my promise to shove something in there.

She can't game.

You suck.

My eyes grow hot again, and I'm not ready for it. I give a hitching breath before I get it together.

My phone chimes with an e-mail. I loop the leash around one wrist and fish my phone out of my pocket.

It's a message via 5Core. From Ethan.

Thursday, March 15   6:46 p.m.

From: Ethan_717

To: Azure M

Hey, here's the screenshot I promised.
   Also, that guy was an ass. I booted him. I'm really sorry.
Message me if you get back on.

The message chases away my tears. I smile.

I pull up the screenshot Ethan sent.

At first it takes a moment to see what I'm looking at, but when I figure it out, I giggle. His burly hero character is bisected by the slope of a mountain, and one sword-heavy arm is lifted in the generic /wave/ command. In the image, he looks like he's waving for help.

I've come to the corner by St. Patrick's Catholic Church, and there's a huge open stretch of grass in front of the parking lot. When I was a kid, we used to come to Mass here as a family, until one day Mom and Dad stopped bothering. It seems like an extra kick in the teeth that we let the dog crap on their lawn. I bring bags. Does that count?

The street is a well of silence, so I stop under the streetlight to let Texas off the leash to do her thing. While I'm waiting, I tap out a reply.

Emma: Thx. I'll fix it when I get back from walking the dog.
Around 9?

He must be online now, because his message comes back almost instantly.

Ethan: 9 is good. No d-bags this time.

I smile at the face of the phone. "Come on, Tex. We've got a date."

Texas doesn't come.

I lift my head. The field is empty.

I look around. The street is empty. A faint light glows from inside the church.

A breeze rushes through the trees, sliding under my jacket to make me shiver. The air smells like rain might not be far off.

I listen for Texy's dog tags to jingle. Nothing.

"Tex!" I call. "Texy! Come!"

How could I lose a nine-year-old dog in less than thirty seconds?

Get away from that technology.

Mom is going to kill me.

Then I hear it, the faint jingle of dog tags in the distance. She must have gone around the corner of the building. I break into a jog and spot her down by the back of the church, under the stained glass windows. It's nearly pitch-black out here, but she looks like she's eating something.

OMG. If she's found a dead animal, I am going to throw up.

"Texas!" I shout, sprinting in the darkness. "Tex. Get away from that!"

"She's okay," says a male voice. "I gave it to her."

I give a short scream and skid in the grass, coming down hard.

"I'm sorry," the guy says, and his voice is quiet. Now I see him, a dark huddled shape beside the church wall. He's wearing dark jeans and a hoodie, and the hood is large enough to put his entire face in darkness. I feel like I'm talking to a Sith lord.

"I'm sorry," he says again. "I didn't mean to scare you. I thought you saw me."

I scramble and somehow manage to find my feet. My phone went somewhere in the grass, and I have nothing with which to defend myself.

I can't believe I'm worried about my *phone*.

"Who are you?" I demand breathlessly. "What are you doing to my dog?"

"Nothing! They're chicken nuggets."

To the guy's credit, Texy looks thrilled. Her tail is wagging, and she looks up at me, chomping happily.

My pulse isn't ready to take him at his word. "So you're just randomly sitting beside a church eating chicken nuggets?"

"Yes. Well, the random sitting. Your dog is eating." His voice is dry and quiet. He hasn't moved.

I swallow my heartbeat. "Those aren't laced with rat poison or something, are they?"

"Of course not." He sounds offended.

"What are you doing here?"

"I like it here."

"A good place to bury a body?"

"What?"

"Nothing."

Texas finishes her nuggets and goes to him, nosing at his empty hands. Traitor dog. He rubs her behind her ears and she flops down next to him. Something is familiar about him, but I can't quite put my finger on it.

I lean in a bit. "Do I . . . do I know you?"

"I don't think so." The way he says it is almost self-deprecating. "But maybe. Do you go to Hamilton?"

"Yeah. You?"

"I'm a senior."

He's a year ahead of me. I study his shadowed form.

And then I have it. I don't know what his name is, but I know who *he* is. The hoodie should have been an immediate giveaway, because he's always wearing them. I've heard kids call him the Grim Reaper, but I'm not sure if he knows that. He doesn't have a dangerous reputation, just one of freakish interest. I don't really *know* him, but I'm *aware* of him, the way outcasts are always aware of each other.

I completely realign my immediate fear and start to think of other reasons a teenager might be sitting in the darkness.

"Are you okay?" I say.

He shakes his head. "No."

IIe says the word so simply, without much emotion, that it takes me a moment to process that he said *no*. His hands are buried in Texy's fur, and she's leaning into him.

I glance at my phone lying in the grass. "Do you want me to call someone?"

"I don't think so."

I sit down in the grass. It's cold and almost damp. "Did something happen to you?" I ask quietly.

He hesitates. "That's kind of a loaded question."

It is? "Are you sure you don't want me to call someone?"

"I'm sure."

We sit there in silence for a while. Texy rests her head in his lap, her neck under his arm. His hand remains buried in her fur, until she begins to look like a life preserver, and he's clinging for dear life.

Eventually, he looks up at me. I'm not sure how I can tell—the hood only moves a few inches. "Do you believe in God?"

My night could seriously not be more surreal. I wet my lips and answer honestly. "I don't know."

He doesn't challenge me, which I was worried about. "There's this verse I like," he says. " 'The one who doubts is like a wave of the sea, blown and tossed by the wind.' "

My eyes narrow. "Are you quoting the Bible?"

"Yes." He says this like it's the most normal thing in the world. "You know what I like about it? I like how it makes doubt seem inevitable. It's okay to be unsure."

I blink and let that sink in. This should be off-putting, but somehow it's not. It feels like he's sharing a piece of himself.

I wish I knew his name.

"I like that, too," I say.

He says nothing for the longest moment, but I can feel him evaluating me. I stare back at him—well, at where I think his eyes are. I've got nothing to hide.

"Did you figure out how you know me?" he says.

"I've seen you around school."

"Do you know anything about me?"

The question feels heavier than it should be, which tells me there's a lot more to his story than the fact that he wears hoodies. "So far, all I know is that you like to sit beside churches and quote the Bible," I say. "And I've learned that in the last two minutes."

He gives a soft laugh that carries no humor.

"Why did you ask if I believe in God?" I ask.

He grimaces and looks away. "I forget how much of a freak I sound like when I say things like that."

"You don't sound like a freak."

He reaches into a pocket and pulls out a folded piece of paper. "I got this letter in the mail, and I was sitting here trying to figure out what to do."

He doesn't extend the letter toward me, and I wait for him to say more. When he doesn't, I say, "Do you want to share?"

He hesitates, then holds it out. I unfold the creased paper, and dark flakes drift off into the grass. I read the three short lines and try to figure out why they're upsetting.

I glance back at him. "Someone sent you a burned letter?"

"I did that. The burning."

I wet my lips. "Why?"

"Because that letter is from my father." A pause. "I haven't seen him in ten years." Another pause, a heavier one. "For reasons."

"Reasons," I echo. I study him, trying to identify the emotion

I hear in his voice. Trying to figure out what would inspire someone to burn a letter after not seeing someone for ten years. At first I thought it might be anger, because there's a thread of that in his voice, but it's not.

When I figure it out, I'm surprised. "You're afraid," I whisper.

He flinches—but doesn't correct me. The fingers brushing through Texy's fur are tight, almost white-knuckled.

I consider my hypercritical mother, my laid-back father. We've argued, but I've never been *afraid* of them.

For reasons.

Abruptly, he unfolds from the ground. He's bigger than I expected, tall and lean with broad shoulders. He moves like a ninja, all silent, fluid motion.

Looking at him now, I can't imagine him being afraid of anything.

But then he says, "I need to go home."

He sounds a little spooked, so I'm surprised when he puts out a hand to help me up. He's strong. His grip makes me feel weightless.

Once I'm on my feet, he doesn't move. Light from somewhere catches his eyes and makes them glint under the hood. "Thank you."

"For what?"

"For seeing me." Then he turns, jogs across the street, and disappears into the darkness beyond.

FOUR

Rev

Thursday, March 15   7:02:08 p.m.

FROM: Robert Ellis <robert.ellis@speedmail.com>

TO: Rev Fletcher <rev.fletcher@freemail.com>

SUBJECT: RE: Leave me alone

Where did you come up with "Rev Fletcher"?

Regardless, I'm glad to hear from you. If you wanted me to leave you alone, you wouldn't have sent me an e-mail at all.

He's right, of course.

You're afraid.

She's right, too. This e-mail seems to double down on the fear.

I can't believe I showed her the letter. I'm halfway home

before I realize I never asked her name. She goes to Hamilton, but I don't even know what grade she's in.

Not like it matters. I've long since abandoned any hope of a relationship with a girl.

I keep thinking of her eyes. The way she saw right through the anger and uncertainty and pinned me down with two words.

You're afraid.

And then I proved it by running.

I am such an idiot.

My phone chimes with a text. It's Kristin.

I wince. It's *Mom*.

I expect her to be checking up on me, because I'm sure Dad told her I was playing the role of petulant teenager after school. To my surprise, she's not. Well, not really.

Mom: Are you coming home soon? We've got an
emergency placement. I'm getting things ready now.

I stop in the middle of the street.

An emergency placement means a kid needs immediate foster care. Geoff and Kristin are certified for special needs infants and toddlers, so we get a lot of those. Some kids stay for short periods of time—maybe the parents were in a car crash, or there was a medical emergency, and it takes time to work out the legalities of who should take custody. Some kids stay longer—like if the mother has been arrested or is in rehab. The last baby we had stayed for nine months. The spare room has been vacant for less than a week—but it never stays empty long.

Normally, I'd rush home to help.

Tonight, my twisted emotions are in the way. I keep worrying about my father, wondering when something is going to snap inside me. Wondering when I'm going to turn vicious and cruel, just like he did.

I want to text Declan to see if I can crash there, but our last text exchange sits on the screen, making my insides twist. I can't explain myself without talking about my father. I'm not ready for that. He wouldn't mean any harm, but it's his personality. Declan ignites. I extinguish.

I'm probably not being fair to him. Everything seems upside down.

Maybe I'm overreacting. I can go home. I can sit on the couch and make faces at a baby.

I can forget about my father for a little bit.

Once we got an infant who was four days old—the youngest baby I've ever held. Her mother had a seizure during childbirth, and died a day later. We kept the baby for six months while the grandparents battled in court over who would get custody. We saw her first smile, fed her the first spoonful of baby food.

Kristin cried for days after she was taken away.

She always cries after they're taken away. Even when it's only twenty-four hours.

Then she wraps her arms around my shoulders and says they're so lucky they get to keep me forever.

That's never made me uncomfortable until this very moment, when I realize what a monumental secret I'm keeping from them.

My father's letter burns a red-hot brand into my brain.

I hope you'll make me proud.

I can't tell them.

A police car sits in front of my house when I turn the corner. That's not uncommon, especially with an emergency placement. I come through the front door, expecting to hear a baby or toddler crying, but the house is oddly quiet. Maybe it's a really little baby, asleep in a carrier.

Low voices speak down the hall, by Geoff and Kristin's bedroom. I begin to climb the stairs.

Geoff appears from the hallway. "Rev," he says quietly. "Come downstairs. Let's talk."

I hesitate, and our confrontation over the Pyrex bowl flashes to the forefront of my mind. My father's letter is hot in my pocket. "I don't—I'm sorry I yelled."

"It's all right." He comes down the steps and claps me on the shoulder gently. "You're allowed to be a teenager. Are you okay?"

No. "Yes."

"Come on downstairs. I need to talk to you."

He heads into the lower level, but I hesitate on the landing, staring down at him. Suddenly I'm seven, staring down another flight of stairs, not knowing what I'll face at the bottom.

"Rev?"

I blink and I'm me again. "Sorry."

I still haven't heard a baby cry upstairs—and it has to be a baby, because toddlers make an insane amount of noise. Geoff sits on the couch and gestures for me to do the same.

He looks like he wants to have a *talk*.

"I'll save you some time," I say. "I know what sex is."

He smiles. "You're funny." A pause. "Bonnie called earlier. They needed a spot for an emergency placement."

Bonnie is a social worker. She's close friends with Kristin. "Mom texted me. I saw the police car."

"His name is Matthew."

"Okay." I'm waiting for him to drop the hammer, because bringing a new kid into the house isn't a sit-down-and-talk-about-it event. I'm used to it. I usually *like* it.

"Matthew is fourteen."

I freeze. "Oh."

I'm not sure how to react. They've never taken in a teenager before. The oldest kid we've ever had was nine, and he stayed for one night after his father fell down some basement stairs and his grandmother couldn't catch a plane into Baltimore until the morning. I turn the idea over in my head and imagine I should be glad I won't need to change any diapers.

I'm not opposed to an older kid living here. At least I don't think I am. Part of what I love about Geoff and Kristin is how they welcome everyone.

But as soon as the thought enters my head, doubt crowds in with it. Another teenager will mean someone with questions and judgments about our family. About me. I felt it the instant that girl beside the church realized who I was. Everyone at school knows who I am, even if it's only distantly. It's hard to hide your freak status when you wear long-sleeved hooded sweatshirts in the dead heat of summer. It's harder to hide that you're adopted when you're white, and your parents are black.

Not that I've ever wanted to hide it. But people talk.

"Matthew has been in four foster homes over the last year," says Geoff. "He started a fight this afternoon, and the family called the cops. No one pressed charges, but they don't want him living there anymore."

Four foster homes over the last *year*? I'm not sure what to say to that.

"What happens if he doesn't stay here?" I say.

Geoff hesitates. "He'd go to Cheltenham. He's already got two strikes with group homes."

The juvenile detention facility. "Wow," I say softly.

"Bonnie doesn't think he'll be a problem," Geoff continues. "And you know Kristin would open the door to every child in the county. But I want to make sure you're okay with it."

"I'm okay."

Geoff leans in. "Are you sure?"

I have no idea. My emotions are scattered in a million different directions. I'm not sure about any of them.

"He can stay." My voice is rough.

"Rev. I need you to be honest with me."

He's talking about Matthew, not the letter hidden in my pocket, but the words make me flinch.

I need to speak to cover it up, because I can see Geoff's expression shift in response. "It's fine," I say quickly. I have to clear my throat. "It'll be different, but it'll be okay."

Then I look up. "Where's he going to sleep?" The spare room is made up for younger children. There's a toddler bed and a crib, with a dresser, a changing table, and a rocking chair. The color scheme is peach and white, with alphabet letters stenciled along the ceiling. Aside from the rocking chair, there's not a single piece of furniture in that room that would support a teenager.

Geoff sighs. "That's part two of why I needed to talk to you."

• • •

This is not my first time sharing a room. Declan spends the night all the time. Geoff and Kristin put the futon in here specifically for him. Geoff said it's only until Saturday, when he can buy a full-size bed, but by law, Matthew needs a bed, so here he is.

It's after midnight. He's not sleeping.

Neither am I.

He's smaller than I expected, though he's got some muscle. Geoff said Matthew started a fight, but he clearly wasn't the one to finish it. The entire left side of his face is a mess, swelling and bruises running from temple to jaw. His cheek split and bled at some point, and flecks of dried blood cling to his face where it was probably too painful to scrub. His movements are stiff and careful. I wonder who he fought with.

I'll probably wonder for a while. He's said exactly two words to me.

"Hey" when Kristin introduced us.

"Okay" when I told him where he could put his things, which he carried in a white kitchen trash bag.

And that's it. He brushed his teeth and climbed into bed. Fully clothed. Jeans and everything.

I'm not in a position to judge. I'm wearing long sleeves and sweatpants.

After Geoff's description, I expected . . . something else. Belligerence. Anger. Defiance. Some swagger.

Matthew is quiet, but watchful. He's watching me now, peripherally, though his eyes are focused on the ceiling. Tension has settled over the room like a too-heavy blanket.

"Go to sleep," I say quietly. "I'm not going to mess with you."

He doesn't answer. He doesn't move. He doesn't even blink.

My phone *pings*. Declan.

Dec: How's your new roommate?

I texted him earlier to let him know what was going on, but I never answered his first text about what was wrong. Now it sits above our more recent messages, a giant elephant in the room. On the screen. Whatever.

I stick to the matter at hand.

Rev: Quiet
Dec: What's his name?
Rev: Matthew
Dec: Is he going to school with us tomorrow?

That's a good question. I always ride to school with Declan. I'll have to ask Kristin.

"Are we locked in?" Matthew's voice is rough and low.

I look over. He's finally broken his staring match with the ceiling.

I don't understand his question. "Locked in?"

"In the bedroom." His eyes flick to the closed door. "Are we locked in here at night?"

It takes me a second to work through what he's implying. I set my phone down. "No."

"Am I allowed to go to the bathroom?"

"Yes." I try not to let my voice show what an unusual question this is, but also that I'm just answering his question, not giving permission. It's a lot to demand from a three-letter word.

While he's gone, I look back at my phone.

Rev: He just asked if mom and dad lock us in the bedroom at night.
Dec: wtf

Exactly.

I bite at the edge of my lip and study our text messages. Maybe I'm imagining a distance between us, but I hate hiding something from him. It's hard enough to hide from Geoff and Kristin.

But now that I've kept this monumental secret, I'm not sure how to unravel it.

While I'm deliberating, I realize that Matthew has been gone for a while. I haven't heard water run or a toilet flush.

I slide the phone into my pocket and pad barefoot out of the room. The bathroom door is open, the lights off. Geoff and Kristin's bedroom door is closed. The entire house is dark.

Silence swells around me. I head down the hallway, to the kitchen.

Then I spot him, down on the landing, staring at the door—which is locked with a double-cylinder dead bolt. You need a key to open it from the inside.

I stop at the top of the staircase. "We *are* locked in the house," I whisper.

He whirls and flattens his back against the door. There's a knife in his hand.

My brain does a double take.

There's a *knife*. In his *hand*.

It's a paring knife from the kitchen block—but it's still a knife.

We have never had a toddler go for a weapon.

This has been the longest day. I almost say so, but then I look at his face and realize his day has been longer. I got a letter. He got a busted face.

I have no idea what to do. Yell for Geoff and Kristin? Would they send him to juvie? Do I cut him some slack, or do I end this right here?

I consider how I found him. He was taking the knife and going out the front door. He wasn't coming after me. He wasn't going after anyone in the house.

In another minute he probably would have tried for the back door—which slides and locks with a simple latch—and he would have been gone.

I drop to sit on the top step. "I told you I'm not going to mess with you." The words are meant to reassure him, but I'm also reminding myself. I could mess with him. I could mess with him a lot more than whoever messed with his face.

These thoughts link me with my father, and I force them out of my head.

"Put the knife down and go back to bed and we can pretend this didn't happen."

Matthew stares up at me and says nothing. His chest rises and falls quickly.

I don't move. I can be patient.

Apparently, so can he.

Ten minutes pass. Twenty. I lean my head against the wall. His breathing has slowed, but he hasn't changed his grip on the knife.

Thirty minutes. He slides down against the door until he's sitting on the welcome mat. I raise my eyebrows, but he holds my gaze and keeps the knife in his hand.

Fine.

An hour passes. The silence has turned heavy. Against my will, my eyes begin to drift closed.

His must, too.

Because that's exactly how Kristin finds us, sound asleep, at six o'clock the next morning.

FIVE

Emma

Friday, March 16   3:28 a.m.

From: N1ghtmare

To: Azure M

Don't make me find you, bitch.

And a good morning to him, too.

I don't delete this one. I don't ban him yet either. No banning before coffee.

Mom is in the kitchen when I go downstairs. She's standing at the counter, eating a breakfast of fruit and cottage cheese. It's barely six thirty, but she's already showered and dressed for work. She runs five miles every morning, too. The very picture of discipline.

"You look tired," she says to me.

I debate whether that's worse than some rando on the Internet calling me a bitch.

I shrug and find a mug. "Tell that to the county school system. I don't make the schedule."

"How late were you up?"

Until two. I ran missions with Ethan until my eyes went blurry. Cait joined us after her mom was in bed and there was no one to guard the family computer. We started on OtherLANDS and then moved over to Battle Guilds when he asked if we wanted to do something new. It's not a game I play often, because it was built by a competitor of Dad's company, but I wasn't turning down an invitation. That's never happened before. Usually guys sign off to go play with someone else.

I shrug and pull the creamer out of the refrigerator. "I don't remember. I was reading."

"I've told you before that I don't like you drinking coffee, Emma."

I've ignored her before, too. I dump a quarter of a cup of sugar into my mug. "I'm sorry, what?"

Her lips purse. "I know your father stays up until all hours of the night, but he doesn't need to be in class at seven thirty."

"That's because he's *lucky*."

"That's because he's an adult." She pauses. "Or at least he *pretends* to be—"

"Mom." I glare at her. She knows I don't like the sniping.

"I know you're enjoying the computers and the games, but I hope you're aware what a competitive field—"

"Because you slid right into medicine?" I sip at my coffee and head for the stairs. "I forgot how easy it was for you to get into Columbia."

"Emma. Emma, come back here."

I'm already halfway up the stairs. "I need to take a shower."

I'm grateful for the fan and the rattle of water against the bathtub. I turn the water as hot as I can tolerate and step into the steam. It burns my scalp.

Don't make me find you, bitch.

My eyes burn, and I turn my face to the stream of water. I hate that there are people like him. I hate it.

Dad has a female coworker who gets a lot worse. Death threats. Rape threats. It's rampant in the industry. I need to learn to deal with it now if I want to make a career out of this.

But still. The words have set up shop in my brain, a constant thrum of warning. *Don't make me find you.*

I remind myself that he's probably thirteen and bored.

The doorknob clicks. "Emma. I want to talk to you—"

"Mom! Oh my god, I'm in the shower!"

"You do realize there's a curtain. And I'm your mother. And a doctor. I have seen—"

"Mom!"

"Emma." She sounds closer. "I don't have a problem with the computers or the coding. I hope you know that. But I worry that your father's habits may have given you an unfair expectation—"

"Mom." I pull the curtain around my face and look out at her. She's sitting on the closed toilet. The steam has already curled the tendrils of hair that escaped her ponytail. "Dad works just as many hours as you do. I know it's not all fun and games."

"I just want to make sure that you realize that creative endeavors are always more complicated. We would be having the same conversation if you wanted to be an artist . . . or a writer . . . or an actress . . ." Her voice trails off, and she sounds more displeased with each progressive career.

Shampoo finds my eyes, and I duck back into the shower. "Wow, thanks for the pep talk about following my dreams."

"Dreams won't pay a mortgage, Emma. I just want to be sure you're thinking objectively about this. You're a junior in high school."

"Mom, I'm pretty sure knowing how to write code will help me find a job."

"I know it will. Playing games until two a.m. and scraping through the day won't."

I can't say much to that. She makes me feel like such a slacker.

Combined with the e-mail I received this morning, the burn in my eyes returns.

"Is your homework done?" she asks.

"Of course." My voice almost breaks, and I hope the shower is enough to cover it up.

"Emma?" She sounds surprised. "Are you upset?"

"I'm fine."

She begins to pull the shower curtain to the side.

I grab it and yank it shut. "Mom! Are you kidding me right now?"

"I just wanted to make sure—"

"Would you get out of here? I need to finish getting ready for school."

For a long moment, she says nothing.

During that moment, I think of all the things I want to say to her.

Do you know I wrote my own game? I wrote the whole thing. And people actually play it. Hundreds of people. I did that. I DID THAT.

I'm terrified she'd find the whole thing a waste of time.

And then she'd make me delete it so I could focus on something "more productive."

"Emma," she says quietly.

I push the water off my face. "Mom, it's fine. I'm fine. Go to work. I'm sure you have patients to see."

I hold my breath, and in that moment, I'm torn between hoping she'll stay and hoping she'll leave.

I don't know why. It's ridiculous. She has so much contempt for everything I love.

Then the door clicks, and it doesn't matter. She did exactly what I asked.

• • •

"Why don't they sell coffee at lunch?" says Cait. She's paying the price for our two a.m. gaming, too. We're all but slumped on the lunch table. Even her makeup seems lackluster this morning: glitter eyeliner is about as daring as she got.

"Because they're sadists." I poke at a slice of pizza on my tray. "Want to ditch next period and walk to Dunkin' Donuts?"

"If I got caught cutting class, my makeup would be in the Dumpster, and Mom would sell my camera."

"And what a tragedy that would be."

She startles a little, and I realize what I've said. I wince. "Sorry. I didn't mean—I don't even know what I'm saying."

Her expression is frozen in this space between hurt and confused. "What did you mean?"

"I didn't mean anything, Cait. Really."

She's staring at me like she's trying to decide whether to push or to let it go.

I don't even know why I said that. My mouth needs to be reconnected to my brain. "It was stupid. I was trying to make a joke but I'm too tired to make it happen."

A tiny line has appeared between her eyebrows, but she sits back. "Okay." She pauses, and the slowly growing wall between us gains a few more bricks.

I had considered telling her about Nightmare, but the air between us is full of tension now. Cait wouldn't understand anyway. The worst kind of troll she faces is someone who accuses her of copying makeup designs or calling her ugly. She has no problem shutting them down. She wouldn't understand why I can't do the same.

Motion across the cafeteria catches my eye. That guy from behind the church is sitting at a table in the corner. He's wearing a maroon hoodie today, the hood low enough to block his eyes from view. He's got half a dozen plastic containers spread on the table in front of him. It looks like he's sharing with another guy, someone with reddish-brown hair.

I can count on one hand the number of times I've seen two guys share a lunch.

Check that. I can count on one finger.

It's about the same number of times a guy has quoted the Bible to me.

I pull a purple pen out of my bag and draw stripes across my fingernails, just to give my hands something to do while I stalk Mr. Tall, Dark, and Hooded. A girl joins the two boys in the back corner. She's pretty, with long, shining dark hair and trim-fitting clothes. Preppy. Glossy. The type of girl I usually avoid, for the simple reason that they always look completely together, and I generally need a computer in front of me to communicate. I have no idea who she is.

Then again, she's sitting *with* the Grim Reaper, not sitting on the quad gossiping about him, so maybe she's not *all* bad.

"Why is it okay for you to draw on your nails, but it's not okay for me to do it with real makeup?" says Cait.

My hand stops. "You can do whatever you want with makeup," I say tightly. "It was a stupid comment."

"Okay."

It doesn't sound okay at all. I hesitate, wishing I could fix this. "I was watching that guy over there. Do you know who he is?"

She twists on the bench to look. "Yeah," she says. "He's in my Sociology class. Why?"

"What's his name?"

"Rev Fletcher. *Why?*"

I watch him eat from a container with a fork. A real metal fork. "Is he gay?"

"Wait. Let me check." She screws up her face. "Oops. Sorry. Telepathy is down again."

I can't decide if she's trying to lighten the mood or darken it. "Do you know what's up with him and the hoodies?"

She glances over her shoulder again. "No. Mrs. Van Eyck makes him take the hood down during class, though."

"Does he wear it every day?" I don't know why I care, but it's like I've found a source of information, and the download speed is pathetic.

"Yes. Not the same one, though. He doesn't smell or anything. He's very quiet. Doesn't say a lot." She pauses. "Why are you interested in Rev Fletcher?"

I don't know. I can't pin it down.

Are you okay?

No.

He seems fine now. But also . . . not. Some small, hidden part of me wants to walk over there and ask him again.

I can see it now. *Hey, remember me? You scared me beside the church. Fed my dog some nuggets. Discussed existentialism?*

Sure.

He has friends. He's eating lunch. He doesn't need me.

But if he has friends, why was he hiding beside the church with that letter?

"Emma?"

"It was nothing," I say to Cait. "I ran into him when I was walking the dog."

"Was it weird? I feel like he'd be weird outside of school." She makes a face. "I mean, he's weird *inside* of school—"

"Not weird." I pause. "Unusual."

"There's a difference?"

"You wear a different face every day. You tell me."

She jerks back, and I wish I could suck the words back into my mouth. I didn't mean the words as an insult—or maybe I did. I'm too tired to know.

She shrugs her backpack over her shoulder. "I need to go change out some books before class. I'll see you later, okay?"

Before I can say anything, she slides through the crush of students.

With a sigh, I gather my things and head to class myself.

I'm the only junior in AP Computer Science. I'm also one of only three girls. I slept through Introduction to Coding last year, but it was a mandatory prerequisite. I could have taught the class. When Mr. Price noticed that I was doing homework for other classes while he was droning at the Smartboard, he offered extra credit if I designed something myself. I think he expected something pathetic and basic so he could pat me on the head and pretend he was challenging me. When he logged in to OtherLANDS, he choked on his coffee.

Seriously. He almost sprayed me with it.

This isn't my first game. It's my sixth. No one comes out of the gate with an online RPG. Well, no one I know. Not even Dad. He started teaching me to write code when I was seven years old, showing me Pong and telling me to see if I could re-create it. By the time I was ten, I was making basic two-dimensional games. By the time I was thirteen, I could handle 3-D graphics. Other-LANDS is the hardest thing I've ever done.

Dad has never played. He doesn't even know about it.

He's a senior programmer for Axis Gaming. His next release is supposed to integrate with mobile, allowing people to switch from desktop gaming to their phones seamlessly, going from battle missions to scouting missions. I've seen some screen shots, and it's amazing.

I can't wait to show him OtherLANDS. But it has to be perfect first.

Meaning, I can't have characters disappearing into the side of a mountain.

Mr. Price is typing some code into the overhead projector. All the computers have a screen protector to prevent cheating, so I can do whatever I want back here. I log in to my OtherLANDS server and get out a notebook to start "taking notes."

And there, waiting right on top, is this morning's e-mail from Nightmare.

My finger hovers over the Ban Player button.

I do it. I click it.

And then I delete his e-mail.

It's over. It's done. He's gone. He can't bother me on here anymore. The relief is almost potent.

He can bother me on 5Core, but that site is maintained by the county school system. I can report him to an admin on there if he sends harassing messages.

I glance at the board. Mr. Price drones on, so I start sketching a map. I want to try to build an insect realm. I haven't done anything that can fly yet, and I want a challenge. I could have swarms of bees, spiderwebs, stinging scorpions, butterflies that drop healing potions . . . *Hmm.*

My computer flashes at me.

A new message. My eyes lock on the sender, and I freeze.

Friday, March 16   12:26 p.m.

From: N1ghtmare2

To: Azure M

Nice try.

You've just made this personal.

SIX

Rev

Friday, March 16   5:37:56 p.m.

FROM: Robert Ellis <robert.ellis@speedmail.com>

TO: Rev Fletcher <rev.fletcher@freemail.com>

SUBJECT: Silence

I believe the quiet moments are the loudest.
     Your silence speaks volumes, Son.

Two sentences, and guilt cramps my insides. My silence feels like a crime against everyone in my life.

I haven't answered my father.

I haven't told Geoff and Kristin.

I haven't told Declan.

Tonight, I'm smothered by loud silence. We're having dinner

as a "family," but no one is talking. Kristin made breakfast foods: French toast and fried eggs, sausage gravy and bacon, roasted potatoes, and sliced fruit with whipped cream. Comfort food, because the house feels so *un*comfortable. I shove food around my plate and keep my eyes on my place mat.

Matthew sits on the other side of the table, doing the exact same thing.

I was surprised to find him here when I got home. I thought for sure the knife thing would send him back into CPS's clutches. When Kristin found us this morning, she sized up the situation, then put her hands on my shoulders and quietly told me to go get ready for school.

I glance across the table. Matthew looks exhausted. The bruises along his face are darker, fully set now. Apparently, Bonnie, his social worker, came back to the house and they all had a long talk.

I don't know what they said, but whatever it was bought him another night here. He sure doesn't look contrite. He doesn't look aggressive either. Point in his favor? I have no idea.

Geoff said Matthew promised to ask before leaving the house.

So reassuring. Time for confetti.

"Rev, honey, can you pass the sausage?" Kristin's voice is falsely bright. This is her voice for when toddlers are defiantly smearing food—or worse—on the wall.

Passing food requires me to look up, and I find Matthew watching me without really looking at me, the way he was last night.

A familiar tension settles into my shoulders. I feel defensive and nothing has even happened yet.

Geoff sits at the end of the table, studying both of us. He hasn't said a word either. He doesn't look happy.

Kristin's voice is still casual. "You haven't said anything about school today, Rev."

"It was fine." I shove a piece of French toast in my mouth so I don't have to say more.

"Declan didn't want to join us tonight?"

My best friend usually eats here on Fridays, a long-standing tradition from when he needed to avoid his stepfather. I force my throat to swallow. "He's out with Juliet."

Again.

Which is fine.

"I spoke with Mr. Diviglio this afternoon. Matthew is going to start on Monday. I thought it would be nice if you could help him learn his way around."

Mr. Diviglio is the vice principal. The French toast turns to stone in my mouth and it hurts to swallow. Once I can speak, I lock my eyes on Matthew's, almost forcing him to make eye contact. "If you get caught with a knife at school, you'll be suspended."

"Rev," Kristin says softly. Not quite chiding, but almost.

"I've been to Hamilton before," Matthew says, his eyes on his plate. "I know my way around." A pause. "And the rules."

Geoff clears his throat. His voice is low and calm, easing some of the tension in the room. "Good. That should make things a bit easier, then."

His calm manner reminds me that a lot of the strain in the room is coming out of my own head. I need to back off. I shrug and stab at another piece of French toast. "He can ride to school with us. Declan won't care."

Actually, Declan probably will care, and he won't make a secret of it. I imagine my best friend finding Matthew in the hallway with a knife.

Declan would put him through the wall.

"Isn't there a bus from here?" Matthew says. His eyes are still locked on his plate.

The table is silent for a beat.

"There is a bus," says Kristin carefully. "But it's a forty-minute trip. You'd have to be at the stop at six twenty."

He says nothing.

I study him. I feel like I've screwed this up without even trying. "You don't have to ride the bus. You can ride with us."

"Six twenty is fine." He takes a slow bite of food and speaks quietly. "I can get up early."

His words sound deliberate and calculated, and I can't figure out if that's real or if it's my own screwed-up mental process taking everything the wrong way.

Your silence speaks volumes, Son.

I shove my chair back from the table. "May I be excused?"

Geoff and Kristin exchange a glance, and then she looks up at me. "You've hardly eaten."

"You packed me a big lunch." I hesitate, not wanting to be a jerk. "Let me know when you're done. I can clean up."

She leans over and rubs my hand, giving it a gentle squeeze. "Don't worry about it. You do what you need to do."

● ● ●

I throw on clothes to head to the gym, but at the last minute, I change my mind. I desperately need to get out of the house, but the thought of leaving turns my stress dial all the way to the right. I wish I could go to Declan's. I wish I could tell him.

At the same time, I don't. I feel too exposed. Too raw.

No. I feel ashamed.

I think of the girl beside the church.

You're afraid.

I've spent years learning how not to be afraid. And now, with a few short sentences, my father has sliced through all my defenses.

I attack the heavy bag in the basement. I start with kicks, then punches, then hooks and knee strikes, before starting the whole cycle over again. At first, my rhythm is off, leaving me clumsy in a way I haven't felt in ages. Eventually, my brain realizes I'm serious, and muscle memory takes over. I lose myself in the force of each movement.

When I was young, when Geoff and Kristin were new foster parents and I was their first foster kid, I spent each night terrified my father would get me back and torture me for liking them even a little bit. Kristin would come into my room every night and read me a story while I stared at the ceiling and pretended not to listen. I had never been allowed books about magic or fantasy or anything that wasn't based in religion, so I listened as she read *Harry Potter and the Sorcerer's Stone* and felt certain the devil was going to crawl through the floor and drag me straight to hell.

That didn't happen. Obviously.

By the second month, she had moved on to *Harry Potter and the Chamber of Secrets*, and I stopped staring at the ceiling. I laughed at something. She moved her chair closer to the bed so I could see the chapter illustrations.

I barely remember the story.

But I remember when she closed the book, I burst into tears.

"What's wrong?" she said.

"I don't want to go back."

She didn't need clarification. She knew what I meant.

It was one of the few times I've ever heard her voice turn to steel. "You are *never* going back."

Your silence speaks volumes, Son.

My throat tightens, and my eyes suddenly blur. His words work against me in both directions. I'm not just avoiding him. I'm avoiding Geoff and Kristin. I'm avoiding my best friend.

I slam my fist into the bag, and my arm shakes with fatigue. I draw back, panting, and shove hair out of my eyes. Geoff and Kristin are talking upstairs, their voices a low murmur.

I drop onto the weight bench, strip off my gloves, and drain half my water bottle without thinking about it. The cold almost burns, both amazing and terrible. The cool quiet of the lower level presses in around me.

And then, like a switch flips in my brain, I'm aware I'm not alone. Maybe the air shifts or a shadow moves, but the atmosphere changes.

I take another sip of water, my focus razor sharp. It has to be Matthew.

I can't hear him breathing, but he's here somewhere. I'm not afraid of him. Not exactly. Intellectually, I know he's not much of a threat to me.

But a darker, primal part of my brain does not like anything resembling a threat. Especially not now, with memories of my father clawing their way to the surface.

"Come out," I say, my voice low and leaving no room for argument.

Everything goes more still somehow. More silent.

"Come out," I say again.

Nothing.

My heart rate has gone up a notch, a hammer inside a cage. A fresh line of sweat crawls down the center of my chest. The longer he stays in the shadows, the less I like it.

I stand up, turning full circle, because this kind of anxiety won't let me sit. "You do not want to sneak up on me."

Silence.

Your silence speaks volumes.

Maybe it's not Matthew at all. My father has this address. My father knows how to find me.

Fear is a quick and deadly vise grip on my chest. I can't speak. I can't move.

It's not my father. It can't be my father.

It can't be.

It can't be.

My fingernails dig trenches in my palms. The room shrinks by half. I'm trapped.

I bolt from the basement. My feet don't feel the stairs. I grab a hoodie from the rack by the door and fling the front door wide. The cool night air feels like a wall. I tear through it.

The moon hangs high above, the stars swinging in arcs. Breath can barely squeeze into my lungs.

"Rev!"

Kristin's voice behind me.

I turn and look at her. She stands on the front steps. She seems a mile away.

She can't come after me. I don't know what I'll do if someone comes after me right now.

"I need some air." I sound like I've run a marathon. I yank the hoodie over my head and thrust my hands into the sleeves.

"Wait," she says. "Dad will walk with you."

"No." I grit the word out. "No. I need to go."

"Do you have your phone?"

Maybe. Who knows. We could be on Mars right now and I wouldn't be aware of it.

But the question is so normal that it throws a deflating dart into my panic attack. I can take a breath. I can slap my pocket. I can answer. "Yeah."

"Text me if you're going to be longer than an hour."

The air turns colder. My body turns hotter. "Okay." My voice almost breaks. "Okay."

She glances behind her, then looks back at me. "Dad says he

needs a walk, too. Why don't you wait a second? He's getting his shoes."

If she keeps talking to me I'm going to pass out. Or start crying.

Or put my hand through a car window.

"I'm going for a run, okay?"

I don't wait for a response. I turn on my heel and sprint down the street.

SEVEN

Emma

I'm playing OtherLANDS again. Mom would be so proud.

Some of the joy has been sucked out of it, though. It's not just that idiot troll—whom I've banned a second time. It's this bizarre tension with Cait, who used to sign on and play with me but who's probably doing a live video about false eyelashes. It's Mom's comments this morning about how dreams won't pay the mortgage, like I don't know that.

I don't understand what her whole deal is anyway. Dad makes a good living. He works long hours, too. Just because he's crouched over a computer and she's crouched over a hospital bed doesn't mean his time is worthless.

Ethan's voice comes through my headphones. "You seem distracted."

We're running a mission in the elven realm. I've never played with him one-on-one before, but after what happened with

Nightmare, when Ethan added me, I said, "Can we just keep it to two? I want to check for more holes in my code."

He didn't say anything; just activated the mission.

I didn't realize how tense I'd been about it until the knot in my stomach uncurled.

"Sorry," I say. "Just thinking."

"School or parents?" His avatar quickly slashes through an elf that steps from behind a tree.

"What?"

"Are you distracted by school, or by your parents?" He pauses. "Or a boyfriend?"

"No boyfriend." My cheeks warm, though his voice wasn't in the least bit flirtatious. This feels solidly friend-zone. If it's even that.

"Or girlfriend?" he adds. "I don't want to assume."

I laugh. "No girlfriend either. And school is fine. It's parents. Well, Mom. Dad's okay." My avatar follows his, running across the green terrain. "Hold on. I want to add more texture here. I need to make a note."

His avatar stops. "Let me guess. Too much gaming, not enough focus on school, get some sunshine before you need vitamin D supplements—"

"Yes! How do you know that?"

A disgusted noise. "I live it." He pauses. "But I just play. Does she know you're actually writing these games? I think my mom would back off if she found any of this productive."

I make my own disgusted noise. "My mom would find a scholarship to Harvard Medical School productive."

"Who wouldn't?" His character moves forward a few steps. "Are you ready?"

"Yeah." We run. Well, our avatars do. "No, she doesn't know about OtherLANDS."

"Are you kidding me? You wrote a *game*."

"I know." I pause. "She thinks it's stupid. I'm worried she'd make me delete it."

"She wants you to be a doctor?"

"I think she knows I don't want to go into medicine."

"I have no idea what kind of doctor you'd be, but as a game designer, I think you're pretty badass."

His voice is just as dispassionate as everything else he's said, but the comment lights me with a little glow. No one has ever called me badass before. Certainly not in a game.

Then he says, "I mean, it's kind of basic, and the graphics aren't that intense, but—"

"No, no," I say. "Leave it at badass."

He laughs.

He has a nice laugh.

I need to stop blushing.

My in-game in-box flashes with a message. I freeze. On the screen, my avatar stops running.

"M?" says Ethan.

"Hold on. I have a message." I click the flashing button.

Friday, March 16   7:29 p.m.
From: N1ghtmare3
To: Azure M

I can do this all day, baby. Tell me, do you charge for
sucking?

My breathing goes shallow. I hate this.

I can't ban him from here. I have to log in to my admin
dashboard.

"I have to go," I say to Ethan.

"Are you okay?" He must hear the change in my voice,
because he sounds concerned.

"I'm okay. I just—I have to go."

The laptop slams shut.

I should reopen it. I should log in and ban that jackass.

I just can't look at it again. Not right now.

My eyes are burning again. I need to get out of the house. I
shove my phone in my pocket and jog down the steps. Texy is
waiting at the bottom of the steps with a wagging tail.

"Come on," I say to her. My voice breaks. My eyes have blurred
over. The dog follows dutifully, ignoring my fumbling hands as
I struggle to clip the leash to her collar. She's excited to be going,
and her nails click all over the marble floor of the entryway.

"Emma?" Mom calls from the kitchen. She appears in the
doorway with a glass of wine in her hand. "Where are you
going?"

I can't look at her. "I'm taking the dog for a walk." I hope I
sound congested instead of emotional.

"Good!" she says. "I'm glad you're getting some exercise."

Mission accomplished. I guess.

Then we're outside.

I need to calm down. I'm being ridiculous. Women get these messages *all the time*. It's not right, it's not acceptable, but I can't fix it. I can only block him. My game is free and publicly available. It's not like people need a credit card to play. Like Ethan said, it's pretty basic. All my efforts at security went into making sure no one could hack my network. Not making sure I knew the identity of players. I never thought I'd have a reason to care.

And I don't really care now. I don't care who he *is*. I just want him to stop.

Ethan's voice rings in my ears, but now it sounds like a joke. *I think you're pretty badass.*

The last thing I feel right now is *badass*. My breath hitches. I need to get it together.

My phone vibrates in my hand, so suddenly that I almost drop it. The display is lit up with an incoming call. *Dad.*

I swipe to answer. "Hello?" My voice sounds thick with tears and I can't help it.

"Emma?" He sounds concerned. "Are you okay?"

"I'm okay." My voice breaks.

"You're not okay." His voice is rich and warm in my ear. "What's going on?"

I can't tell him without telling him about the game.

And even then, I know what he'll say. I've heard it before.

It's horrible, he'll say. *But people get online and they take out all their rage, just because they can. It makes me sick. But the only thing you can do is block and ban.*

And he'd be right. That's the only thing I can do.

"I'm okay," I say. "Some jerk is trolling me online. I keep blocking him but he keeps coming back with new screen names."

"Have you reported him to the admin? Sometimes they can block a user from registering with an e-mail address."

Great idea. Too bad I'm the admin. And I don't require an e-mail address.

"I'll try that," I say. I sniff.

"How bad was it?" he says. "Is he threatening you?"

"Well, it's kind of—"

"Hold on, M&M. Someone just walked in." He must have put his hand over the phone because his voice gets muffled. A minute goes by. The tears on my cheek go dry.

I begin to wonder if he forgot I'm on the line.

Finally, he comes back. "Hey, kiddo, I need to go. We just discovered a critical issue on the server, and you know it's crunch time until release. Are you okay?"

"Yes. Yes, of course."

"I'll probably be late, but I'll see you in the morning, okay? Don't let the dragon lady get you down while I'm gone."

The dragon lady is Mom. When I was small, it used to make me laugh. Lately, it sounds a little too real. "Okay, Dad."

"I just wanted to hear your voice, baby. Okay?"

These moments are so few and far between now. When his words are just for me. "Okay, Daddy. I love you."

"I love you, too. No matter what." He disconnects the call.

No matter what? What does that mean?

Texy bounces on her front paws and woofs. She must see a

squirrel. I've barely got a grip on her leash, but I give it a tug. "Come on." I sniff. "Leave it."

She barks full out. Then she bolts. The leash snaps out of my hand.

UGH.

She doesn't go far. She tears across the street to stop on the opposite corner, leaping against a guy who stands just out of range of the streetlight. Her entire body wags.

I jog after her. She's still on her hind legs, her front paws against his chest, but the man is rubbing behind her ears. Sneakers and black track pants—a jogger. Her head hangs sideways, her tongue hanging out of her mouth. She's like, *Don't you see? This is why I was so excited.*

I bend to scoop up her leash. "I'm sorry. I'm so sorry. Texas. *Texy*. Down."

"She's okay."

I recognize his voice, and my head snaps up again. The ever-present hoodie blocks most of his features from the light, but it's definitely him.

"Oh," I say in surprise. "It's you."

"It's me."

"Rev Fletcher," I say without thinking. Like he doesn't know his own name.

He's still rubbing Texy behind her ears, but that draws his attention up. "Yes." A pause. "Rev Fletcher." The way he says it is interesting, like he's reminding himself. Which is weird.

Then he leans forward, just enough for the light to catch his eyes. "Are you crying?"

I jerk back and swipe at my face. I forgot. "No." My voice sounds nasally. Of course I have to sniff. "It's just—it's allergies."

But standing this close to him, with his face turned toward me, I see that his cheeks are flushed, too, his eyes a little wild.

It's enough to chase me off my own drama. I think of the letter he shared last night, the fear in the air. "Are *you* crying?" I ask in surprise.

"No," he says, a dry mimic of my own tone. "It's just allergies."

I don't buy that for a minute.

Texy finally drops to the ground, and Rev hides his hands in his sweatshirt pockets.

The night wraps around us like a cloak, pooling all this emotion in the space between us. I know I build walls around myself, but I've never met someone whose own walls seemed equally impenetrable.

For the first time ever, a little prick of fear sets up shop in my chest. I'm reminded of Nightmare's message.

Don't make me find you, bitch.

But Rev didn't find me. I found him. Well, Texy did. And when he speaks, his tone is rich and full, almost tangible. Nothing like Nightmare in the game.

The hoodie seems unfair. I squint at him. "Can you put the hood down so I can see you?"

I expect him to refuse, but Rev lifts a hand and shoves it back. "Nothing to see," he says.

He's wrong. There's a lot to see.

His hair hangs just past his chin, the color dark and muted in the moonlight. There must not be an ounce of body fat on him, because his features are sharp, from the angle of his jaw to the slope of his cheekbones. Dark eyes, their color a mystery in the moonlight. He's built and moves like an athlete, but nothing about him screams *team spirit*, so I'm not sure.

"You're staring," he says.

"So are you."

His eyes flick away. "I'm sorry."

"Don't be sorry," I say quickly. "You're allowed to look."

Ugh, I'm so awkward. This is why I'm better with a keyboard and a screen, especially when my thoughts have been shaken and scattered like Scrabble tiles.

I fidget and glance away. "I mean—it's fine. We're standing here. I wasn't complaining. I expect you to see me."

His eyes find mine again, and he doesn't say anything to that. I can't read his expression.

Oh, good. I've made it more awkward.

I give Texy's leash a tug and start to move away. "I didn't mean to hold you up."

"Wait."

I wait.

He's frowning. "I find it interesting that we've run into each other twice now."

"Like I'm stalking you?"

That startles a smile out of him, but it's hesitant. "No. Not like that at all."

It takes me a second to figure him out. Considering our

conversation last night, it's a second too long. "Are you talking about fate?" I study him. "Or God? You think there's someone up there controlling my dog?"

"Not exactly." He pauses. "But I'm not sure we should run away from it."

I don't know what to say. Maybe he doesn't either, because we stand there for the longest moment just sharing the night air.

When he speaks, his voice is quiet. "Do you want to go sit by the stained glass windows again?"

"To talk?"

"Either that, or we can bury a body."

His voice is deadpan. He's teasing me, after what I said last night.

"Yes," he adds, his tone deliberate, as if I might have misunderstood that was a joke. "To talk."

Let me make a list of the times a boy has ever asked me to sit and talk.

1. Right now.

If fate does exist, maybe this is her way of telling me to take control of my own destiny.

God, I'm starting to sound like him. I'm not sure I mind.

"Sure." I look up at him in the darkness. "Let's go."

EIGHT

Rev

The girl follows me to the grass behind the church, and we sit, hiding in the darkness where streetlights won't find us. We lean against the brick wall, and the cool masonry feels good against the heat of my back.

I have no idea what I'm doing. I don't even know this girl's *name*.

The dog flops in the grass beside me, and I bury my fingers in her fur. She shifts closer to me, laying her head in my lap. I've always wanted a dog, but Geoff and Kristin worry about small children being afraid or having an allergy, so we've never gotten one.

I peek over at the girl. Auburn hair hangs over one shoulder in a long, loose braid, and she fiddles with the end, twisting the strands between her fingers. Soft features, though her eyes are guarded, framed by dark glasses. Freckles are *everywhere*. She's used a metallic marker to create constellations out of them on the back of her hand. She's relaxed against the wall, looking out at the street.

It's some kind of miracle she agreed to sit and talk. I'm such a freak. Declan would never let me hear the end of this.

So you finally asked a girl to talk to you . . . and you chose the grass beside a church? Dude.

Then again, this is probably exactly what he'd expect.

I glance over again. "Can I ask you a personal question?"

"Shoot."

"What's your name?"

"Emma Blue. That's not really a personal question."

"You knew mine. I felt bad for not knowing yours."

"I only know yours because I asked a friend—" Emma blushes and breaks off, but she must know there's no point in back-pedaling. "We saw you in the cafeteria this morning. She's in your Sociology class."

"I saw you, too."

She winces and glances over. "Sorry for staring. Again."

"I'm used to people staring." A pause. "I wondered if it was a sign I should talk to you."

She turns her head and looks at me in the dark. "You could have talked to me."

"You could have talked to me, too." I pause. "I thought maybe I weirded you out last night."

"I think I've got a different standard on what's considered weird." Her blush deepens. "And I don't know if you've noticed, but I'm not the kind of girl who walks up to boys and starts talking."

"We have that in common."

"You get nervous talking to boys, too?"

"I lose sleep over it."

She smiles. I don't know if this is teasing or flirting but I do know it's the first time in two days that I haven't been on the verge of a panic attack.

Then she says, "Can I ask *you* a personal question?"

I hesitate. I know what it's going to be. "Sure."

"What's with the hoodies?"

I have to resist the urge to curl in on myself. To hide. "That . . . has a long and complicated answer."

She's quiet for a moment, then makes a guess. "Are you super hairy?"

It's so unexpected that I laugh. "No."

She thinks for another moment. "Cyborg?"

I like that she's keeping this light. "Now that you know, I might have to kill you."

She smiles, but her voice turns serious. "Scars?"

I hesitate. That's closer to the mark. "Not exactly."

"Not *exactly*?"

"Well." I pause as tension latches into my shoulders again. Thinking about my scars makes me think about my father. I draw my knees up and rest one arm on them. The other hand stays buried in the dog's fur. "Some scars. I had . . . a rough childhood. But that's not why I wear them."

I brace myself for her to push, because she knows about the letter—but she doesn't. She crosses her legs and leans back. "Okay. Your turn."

I frown. "My turn?"

"Personal question."

She reminds me of Declan. A little. In a good way. "Why were you crying?"

She hesitates. "That . . . has a long and complicated answer."

I deserve that. I sigh and look out at the night.

Beside me, she does the same thing.

"Your turn," I say quietly.

She's quiet for a few beats. "Is your father the reason for the rough childhood?"

"Yes."

"Did he send you another letter?"

I swallow. "An e-mail."

"An *e-mail*?"

"I wrote to him." I pause. "I told him to leave me alone. He wrote back."

"Is he the reason for the hoodies?"

"Yes." My tension dials one notch higher, my fingers gripping tight on my knees.

But then she says, "Aren't you hot all the time?"

I let out a breath. "Sometimes."

"Are you hot now?"

"A little." I was running before her dog found me, and that was after an hour of attacking the heavy bag.

"You can take it off," she says. "Your father's not here now."

Her voice is so pragmatic. This isn't a challenge. It only feels like one inside my head.

I'm wearing a long-sleeved athletic shirt under the sweatshirt, so it wouldn't be a big deal. She wouldn't see anything.

I think of that feeling in the basement, when I was so certain Matthew was watching me.

Right now, wearing this sweatshirt makes me feel like a coward. Makes me feel like I'm hiding.

Your silence speaks volumes, Son.

I *am* hiding.

"I didn't mean to throw you into a crisis," Emma says quietly.

"You didn't." But she did. Sort of.

And that's ridiculous. We're talking about a *sweatshirt.*

I grab the hem and yank it over my head.

"Whoa." All the breath leaves her in a rush.

I freeze. The sweatshirt is a crumpled ball on the ground beside me.

She's staring at me. Her eyes might as well be laser beams, the weight of them so potent. "Rev . . . I didn't . . ."

"Stop," I say. My shirt must have pulled free with the sweatshirt. She must have seen some of the marks my father left. This was such a mistake. I'm so *stupid.*

I tug at my sleeves, but the shirt is snug and they're already at my wrists. "Please. Stop."

"I'm sorry." Her voice is hushed, and she turns to look at the street. "I'm sorry."

Tension has buried claws in my shoulders. "What did you see?"

"Nothing."

"You saw something." My voice is tight and angry and afraid, and none of that has anything to do with her, but she's here and I feel exposed and none of this is going the way I thought it would. "You said *whoa.*"

"Hey," she says quietly. "Rev. I didn't see anything."

Memories of my father flash in my brain, so quickly I can't pin any of them down. It doesn't matter—none of them are good. My fingers clench around my abdomen. I'm deathly afraid she's going to touch me and I'm going to lash out and hurt her.

"Don't touch me," I force out, keeping my voice as low as possible. "Don't—you should just go home."

She shifts in the grass, like she's moving away. Good. I can inhale.

Then she speaks, right in front of me. "Hey. Open your eyes. Look at me."

I don't remember closing my eyes, but I must have. I obey.

She's kneeling in the grass, holding out my sweatshirt. "I didn't see anything," she says again. "Really."

I swallow. "It's okay. I'm okay." It's not. And I'm not. I still can't move.

"Okay. Look. I don't know what you think I saw." Emma speaks fast. "And I can't believe I'm going to admit this out loud. But I said *whoa* because you have an amazing body."

My thoughts freeze.

The world stops spinning.

She keeps babbling. "I've only ever seen you in big hoodies. I was unprepared for . . ." She gestures. "*This.*"

I frown. "Are you messing with me?"

"Are you kidding? Looking like that, I would be an absolute *idiot* to mess with you. Haven't you ever looked in a mirror?"

I flinch. "Stop it."

"It's like watching Clark Kent turn into Superman."

"Hey." My jaw is tight, making my voice turn sharp. "*Stop it.*"

She sits back on her heels. A few strands have come loose from the braid to hang across her face. She impatiently blows them out of the way. "I'm not making fun of you, Rev."

I feel like such a fool. I look down at the crumpled mess of my sweatshirt. I don't know what to say.

Your silence speaks volumes, Son.

My eyes burn, and I have to hold my breath. My fingers dig into the jersey fabric.

Emma shifts until she's sitting with her legs crisscrossed. "My turn."

It brings me back to earth. My voice is barely a rasp. "Your turn."

"I'm getting e-mails, too," she says quietly. "Not from my father. From some jerk in a computer game. He's not threatening me but—but they're not good."

I go still.

"I don't know him," Emma continues, her voice soft and heavy. "And I know that sounds crazy. But it's common in online gaming. Girls always seem to be a target. So he thinks he can send me e-mails that say things like—"

Her voice breaks off. The night is so quiet, I can hear distant cars in the neighborhood.

"Like what?" I say.

"I can't." Her voice breaks, and I jerk my head up.

Her eyes glitter with tears, but she's not crying.

"You can tell me," I say carefully. I borrow her own words. "He's not here now."

For a moment, I don't think she's going to answer, but then she fishes her phone out of her jeans pocket, and swipes her finger across the screen.

Then she turns it around to show me.

I can do this all day, baby. Tell me, do you charge for sucking?

The words hit *me* like a fist to the gut, so I can't imagine what they must be doing to her. It chases any concern for myself right out of the air. "Emma—this is from someone in a *game?*"

"There's more." She reaches over and swipes the screen. "This was yesterday."

You suck. And that's what I'm going to say when I shove it in your mouth hole.

Anger chases my own fears away. "How many of these are there?"

"It's not a big deal. It's just some loser with too much time on his hands."

"Emma—these are *threats*—"

"But they're not. He doesn't know me. He doesn't know anything about me. It's just some douchebag with an e-mail account." Despite her cavalier words, tears are bright on her cheeks. "Stupid, right?"

"It's not stupid." I wish I had a tissue to give her. "It's—horrible."

"No." A big sniff. "It's common. It happens all the time. He's just a troll. I shouldn't be this upset."

"Emma—this is a big deal."

"It's not." She swipes at her face. "Really. It's not. You're dealing with PTSD or something, and I'm crying over a dumb *troll*."

I flinch. "It's not a competition."

"No! That's not what I meant." She straightens. "I didn't realize asking you about the sweatshirt would turn into . . . into *that*."

"I think you can cry over a dumb troll if I can lose my mind over a stupid sweatshirt." I drag a hand through my hair. I feel wrung out.

She levels me with her eyes. "It's about more than the sweatshirt."

"Well." I pull the sweatshirt over my head and force my hands through the sleeves. "I think it's about more than the game."

She swallows. "You're right."

"So are you."

We sit in the dark facing each other. Challenging each other, without risking anything.

My cell phone chimes, and I fish it out of my pocket. Kristin.

Mom: Just checking on you.

I shove it back in my pocket. "My mom."

"She doesn't know about the messages from your dad?"

I shake my head. "No—not my mom that way. She doesn't know him. She's—I'm adopted."

She frowns like she wants to push for more information, but then *her* cell phone chimes, and she yanks it out of *her* pocket.

"*My* mom." She sighs.

I hesitate, then get to my feet. "We should probably get back before they send out search parties. I was pretty messed up when I walked out of the house."

"Me too." She gets to her feet, wrapping the dog's leash around her wrist.

Then we stand there, not moving, sharing the same air.

"Do you—" I begin, then stop short. I have no practice with this. I'm not even sure what I'm asking.

She waits.

I take a breath and try again. "Would it be weird if I asked if you wanted to do this again?"

"You mean, meet behind the church to freak out together?"

I let out that breath. "Yeah?"

"Probably. Would it be weird if I said yes?"

I smile. "Probably. Tomorrow night? Eight o'clock?"

"Sure." She turns to go.

I watch her walk across the grass, the dog trotting lazily by her side.

"Hey, Emma!" I call.

She whirls. "Yeah?"

"That's not okay," I say. "What he said to you. You know that, right?"

"Yeah." She turns and keeps walking.

Then she turns around, but continues walking backward. "Hey, Rev."

I haven't moved, but it makes me smile. "Yeah?"

"Whatever your father did to you. That's not okay either. You know that, right?"

The words hit me hard. I can't speak. I nod.

"Good." Then she turns around, breaks into a run, and she's gone.

NINE

Emma

The message from Nightmare is right in the middle of the screen when I open my laptop.

It's lost a little bit of its power, though.

That's not okay. What he said to you. You know that, right?

I did know that. I do know that. But for some reason, hearing the words from a complete outsider gives them a little more weight.

Hearing the words from *Rev* gives them a little more weight.

I've never met anyone quite like him. He's intriguing. I said that watching him lose the sweatshirt was like watching Clark Kent turn into Superman, but that was almost an understatement. It's more like finding the dark and brooding Oliver Queen under the hood of the Green Arrow.

I don't usually tell anyone about in-game harassment—it's

so common that I rarely think to mention it. If someone hassles you in person, you can tell a teacher, or talk to a manager, or call the cops. It's one person, and you can recruit other people to help stand against them.

If someone harasses you online, you can have them blocked— but they can reappear in seconds, pretending to be someone else. Over and over again.

Anonymously.

I close Nightmare's message, log in to my admin panel, and block him again.

This is beginning to feel a bit fruitless, though. Nightmare has already demonstrated a willingness to create new accounts to harass me. I'm stuck in this space where I'm giving him what he wants—attention—and wishing I had a more effective means of attack.

I don't. So. Here I sit.

A message is waiting from Ethan, too.

Friday, March 16   8:11 p.m.
From: Ethan_717
To: Azure M

What happened? All OK? I'll be on for a while if you get a chance to log in. If I'm not here, check Battle Realms.

It makes me smile. He's turning into a friend.

What a weird night.

The moment I have the thought, there's a tap-tap-tap at my door. I slide my headphones onto my neck and sigh. It has to be my mother. "Come in."

Mom eases the door open. She's in loose pajama pants and a tank top, her hair in that signature ponytail. Sometimes I wonder if she's trying to send a statement to the world that she has no time for feminine standards—but really, she's probably just too busy to bother with more.

Texy gets up from where she was flopped out and noses at Mom's hands.

She rubs the dog absently behind her ears. "Are you playing?"

I bristle. "It's a Friday night." I glance at my clock. "And it's not that late."

"I wasn't criticizing. I was asking if I was interrupting."

Sure. "No. It's fine."

"Can I come in?"

I close the laptop and wish I could say no. I don't want a lecture, so it's better to just get this over with. "Okay."

She eases into my desk chair and looks around. "I wanted to talk about what you said this morning."

"Oh. When I was in the shower?"

"Yes, Emma." She sounds a little exasperated at my attitude. "When you were in the shower." Texas is leaning against Mom's legs, her head resting in her lap. I want to call her away, but Mom is rubbing her head now. It reminds me of how Rev was doing the same thing. Maybe it's a tension release.

"We don't need to talk," I say. "I know you don't like the gaming."

"Emma—it's not that I don't like the gaming. It's that I want you to be realistic about your goals."

I scoff. "What do you know about my goals?"

"I know you think your father has an amazing job. I know you'd like to be a game designer yourself. But sometimes luck plays a role, and that's not something you can count on."

"I know, Mom."

"I'm very much in favor of furthering women's advancement in STEM fields, but I think it would be prudent for you to have some practical—"

"I know. I get it."

"I don't think you do. I'm asking you to keep an open mind—"

"If I'd said you *were* interrupting, would that have stopped this conversation?"

"I don't appreciate that, Emma. Every time I try to talk to you—"

"Look." My throat tightens, because she'll never understand why this is important to me. "I don't want to be a doctor. I'm sorry, okay?" I put the headphones back on my head and open the laptop before emotion can crowd into my voice. "I'm sorry I'm such a disappointment."

Her expression seems frozen between surprise and irritation. "Emma. What—"

I press a button. Hard rock courses into my headphones. She keeps talking, but I have no idea what she's saying.

I lock my eyes on my monitor. If I listen to one more word, I'll start crying.

She's still talking. I wonder how long I can get away with this.

I log in to OtherLANDS and keep my eyes on the log-in message.

An iMessage from Cait appears on the screen.

> **Cait:** Are you gaming?
> **Emma:** No, I'm ignoring my mother.
> **Cait:** What do you mean?
> **Emma:** I mean she's sitting right here and I am not listening to her. What's going on?
> **Cait:** I got all set up to do a video, but then Calvin needed the laptop for homework. Now I'm just killing time.

Calvin is her younger brother. I should ask what her video is about, but I really don't want to talk about eyeliner or cosplay or foundation right now.

At the same time, I don't like this weird distance between us. I type quickly.

> **Emma:** Do you want to come over?
> **Cait:** Doesn't sound that happy at your house right now.

She's right. I glance up. Mom is still there. She's glaring at me now.

That's actually helpful. A glare means she's angry instead of pretending to understand. I can deal with angry.

I pull the headphones down. "What?"

"I'm trying to have a conversation. If you're trying to demonstrate your maturity, ignoring me won't do the trick."

"Look, I know you think Dad is a waste of space right now. Sorry I got the bulk of his DNA. Must be so rough for you." My voice threatens to waver. I pull the headphones back up.

I force my eyes to stay on the screen, but I can see her in my peripheral vision. Her face is red, her jaw clenched. She looks like she's ready to yell. Or to hit something.

I hope she does. I'd love to see her lose it.

Instead, she walks out.

Emma: Mom just walked out. That didn't take long at all.
Cait: What's going on?
Emma: She's mad that I don't want to be a doctor.
Cait: Have you showed her the game?
Emma: I don't think it would matter.

The little dots appear below my message, showing that she's writing back, and they seem to go on forever.

And ever.

And ever.

I log in to my game while I'm waiting.

A message flashes at me immediately. *No connection found.*

What? I glance at my bookcase, at my flashing router.

Which isn't flashing.

WHAT?

I get up and pull the plug, then wait a full minute.

When I plug it back in, it still doesn't work.

I go to the door and fling it open.

Before I can say a word, my mom calls from down the hall. "Problems, Emma?"

Irritation stabs me right in the back. I can tell, just from her voice, that she's done something. "Did you cut the Internet?"

"Maybe you would have noticed if you weren't so busy ignoring me."

I want to punch the wall. "And you called *me* immature?"

She comes to the doorway of her bedroom. She's rubbing lotion into her hands. For a moment, I feel as though we're having some kind of standoff.

"Maybe a night without the Internet will do you some good," she says. "Some time to think."

"I don't know why Dad puts up with you," I snap.

She jerks back, like I've hit her.

Turning off the Internet feels like she's hit *me*.

I slink back into my room and push the door closed. My throat refuses to loosen. I've already started regretting what I just said.

The worst part is that I sound just like her. The gaming DNA might have come from my father, but the biting one-liners are all her.

I close my laptop and pick up my phone. I could connect to the phone via Bluetooth and get Internet that way, but it would never support gaming. The only place she could have disconnected the Internet is at the Verizon box in the basement, so I just need to wait until she's asleep to reconnect it. Not a crisis, but a pain in the ass.

Emma: My mom just cut the Internet.

Cait: I guess she wasn't happy about the ignoring.

Emma: Whose side are you on?

Cait: I wasn't taking sides! I'm just saying.

I don't know what to say. My mental state has gone straight to hell in a matter of minutes. I want to pick a fight with everyone right now.

Where's Nightmare when I need him?

There's a long pause before the little gray dots appear from Cait's side of the conversation.

Cait: Thanks for the invite. I think I'm going to bed.

Emma: OK.

I sit in absolute silence for the longest time. Texy climbs up on the bed and flops her lumbering self down beside me. Her head drops in my lap.

I log in to my messages on my phone to write back to Ethan through 5Core. I don't want to complain about Nightmare. It makes me feel weak, like I can't handle a little trash talk.

Friday, March 16   9:14 p.m.

From: Azure M

To: Ethan_717

Mom cut the Internet. I'm waiting for her to fall asleep so I can reconnect it.

His response comes back almost immediately.

Friday, March 16   9:15 p.m.
From: Ethan_717
To: Azure M

That's a new one. I'll be here all night. Yay, Friday.

I smile. *Yay, Friday.*

Friday, March 16   9:16 p.m.
From: Azure M
To: Ethan_717

Give me an hour. Depending on how many glasses of wine she's had, it might be less than that.

A new message appears almost instantly. I grin.
But then I see the message header.

Friday, March 16   9:16 p.m.
From: N1ghtm@re4
To: Azure M

Hey, look, I found you on 5Core.
   Nice pic.

I freeze, staring at the message.

My screen names are the same in both places. That's not too big a deal.

It's the content of his message that's so unsettling.

No one has ever connected Azure M to Emma Blue, but as I stare at his message, I realize how simple it could be to connect the dots. And my profile pic doesn't show my face, but it does show my back. Cait took it last October, at the Fall Festival. My arms are up, and I'm cheering after throwing a whipped cream pie at the quarterback and hitting him square in the face.

In the picture, my braid hangs down my back.

I'm wearing a Hamilton High School T-shirt.

I can't delete it from here. I need to go downstairs and reconnect the router. My heart beats so hard it's almost painful, and adrenaline has taken over my bloodstream. My fingers shake over the screen of the phone.

But then I talk myself down.

Azure M isn't *that* obvious.

Hamilton High School isn't either. My braid covers half of the words. I know what it says because it's my T-shirt, but in the tiny thumbnail, it's almost unreadable.

Not to mention, I go to school with two thousand other kids.

And he didn't threaten me. He just said *nice pic*. He could be commenting on my butt. He probably *was* commenting on my butt.

This is a calculated attempt to make me uncomfortable. It's working, but it's not criminal.

It's not even a message I can report. What would I say? *Some guy said I have a nice pic.*

I can click on his name, though.

Annnnd of course his profile is almost completely blank. His "name" is Night Mare. Hilarious.

I sigh. I hate this. I delete the message.

All of a sudden, I don't want to reconnect the Internet at all. I don't want to see what else he might have sent me in the game.

That's not okay. What he said to you. You know that, right?

I do know that.

I just can't do anything about it.

TEN

Rev

Saturday, March 17   12:06:24 a.m.
FROM: Robert Ellis <robert.ellis@speedmail.com>
TO: Rev Fletcher <rev.fletcher@freemail.com>
SUBJECT: Midnight

Do you remember the story of the Prodigal Son? Which
brother are you? I wonder.

Yes, I remember.
I can practically recite it verse for verse.
Basically, a father has two sons. The younger son is eager to
live his life and go off into the world, so he asks his father for
his inheritance early. The father gives it to him, and the younger
son goes off and blows all his money, until he's destitute and

living in the streets. Meanwhile, the older son never leaves his father's side.

When the younger son remembers that his father's servants have always had food to spare, he decides to return home to beg for the opportunity to work as a servant in his father's house. The father sees him coming, and throws a huge party to welcome his son home.

The older son is pissed. He's been there all along, but no one's ever thrown him a party for being the good son. His younger brother insults the father, blows all his money, and now he gets a celebration?

In the end, the father tells the older son, "My son, you are always with me, and everything I have is yours. But we have to celebrate and be glad, because this brother of yours was dead and is alive again; he was lost and is found."

Honestly, neither son sounds like that great a guy.

Which brother are you? I wonder.

I don't like either option. I turn my phone off.

I'm exhausted, but sleep feels miles away.

It must be miles away from Matthew, too, because he's lying in bed, staring at the ceiling.

He has said nothing to me since I got home. I've said nothing to him. The moment of peace I found with Emma seems miles away.

My bedroom has turned into this cube of anxious silence. I want to take my pillow and my blanket and go sleep on the couch, but I don't like the idea of being on the other side of the house, or being in the basement.

I don't understand his issue with the bus. I don't understand why he was hiding in the dark, watching me.

I don't understand the knife, or the question about the locked door, or why I found him trying to sneak out.

I turn my head and look over at him. I keep my voice soft. "Hey. Why did you need the knife?"

Matthew says nothing.

"You were trying to get out the door, so I don't think you were going to hurt Geoff and Kristin."

Nothing.

"Were you going to meet someone? Were you going *after* someone?"

Nothing.

This is exhausting. I sigh. "I know you can hear me."

Nothing.

I sigh and roll up on one elbow to look at him directly.

Matthew shoves himself upright. He looks ready to bolt from the bed. I can hear him breathing.

But I don't move, and he freezes in place. He watches me, his eyes shining in the moonlight from the window.

"I told you I'm not going to mess with you," I say to him.

He doesn't move. Surprise, surprise. I can't stay in this bedroom if either one of us is going to get any sleep.

My phone tells me it's half past midnight. Declan might still be up.

I hesitate.

Three days ago, I wouldn't have hesitated.

I need to get over myself. I shoot him a text.

Rev: You awake?

I wait a full minute, my heart pounding, but he doesn't respond.

I call him.

He answers on the third ring, and he was very obviously asleep. His voice is slow and lethargic. "Rehhv?"

"Can I come over?"

"Yuh."

Close enough. I end the call. Matthew is still watching me. It's freaking me out.

I throw back my quilt. "You're in luck," I tell him. "The bedroom is all yours."

● ● ●

I cross our yards barefoot and use the hidden key to let myself in through the back door. I'm careful to close it slowly because it sticks and squeaks. Declan's parents won't care that I'm here, but showing up after midnight will invite questions I don't want to answer. I creep through the darkened house and pad up the steps to his bedroom.

He's already fallen back to sleep.

"Hey," I whisper. "Dec."

He shifts and runs a hand over his face. "Hey."

I ease his door closed so I won't wake his parents, then lean against the wall. "I need to talk to you."

His eyes don't open. "I'm awake." Barely. "D'you want the air mattress?"

"No." My brain is ticking along at high speed, leaving sleep way in the distance.

"'Kay. Here." He pulls a pillow out from under his head and flops it on the other side of the bed.

We haven't shared a bed since we were little, but it's a testament to our friendship that he tosses a pillow over so casually.

I prop the pillow up and sit down on the bed cross-legged, then lean against the wall. I keep my voice low. "I'm sorry I woke you up."

Declan says nothing, and it takes me a minute to realize he's fallen asleep *again*.

That's okay, though. This house is so different from my own right now. Instead of anxiety and mistrust, Declan's room is full of silence and sleep. I sit in the darkness for a few minutes and allow my tightly wound thoughts to uncoil.

"Rev?"

I look down. Declan blinks up at me in confusion.

"How long have you been here?" he says, his voice groggy.

Any other night and I'd find this hilarious. "Not long."

He rubs at his eyes, then glances at the clock. "What's going on?"

As soon as he asks the question, I realize how far we've drifted apart over the last few days. All because of one tiny secret. "Matthew won't stop watching me. It's freaking me out."

"Watching you how?"

"Just . . . watching me. It makes me nervous."

"Hold on." Declan rubs at his eyes again. "I'm not awake enough yet."

"And I met a girl. Sort of."

"Did you say 'sort of'?"

"We keep meeting behind a church."

He stares at me like he's having trouble tracking this conversation. "Rev."

"You know what your room reminds me of right now?"

"I have no idea what is happening right now, so no."

"One of the psalms. 'He stilled the storm to a whisper; the waves of the sea were hushed.'" I pause for a moment, just to savor the silence. "All night, my brain has been a war zone. Now I'm here, and it's quiet."

"You walked yourself over here, Rev. And it's quiet because I'm sleeping. Not because of God."

I frown. "Why do you always do that?"

"Dude. Seriously." His expression is a mixture of incredulity and irritation, but at least he looks more awake. He glances at the clock on his dresser. "It's almost one in the morning. You want to argue about religion?"

"No." But now I don't want to talk about any of it. I look away from him to stare out at the moonlit street. I wonder if Matthew fell asleep.

I wonder if he's taking the chance to escape.

Declan sighs, then sits up, propping his pillow to sit against the wall, too. He lets out a breath and runs a hand back through his hair. "Did you say you met a girl behind a church?"

"Forget it."

"Rev, I swear—"

"Answer my question." I turn to look at him. His eyes are

still heavy lidded, his hair standing up in tufts. He's shirtless, and while I don't care—in fact, I envy his comfort with it—all I keep hearing in my head is Emma's voice saying *I said* whoa *because you have an amazing body.*

In truth, my body is a testament to all the ways I failed my father.

"What question?" Declan says.

"Why do you always do that? Why do you always . . ." I search for the right word. "*Deflect.* When I talk about God, or the Bible, or anything that's not concrete."

"Can I go sleep in your bed and you can have this argument alone?"

I don't answer. Anger begins to build in my chest, a slow burn I can't ignore.

The doorknob clicks and turns, and Declan's stepfather, Alan, pokes his head into the room. They don't have a great relationship, but they've learned to tolerate each other. He does a complete double take when he sees me sitting on the bed. "Rev. How long have you been here?"

Ten minutes is not an answer that would go over well. I shrug. "Awhile."

He looks like he's going to demand a better answer, but then he grimaces and glances back out into the hallway. "Declan, I'm taking your mother to the hospital. She thinks she's having contractions."

Any attitude just *falls* off Declan's face. His eyes widen. "Is she okay? I can get dressed."

"No, no, stay here. She's not sure. We're just going to check.

It'll be a lot of waiting." He pauses, and his expression softens. "I'll text you and let you know what's going on. Okay?"

"Yeah. Okay."

Alan eases the door closed, trapping the silence in here with us again.

Declan doesn't break it. There's another splinter in our friendship, and I don't like it at all.

"I'm sorry," I say quietly. "I didn't come over here to pick a fight."

"Rev—" He breaks off and sighs. He yanks open the drawer to his bedside table and fishes out a box of orange Tic Tacs. He pours out a handful. "There are days I hate Juliet for making me quit smoking."

I hold out my hand and he pours some for me. "No, you don't."

"Trust me. I do." He tosses them into his mouth. I do the same. We crunch for a while.

Finally, he says, "I don't know what's out there. You know I have a hard time with the whole God thing. Especially since Dad . . . since Kerry died."

His sister. She died five years ago, when Declan's father got drunk and crashed the car they were riding in. Declan hasn't seen his father since it happened, but I know he feels some responsibility for all of it.

He hasn't seen him because his father has been in prison.

Declan looks at me. "And you know I don't understand how *you* can believe any of it. After what your father did." Another pause. "But I don't mean to *deflect*. It's important to you. I don't need to be an ass about it."

He stops, but he sounds like he has more to say, so I wait.

"You've got that scar on your wrist," he says. "Looks like half circles."

I go very still. I know the scar he's talking about.

I remember getting it.

I was seven. We'd been fasting for two days. I was so hungry that the thought of food made me dizzy. Even the memory is hazy.

"Please," I said to my father. "Please can we have some food?"

He turned on the stove.

And I stupidly thought that meant he was going to cook something.

"Rev." Declan's voice is soft. "We don't have to talk about this."

My hand grips tight around my wrist, covering the scar through two layers of fabric. I'm not breathing. It was one of the last things my father ever did to me.

I force myself to inhale. I stare down at my fingers. "What about it?"

"I didn't figure out what made that scar until we were like fifteen years old. A coil burner on a stove, right? I know about everything else, but that—figuring it out—I've never hated someone so much, Rev. I asked Geoff where to find him. I wanted to kill him." He shakes more Tic Tacs like he wants to murder the container. "Damn it, thinking about it makes me want to find him and kill him *right now*."

"You asked Geoff?" I stare at him. "You never told me that."

"He told me not to. He said it would upset you."

It's very strange, to hear that they had a conversation I knew nothing of. "But that scar—that's not even the worst of it."

He flings the container against the bedside table and rounds on me. "Oh my god. Are you kidding me? It's *all* the worst of it, Rev. All of it! You can't even wear short-sleeved shirts! Have you ever been in a pool? You can't tell me Geoff and Kristin haven't wanted to go to the beach once in the last ten years. We're two hours from the ocean! And that asshole defended himself by saying everything he did to you was the work of God, and somehow you believe that's true. You think God saved you from him. Hell, you find some peace and quiet in my house, and you think God led you here. Do you have any idea what that sounds like?"

I flinch.

"Rev," he says. "If you want to believe in God, fine. If you want to debate theology, fine. If you want to believe a higher power offered you some protection, *fine*. But every mark on your body—your father did that. Your *father*. You survived what he did to you. You got yourself out of there. And *you* walked yourself over here tonight. You, Rev. You did that."

I can't breathe. He's never said these things to me. I feel as if I'm made of stone, and Declan has struck me with a chisel, sending cracks along my surface.

And suddenly, I know I can't tell him about the letter. About the e-mails. Not tonight. He won't understand why I sent the first e-mail. He won't understand why I let it go on.

"Are you okay?" he says.

My breath shakes. "Do you know the story of the Prodigal Son?"

"Oh my god. Rev—"

"Do you?"

He sighs. "I don't remember the whole thing."

So I tell him the story.

He listens. When I'm done, he says, "What does that have to do with anything?"

"Which one am I?" I finally ask.

"Rev—"

"I didn't stay with my father. So I'm obviously not the devoted son."

"Dude."

"But is that saying that if I went back to him, he'd welcome me with open arms? Am I supposed to be that son?"

"Are you listening to yourself right now?"

"No." I study him. My voice is a breath away from breaking. "Help me, Dec. Which one am I?"

His eyes are dark and serious. "Neither. Is that what you need me to say? You're neither son."

"But—"

"You're not selfish. You wouldn't be the son who asks for his money and leaves. And you're not spiteful. You don't resent anyone, even the one person you *should*."

I flinch again. "Don't you understand? I have to be one or the other."

"No, you don't! You moron, there are three people in the story."

"What?"

"You're neither son, Rev. If you're anyone, you're the man

who watched his kids act like total dicks, only to stand there with open arms and forgive them."

I'm speechless. I might be gaping at him. As many times as I've read that parable, I've never considered a third perspective. But of course it's right there. It's so clear.

Declan pulls his pillow away from the wall, fluffs it up, and lies back down. He yawns. "Now. Tell me about the girl."

ELEVEN

Emma

Saturday, March 17   3:22 a.m.

From: Ethan_717

To: Azure M

I don't want to sound like a stalker, but I didn't see you. I hope everything is OK with your mom. Signing off for the night.

The Internet is back. I wake to flashing lights on the front of my router.

When I saw the 5Core message on the face of my phone, I was almost afraid to click on it. Thank god it was just Ethan.

That said, I don't want to sign on. I don't want to deal with Nightmare yet. I know I need to block him, but it can wait another ten minutes. I go downstairs to find coffee.

Mom is in the living room doing yoga. Country music pours out of the speaker near her, which I find amusing. She never listens to anything tranquil. It's like she has to be contrary, even when she's supposed to be mindful.

She's in this pose called Dhanurasana, where she's on her stomach, her arms and legs curled up to meet over her back. She used to make me do this with her every Saturday until I realized I could just stop showing up.

"You're up early," she says. "Get a good night's sleep?"

I scowl and head into the kitchen. It shouldn't be a dig, but it is.

What she means is, *Get a good night's sleep without your game?*

I pour coffee into a mug.

"Do you want to join me?" she calls.

"I like my spine the way it is, thanks."

"The recycling needs to go out to the curb."

It's not a request—but at the same time, it is. I don't want to do it, but I also don't want her to call Verizon and kill the Internet entirely. I leave the coffee on the counter and head into the garage. The large yellow bin sits by the wall near Mom's BMW.

Dad's car isn't there.

Huh. I'm not sure what to make of that.

I drag the recycling to the curb, then head back inside.

I really don't want to talk to Mom, especially about Dad, so I grab my coffee and head back up the stairs.

"You shouldn't be drinking that!" she calls.

"Okay!" I call back. Then I shut myself into my room with my mug.

I open my laptop and go into iMessage.

I was going to send a message to my father, but my last messages with Cait sit right there in silent judgment.

Thanks for the invite. I think I'm going to bed.

I message her now.

Emma: Hey. You there?
Cait: Yes. What are you doing up?

Is it really *so* shocking? I scowl.

Emma: You sound like my mother.
Cait: It's 7:30. I don't usually hear from you until noon.
Emma: OK.

She doesn't say anything. I don't know what I expect her to say.

I don't like this feeling.

I start a new message to my father.

Emma: Hey, Daddy. You're out early. ♡

I wait. And wait. And wait.

He doesn't respond.

A new message from Cait appears.

Cait: Are you OK?

Emma: I don't know.

Cait: You don't know if you're OK? You texted me. What's going on?

I don't answer her. I close iMessage. I don't know what's wrong with me.

OtherLANDS takes a minute to load. No new messages from Nightmare. I leave his account alone. Maybe blocking him has been the wrong strategy. Maybe I've been giving him attention he doesn't deserve. Ignoring him might be the better bet.

My phone rings.

I check the display. Cait.

I slide the button to silence the ring.

I am such a horrible friend.

At the last second, I slide the bar to answer.

"Hey."

"Hey," she says back, her voice low. "Are you okay?"

"I'm fine."

"You don't sound fine."

"Yeah? What exactly do I sound like, Cait?"

She's silent for a beat. "You sound angry."

"I am angry."

"Okay. Are you angry at me?"

"I don't think so."

"You don't *think* so?"

"Are you going to repeat everything I say?"

"Em?"

I can practically hear her frowning over the phone. "I'm not angry at you, Cait." I can't even think why I would be. She's done nothing wrong. And I'm certainly not jealous of her.

For some reason, this is not a good feeling.

"Is the Internet still off?" says Cait. "Are you mad at your mom?"

"No. She turned it back on. Probably for herself."

Another few beats of silence. "Do you want to come over?"

"No."

"Do you want *me* to come over?"

Maybe. I don't know. "I need to finish waking up first."

She sighs. "Did something *else* happen? I'm just . . . I'm trying to figure out what's going on."

My father's not home, and it doesn't feel right. My mother is constantly on my case. I have some weirdo sending me bizarre messages through my game. I'm a slacker who's good for nothing more than late-night gaming.

"I'm fine," I say. "I'm just PMS-ing."

"Mom is making chocolate-chip pancakes," she says. "Are you sure you don't want to come over?"

"Of course she is." I'm sure Cait and her family will be lining up to share a lovely weekend breakfast. My parents can't even be in the same room without arguing.

"Are you going to have a snippy comeback to everything I say?" says Cait.

"Maybe. Keep talking."

I mean it as a joke, but instead, it comes out exactly like everything else I've said.

"Mom's calling me," she says resignedly. "I need to go."

"Wait," I say.

"What?"

I need to apologize. I think.

This has gotten so complicated. I don't know why I'm taking everything out on Cait.

I do know that I don't want her to hang up. If she hangs up, I'm at my mother's mercy. Ethan won't be awake if he was still online at 3:30 a.m., and I don't want to take my chances with Nightmare.

I take a deep breath. "I'm supposed to see Rev Fletcher tonight."

There's a moment of stunned silence. "Like . . . a date?"

"Sort of."

"Is that what you're so keyed up about?"

"No. Maybe." I clench my eyes shut. "I have no idea, Cait."

"How did this come about?"

I pause. "I ran into him again. We . . . talked."

"He said more than two words to you?"

I had a rough childhood.

"Yeah. He . . . I think maybe he's misunderstood. I think he's quiet for a reason."

Her voice turns wry. "You mean he's not really the Grim Reaper?"

"Stop it."

"Jeez, Em. I'm just kidding." She pauses. "He doesn't strike me as the 'date' type."

"We're meeting behind the church." I realize how that sounds, and heat finds my cheeks. "To talk."

"Wow, that doesn't sound incredibly sketchy."

"It's—I don't know. He's very thoughtful."

"Like, he gives you presents?" She sounds confused.

"No! No. I mean—thought provoking. He feels—I don't know, Cait." I flop back against my pillows. "He feels real."

Now there's a long silence.

So long that I say, "Are you still there?"

"Yes. I think that's an interesting statement." She pauses. "I don't want you to snap at me, but . . ."

"But what?"

"I think it's a good statement." Another pause. "I think you need someone real, Em."

It doesn't make me want to snap.

In fact, it makes me want to cry. "I think I need someone real, too," I say.

She must hear emotion in my voice because she says, "Are you *sure* you don't want me to come over?"

Yes, I realize. I do. I so desperately do.

I don't like being desperate for anything. I sniff and get myself together. "No," I say. "I'll let you go . . . before your brothers eat all the pancakes."

TWELVE

Rev

Saturday, March 17   04:09:29 a.m.

FROM: Robert Ellis <robert.ellis@speedmail.com>

TO: Rev Fletcher <rev.fletcher@freemail.com>

SUBJECT: Disappointed

Do you remember your lessons? Perhaps you were too young.

   Here is one from Proverbs I remember well. "If one curses his father or mother, his lamp shall be put out in utter darkness."

The e-mail doesn't wake me, though it's a nice little morning surprise when I find it. Does my father ever sleep?

   Kristin texts me at 8:00 a.m. I've been staring out the window, watching the sun rise for an hour.

Mom: Please tell me you're at Declan's.

Rev: Yes. Sorry. Should have left a note.

Mom: Did something happen?

How am I supposed to answer that?

Rev: No. All OK.

I bite at my lip, waiting. She doesn't write back.

Matthew must not have left, because I'm sure she would have mentioned it. I should feel relief, but I don't. I don't feel dread, either. I don't know what I feel.

Declan continues snoring beside me, but there's no way I can go back to sleep. I ease off the bed and move to the desk chair, sitting in the dim light of early morning, thinking.

My father's e-mail shouldn't be a fist to the gut, but it is. I wish I had a shred of Declan's attitude, his ease with bucking authority. For Declan, there'd be no hesitation. He'd take a selfie of himself flipping off the camera and reply with that.

I don't like bucking authority. You don't need a degree in psychology to figure out why: when your father tortures you for breaking a rule, it's hard to let that go.

But that's just one side of it. My father wasn't always horrible. When I earned his praise, he made me feel like the most cherished child alive. I learned to crave it.

I crave it now. And I hate myself for it.

Without warning, Declan rolls over and rubs his eyes. He finds me sitting in the chair. "Have you been up for a long time?"

My eyes flick to the clock on the dresser. It's almost nine. "Yes."

"You should have woken me."

"It's okay." I pause, keeping my voice low. "Alan and your mom got back a little while ago. No baby."

He sits up and looks at the door. "Are they awake?"

"I don't think so. I heard their door close."

"Okay." He rubs his face again. "I need ten minutes. Do you want to go make coffee?"

Good. A task. I need a task. "Sure."

I know my way around his kitchen as well as my own. The white cabinets, the drawer that sticks, the one loose handle that'll come off if you tug. I could do this with my eyes closed. Making coffee takes no time at all.

Which sucks.

I read the e-mail again. I know the verse by heart. It was one of my father's favorites.

I want to twist this phone in my hands to watch the screen shatter. Worse, I want to write back and beg his forgiveness for ignoring the last three.

I slide my sleeve back and trace my fingers over the arcs burned into the skin. I don't remember everything, but I remember the stove. The pain was so strong it became more than pain: a scream in my ear, the brightest light in my eyes. I could *taste* the pain.

I never ran from my father before that day.

He caught me, of course. I was seven. He caught me and spun me around so hard that it caused a rotational fracture in my forearm.

I made it outside before he caught me. My screaming drew a lot of attention.

That, and the fact that I'd thrown up all over myself.

"Rev."

I jump and yank my sleeve down. Declan stands in the kitchen doorway.

"The coffee's almost ready," I say, though I have no idea whether that's true.

He comes into the kitchen and pulls down steel mugs from a cabinet. "Something else is up with you."

I blink at him, startled. "What are you talking about?"

"I don't know. But you were fine when we fell asleep and now you're a wreck."

He's right, but I have no idea what to say to that. He pulls a spoon from the drawer, then dumps an obscene amount of cream and sugar into both mugs.

Once he's done stirring, he holds one out to me. "Do you want to talk about it?"

"No."

"Okay, then come on."

He turns and heads for the back door, not even waiting for me to follow.

I go after him. The air is cold, with just a hint of warmth to come. Clouds thicken the sky, and the humidity promises a rainstorm later. "Come on, what?"

Declan stops to unlatch the gate between our yards. He looks back at me. "The girl you met at the church doesn't have you this keyed up. You said you barely know her."

I don't move. "Yeah, so?"

The latch gives, and he pushes through. "There's only one more variable."

A chill locks into my spine. Did he figure out the e-mails somehow? "One more—what?"

"I think I need to meet Matthew." Then he sprints up my porch steps and goes through the sliding door, without waiting for me to catch up.

Oh. Oh, *wow.*

In the ten seconds it takes me to cross the yard, I consider how this will go. Every scenario I can imagine ends badly. By the time I get into the kitchen, I expect to find Declan cornering Matthew while Kristin and Geoff wring their hands and beg him to stop.

But I really should know my friend—and my parents—better than that. Declan has helped himself to a slice of bacon from a plate on the counter, and he's dropped into one of the kitchen chairs. Kristin has two quiches cooling on racks by the stove. Matthew is nowhere to be seen.

"How is your mom feeling?" Kristin is asking Declan when I burst through the door.

She gives me an odd look, but Declan acts like nothing is amiss. "She's fine," he says. "Alan took her to the hospital last night, but nothing happened."

"She must be getting close."

"I told her that I'm going to move in here so I don't have to listen to a baby crying." He takes another piece of bacon. "But I guess Rev's already got a roommate."

"Maybe we can trade," I say. "I don't mind crying babies."

Kristin glances between us, but she lets the comment go. She picks up a pan to wash from the overflowing sink. "Rev doesn't have a roommate for long. We're going to pick up a twin bed for the other bedroom this afternoon. We'll put the crib and the rocker in the garage for now."

Good.

As soon as the thought hits me, I frown. So much for welcoming everyone with open arms.

"Where is he?" I ask. It sounds like a demand. Or a threat.

"Taking a shower." Kristin holds out the pan and a dish towel. "Dry this, please."

I do, and she moves on to the next dish. My movements are tense and forced.

"Tell me what's going on," she says quietly.

"I don't know."

As soon as I say the words, I realize how true they are. I *don't* know what's going on. What am I supposed to say? Matthew won't talk to me in the middle of the night. I think he might have been watching me work out. He doesn't want to ride to school with me and Declan.

It all just sounds so . . . *juvenile.* Maybe I could whine about eating broccoli or cleaning my room next.

Kristin is looking at me while she washes the next pan, and she holds it out for me to dry. Her voice remains quiet, nonconfrontational. "Did something happen?"

Kristin has always had this magical way of making people talk, and now is no exception. I sometimes tease her that she should have been a therapist instead of an accountant. I have a great relationship with both of them, but with Kristin, her warm acceptance of everything makes it so difficult to keep my father's e-mails a secret.

I take a breath and hold it for a moment, though I know she won't judge me for anything I say. "Matthew makes me nervous."

Another dripping pan extends across the counter. "That's interesting."

"Why?"

"Because half an hour ago, he was sitting here telling me that you make him nervous."

My hands go still with the dish towel. "Why do I make *him* nervous?"

"He didn't say." She pauses, then holds out another dish. "I just thought you should know."

I consider Matthew's reaction when I barely moved last night. I realign what he's said—and what he hasn't said—over the last two days. Geoff said he's been in and out of four different foster homes so far this year. He said Matthew started a fight in the last one. I took all that to mean Matthew was the problem.

It's not like he's done anything to correct my assumptions.

Declan was wrong. I'm totally the resentful son.

"Hey, man," Declan says, and the tone of his voice says he's speaking to someone new. "Want some bacon?"

I turn to look. Matthew hovers in the shadowed hallway. His wet hair is slicked back, making him look even younger, the bruises along his face more pronounced.

His gaze bounces from me to Declan and back. Then to Kristin.

"There's plenty left," she says brightly.

"No, thank you." He turns and disappears down the hallway.

I hand Kristin the dried pan and take another wet dish. She doesn't say anything, so I don't either.

Declan rises from his chair and comes to get more bacon. He keeps his voice low. "Rev. Seriously. You've got that kid by like forty pounds."

"He doesn't make me nervous that way."

"What other way is there?"

I'm not sure how to answer that.

Kristin holds a dripping measuring cup out to Declan, along with another towel. "If you're going to eat all the bacon, you can help with the dishes."

He shoves another piece into his mouth and takes the dish readily. "Who did that to his face? Hell, if I looked like that, I'd be afraid of you, too."

"Shut up."

"I'm not kidding."

I dry a cookie sheet. Tension has settled across my shoulders again. I don't know what to do with this.

"Can you boys help move the furniture this afternoon?" says Kristin. "Dad won't admit it, but his back is bothering him again."

"Sure," says Declan. He takes what must be his tenth piece of bacon. "Keep feeding me and I'll move the whole house."

"Deal. You can start clearing out the furniture now if you want. The only thing we're leaving in there is the dresser."

I don't look at her. I keep drying dishes. I can stand in the kitchen and dry dishes all day if it means I don't have to deal with any of this.

Declan forcibly pulls the bowl out of my hands. "We've got our orders. Move."

● ● ●

I don't know why I was worried. Matthew doesn't help. I don't even know where he went. He's probably hiding in my bedroom.

Hiding.

I don't like that.

Shame curls through my chest like something alive. I've wondered how my father turned into the man he was. The man he is. I know about the cycle of abuse, and I've spent a lot of hours wondering when I would start to change.

Did I do something I'm not aware of? Does Matthew sense something in me that makes him nervous? I think of the day I found the letter, how darkness wove through my thoughts and turned my anger on Geoff and Declan.

I'm glad for an excuse to bury my worries in something physical. Cleaning out the baby furniture is a bigger task than I anticipated, because we need to make room in the garage first, which requires moving plastic boxes of clothes and toys into the house and up into the attic. Kristin wants us to sweep and blow all the dust and dirt out of the garage before we move the furniture in.

Then Geoff comes back from Big Lots, and we have to unload the *new* furniture.

By the time we're done, it's midafternoon and we're filthy. Dark clouds have rolled in, promising rain. Declan collapses in the backyard grass with a bottle of Gatorade. He's flat on his back, staring at the sky.

Thunder cracks. Raindrops fall.

He doesn't move. "This figures."

I don't move, either. The raindrops feel good. I'm sitting cross-legged with my own bottle of Gatorade. I ditched the hoodie hours ago, when the humidity got to be too much, but I kept the long sleeves. I only own one short-sleeved T-shirt. I don't own *any* shorts.

"I'm supposed to meet Emma tonight," I tell him.

"Another hot date at the church?"

"Shut up." He was half asleep when I told him about her, but of course he'd remember that detail. "But yeah."

"Do you like her?"

"Yes."

My answer must be too easy, too literal, because he turns his head and looks over at me. "Do you *like* like her?"

Raindrops collect in my hair as I try to figure out the twisting pathway of my thoughts. I like the way her questions push me without pushing too hard. I like how she offered vulnerability when my own emotions were clawing at me from the inside.

I like her freckles and her braided hair and her analytical eyes. The soft curve of her lips.

Declan hits me with his Gatorade bottle. "Yeah. You like her."

"I don't know what I'm doing."

"Just be yourself."

"Thanks, Mrs. Vickers. You have a pamphlet for that?"

Declan makes an aggrieved sound. "Man, I don't know. Half the time I think it's a miracle that Juliet will give me the time of day." He swipes rain off his cheeks. "I'm probably not the best resource for relationship advice."

Maybe not, but he's the only resource I have.

We sit in the rain for the longest time. Lightning flashes, but it's a while before the thunder rolls.

"Thanks for helping," I tell him.

"I did it for the food." Kristin made us tuna melts for lunch. I think Declan really would move in if he thought he could get away with it.

The back door slides open behind us, and I'm sure it's Geoff or Kristin coming to tell us to get in the house and out of the thunderstorm.

Instead I hear Matthew's voice. "Kristin says to come inside."

Then the door slides closed.

I sigh.

Declan sits up. He hits me in the arm. "I'm going home. Go fix that."

"I don't know how to fix that."

He's quiet for a moment. "Sure you do. You remember how to play with Legos, right?" Then he uncurls from the ground and heads for the gate.

THIRTEEN

Emma

Saturday, March 17   4:16 p.m.
From: N1ghtm@re4
To: Azure M

What's wrong? I haven't seen you in a while. All tied up?

And then there's a picture. It's a screenshot of my avatar, Photoshopped to look like she's bound and unconscious. Or maybe dead. I don't bother to figure it out before slamming my finger on the trackpad to close his message.

I'm breathing so hard I'm worried I'm going to hyperventilate.

I block him again.

My heart needs to slow down.

I'm glad I'm alone in the house—but at the same time, I'm not.

I imagine the conversation.

Mom, a guy sent me a picture of my avatar and she's all tied up.

Emma, I told you to stay away from technology. When will you ever learn?

I swallow. No, thank you.

I click over to iMessage. My father still hasn't written back.

I can't talk to Cait about this. She wouldn't understand.

Then I remember the message from Ethan this morning. He might be online. I pull on my headphones and log in to my game.

Nope, he's not there. But I switch over to Battle Realms to see if he's playing there.

Bingo! I send him a team request.

"Hey," he says, sounding surprised. "All okay?"

"Hey," I say. "Yeah, just—family drama."

He snorts. "I know all about it." A pause. "You sound upset."

I am upset. I need to move past this. It's an altered screenshot. I've gotten them before. "It's fine. I'm fine."

"You want to talk about it?"

"God, no. I just need to play."

Ethan laughs. "That's my girl."

I barely know him, but hearing his voice makes me feel less alone. In-game, with my headphones on, I'm never alone.

I take a deep breath and start playing.

FOURTEEN

Rev

When I was seven, when I was first brought to Geoff and Kristin's home, I had never been in the care of anyone but my father. People have asked me why I didn't report him earlier, and to me, that's such a bizarre question. How do you report someone for doing something you've always been taught is *right*?

My father wasn't stupid. I know that now. My first experience with school didn't happen until I was living with Geoff and Kristin—my father had homeschooled me before that. I sometimes wonder if a teacher would have reported something, but I doubt it. My father had this bizarre charisma that made people love him. He was honored and respected as a man of God. I didn't realize it at the time, but his church was an offshoot of what people consider *organized* religion. We followed the Bible, we believed in God, but really, we belonged to my *father's* church—and at the time, it was all I knew. Everything I lived

was by his interpretation. Everyone who didn't was a sinner—
or worse.

I remember sitting in a pew at the front of the church while
he gave a sermon about being a father, how discipline was the
truest act of love. An older woman had leaned down and whispered in my ear, "You are so blessed."

I believed her. No matter what my father did to me, he
claimed it would make us closer to God. It was my *duty* to welcome it.

When my father put my skin to that stove burner and broke
my arm, I ran from the house screaming. A neighbor saw me
and asked what was going on—and my father almost talked himself out of the situation. I was standing there with my arm
twisted and bile on my shirt, and my father was talking about
how the flu had made me so disoriented that I'd fallen down the
stairs. At some point, the neighbor must not have believed him—
or maybe I just looked too pathetic. My memories are hazy, and
it's probably some combination of the pain and the hunger I felt
at the time, and my mixed terror over whether someone would
take action.

Here's the thing: At the time, I was ashamed of running. I
didn't want to be taken away.

Then I was. I was taken to a hospital, a place I'd never been.
I knew nothing of doctors and nurses and immunizations and
X-ray machines. I remember needles and people holding me
down. At the time, I would have given anything to be returned
to the "safety" of my father. I remember screaming for it. I'm
sure they sedated me.

The next morning, a social worker left me with Geoff and Kristin, who could not have been kinder and more welcoming. Kristin almost always smells like pies or cookies, and no one is immune to her warmth.

I was, though. At first. I thought I was in hell. My father had taught me black people worked for the devil. I believed him.

As soon as their backs were turned, I ran.

I ended up in Declan's house, because the back door was open. His mother had been gardening, her back to me. I slipped through the house, found a bedroom, and hid in the closet behind a massive box of Legos.

I was good at hiding.

Declan found me. I remember the burst of sunlight when he opened his closet door. The panicked fear in my chest. The surprise on his face. We were seven.

Declan said, "Hey! You want to play?"

I had never played with another child. I had never had toys.

"I don't know how," I whispered.

"It's easy. I'll show you."

And just like that, he started building.

• • •

I find Matthew in his new bedroom, sitting on his crisply made bed. Geoff picked up gray sheets and a navy-blue quilt at Target. A new desk with a lamp sits against the wall beside the bed. Everything smells fresh and clean—not that the room smelled bad before. But now it's all fabric and furniture instead of baby powder and Desitin.

A book sits on the comforter beside him, but Matthew isn't reading. He stares out the window at the rain.

I stop in his doorway, but I don't go farther than that. "Hey."

He doesn't look at me, but his body takes on a certain stillness.

I am not Declan. I don't know how to do this.

I tell myself to stop being such a wuss. "Can I come in?"

He says nothing.

I frown and try to keep an edge out of my voice. "If you don't want me to, just say so."

He doesn't say so. I don't like to push, but I'm going to have to, or we'll be forever trapped in this silent discomfort.

I go through the doorway, and he moves just a fraction of an inch. It's small, but it's a defensive motion.

The only chair in the room is at the desk, which is right beside the bed. I don't want to push that hard, so instead, I sit on the floor, against the wall. I'm opposite the door. He can walk out of here if he wants.

I say nothing. He says nothing.

There's no knife between us, but this feels like the other night. A standoff.

The bruises on his face and neck have started to yellow around the edges, and most of the swelling is down. "Did you really start a fight?" I ask.

Nothing. Rain batters the house, punctuating his silence.

"I don't think you did," I say.

That gets his attention. It's barely a flicker, but his eyes shift to me.

"If you were the type of kid to pick a fight, you'd have started one already." I pause. "Did someone pin you down and do that to you?"

His expression is completely blank, but I can feel him evaluating me.

I shrug. "Those marks on your neck look a lot like fingerprints."

His hand goes to his throat.

I keep my voice mild. "Why did you let them think you started it? Kristin said you risked being sent to juvie."

"Juvie would have been better." His voice is rough and very soft.

My eyebrows go up. "Better than *here*?"

He shakes his head, the tiniest movement. He speaks like he's not sure he wants to be talking. "Better than there."

We lapse into silence again. Thunder cracks hard outside, and he jumps. The storm rolled in so fast, and the afternoon sun is gone. His arms fold against his stomach.

"Do you want me to get out?" I say.

He doesn't answer.

In a flash, I think of my father's e-mails, sitting unanswered in my in-box. I wonder if Matthew doesn't know how to answer me, the way I don't know how to answer my father.

Sitting here questioning him suddenly seems like the worst kind of cruelty.

"It's okay," I say. "I'll go."

He doesn't stop me. I go down the hall to my bedroom and fall onto my bed.

This has been the most exhausting day, and it's only the middle of the afternoon. My cell phone lights up on my bedside table, and I can tell it's an e-mail from the color of the little icon.

I don't even want to look.

I have to look.

It's just something for school.

When I put the phone back down, I notice Matthew standing just outside my doorway. He's clinging to the door frame like a shadow.

I act like this isn't the weirdest thing ever. "What's up?"

"Are you the type?"

I hesitate. "The type of what?"

"The type to pick a fight."

"No."

He thinks about that for a minute. "Okay."

Then he turns around and slips back down the hallway.

FIFTEEN

Emma

I've been counting the minutes until 8:00 p.m., and now it's pouring rain.

This is so my life.

I press my nose against the window in the dining room, blowing steam against the glass. Mom would bitch at me about dirtying the windows. If she were here. I have no idea where she is. After yoga, she put on a pants suit and said she needed to make rounds. She's been gone all day.

So has Dad. He still hasn't responded to my text from this morning.

Rain pelts the siding.

Am I *not* supposed to meet Rev now? Then what was the point of fate putting me in his path twice?

This is what's wrong with relying on fate. Or God. Or whatever.

I whistle through my teeth. "Come on, Texy. We're going to get wet."

The rain is colder than I expect—which is ridiculous, since it's March. My cheeks are freezing by the time we go two blocks, my hair has a sodden weight on my shoulder. My glasses are so wet I need to shove them in a pocket. I threw Mom's pullover windbreaker over my sweatshirt before leaving the house, thinking it would be waterproof, but I am so wrong.

By the time I make the final turn for the church, I wonder if I'm stupid for being out here. It's pouring so hard that a haze has formed around the streetlight, and I can barely see anything through the darkness.

My sneakers squish in the grass. I get to the spot where we sat for the last two nights.

And of course he's not there.

I sigh. Only a complete moron would go meet in the rain.

Then Texy woofs and bounces on her front paws.

I turn, and it's like I'm in a chick flick. His shadowed figure lopes across the grass.

Okay, maybe the dark and rain make it more like a horror movie than a romantic comedy, BUT STILL.

He draws to a stop in front of me. He had the sense to wear a heavy, waterproof coat over his hoodie, but the hood is soaked and rain drips down his cheeks.

"Hey," he says, his voice a little loud over the rain.

I'm blushing. I tell my cheeks to knock it off. "Hey."

"I wasn't sure you'd show up, but I didn't have a way to text you . . ."

"I had the same thought process."

Texy presses her nose against his hand. Rev rubs behind her ears, but his eyes stay on me. "Do you want to go sit out front? There's an atrium. We can get out of the rain."

"Sure."

The church underwent a partial renovation a few years ago, and now sports a large timber and stone entryway that forms a covered courtyard. Several stone benches flank the doorway, set undercover. A security light shines overhead, throwing a sallow tint over everything, but it's still very shadowed on the benches.

Rev curls onto a bench sideways, his side to the glass wall of the church, his legs crisscrossed. I'm not as limber, but I manage to sit cross-legged on the bench to face him. Texy flops down on the concrete below us.

Rev pushes his sodden hood back and wipes his hands against his jeans. His hair is a wet, tangled mess, but the light throws sparks along the raindrops that cling to his face, making him look almost ethereal.

I probably look like a drowned rat. My braid hangs like a limp rope over my shoulder. I hug my arms to my body and shiver.

He frowns. "Are you cold?"

I tug at the windbreaker. "I don't know why I thought this would be waterproof."

He shrugs out of the coat. "Here. Take this."

He does this like it's nothing, but no one has ever offered me a coat before. My own mother would lecture me on not dressing appropriately for the environment, and then tell me to toughen up. I shake my head. "I can't. You'll be cold."

"I have a dry sweatshirt. I'm okay." He holds it out and gives it a little shake. "Really."

There's a part of me that wants this to be some grand romantic gesture—it's the same part of me that's sending warmth to my cheeks. But I also know he's not flirting. He's just being kind.

I drag the windbreaker over my head so I don't get the inside of his coat wet, and then slide my arms into the sleeves. They're about six inches too long, but the coat is heavy and warm from his body. I want to snuggle down into it and revel in this feeling.

"Better?" he says.

"Yes." I'm still blushing. "Thanks."

"You're welcome."

Then we lapse into silence, almost by accident. The rain forms a rhythmic lull, cocooning us with white noise, making this courtyard feel very private.

I study his hands where they rest in his lap. He has long fingers, the nails short and even. On his right wrist, the edge of a scar peeks from below his sleeve, almost pointing toward his thumb. The tiniest line of black ink sits above it.

A tattoo? I can't tell. It could be a pen, but it seems embedded in the skin.

My eyes lift, and I find him watching me.

I swallow. I don't know what to say.

He shifts, just a bit, but enough that his sleeves cover the scar and the mark. The movement seems very deliberate. "Any new e-mails from that guy in the game?"

"Yes." I force my voice to remain light, but the mention of Nightmare is enough to make me tense. "Any more e-mails from your father?"

His eyes level with mine. "Yes."

I slide my phone out of my pocket and unlock the screen, then tap a few times to pull up Nightmare's latest message. I almost don't want to share, but he's the only one who knows how bad the e-mails have gotten, and I've been desperate to tell someone all day.

I hold the phone up to face him. "Want to swap?"

He looks like I just asked if he wanted to rob a bank, but he pulls out his phone anyway, presses the obligatory icons, and hands it over.

I read. His dad sounds like a real winner.

Then Rev says, "Emma."

I look up. He's staring at me over my phone. His eyes are shadowed, his expression tense.

"What?" I say.

"Why would someone send you a picture like this?"

The image Nightmare sent is practically burned onto the insides of my eyelids. "It's fine. It's nothing. It's not even a picture of a real person—"

"This image—this is your character in a game?"

All of a sudden, I regret swapping phones, as if I've shown him a picture of myself bound and naked. My cheeks feel hot. "Forget it. I shouldn't have shown you."

"Have you told your parents?"

I glare at him. "Your e-mail is from someone you *know*. Some-one who obviously *hurt* you. Have you told *your* parents?"

We glare at each other for a long minute. Then he makes an aggravated sound and looks away. "I'm sorry. I'm not good at this."

"Not good at what?"

He gestures between us. "This. I'm not—I'm not good with people."

"I'm not either." I take a deep breath and blow it out. "I am *so* much better with a screen and a keyboard."

"My best friend met his girlfriend by exchanging letters for a month. Right now I am so envious of that."

"Really?"

"Really."

"Okay," I say. "Turn around. Look the other way."

He gives me a look, like, *Seriously?*

But I'm already scooting to turn around. He's completely silent, so I have no idea whether he's moving.

Then his back is a warm weight against mine, and I catch my breath. I didn't mean to sit *against* each other, but now that he's doing it, I can't imagine moving away.

"Now," I say, and my voice is a little breathless, "give me your number."

He does.

I quickly tap out a text.

Emma: Better?

Rev: Much. If I'm too close, I can move away.

I flush, and I'm glad he's looking the other way. I can feel each breath he takes. Despite the fact that we're texting, this suddenly feels more intimate than it was a minute ago.

Emma: You're not too close.

I'm blushing again. I need to get over myself. It's his *back*.

Rev: You're right about my father's e-mail. I haven't told anyone. It's complicated.
Emma: So is that e-mail from Nightmare.
Rev: I don't understand why. Especially if you don't know him.
Emma: Do you play any kind of video games?
Rev: Sometimes I kill zombies on Xbox with Declan.
Emma: You ever play online? With other people?
Rev: Sometimes.
Emma: You ever play with a girl?
Rev: I've never really paid attention. But I would never send someone a message like that, even if I was a hard-core gamer.
Emma: A lot of guys feel like it's a male space. They get angry if a girl comes in and beats them.
Rev: The same thing happens in jiu-jitsu. Usually the guys just need to get over themselves.

My eyebrows go up.

Emma: You know jiu-jitsu?
Rev: Yes.

I swear to god, I almost type, *No wonder you have an amazing body.*

But seriously. No wonder.

Emma: So if a girl came in and kicked your ass, you wouldn't get all bent out of shape about it?

Rev: No. I'd probably ask her to do it again so I could study her technique. But jiu-jitsu is face-to-face. This is not.

Emma: I think that's part of the problem. I read once about how fighting in a game releases the same brain chemicals as fighting in real life—but fighting online removes any humanity from it. It's all in your head. Even with a headset and a voice, no one feels real. It's easy to drop your guard and make friends. And it's just as easy to tear someone down. I don't just mean from my side. If I win a mission, I'm happy—but to someone on the other side, do they feel even worse because they were defeated by someone who their brain doesn't think exists? And when they pair that anonymous defeat with a woman's real voice/likeness, is that somehow emasculating? Like, where does the rage come from?

After I send the message, he's very still. I can still feel each breath as it enters his lungs. Rain pours down around the atrium.

"I'm thinking," he whispers.

I smile. "Okay."

Finally, his upper arm brushes mine as he writes back.

Rev: I think rage comes from a lot of places. I worry about my father sometimes, that I inherited his violence, that it will somehow find its way out of me. When I was young, when I was taken away from him, I was afraid of anyone else hurting me. Geoff and Kristin offered to sign me up for Tae Kwon Do, but when we went to register, I saw a Brazilian jiu-jitsu class, and I wanted to do that. It's all grappling. Very physical. They almost refused to let me do it. But the instructor convinced them to let me give it a try. I loved it.

"There's more," he says.
"I'll wait."

Rev: I see a lot of people come through the gym. I think a lot about what they bring to the mats. When I was young, I brought a lot of fear. Sometimes, people bring a lot of anger. They just want to fight—and that's okay, too, because they quickly learn that there's no place for rage on the mats. There's really no place for fear, either. It helps teach control. I think that's what I like so much about it. But if someone on the mats gets into trouble, it's easy for someone to see and step in. How can someone step in here, if you don't ask for help?
Emma: But that's the thing—do people on the mats ask for help? Or do you just step in? Do they want help?
Rev: I think it would depend on the situation.
Emma: What if a woman said she didn't want help?

Rev: Then I wouldn't help.

Emma: What if I tell you, right now, that I don't want help?

His back rises and falls as he takes a long breath. I'm tense, expecting him to push.

But then he doesn't.

Rev: OK.

Emma: Thank you.

Rev: This was a good idea. The back-to-back.

That makes me smile. "I do what I can," I whisper.

"*Shh*," he says. "I'm texting with someone."

I grin and slide my fingers across the screen. I don't want to talk about Nightmare anymore.

Emma: I didn't expect you to be some kind of martial arts junkie.

Rev: What did you expect?

Emma: I have no idea. I didn't expect you to be a sports junkie, either, but then you look like *that.*

Rev: It's not just jiu-jitsu. I also do Muay Thai and yoga.

I laugh and turn my head. "You do not do yoga. My *mother* does yoga and she does not look like you."

His arm brushes mine again as he texts a response.

Rev: It helps with flexibility.

Emma: What's Muay Thai?

Rev: Kickboxing. And *you* didn't strike me as a gaming junkie.

Emma: Inherited. My father is a game designer.

Rev: You and your dad are close?

Emma: Yeah. He's busy all the time, but . . . yeah.

He doesn't respond for a moment, and I realize that maybe this is a painful line of conversation for him. For the first time, his back is tense against mine.

I slide my fingers across the screen.

Emma: I saw the scar. At the edge of your sleeve. Your father?

Rev: Yes.

Lightning flashes in the sky, followed by a loud crack of thunder. I jump and catch my breath. Texy whines and crawls under the bench. The light reflects off the rain, closing us into this space.

Rev turns his head, and I can see just the edge of his profile. "Are you all right?"

I laugh a little, but nothing is funny. "I just don't like thunder. Are *you* all right?"

"No." The side of his hand brushes mine where it hangs by the bench. Sparks travel up my arm, and I have to remind my heart that it's just a casual motion.

But then his hand closes on mine. I freeze.

"Is this okay?" he whispers.

This would be so mawkish and unbelievable if I tried to explain this moment later. The rainstorm, the bench, the darkness. But his breath is fractured and his manner is uncertain and this feels as significant for him as it is for me.

"Yes," I say. "Do you want me to let go so you can text?"

He inhales—and his breathing steadies. He turns his head, and his breath brushes my neck. "I don't want you to let go."

"Okay."

"I've never told anyone about this," he says. "My parents know. My best friend. That's it."

"You don't have to tell me."

His fingers grip mine just a little more tightly. "I want to. I want you to understand why—why it's so hard for me to tell anyone."

"I'm listening."

"My father ran his own church," he says. "I don't know how many people followed him, because I was very young, but to me, it seemed like there were a lot. He would ask for blessings every week—*money*, in other words. He would tell me that God was providing for us, and I believed him. Now, I'm aware he was a skilled con man—but maybe not. Maybe he really did believe that they gave him money because he was blessed by God.

"Whichever, it was enough to keep us in a big house, in what I now know was a fairly nice neighborhood. At the time, he told me we were surrounded by sinners. He said the devil lived in those houses. If kids were playing in the yard, the devil had lured them there. If people were jogging, the devil was chasing them. I was afraid to go outside without my father, because it seemed the devil was *everywhere*." A pause. "Now, when I think back, I think the devil was in the house with me."

His fingers are wound through mine, his grip firm. Not too tight—just enough that I know he's not letting go anytime soon. I wonder if he needs the anchor.

"My father would set up these tests," Rev says. "He would say that if God wanted me to succeed, I would succeed. If I wasn't devout enough, or holy enough, or *whatever* enough, it was my father's duty to solve the problem." His voice tightens, and I'm not sure if it's anger or fear or shame. "When I was six, he wanted me to copy an entire page from the Bible. My hand started to cramp, and he decided the devil had taken control of my arm. He took a knife, and he started cutting, and he said my screaming was the devil fighting to stay inside—"

"Rev." Emotion grips my throat, and I feel like I'm a heartbeat away from crying. "Oh, Rev."

He turns his head again and I can see his profile. "Sorry." He sounds abashed. His fingers grip mine. "I didn't mean to get so graphic."

I turn on the bench, then wrap my free hand around his. My little finger brushes the scars under the edge of his sleeve, and his breath stops.

But he doesn't pull away.

"Can I ask you a question?" I say.

"Always."

"Did your mother—I mean, your birth mother—do anything to stop him?"

A breath. "She died when I was born. He used to tell me that she died fighting off the devil. Once I got away from him and started learning how to be normal, I wondered if he'd lied about her death. I had this moment where I was sure he'd made it up, that she was out there somewhere missing me. But Kristin—Mom—has a huge file on me, and my mother's death certificate is in there. Cause of death: uterine hemorrhage. So that much is true."

"I'm so sorry."

"That's why his e-mails have me so rattled. Even after all this time—it's like he still has this hold on me. I'm afraid to disobey. It's getting harder and harder to not answer." He swallows.

"Is he in prison?"

"No. He surrendered parental rights as part of a plea bargain. He served one hundred and eighty days. I have no idea where he is now."

One hundred and eighty days, after torturing Rev for years. It feels like a joke.

"Are you worried he'll come after you?"

"Yes. I worry about it every day." A long breath. "I've been afraid to leave for too long, like he might show up at the house or something. I worry that all of this is a test. I worry that I'm failing."

"And you don't want to tell your parents?"

His breathing is fractured again. "I don't know what they'll do, Emma. I've never hidden something from them."

"Do you trust them?"

He sniffs, and I realize he's crying. Not full out. Just a tear. He might not even be aware of it. He doesn't answer.

I turn on the bench to look at him. "Rev," I say. "This is a big deal."

"I know."

Nightmare is anonymous. His e-mails suck, but I can close my computer and pretend he doesn't exist. Rev's father is real. A true threat. "Do you want to tell them? I can go with you if you want."

For the longest moment, I feel like a total fool. Rev's going to scoff. He's going to tell me I don't understand.

He's going to do exactly what I did to him, when he pushed about the Nightmare e-mails.

He doesn't.

Rev stands up. "Okay," he says. "Let's go."

SIXTEEN

Rev

Saturday, March 17   9:06:16 p.m.

FROM: Robert Ellis <robert.ellis@speedmail.com>

TO: Rev Fletcher <rev.fletcher@freemail.com>

SUBJECT: Question

Do you ever think of me at all? Or have you been tempted away so thoroughly?

I'm having the most bizarre emotional experience.

There is another e-mail from my father on my phone.

There is a *girl* walking next to me.

I'm taking her to my house.

It's pouring rain and we're holding hands and I'm soaking wet. I'm freezing on the outside and warm on the inside, and I both want this moment to end and go on forever.

I shove my phone into the sodden pocket of my hoodie. I only checked because I thought it might be Geoff or Kristin.

"What just happened?" says Emma.

My movement must have been a little too forceful. "My father sent me another e-mail."

"Do you write back to any of them?" She looks up at me. Her hair is plastered back from the rain, and her eyes are huge.

"Only the first." I wince. "I told him to leave me alone."

She doesn't respond to that. We walk in silence for a while.

"Do you think there's a part of you that wanted to talk to him?"

"Yes." No mystery there. "And I know that sounds weird."

"No, I think I get it." She shrugs. "I don't like my mother, but she's still my mother."

"You don't *like* her?"

"She doesn't like anything about me either. She thinks I'm a slacker wasting all my time playing games on the Internet. It's basically the same way she feels about my father, but she knows she can control me."

"Your parents don't get along?"

She snorts. "They must have gotten along at some point, but not now. Mom is all about eating healthy, working out, and spending seventy hours a week at her job. Dad is all about eating nachos, staying up all night, and also spending seventy hours a week at his job."

"So they're never home."

"Not a lot, no. But really, that's better. When they're home they snipe at each other. When he's not home, Mom snipes at *me*."

No wonder she doesn't feel like she has anyone she can tell about the guy sending her those hateful messages.

"So you think your mother is disappointed that you're doing what your father does?"

"I know she is. And it sucks. I'm *good* at game design. I love the creativity of it. I write out whole storyboards. I have my own game, and a whole community! But she—"

"Wait." I use our joined hands to pull her to a stop. "You have your *own* game?"

Her cheeks turn pink, even in the rain. "It's nothing. It's small."

I stare at her. "Your own game. Like—you built a computer game?"

"It's nothing. Really."

It's literally the most fascinating thing in the world and she says this like it's nothing. "Emma—I don't know *anyone* who can write a computer game. Are you kidding me? Can I play it?"

"No!"

"Why?"

She glances away. "It's silly. Like I said. It's ridiculous."

"It's not. I want to see."

"I don't want you to see."

Her words stop me in my tracks. I'm not entirely sure how to take them, and my brain is such a twisted, screwed-up place already. "Okay."

Her blush deepens. "It's not perfect yet. I haven't even shown my father. It needs to be perfect before I show it to him."

"And probably not your mother, either?"

"God, no. She wouldn't be impressed by any of that. She finds it disappointing. So I spend all my time resenting her but also wishing I could please her. If that makes any sense."

"Of course."

"Of course." Light and shadows play games with the trails of water on her face. My eyes trace her lips, the lines of her face, the soft curve of her jaw. I want to touch her so badly that my hand aches for it.

"Are you stalling?" she whispers.

It breaks the spell. I blink and look away. "No. Come on." We start walking again.

Are you stalling?

Much like her refusal to let me see her game, I don't know what to make of that. Maybe this attraction is one-sided. Maybe my head can't even wrap itself around normal social cues.

Then again, she's still holding my hand.

Maybe she's not ready to talk about her mother any more than I wanted to talk about my father.

Maybe I really *am* stalling.

"Are you sure your parents aren't going to mind you bringing a friend home this late?" she says. "A friend with a *dog?*"

"Don't worry." I glance down at her. "My parents are used to me doing bizarre things." As we turn the corner to my street, anxiety has my stomach in knots. My father, my parents, Emma at my side. I don't know if I can do this.

I wish I could take her to Declan's house instead.

I have to clear my throat. "I live just up there. The blue house." Lightning flashes.

Emma shivers. "You sound like you want me to just go tell them for you."

"Is that an option?" I mean it as a joke, but the words come out too heavy, too serious.

"No." She peers up at me. "Or . . . yes? I mean, if you really want me to?"

The scenario plays out in my head. Geoff and Kristin have never flinched at anything I've ever done or asked, but this would be a new level.

"No," I say. "I was kidding."

I don't sound like I'm kidding at all.

"Would you have really done that?" I ask her.

"Sure. I mean—I don't have anything to lose. Any reaction wouldn't be about *me*, really."

My mouth goes dry. "Do you think they're going to have a reaction?"

"That your abusive father is e-mailing you? Um, yeah, I'm pretty sure they're going to have a reaction. What other things has he said to you? Does he threaten you?"

The very existence of his e-mails feel like a threat. I stop in the rain again. "Here. I'll show you the rest."

We're on the sidewalk in front of the house now. Geoff or Kristin could look out and see me standing here. It's unlikely, though. Their bedroom is at the back of the house. So are the kitchen and the family room. I told them I was going to Declan's, so they're not going to expect me to come home from this direction. We have time.

Emma reads quickly—but it's not like his e-mails have a lot of text. It's the underlying messages that hit so hard. Her hand hovers over the screen as she flicks to scroll.

"I thought his e-mails were going to sound nuts, but they don't. He sounds pretty lucid. I can see what you mean. It's almost diabolical."

Diabolical. That's such a good word for my father—and one he would hate, because it means *devil-like* at its root.

I love that Emma used it to describe him. It brings me a measure of comfort. When people dismiss him as crazy, I know they don't understand. He wasn't crazy. He was . . . deliberate. Calculated.

Then she looks up again. "Is Rev Fletcher not your real name?"

I blink, thrown. "What?"

"In his first e-mail, he asks where you came up with Rev Fletcher." She winces. "Am I not allowed to ask that?"

"No. No, you can ask me anything." I run a hand through my hair. I'd forgotten that. "Fletcher is Geoff and Kristin's last name. I took it when they adopted me."

"And Rev? Is that short for something?"

"Yes. Sort of." I pause. "When I first came here, I used to jump every time Geoff and Kristin said my name. Because my father would only use it when—" I have to stop. Close my eyes. Take a breath and shake off the memory. "They let me choose a new one."

"Do you have a brother?"

It's not the next question I was expecting. "What?"

"A kid just came around the back of your house, saw us, and ran back into your backyard."

"What?"

Emma points. "You said you live in the blue one, right?"

My eyes zoom in on the house with laser focus. The garage, the trees between our house and the neighbor's, the shadows along the shrubbery. No motion at all.

"Wait here." I sprint up the lawn.

"Hey!" shouts Emma. Texas barks.

And then the dog is beside me, and we're sprinting into the backyard, her leash trailing in the grass. There's no one here.

Texas bounces on her front paws, panting excitedly. Then she stops, one paw raised. Her ears are trained on the backyard of the house next door.

With a loud *woof*, she bolts.

I follow her.

She finds Matthew crouched behind an air-conditioning unit. She's barking like crazy, her tail wagging fiercely.

Matthew flattens back against the siding. He's already soaked from the rain. He looks from me to the dog and back. One hand is behind him, against the house.

I think of the first night, when I found him with a knife.

Emma appears around the side of the house. She's panting. "Rev. What's—what's going on?"

Matthew takes advantage of the distraction. He bolts.

Texas is not a police dog. She barks and gives chase, but she doesn't tackle him or anything.

That's okay, because I do.

We roll to the ground in a tangle of limbs. He goes down fighting. I'm ready for a blade to catch me somewhere, but he either dropped it or he never had one. Matthew hits with power, like he's learned how. He gets some solid jabs into my ribs. The rain makes his skin slick and difficult to grab.

But I'm stronger than he is. I get an arm around his neck and pin a leg so he can't get free. He's got one arm loose, and he's trying to pry at my arm, but I've got leverage and I know what I'm doing. He struggles until I tighten my grip.

"Knock it off and I'll let you up," I say.

He tries to drive his elbow into my rib cage in response.

"Rev!" cries Emma. She's still panting. Rain pours down around us. "Rev—"

"Go to my house," I tell her, my voice tight with strain. "Tell my parents where we are."

She turns and runs. I love that about her—no hesitation. No second-guessing.

Matthew finally goes still. His breathing is rough and ragged. "Let me go."

"Do you have a weapon?"

"Go to hell."

"Do you want me to let you go or not?"

"I don't have anything." He grinds the words out. "Let me *go*."

I let him go. He *immediately* digs his feet into the ground and tries to run again.

I catch his arm. He swings around and drives a fist right into my face.

Stars explode in my eyes. He breaks free.

I'm still faster than he is. I tackle him again, and this time I trap him more effectively. I've got an arm around his neck and his lower body pinned. He can't even struggle.

My jaw hurts. No one has hit me in anger since my father. A dark thought flashes through my mind, that I could break Matthew's neck right now.

"Rev!" Geoff's voice. "Rev! Let him go!"

I open my eyes. I don't remember closing them. Matthew's fingers dig into my forearm, almost a panicked clawing. Geoff, Kristin, and Emma stand in the rain, staring down at us. Texy is straining against her leash, barking wildly. Emma holds her back.

"Rev, honey," says Kristin. Concern threads through her voice. She touches my arm. "Rev, let him go."

I let him go. I fall away into the grass.

Matthew doesn't run this time. He's making choking sounds, coughing into the grass.

I did that. I hurt him.

Shame hits me like a sledgehammer.

Geoff and Kristin go to Matthew. I'm glad. I don't deserve their attention right now. I can't look at any of them.

"Hey." Emma speaks right beside me.

I turn my head and find her crouching in the grass. Texas thrusts her nose into my face and starts licking my cheek.

It hurts, and I wonder if I'm bleeding. I push the dog's muzzle away.

"Are you okay?" Emma says.

"No," I say. "I'm not."

Then I get to my feet.

Emma reaches out and touches my hand. "I'm still here," she whispers.

"I know." I don't want to look at her.

She frowns and leans in a bit. "Rev, you—"

"Don't," I say. I wish she hadn't seen any of this. "I'm a mess, Emma."

"But—"

"Please go home. Please forget this happened. Please—" My voice breaks. I can't take much more of this.

"Rev." She says my name softly. "It's okay. I can stay."

I force my eyes to open. Geoff and Kristin are helping Matthew to his feet.

I don't know what they're going to do.

I don't know what's going to happen.

I do know I don't want her to see it. I run a wet hand across my face. "Please, Emma. Please just go."

"Okay," she says softly. "Here."

She slips out of my coat. It pools in my lap.

It feels warm and smells like her, something fruity, like oranges and sunshine.

The rain pours down to steal the warmth and scent.

"Are you sure?" she says.

I hold my breath. I'm not sure of anything.

I'm always worried I've inherited his violence.

I have. It's always waiting inside me.

I nod. "Go. I can't do this."

"Okay."

And that's it. She turns and walks out of the yard.

SEVENTEEN

Emma

The walk home feels miles long, even though we only live five blocks apart. I keep wanting to go back, to make sure he's okay. My hand tingles from where his fingers wound through mine.

He told me so much about his life—but everything that happened in the rain shows that a lot is still a mystery.

Was that boy his brother? He didn't mention a brother during all the talk about his father and the years of abuse he must have suffered.

My head is so twisted in knots. A week ago my entire life made sense. Now *nothing* makes sense.

I've never seen boys fight before. The movies make it seem exciting, with clear stakes. A good guy and a bad guy. This was dirty and frightening and I didn't understand what was going on *at all*.

And now I'm walking home alone. At least the rain has slowed to a drizzle.

I shiver and jog a little. My body needs to spend an hour in a hot bath, just to soak the cold out of my bones. When I turn the corner onto my street, even Texas lags a bit. It's been an exciting night for her.

Both my parents' cars are in the driveway. The lights in the main level are on.

I almost fall over in the street. My father is *home*? At a decent hour?

"Come on, Texy." I sprint for the door, bouncing up the porch steps.

They're just inside, sitting in the living room. They both look up in surprise at my entrance.

My mother frowns. "Emma. What on earth happened to you?" Her eyes go to my shoes, which are streaked with mud from the adventure in Rev's backyard. "Have you been out in this storm?"

Where did she think I was?

"Yeah." I'm breathless. "Got caught in the rain with Texy. What's going on?"

She exchanges glances with my father. "We've been talking things over, and we both agree some changes need to be made to keep the peace—"

"The peace?" I say.

She nods. "Among all of us."

"Catharine." My father's voice is a low rumble. His tone is mellow. Calm. "Why don't you let her go get changed first."

Calm. It's so foreign in this house that I want to lie down and bask in it.

"Okay." I fling the leash at the hook by the door and kick out of my sneakers. "Okay. Just give me a few minutes."

The bath can wait. I jog up the stairs and strip out of my wet clothes.

Some changes need to be made to keep the peace. Among all of us.

She could break out a detailed chore chart and I'd be okay with it. I'll cook every day if it means the sniping will end. We'll have to eat macaroni and cheese for every meal, but whatever. I'll vacuum every night if it means my father will come home at a decent hour.

They're proposing a change. I can feel it.

Maybe I can show OtherLANDS to my father. Maybe he'll finally have a few minutes to spare.

He'll be so proud. He'll be *so* proud.

I have to brush a tear away. I don't know what he'll do, but it'll be amazing.

They're still not yelling. No one is drinking. I can't believe this.

Maybe they've been with a marriage counselor all day! Maybe they've learned to effectively communicate.

I don't even know if my clothes match, but they're dry. I almost fall down the stairs to get back to them.

Once again, they stare at me in surprise.

I need to be chill. "Sorry." I drop onto the couch. "I'm just happy that you're both here."

They exchange glances again.

"Emma," says my father, and his voice is gentle.

"Emma," says my mother.

And then the room shifts. Tilts. Changes.

Something here isn't good.

"What's going on?" I say.

"This isn't working," my mother says. Her voice is deathly quiet.

"We can't do this anymore," says my father.

My heart is pounding in my head. I can't hear what they're saying. I can't hear anything.

"Emma?" my mother's tone takes on a familiar note of impatience. "Emma, do you understand what we're telling you?"

"You just said you wanted to make a change. You wanted to keep the peace."

"We do," says my mother.

"We're getting a divorce," says my father.

I watched Rev tackle that boy in the rainstorm. The boy was running, and Rev plowed into him, full out, and brought him down.

That's what this feels like.

I don't know how I'm on my feet. I think I'm going to be sick.

I try to speak, but my mouth is too thick.

"I'm going to take a few things and stay with Kyle," my father says. Kyle is another guy who works for Axis Games.

"Don't do this," I whisper.

"I've told your father we'll have to put the house on the

market." My mother's lips are pursed. "We can't support a mortgage and an apartment—"

"Could you wait before we start talking about money?" My father heaves a sigh and rubs at the back of his neck. "She doesn't need the details—"

"Well, *someone* has to worry about the details," my mother snaps.

"Of course," my father scoffs. "You're so good at details."

"And it's a lucky thing for you, or we'd have *nothing*. I'm going to carry you through this divorce just like I carry you through everything."

"Can't you get one of your doctor friends to write you a prescription for something that would make you less of a controlling—"

"Don't you *dare* call me names in front of my daughter."

Her daughter. *Her* daughter.

"I'm not your daughter," I snap. "I'm his." I look at my father. "I can pack a bag, too."

He looks taken aback. "Emma—sweetheart—I'm going to Kyle's. He doesn't even have a second room. I'm sleeping on the couch—"

"I can sleep on the floor."

My mother makes a disgusted sound. "You are not going over there."

"I don't want to be *here*," I yell. "Don't you understand? I don't want to be here with *you.*"

Her face pales a shade. She looks stricken. "Emma—"

"Catharine. Stop." My father looks at me. "Em. I'm sorry. You need to stay here. When I find a place, we can talk—"

"She is *not* coming to live with you." My mother has recovered and her voice is full of ice.

Even now, she's trying to control me. Even in this. I can't speak.

My legs don't want to move anymore. Maybe I can go back upstairs and do this again. I can come back down and we can have an entirely different conversation.

I saw this image online once. It was a picture that said, *If you're seeing this, you've been in a coma for twenty years, and we're trying a new way to reach you. Please wake up.*

I stared at that meme for a full minute.

I've never wished for something to be so true.

Wake up. Wake up. Wake up.

My parents are still bickering. I'm still here. Or not here.

"Can't you—" My voice breaks. They don't even hear me. "Can't you—can't you go to a counselor?"

"We've been to a counselor," my mother says.

"You've—what?"

"For the last year," my father says. "It's not working, M&M. We have to do this."

The nickname is like a punch to the face.

Now I'm awake.

"Don't call me that," I seethe. "Don't ever call me that again."

"Emma—"

"You're both so *selfish*." I turn for the stairs.

"Come back here!" my mother yells.

"Let her go," says my father. "Let her process this."

I hate him. I hate her.

I HATE THEM.

My room is cool and silent. Lights flicker on my routers. Texy barrels in beside me and shoves her nose under my hand.

I ignore her and fling my laptop open.

There are my text messages. The message my father never answered.

The tense messages with Cait. She lives with parents who are so in love with each other that it makes me want to vomit when I'm over there. Her mother comments and likes her makeup videos, for god's sake. The last thing I need right now is an offer of chocolate-chip pancakes or someone to give me a hug, and that's all I'd find at Cait's house.

After a moment, all my messages with Rev filter onto my screen, too, loading from my phone.

You and your dad are close. One of his last text messages. The words made me feel warm inside an hour ago.

Now they feel like molten lava, melting my organs.

He might understand—but all my brain hears are his parting words.

Go. I can't do this.

I can't text him either.

My father knocks on the door. "Emma. Please. Talk to me."

His tone is always so quiet, which goes with his no-big-deal manner. I used to think it was a sign of strength, that he could take anything in stride.

Now it just pisses me off. I put my gaming headset on. The padded earphones muffle any sounds.

"Emma," my father calls.

I log in to OtherLANDS.

And there, right on top, is another message from Nightmare.

Saturday, March 17   9:36 p.m.

From: N1ghtm@re4

To: Azure M

Are you blowing me off?

This one has an attachment, too. It's the same naked, bound avatar, but now her head has been blown up. The graphic design work is impressively visceral.

Rage fills every cell of my body. If molten lava were eating my insides before, it's turned into a supernova settling somewhere in the center of my chest.

I don't think about it. I type back.

Saturday, March 17   10:47 p.m.

From: Azure M

To: N1ghtm@re4

I HATE YOU.
I HATE YOU.
I HATE YOU.
I HATE YOU.

I HATE YOU.

LEAVE ME ALONE.

I block him.

Then I slam my laptop shut. I flip over in bed and scream into my pillow.

I scream so loud and so long that I forget what silence is like.

I scream until I run out of breath.

And then the silence falls and pours in around me. So much silence I almost can't stand it.

I don't know where my parents are. I don't care. I don't care.

My phone chimes. I almost throw it.

It's almost eleven now. I hope for Cait, though I know that's impossible. I hope for Rev, somehow.

No. It's a message through 5Core.

For a moment, I panic that Nightmare has written back, but it's not him. It's Ethan.

Ethan_717: Are you around tonight? Want to get on OtherLANDS or Battle Realms?

I'm so stupid. I burst into tears.

I'm sobbing openly, but I log in to my game. Mom knocks on the door. "Emma. Can I speak with you, please?"

"Why?" I yell. I sound hysterical. "So you can tell me what a slacker I am? Or are you going to tell me how evil gaming is? Or what a loser Dad is? Or have I covered it all?"

"Emma." Her voice is so quiet that I can barely hear her. "Emma—"

"Forget it!" I yell. "Go away."

Then something else occurs to me. "If you turn off the Internet again, I will hack your laptop and delete everything on it."

"Emma." Her voice is sharp.

I turn on music and drown her out. It's so loud that my ears hurt.

I look for Ethan_717. He's online. I send him a team request. He doesn't respond, but he opens a private chat link.

Ethan_717: I'm in a group already. Want me to add you?

Of course. Like I can join a group while openly sobbing.

Azure M: No. It's OK.

Then I sit there and stare at the screen. My parents' words spin in my head.

Divorce.

We'll have to put the house on the market.

We can't support a mortgage and an apartment.

Divorce.

Divorce.

Divorce.

My screen blips with a private team request.

I send Ethan a quick chat.

Azure M: I really can't deal with a team right now.
Ethan_717: It's OK. It's just me.

Oh. I click Accept.

His voice is warm in my ear. "What's up?"

I don't want to talk. I just want to play.

But then I inhale, and I break down sobbing. I tell him every-thing. My mother. My father. Their divorce. Nightmare and his messages.

It takes me a long time.

"I'm sorry," I say when I get to the end. "I didn't mean to unload all of that."

"Don't be sorry." He takes a long breath. "I'm sorry about your parents." A pause. "And I'm sorry about that other guy."

"It's fine." I sniff. "I keep blocking him. He'll get bored eventually."

"Probably." He pauses. "Is there anything I can do?"

I think of the feel of Rev's fingers wound through mine. I swipe at my cheeks and turn down the music. My parents have gone quiet.

"Can we just play?" I say.

"Absolutely."

So I load up a mission to do exactly that.

EIGHTEEN

Rev

It's after midnight, again.

I'm not sleeping, again.

Quiet has overtaken the house, but it's a false quiet. No one is asleep. Geoff and Kristin are talking, their voices a low hum down the hall. The door to Matthew's room closed a short while ago, but I know—just *know*—he's not sleeping.

My jaw aches something fierce, but I welcome the pain. When I was a child, my father always told me pain was evil leaving my body, and I find a measure of reassurance in that now.

I haven't talked to Geoff or Kristin. After they brought Matthew into the house, I headed straight for my room, while they dealt with him in the kitchen.

He didn't have a knife. I attacked him like that, and he didn't have a knife.

I can't face him. I don't want to face him. I told him I wouldn't mess with him, and then I *did*.

Have you been tempted away so thoroughly?

The words from my father's e-mail are haunting. Have I been tempted? Who is tempting me? I feel this pressure to satisfy everyone, and I can't. Everything is so confusing.

I keep flashing on that moment in the rain and the dark when I knew I could hurt him. I wonder if Matthew knows. I wonder if he could sense it.

It all happened in front of Emma, too.

Shame has taken up residence in my belly, a dark and curling feeling that won't leave me alone.

I need to apologize. I don't know how to apologize for what I am.

A knock sounds at my door. It's very soft, so I think it's Kristin.

"Come in."

I was wrong. It's Geoff. His frame fills the doorway, darkness and shadows at his back.

"I thought you might be sleeping," he says.

I shake my head and study the quilt on my bed. I haven't even lain down. Sleep has been an elusive creature lately.

"Can I sit down?" he asks.

"Yes."

He sits in my desk chair and wheels it around to face me. "That's quite a bruise." Before I can say anything, he turns his head and calls out to the hallway. "Hey, Kris, he needs an ice pack."

My jaw tightens, but that hurts, so I force myself to relax. "I don't need an ice pack."

"Humor me."

Kristin appears in the doorway with a bag of ice wrapped in a towel. She takes one look at me and her face falls. "Oh, Rev, you should have said something. We've been out here talking, and I didn't realize—"

"I'm fine. It's fine."

She comes into the room and sits beside me, then puts the ice pack against my face. "I didn't realize he hit you that hard."

"Stop." I push her hand away and hold the ice there myself. I don't want to, but she'll pick it back up if I don't. "I'm fine."

She puts a hand on my shoulder. "You're not fine."

I go still. I don't know what that means.

My breath quickens.

"We didn't mean to cause this," she says quietly. "When we told Bonnie that we'd welcome Matthew staying here, I don't think we considered what it would do to you."

These words take the longest time to sink in.

They're not here to yell at me.

They're not mad.

Somehow, this is worse.

I lower the ice pack. "Stop. Stop."

"Rev—"

"I hurt him. Don't you understand? I hurt him."

"You didn't hurt him." Kristin leans into me. Her voice is so gentle. "You stopped him from hurting you. You stopped him from running away—which could have been so much worse."

They can't paint this a different way. I know what I did. I know what I felt.

"Rev. Sweetheart." Her arm comes around me. "You didn't—"

"I *did*." I shove myself away. It's a motion full of fear and fury and I wish I could take it back immediately.

I curl into myself. "I'm sorry. I'm sorry." My voice breaks and I wait for Geoff to grab me, to protect Kristin.

He doesn't. He wheels the chair closer to me. "Rev. Look at me."

I don't want to look at him, but he's got a good voice for when he has no patience for nonsense. Deep and solid. I look at him and meet his eyes.

"You didn't hurt him," Geoff says. "Do you understand me? You did not hurt him. He's fine."

"I hurt Mom—"

"You didn't hurt me." Kristin moves toward me again, and I put up a hand.

"Stop." I can't look at them now. I can't look at anything. "Please. Stop."

"Okay." But she doesn't move from the bed.

We all sit in absolute silence, broken by nothing but my ragged breathing.

But they sit, and they don't leave me.

I can't handle all of this alone anymore.

It takes three attempts for me to force the words out. "Do you know where my father is?"

"No," says Geoff. He wheels even closer to the bed, but not so close that the distance is threatening. "Do you want me to find out?"

I look up at him. "Can you do that?"

"Maybe." He pauses. "Would it be okay if I ask you why?"

I inhale to tell them about the letter. About the e-mails.

But I can't. It feels like such a betrayal on so many levels.

But if I know where my father is, I can judge whether he's a threat. He could be on the other side of the country. He could be in jail. He could have another child.

The thought turns my blood to ice. "I just want to know." My voice is a broken thing, the words squeezed out of lungs that don't want to work. I feel wrung out and exhausted. All that's holding me upright is the frozen blood in my veins. "I need to know. Okay?"

"All right." He pauses, and his eyes are full of concern. "Rev—it's okay to talk about your father. Do you know that? It's okay."

No, it's not. "I don't want to talk about him."

I know I sound crazy. I'm the one who brought him up.

But it's not like you can Google "Robert Ellis" and have any hope of finding the right guy. He might as well be named John Smith or Jack Baker.

"Do you want to talk about Emma?" says Kristin.

Hmm. Do I want to talk about how I completely lost control and attacked Matthew in front of her? How I will never trust myself around her now?

I shake my head.

"Rev, I need you to answer me honestly," says Geoff. "Should I call Bonnie and have her start making arrangements for another home for Matthew?"

I blink and stare at him. "You want to find another home for *him?*"

"No. I don't. I think he needs time to figure out he can trust us. But I will call her right now if it's causing too much stress for you."

"No—" I shake my head. "That's not what I mean. I did this. You had to know I would do this."

He straightens in the chair and studies me, nonplussed. "Rev." His voice is almost hushed. "I don't understand what you think you did."

"I'm going to turn into my father. I keep waiting for it to happen. I've read about the cycle of violence, and the way certain traits are carved into your genetic makeup." My forearms are clenched tight against my abdomen, like I need to physically hold myself together. "It's like how Dec swears he'll never touch alcohol again. I have to do that somehow. Because I don't know how it starts, and I won't know how to stop."

They're silent, and my eyes are on the quilt again, and I don't know if I want to look up to read their expressions. I've discussed this with Declan, but never with them.

I think of that flash in my head when I pinned Matthew in the grass. How I could have broken his neck.

Or the way my father's words have wormed their way into my brain, triggering long-dormant thoughts.

Maybe he's right.

Maybe I'm the one who belongs in juvenile detention. Locked away where I can't hurt anyone.

Geoff moves a bit closer, and rests a hand on my knee. It makes my breath catch, but I don't pull away, and he doesn't react.

"You said you know about the cycle of violence," he says. "What do you know?"

His voice is very matter-of-fact. Not challenging. Just a question. His teaching voice.

"I know that abused children grow up to be abusers."

"Not always, Rev."

"Almost always."

"Do you know why? Because it's not just genetics."

I hesitate. "I know it has something to do with your brain getting screwed up as a kid, and not learning how to handle emotions the right way."

"Yes. Somewhat. At a very basic level, attachment disorder happens when a child does not develop a normal bond with a caregiver, whether because of neglect, or abandonment, or abuse. You've seen this in some of the children we've had here. Some of these kids have never learned what trust *is*."

He's right. I have seen it. I remember a little boy who never cried because no one had ever responded. He was three years old and couldn't speak.

By the time his mother got clean, he was a chatterbox who loved to sing the alphabet. When she regained custody, Kristin went to visit every single day for months.

Geoff spreads his hands. "Young children are pretty simple,

really. If they're hungry, they need to be fed. If they're sad, they need to be comforted. If they're hurt, they need to be cared for. It's the core of a trusting relationship with adults. But if someone isn't there to do those things, or if those things aren't consistent, those children start missing some of the building blocks for their personality." He pauses. "Or if the response to those needs is *negative*, and not just neglectful, the child begins learning incorrect responses for himself. So if a child asks for food and the response is a smack across the face, the child begins to internalize that as cause and effect."

My breathing has gone shallow, a familiar tension gripping my shoulders again.

I don't know if I can keep talking about this. I don't know if I can stop.

"My father—he wasn't like that. He was—"

Diabolical.

"This is different," I finish.

"Why?" says Geoff.

"Because he wasn't being neglectful. He thought he was doing the right thing. He *believed* in what he was doing. How can I fight against that?"

"Do *you* believe in what he was doing?"

The question draws me up short. "What?"

"Do you believe in what he was doing? Do you believe his actions were directed by God?"

I freeze. It's so obvious, but I can't say the words.

Even after all these years, denying it feels like an act against my father.

I press my hands against the sides of my head. A sudden migraine pulses between my temples. "I can't talk about this."

A brief pause. "Okay. I know it's late." Geoff gives my knee a little shake. "We don't have to talk about this now."

Kristin's hand brushes over my shoulder. She drops a kiss on my forehead. Light touches that remind me I'm here. It's now. I'm eighteen. I'm not seven.

"You've had a long day," she says. "Get some sleep."

She shifts off the bed and moves away.

Geoff doesn't move from the chair. "I meant what I said earlier. If having Matthew here is causing a problem—"

"It's not." I clear my throat and rub my palms against my knees. "It's not."

He hesitates. "Something else is going on, Rev. I wish you would talk to me."

Oh, I wish I could.

"Tomorrow," I say. My voice is weak. All of me feels weak. "Tomorrow, okay?"

"Okay." He rises from the chair and gives my shoulder a gentle squeeze.

When he gets to my door, I stop him. "Wait. Why does he keep running? Where's he going?"

"He won't say." His face screws up in thought. "Sometimes, I think people are so used to negativity that a positive atmosphere is uncomfortable, or even frightening. It goes along with what we were talking about. When you can't trust anyone, the unknown is a very frightening place indeed."

A heavy, loaded pause. "Think about it, Rev. Why did you run?"

I look away. I don't really have an answer for that.

Actually, I do, and the answer is shameful.

Geoff doesn't push me. His voice is kind, even though I don't deserve it. "Good night, Rev."

"Good night."

With that, he pulls the door closed, leaving me alone with my thoughts.

NINETEEN

Emma

Dad: Emma, I don't like how things ended last night. I would appreciate a chance to talk to you. How about brunch? Just you and me? I can pick you up at 11.

I look at the clock.
It's 10:00 a.m.
I turn off my phone.
I roll over.
When they knock at 11, I ignore them.
I don't get out of bed all day.

TWENTY

Rev

Sunday, March 18   1:26:16 p.m.

FROM: Robert Ellis <robert.ellis@speedmail.com>

TO: Rev Fletcher <rev.fletcher@freemail.com>

SUBJECT: Void

I'm beginning to think I'm sending e-mails into the void.
Are you on the other end?

Answer me.

I don't want to.

I turn off my phone.

I roll over in bed and pull the pillow over my head.

I don't get out of bed all day.

TWENTY-ONE

Emma

Ethan_717: It might be too late to send you a message, but I just wanted to check on you.

The message hits my screen after midnight. I have to be up for school in the morning, but sleep is a long way off. I don't even feel tired.

That might have something to do with lying in bed all day, but I don't think so.

Divorce.

We'll have to put the house on the market.

Where will we go? What does that mean?

I don't want to think about it. Messaging is a good distraction.

Azure M: I'm alive.
Ethan_717: I'm glad to hear it. Are you OK?

Azure M: I have not left my room all day.

Ethan_717: I haven't either. Any more messages from the Nightmare guy?

Azure M: No. And I'm glad I'm not the only one who's crazy. What's up with you?

Ethan_717: The usual.

Then he sends me a gif of a crazy woman pulling her hair out, with the caption NO WIRE HANGERS!

It's from an old movie about Joan Crawford, who couldn't deal with the stress of Hollywood and took it out on her children. Mom loves it.

I know, I know. I can see the irony.

Azure M: Is your mom like that?

Ethan_717: She can be.

Azure M: Are all mothers like this? I don't even get it.

Ethan_717: Yes. All mothers are crazy.

Azure M: Then again, my father might have made her this way. I don't know.

Ethan_717: I'm sorry you're going through this.

Azure M: Thanks.

Ethan_717: Are your parents still living in the same house right now?

Azure M: I don't want to talk about it.

Ethan_717: OK.

Azure M: OK.

Ethan_717: I'm assuming you don't want to run a mission?

Azure M: Not right now.

Ethan_717: I wish I could help.

Azure M: You are. Thanks, Ethan.

Then I blink at the screen. I quickly type another line.

Azure M: I just realized that I don't even know if that's your real name.

Ethan_717: It is. I'm Ethan. The 717 is my birthday. July 17. I know it's not a gamer name, but I started using Ethan_717 when I was 9 and now I can't seem to give it up.

Azure M: I'm Emma.

Ethan_717: EMMA! Now I get it. All this time I've been guessing M names. I was torn between Melissa and Melanie.

My eyebrows go up.

Azure M: Dude. You could have just asked.

Ethan_717: No, it was more fun to try to figure it out.

Azure M: Now you know everything about me.

Ethan_717: I'm writing a biography entry for Wikipedia right now.

I almost laugh, but it's like my sense of humor is broken. The thought makes me want to burst into tears again.

Ethan_717: Can I tell you something?

Azure M: Sure.

Ethan_717: It might be better. The divorce.

Okay. I do burst into tears. I'm so glad we're typing instead of on the headset, or he'd think I was this total weepy mess all the time.

Azure M: We have to move. Mom said we have to sell the house.

Ethan_717: It's just a house. You'll see. It's just a house.

Azure M: Did you have to move when your parents got divorced?

Ethan_717: Of course.

Azure M: And it wasn't bad?

Ethan_717: No. It was the end of life as I knew it. It was awful.

Azure M: Gee. Thanks.

Ethan_717: But I survived.

I swipe at my face with the sheet again. My cheeks are raw. After a moment, he sends me another message.

Ethan_717: Hey, I don't want to be too forward, but here's my number. In case you ever want to talk outside the game. I know what it's like.

And then he sends me his number. It chases some of my tears away.

I immediately add him as a contact in iMessage, which will add him on my phone, too. I quickly send him a text.

Emma: Thanks, Ethan.
Ethan: You're welcome, Emma.

I roll over in bed and pull the blankets over my head. And for the first time all day, I smile.

TWENTY-TWO

Rev

Monday, March 19   5:26:32 a.m.

FROM: Robert Ellis <robert.ellis@speedmail.com>

TO: Rev Fletcher <rev.fletcher@freemail.com>

SUBJECT: Answer me

I told you to answer me.

Answer me, Son.

I will not wait forever.

I will not wait forever.

The e-mail is still sitting in my in-box, unanswered. But the words poke at me with unsettling frequency. Every time I move. Every time I inhale. Every time my heart beats.

It feels like a threat.

"You look like crap," says Declan when I climb into his car at 7:00 on Monday morning.

"I look the same as I always do." I'm in jeans and a black hoodie. You know. For a change. I didn't bother to shave because I don't want a lot of questions about the bruise on my jaw.

Declan's hand is on the gearshift. "Am I waiting for Matthew?"

"No. Just go."

The car rocks and shifts as he works the clutch to accelerate down the street. "I feel like I've missed something."

"Do we have time to stop for coffee?" I would have had a cup at home, but Matthew was in the kitchen with Geoff and Kristin. I haven't spoken to him since Saturday night.

I haven't spoken to anyone since Saturday night.

"I guess." Declan makes the right at the end of my street, toward the Dunkin' Donuts.

His radio is tuned to alternative music, which I don't mind, but right now the angsty suggestive lyrics rub me the wrong way. I reach out and twist the silver dial all the way to the left.

Now it's silent.

"You going to talk or what?" says Declan.

I keep my eyes on the windshield. Clouds darken the sky, and rain spits at the glass. "I don't know where to start."

"Why didn't Matthew ride with us?"

"Because I almost killed him."

Declan glances over. "What? Wait." He does a double take, then studies me a little more closely before turning back to the road. "Did someone hit you?"

"He tried to run away again. Saturday night. I went after him. He wasn't happy about it."

"Wow." He stretches the word into three syllables.

Dunkin' Donuts is packed, with at least ten people waiting for the drive-through. Declan pulls into the line anyway.

"I can just run in," I say.

"No way. I want to hear this."

I shrug and bury my hands in the front pocket of the hoodie. "There's not a whole lot to say."

Declan sighs and runs his hand down his face. "Am I awake? This feels like our conversation the other night. I'm sure you didn't almost kill him—"

"I did. I thought about it. I could have done it."

"Rev." His voice is quiet. He must hear the turmoil in my own. "You should have come over."

"I almost did. I thought Geoff and Kristin were going to make me leave."

His eyebrows go up. "You're calling them Geoff and Kristin now?"

"Shut up."

The car revs hard as he pulls forward with the line. "I'm just trying to figure out what's going on here."

"I'm not safe, Dec! I've been telling you that for *months*."

He rolls his eyes. "Okay, Rev."

"Don't do that," I snap.

Declan isn't easy to intimidate. He meets my attitude head-on. "You're not safe? Is he alive or isn't he?"

I grit my teeth. "He's alive."

"Did he hit you first, or did you hit him?"

"That's not important."

"It's *totally* important!"

"He hit me," I grind out.

"So you just hit him back?"

"No. I didn't hit him at all."

"Wow. Sounds like you're incredibly unsafe. Maybe you should get out of the car."

I glare at him. "Stop. Mocking. Me."

We pull up to the speaker, and a woman squawks at us to order. Declan orders coffee for each of us, then glances at me. "Food?"

"No."

He orders two breakfast sandwiches anyway, because he knows me better than that.

When we're in the space between speaker and window, he looks over again. "I'm not mocking you. I'm trying to understand what you're saying."

"I'm saying I had him in a choke hold and I thought about breaking his neck."

"So what. I think about doing the same thing to Alan at least once a month, and that's without having him in a choke hold."

"That's not the same."

"It's exactly the same, Rev. Exactly. You think it's a crime to think about harming someone? You could walk up to any kid at school and I guarantee they've had a violent thought in the last twenty-four hours. Hell, most of them have probably had a violent thought in the last twenty-four minutes."

His words are so simple, but for me, they take a little more examination. This feels different.

"You spend too much time inside your own head," he says then, which shocks me into silence.

We get to the window, and he pays. He doesn't ask me for money, and I wonder if he's feeling guilty about some of his comments.

I don't offer to pay him back, because I'm still irritated.

We drive the few miles to school in silence, but we can blame the food this time. Declan pulls into a parking space just as his girlfriend is getting out of her car. Juliet waits for him to open the door.

"Quick," Declan says to her. "When's the last time you had a violent thought about someone?"

"Three seconds ago," she says. "When I saw you stopped for coffee but didn't bring me one."

He holds out the cup. "Wrong. This is for you."

Her expression lights up, and she kisses him, then takes a sip.

He's such a liar. Probably.

But then she hands it to him and says, "We can share," and I wonder if this was his plan all along. He smiles and takes the coffee, then takes her hand.

He makes it look so easy. I'm irritated again.

Once we enter the school, the hallway splits. Normally, I'd walk with Declan and Juliet to the cafeteria until school starts, but I don't want to continue our conversation in front of her. I barely want to have it with *him*. They head left and I veer right.

"Hey," Declan calls after me.

I don't turn. "I need to grab a book before class."

My locker takes three tries to open. The combination doesn't want to work right. My fingers are too rough, too aggressive. I'm not familiar with this feeling.

Once it's open, I realize I don't really need a book. I didn't even need to open my locker.

I slam it shut. Metal on metal. The sound echoes down the hallway. Students nearby turn to stare at me, just for a moment, before moving on with their own day.

"Looks like someone pissed off the Grim Reaper."

I whirl, one hand clenched on the strap of my backpack, but whoever spoke is long gone.

The hallway is crowded with the typical crush of students who need to get to class, but auburn hair catches my eye. Emma. I've never seen her in this hallway before—but I've never been looking. Her hair hangs loose and shining, but her eyes are dark and shadowed. Her skin is pale, the freckles standing out like she drew them on.

I think about the altercation with Matthew and wish I could duck into my locker.

But my gaze stops on her shadowed eyes again. Something happened.

I step into her path. "Emma."

She looks up in surprise. "Oh." She sounds like she's speaking through a fog. "Hey."

"Are you okay?" I ask. "You look . . ." I hesitate.

She nods.

Then her face crumples.

Then she presses her face into my sweatshirt.

I barely know how to react. I would be less surprised if *Declan* did this.

"Emma." I duck my head and keep my voice low. "Emma, what happened?"

She shakes against me. Students continue to swirl around us, but I ignore them. My hands find her shoulders, and I wonder if it's okay to touch her. At the same time, I can't let go.

And then, all at once, she jerks back and swipes at her cheeks. My hands are suddenly empty. There's a foot of space between us.

"I'm so stupid." Her voice is full of emotion. "Please pretend this didn't just happen."

"Emma—"

"I'm fine."

"You're not fine."

She uses a sleeve to scrub at her eyes. "You were the first person to talk to me, and I wasn't ready." Her eyes are locked on my chest. "I made a wet mark on your shirt."

Like I care. "Is it Nightmare?" I ask. "Did you get another e-mail?"

"I wish." Her voice breaks. "I wish it was him."

And then she bursts into tears again.

The first bell rings. We have three minutes to be in class.

I have *never* been late to class.

Right now, I don't care. I take her hand. "Come on."

Declan is around the corner, standing by his locker with

Juliet. Their voices are low and serious. Juliet spots me first, and I watch her eyes shift to the clearly distraught girl at the end of my arm.

She taps Declan, then nods in my direction.

"Great," mutters Emma. She swipes at her eyes again and almost ducks behind me.

"It's fine," I say.

Juliet is fishing in her backpack, and she comes up with a pack of tissues. "Here," she says, holding them out to Emma. "Are you okay?"

Emma sniffs and blinks in surprise. "Oh. Thanks." She takes some tissues and moves to hand them back, but Juliet shakes her head.

"Keep them. I have plenty."

Declan glances at the clock at the end of the hallway. He doesn't care about his own schedule—much—but he knows I'm supposed to be on the other side of the school right now. "What's up?"

"Can I have your keys?"

"Sure." He digs them out of the front of his backpack and tosses them to me. "You all right?"

The hallways are already thinning. If we're going to get out of the school, we have to do it right now, before we're questioned in the hallway.

"Yes. Thanks." Then I lead Emma toward the side exit.

She doesn't resist at all. Not even when I push through the door and lead her into the rain.

"You don't care about missing class?" I say.

"Right now I don't care about anything at all."

The door slams behind us. We're alone in the student parking lot, though I'm sure it won't last. There are always late stragglers. The rain has kept everyone else indoors, and we're able to slip into Declan's car without being seen.

Emma slides into the front seat and pushes her backpack down onto the floorboards. "This isn't what I expected. Is this a classic car or something?"

"Yes. A Charger. His pride and joy. He rebuilt it himself." And he handed over the keys like it was nothing.

Guilt pricks at me. Declan would never keep a secret like this from me.

"Your friend?"

"Declan." I turn the key to start the engine and get some heat going. The rain has locked a chill into the air. Our breaths fog the glass.

"And that girl . . . his girlfriend?"

"Juliet. Yes."

She pulls another tissue from the pack, then drops the visor. She was probably expecting a mirror, but there isn't one. She snaps it back up and turns on the camera on her phone so she can see herself. She makes a face at the reflection and turns it off. "You said they met by exchanging letters?"

"Sort of." This feels like a deliberate avoidance of the whole crying-on-my-sweatshirt thing, but I can play along. "Dec got in some trouble last year," I say. "He had to work community service at a cemetery. Juliet was writing letters to her dead mother, and he started writing back."

She turns to me with eyes wide. "Like, pretending to be her mother?"

"No! No, nothing like that. Just . . . writing back and talking about losing someone." I hesitate. "His sister died when we were thirteen. His dad was drunk and crashed the car."

"Whoa." Emma crushes the tissue in her fist and stares out the windshield. "Every time I start feeling sorry for myself, I realize someone else has something bigger. And then I feel like a real ass." Another tear slips down her cheek. "And then I feel resentful, and then I feel like *more* of an ass for feeling resentful."

"Life isn't a competition."

"My parents are getting a divorce. They're not *dead*. There's no competition."

I swing my head around. After all the tears, she drops this like it's nothing. "They're what?"

"They're getting a divorce. I don't want to talk about it."

"Wait. What hap—"

"I just said I don't want to talk about it."

This doesn't feel like the kind of thing we should leave sitting in the air between us. "Did you just find out this morning?"

"Saturday night."

"Saturday night." The air slides out of my lungs. I have to look away. "After?"

"After you told me to leave? Yeah. After."

These words poke at me with a little too much accuracy. I'm at odds with everyone today. "I didn't—I wasn't throwing you out, Emma."

"You didn't tell me your parents were black."

The comment stops me in my tracks. It's almost impossible to read her voice, because it's full of emotion from other things. I'm not sure whether this is an accusation or a question.

While my adoption settled things inside of me, sometimes I feel like it unsettled things on the outside. As a foster kid, I was temporary, a child thrust upon them by the needs of the county. As an adopted kid, I was chosen.

I remember one night I was doing my homework, and Geoff and Kristin had another couple over for dinner. They mentioned how excited they were to be going through with the adoption. They probably didn't know I could hear them—or maybe they did. But overhearing those words, knowing I was wanted, was a powerful moment.

The man who'd come for dinner said, "There weren't any black kids you could adopt?"

That was a powerful moment, too.

They don't know that I heard. I remember their answer, that I was a child, and that was all that mattered. I was a child who needed them, who needed them *right then*. His words burrowed deeper. At the time, I was too embarrassed to bring it up. Too worried to bring it up, like maybe that comment had been a needed reminder, and the adoption wouldn't go through.

But it did. And they never invited that couple for dinner again.

I'm sure he wasn't the only one who wondered about our family.

The doorway to the school swings open, and a woman exits, rushing in the rain, holding a book over her head.

A tiny burst of fear ignites in my chest. I have never skipped class before.

At the same time, this dark corner of my brain is intrigued about what would happen if I got caught.

"We can't sit here," I say. "You okay if I drive?"

She buckles her seat belt, which I guess is answer enough. "You can drive a stick shift?"

"Yes." I push the clutch to the floor and start the engine. Officially, Geoff taught me to drive, but I've spent far more hours behind the wheel with Dec. I always worried I'd strip the clutch or take out a mailbox, but he's surprisingly chill about this car. At least with me.

We pull onto Generals Highway, the wipers sliding back and forth along the glass.

"I didn't mean to offend you," she says. "With my question."

"You didn't offend me." I pause. "And you didn't ask me a question."

"When your mom answered the door, I thought maybe I had the wrong house."

I almost apologize, but then wonder if that's appropriate. "I'm never sure how to explain."

Her voice turns careful. "You didn't mention it when you were telling me about how you were adopted."

I'm glad I'm driving, and that the winding road takes a decent portion of my attention. I don't know how her crying turned into a conversation about *me*, but this doesn't feel fair. "I don't think about it until people find out and then dig at me about it."

Shocked silence fills the car and I realize what I've said.

"Is that why you wear sweatshirts?" she says. "Because you're white?"

"No." I glance over in surprise. No one has ever asked that. It's never occurred to me. I wonder if other people think that, too. "I'm not embarrassed that we don't match."

The force of her thinking could probably steer this car. "Is this a sore point for you?"

I can't figure out her tone, whether she's judging me or chastising me. "No." I've never been more grateful for a rainy day and a road that demands my attention. "It's just that it's always this kind of conversation. Do you know, when I was a kid, if I was out with Geoff, people would always stop and ask me if I was okay. My father—my *biological* father—was torturing me every single day, and everyone thought he was the best dad. No one *ever* questioned him. Geoff is the kindest man you could ever meet, and people would stop us in the grocery store and ask if I was okay. Like *he* meant me harm."

Emma stares at me. "I'm—sorry. I don't know what to say."

"You don't have to be sorry. It's not you. It's everyone."

"And that other boy—the one you fought with. Who was he?"

Every time I remember it, my shoulders tense. "Matthew. He's a foster kid. He's only been living with us for a few days."

"So . . . what was he—"

"Stop." I cut a glance her way. This whole conversation has ramped me up, and I was already on edge this morning. "I'm happy to provide a distraction if that's what you really need, but you're the one who was crying in the hallway."

Her eyes flash wide in surprise, but then she turns to look out the window. A clear refusal to speak.

"If you didn't want to talk to me, why did you get in the car?"

Emma turns to face me head-on. "Fine. You have a nice reassuring Bible quote about divorce?"

The words are a weapon, one leveled with deadly aim. I can't speak.

She says nothing. She doesn't even seem to realize the impact her words have.

We drive in silence for miles. Hurt and embarrassment shift until anger swells to fill the car.

"What do you want me to do?" I finally ask.

"I don't want to talk about my parents."

I glance over. She's still looking out the window. Her arms are crossed against her chest.

I already feel closed off from everyone else in my life, but this feels deliberate. I told her about my father's e-mails. I felt safe with her.

I thought she felt safe with me.

I try to shake this off. I fail. My jaw feels tight. "I meant, do you want me to keep driving?"

"Just take me back to school," she says.

"Fine."

"Fine."

The rain stops when I pull into the parking lot. We need to park way at the back, because more students have filled in the available spots.

When she gets out, she heads for the front.

I head for the side entrance.

I don't stop her. She doesn't stop me.

We go our separate ways.

And somehow I feel like I'm carrying more baggage than I started with.

TWENTY-THREE

Emma

My fingers are shaking when I slip into second period. For some reason, my imagination thought maybe the school would have contacted the police and sent out a search party. Between the car and the front doors, I concocted a whole story about oversleeping and forgetting an assignment, leading to the tears in the hallway, when a kind senior—Rev—offered to drive me home to get what I needed.

Unnecessary. Apparently no one noticed. Or no one cares.

Clearly cutting class is a lot easier than I expected. I should do this more often.

Even Cait is oblivious. When I slide into my chair in U.S. History, I find her using a Sharpie to draw designs on her nail polish. Her makeup is stunning, with tiny jewels along her eyelids and vibrant lipstick. Completely out of place for school, but that's never stopped her.

She barely glances over, and her voice is easy. "Hey. I didn't see you this morning."

That's entirely my fault, but right now, it tightens the cords of anger and uncertainty that seem wound around my rib cage.

I ignore her comment. "Do you have a metallic one?"

The tone of my voice must get her attention, because she looks up. "Em?"

"A metallic Sharpie. Have one, do you?" I ask, Yoda-style. I'm trying to dial back the irritation and tension that the ride with Rev created, but instead the words just come out hostile and weird.

Cait raises her eyebrows and tosses one over.

She looks like she wants to talk, so I look down and start drawing a Dalek on my left thumbnail.

Mr. Maron comes in with a loud yodel, then slams his book onto his desk. I don't bother to look at him. He's worthless. Mr. Maron coaches cross-country, and he's constantly leering at girls, making comments like, "Nice legs. You should run." And he totally gets away with it. He gives me the creeps. I have no idea why anyone at all runs cross-country.

In case I'm being too subtle, I hate this class, and I hate this teacher.

"I cut first period," I whisper to Cait, keeping my voice low.

"Do you need a pad or something?" she whispers back.

"What?" I hiss. "I said I CUT FIRST PERIOD."

I draw the attention of at least six other students. All of whom probably heard exactly what I said.

Or they all think it's that time of the month.

Cait is staring at me like I've just confessed to murder. "How?"

"Went for a drive with a friend."

"What friend? Who do you know that has a car?"

"Rev Fletcher."

Her jaw drops so far it hits the desk.

I mean, not literally. But it's pretty far.

Mr. Maron turns away from the whiteboard and we need to pretend to pay attention.

You have a nice reassuring Bible quote about divorce?

This sinking feeling in my stomach will not go away. I am truly awful.

The worst part is that I keep thinking about my mother. I sounded exactly like her.

My cell phone vibrates against my thigh, but I need to wait a minute before I can slide it out of my pocket.

I'm hoping for a message from Rev, but I might as well hope for unicorns to burst through the window. A message from my father would also be welcome, but no dice.

It's Ethan.

At least it's not Nightmare. I haven't heard from him since I went off. Maybe that's all I needed to do, just completely lose it.

Ethan: How are you doing?
Emma: I'm OK. I snapped at a friend and I'm feeling like a real bitch.
Ethan: You're allowed. If she's a good friend, she'll understand.

He. I almost type back to correct Ethan, but . . . I don't. I'm not entirely sure why.

I'm not sure what I have with Rev, either, but it's not like we have anything real.

After what I said in the car, we might not have anything at all.

Emma: My head is a mess.
Ethan: Are your parents fighting constantly?
Emma: No. My dad is staying with a guy he works with. I'm avoiding my mother.
Ethan: You're lucky. Mine couldn't afford it, so they stayed in the same house until everything was finalized. Dad stayed in the guest room. He'd wake me up and ask me to tell Mom something.

I stare at his message and imagine Mom and Dad devolving to the point of using me as a carrier pigeon.

I can imagine my mother would like this idea.

The thought makes me want to move out myself.

"Miss Blue?"

I shove the phone into my pocket. Mr. Maron is staring at me. The whole class is staring at me.

Cait clears her throat and says something unintelligible.

She's probably feeding me the answer the teacher is expecting, but unless the answer is a garbled whisper, I'm out of luck.

"I'm sorry," I say sweetly. "Could you repeat the question?"

"Is something else demanding your attention?"

"No." I cough. "I'm sorry."

"Could you tell me the general purpose of the Declaration of Independence?"

THANK GOD THIS IS EASY.

"To declare our independence from the British."

"Why did the colonists want independence?"

My brain goes blank. Because tea was too expensive? Didn't they throw it into the Boston harbor?

Right now, it's a miracle I know my own last name. My cheeks warm as time ticks by. I can't even BS the answer.

Just like in the car, embarrassment begins shifting into other, less-stable emotions.

Mr. Maron stands there, letting the silence stretch on, until it's obvious to everyone in the room—to the whole school, probably—that I wasn't paying attention and I'm getting called on it right now. Mom would be so proud.

The sorrow from this morning threatens to overwhelm me again.

If I start crying in Mr. Maron's class, I am going to launch myself out the window. I imagine my body exploding on impact with the concrete. I imagine the custodian getting a mop, muttering, "Damn kids."

A giggle escapes me.

Mr. Maron has a stroke. Or something. His eyes bug out. "Do you find this *funny*, Miss Blue?"

I sober. "No. This is definitely not funny."

"Do you have an answer? Or have you sufficiently wasted everyone's time?"

He was the one letting the silence stretch on forever, but I won't earn any brownie points by saying that. I shake my head, though I can't erase the image of an exploding body from my brain. I don't know what's wrong with me.

"No." I cough. "No, sir. I'm sorry. It won't happen again."

I shouldn't have said *sir*. It sounds completely sarcastic.

I mean, it was. But I thought I made a good attempt to cover it up.

His bug-eyed stare turns into a glare. "Stop by my desk after class." Then he turns around to face the board again.

I should feel panicked. Anxious. Upset.

I don't feel any of those things. I feel numb.

"Are you okay?" Cait whispers.

"Oh yeah. I'm great. Don't leave me alone with him, okay?"

"So you just want me to wait in here with you?"

"Yup."

My phone has been vibrating against my thigh. All messages from Ethan.

Ethan: I just kept reminding myself that it would be over soon. I got through it.

Did I say the wrong thing?

Ethan: I didn't mean to overstep.

I quickly slide my thumb against the phone.

Emma: You didn't overstep. I got caught texting in class.
Ethan: Crap. Sorry.
Emma: It's OK. I don't even care. I don't care about any of it.

There's a long pause.

Ethan: You care.
Emma: Not right now, I don't.

That's a lie.

But if I think about it too hard, the custodian is going to be cleaning up the Emma explosion.

Ethan: Emma. You're lying.

Of course he knows. My throat tightens. I have to press my fingertips to my eyes.

"Em." Cait leans over and rests her hand on my arm. "Emma. Are you okay?"

Damn it. I'm crying.

I grab my bag and run out of the room.

The girls' bathroom is only twenty feet away, and I know Mr. Maron can't follow me in there, so I go through the door. This one is small, with only two stalls, and the bleach smell is gag-worthy, but it's empty and I'm alone.

I sit down on the floor. My shoulders shake with the force of my crying. I should never have come to school today.

After a moment, Cait bursts through the door to the bathroom. She kneels on the disgusting tile beside me. "Em. Em, are you okay?"

"No." I swipe at my eyes and blink at her. "Aren't you going to get in trouble for running after me?"

"No." She smiles, a little tentatively. "Ryanne Hardesty said she heard you say your period started. Mr. Maron thinks you had an emergency. I'm pretty sure everyone is chalking this up to PMS."

It's a shame there's not a window in the bathroom so I can dive out. "This is so humiliating."

"Let me get you some toilet paper."

"It's okay. I have tissues." I yank the packet Juliet gave me out of the front of my backpack. I have to dab at my raw cheeks carefully.

Cait studies me. "Something *is* going on, though." She pauses. "Did something happen this weekend?"

I snort. "You could say that."

"Why didn't you call me?"

"Because I thought you'd be busy with your mom. Making videos or pancakes or something."

Her face twitches, and I can tell she's balancing irritation with sympathy. "I'm pretty sure I could have stopped to take a phone call."

This seems to be my talent. Someone is kind, someone

reaches out, and I turn into a real bitch. I want to fold in on myself and hide, but there's nowhere to go.

"Emma." Cait's voice goes quiet. "Please talk to me."

I open my mouth to tell her about the divorce, but the words won't come out. Cait's life is so easy. She would pat my hand and say *Poor Emma*.

I don't want to be *Poor Emma*. I already feel worthless in my own house. I don't need to be pitied here, too.

I say, "My parents were just fighting a lot."

Cait drops to sit beside me. "I'm sorry, Em." She hesitates. "You could have come over."

"Yeah, maybe you could have given me a makeover." I wipe at my eyes.

She stiffens, then unzips a pouch on her backpack and pulls out a candy bar. "Would a candy bar make you feel better?"

"No." I roll my eyes at the ceiling. "I'm not *really* suffering from PMS." I wish this could all be solved with a Snickers bar and a handful of Advil.

She studies me critically. "I feel like there's more going on here. What's happening with Rev Fletcher?"

"Nothing. I ruined it."

"Emma—"

"God, Cait. What, are you writing a blog?"

She sits back on her heels. "I don't know what's happening here, but I'm trying to help you."

I look down at my nails. "Forget it, Cait. Everything is perfect for you. You have no idea what I'm going through."

She goes still again, but this time it's longer. Her voice is very quiet. "Everything is not perfect for me."

I snort. "Close enough."

"Really?" For the first time, her voice turns sharp. "You think it's so perfect that my best friend thinks that something important to me is a waste of time?"

"What?"

"How about how perfect it is that I spent months playing a game because it was important to *you*, but when I do something, I get a bunch of snarky comments."

I bristle. "Cait, I don't know what you're—"

"You constantly complain about how your mom doesn't respect what you want to do, and then you treat me the same exact way."

The words hit me like a fist to the face. "I do not!"

"You do too!"

"Cait, it's just makeup!"

She shoots to her feet. "Yeah, Emma. And it's just a stupid game." She shrugs her backpack onto her shoulder. "I guess I need to get my perfect self back to class."

I glare at the floor when she pushes through the door. I wait to feel vindicated or justified. I don't.

I have now alienated the first boy I've ever liked *and* my best friend. Go, me.

I don't treat her that way. I've never had a problem with the makeup.

Maybe you could have given me a makeover.

She's right. Tears prick at my eyes.

I slide my phone out of my pocket. Ethan hasn't sent any more messages, but his last one sits on the screen.

Emma. You're lying.

Emma: I just got into a fight with my best friend.

Ethan: ☹

Emma: I'm not having a good week.

Ethan: Would it sound trite if I said it will eventually get better?

Emma: Yes.

Ethan: Would you feel better if I remind you that you're a badass, even without OtherLANDS?

I smile, but it feels halfhearted.

Emma: Yes. Yes, I would.

I really am lying to him.

I don't feel better at all.

TWENTY-FOUR

Rev

The weather matches my mood. Rain pours down in sheets, beating on the cafeteria windows, keeping everyone inside. The fluorescent lights are giving me a headache. Kristin has packed me a huge lunch, as usual, with pita pockets stuffed thick with lunch meat and cheese, bags of grapes, and a container of bean salad.

I don't want to eat any of it. I shove the bag toward Declan.

He starts prying lids free. "I thought for sure you weren't coming back."

I shrug. I don't want to talk about Emma.

Her words hurt more than they should have.

Or maybe they hurt every bit as much as she meant them to.

The cafeteria is packed. Our school does one big lunch hour for everyone, which is nothing short of insanity. Juliet is working in the photo lab during lunch, but it's so crowded that we don't have the table to ourselves. I don't know the guys at the opposite end. They seem content to ignore us, so we can return the favor.

Declan pushes a pita pocket in my direction. "I can't eat all this."

I guarantee he will. "Whatever."

It's not a response I use often. His eyebrows go up. "Emma isn't what I expected."

"Okay."

"I'm guessing you don't want to talk about her."

"You're guessing right."

"Why was she crying?"

I give him a level glare across the table.

"What?" He looks back at me and eats a spoonful of bean salad. "You want to talk about Matthew instead?"

"Dec."

"You just want to sit here quietly?"

"Yes."

He shuts up. He eats.

I study the surface of the table. My emotions are like a cue ball being knocked all over a pool table, colliding with thoughts at random. Emma, the way she clung to me in the hallway, sobbing, then shut me down. My father, the way he promised he would not wait forever, leaving me to wonder what that means. Matthew, who still isn't talking to me, who's somewhere in this school, doing who knows what.

Disappointment and fear and guilt weave a lattice through my thoughts.

And also, a little dark satisfaction. A little aggression. I cut class. I got away with it.

I've never done something like that. An unfamiliar belligerence has set up camp in my head.

"You think Matthew is having a bad day?" says Declan.

That pulls me from my thoughts. "What?"

He nods toward a table about thirty feet away, where Matthew sits. Nothing is on the table in front of him, though Kristin definitely would have packed him something. No backpack sits near him. His face is red, his jaw set. Two boys stand beside him, and I can't hear what they're saying, but nothing about the situation looks friendly. Other kids are at the table, but they're doing nothing. Just watching.

One of the boys flicks him on the side of the head.

I'm off the bench without a thought. I must look intense, because other students clear a path and I draw stares.

I step right into the boys' personal space, putting myself between them and Matthew. They're underclassmen. I don't recognize them at all. "What's going on?"

The bigger one, the *flick*er, gives me a dismissive look. "None of your business, creeper. What are you, his new boyfriend?" He reaches around me to flick Matthew on the side of the head again. "I told you to *move.*"

I don't realize I've drawn back a fist until Declan has a hold of my arm, and he's half blocking me.

"What are you *doing*?" he says low, under his breath.

I don't know what I'm doing.

Seriously, I don't know what I'm doing. My thoughts spin.

My muscles are tight, but I don't want to fight with Declan. Words grind out. "Let me go."

"Rev." He sounds incredulous. I don't blame him. In the past, our positions have always been reversed. "Dude. If you start a fight, you'll be suspended."

I'm embarrassed and angry and I feel like a caged animal. My voice is a growl. "I said, *let me go*."

He hesitates. I jerk free.

"What's going on here?"

A teacher's voice. Mrs. James, who teaches freshman Health and also monitors the cafeteria at lunchtime. She's tall and imposing and doesn't take any crap.

"Nothing," I snap.

The other boy says, "We were just going to eat lunch. He came over and started hassling us."

Mrs. James looks at me. "Is that true?"

"They were hassling *him*." I nod my head at Matthew.

She looks at him. "Is that true?"

He says nothing. His eyes are locked on the tabletop. His cheeks are still red.

We're very much the center of attention in the middle of the cafeteria.

"Maybe you should all go your separate ways," Mrs. James says.

That will solve things for exactly thirty seconds.

"I'm not leaving him alone," I say.

The *flick*er snorts. "Ha. I knew it. Does Neil know?"

Neil?

"Who's Neil?" I say.

Matthew flinches. He shoots up from the table, yanking his backpack from underneath the bench. He all but runs from the table.

"Enough!" snaps Mrs. James. "You boys. Move. Now."

They move, heading for the food line, laughing as they go.

I shift to follow Matthew.

Mrs. James steps in front of me. "No. You go in another direction."

Across the room, Matthew slams through the double doors to exit the cafeteria. I move to push past the teacher.

"Hey." She blocks me again. "I told you to take a walk. Cool off."

"Rev." Declan pushes at my shoulder. "Come on. Leave it."

I don't want to leave it. I'm coiled like a spring, waiting for someone to turn a dial so I can explode. The world feels edged with electricity.

She's tall, but I'm taller. I could force my way past her without too much trouble. I take a step forward.

She takes a step back, one hand up. "Either you take a walk," says Mrs. James, "or I'm calling security."

No teacher has ever threatened to call security about me.

It's terrifyingly addictive. I've stepped over a line I didn't know I had. A part of me wants to know how far I can push this.

"Declan." Another teacher's voice. Mrs. Hillard. Declan's AP English teacher. She's got a tray in her hands, and she's one table away. "What's going on?"

"Rev is losing his mind."

His voice is dry, but he's not kidding.

She puts her tray down and steps around the table. "Come on, boys. Why don't you eat in my classroom? We can talk it out."

Declan doesn't move. His eyes are on me. "Rev?"

"Fine." I turn away, and when no one says anything to stop me, I return to our table to grab my backpack. My hood falls lower over my forehead, blocking more of the light from the room. It doesn't matter. I don't need to see the other students' eyes to feel them on me. The entire room seems filled with whispers. In my head, the whispers aren't just about this moment. They're about my father.

I told you to answer me.

I will not wait forever.

A threat. A promise. There are penalties for failure.

Tension forms a vise grip around my chest. My throat.

My head wants to explode.

A hand grabs my arm. Red colors my vision. I whirl. My arm flies. I make contact.

Declan hits the ground.

I fall back.

My heart is a roar in my ears. I can't speak. I can't think.

I hit my best friend. I hit my best friend. *I hit my best friend.*

They call security.

● ● ●

A parent has to pick me up.

That means I have to wait.

It'll probably be Kristin, since she works from home, but I've been sitting in the front office for an hour. Rain whips against the windowpanes. People have come and gone, attending to their business, but my head is down, the hood low. My hand hurts, but I don't want to ask for ice.

Declan is fine.

I don't know if our friendship is fine.

When I was young, when I failed a test, my father would make me wait, much like this, to see how I could earn a way back into his good graces. You'd think the abuse would be the worst part, but it wasn't.

It was this. The waiting.

Mr. Diviglio, the vice principal, told me that because this was a first offense, I won't be suspended longer than the rest of the afternoon. A letter will be sent to Geoff and Kristin. I have to attend a class on peaceful resolution of conflict.

What a joke. I didn't hit the kids who deserved it. I hit *my best friend.*

I think about the moments before I punched him. My thoughts were almost those of another person. I can't re-create my mental state. I don't even know why I lashed out.

A part of me wishes they'd called the cops, so I could be locked in a cell, away from my phone and my father and all the conflict that's keeping my brain tied up in knots.

My phone chimes. An e-mail.

My stomach twists. I can't make myself pull it out of my backpack. No message would be good right now.

"Rev?"

I look up. Geoff stands at the desk. I expected him to look angry. He doesn't. He looks confused.

That's worse.

I have no idea what to say to him. Apologize? Explain? My feet seem rooted to the floor.

"I've signed you out," he says. "Come on."

I've never been defiant, but as I stand and throw my backpack over my shoulder, I wonder what would happen if I walked past him, out of this building, and just kept right on walking.

I don't.

Geoff is silent as we climb into the car. Rain clings to everything. The doors close, turning the car into a cage, the seat belt into a noose.

My phone chimes again. My breathing goes quick and shallow. I leave it in my backpack.

"Did you and Declan have a fight?" Geoff says.

"No."

"Do you want to tell me why you hit him?"

I swallow and pick at the line of stitching on the door handle. My eyes are locked on the silver strip along the window. "It was an accident."

"An accident?"

I nod. I don't want to elaborate.

"Mr. Diviglio told me that you were involved in some kind of altercation with other students. Do you want to tell me what happened there?"

Confusion still colors his voice. He sounds like he's trying to decide whether to be empathetic or stern.

I get it. This is not the type of conversation we've ever had. I have never been involved in an "altercation." I've never even had a detention.

I shrug a little. "Some boys were hassling Matthew. I tried to stop them."

A pause. "Hassling how?"

"I don't really know. They were just—hassling him."

His hands tighten on the steering wheel. "Do I need to turn around and go back to the school?"

"What?"

"If they're suspending you because you were trying to *defend* him, I'm going to go have a word with that vice principal—"

"They're suspending me because I punched Dec. Matthew is fine."

As I say the words, I realize I don't know if they're true at all.

What are you, his new boyfriend?

Does Neil know?

"Was Declan hassling him?" asks Geoff.

"Of course not."

He sighs. "Okay, then why did you punch Declan?"

Because violence is in my genes. Because my head is broken. Because I'm a threat to everyone around me. A ticking time bomb.

Declan experienced the first detonation.

My fingers are going to peel the upholstery apart.

"Something is going on with you," says Geoff. "I think you need to start talking about what it is."

We make the final turn toward home. I say nothing.

"Rev." He's chosen stern. "Answer me."

I stiffen. My father's words. *Answer me.*

I don't answer him.

"Rev." Geoff glances away from the road, but I refuse to look at him. He rarely raises his voice, but when he does, he means business. "Answer me. Right now."

I don't. Again, this defiance is addictive. Not in a good way.

He pulls into our driveway, and I'm out of the car before he's even put it in Park. Kristin's car isn't here. Rain beats down on me, just like on Saturday night.

I explode through the front door, flinging it closed behind me.

Geoff catches it, dogging me all the way. He's in great shape, but so am I. "Rev. Stop. We are going to talk about this."

Not if I can help it. I try to slam my bedroom door in his face. He catches it. Pushes it open. Follows me in.

I turn on him. "Leave me alone."

"No."

I get in his face. "*Leave. Me. Alone.*"

He doesn't back off. "No."

My hands form fists. "Leave me alone!" I'm shouting now.

His voice grows quieter. "No."

"Leave me alone!" I shove him, and I'm strong enough to push him back a step, but he doesn't move beyond that.

"No." His voice is so quiet. "Rev. No."

"Go away." I shove him again, harder this time. "Go away." My voice cracks. I'm panting like I've run a mile. "I don't want you. I don't want you."

"I'm not leaving."

"Get out!" I shove him again. He's up against the wall now. "I don't want you! Get *out*."

"No."

I put my hands against his chest. I have fistfuls of his shirt. The fear and anger spooled inside of me are beginning to uncoil, and I can't think. I'm not even sure what I'm going to do. Every muscle in my body is rigid, primed to fight.

Geoff catches my hands. Not in a defensive motion. He just puts his hands over mine.

"It's okay," he says softly. His voice is low and calm and sure. "Rev. It's okay."

I'm breathing so hard I might be hyperventilating. I force my fingers to unclench. My arms are shaking.

"I'm sorry." My voice breaks. I'm crying. "I'm sorry."

Geoff doesn't let go of me. "It's okay."

And then I'm crumpling, falling against him.

He catches me. He holds on.

Because he's not my father. He's my dad.

TWENTY-FIVE

Rev

Geoff makes grilled cheese.

No, *Dad* makes grilled cheese. He slathers both sides of the bread with butter, and it sizzles when it hits the pan. Four slices of cheese go on each sandwich. The crack and spit of butter in the pan mixes with the patter of rain against the sliding glass door. It's the only noise in the house, but it's a good sound.

Mom is apparently meeting a client on the other side of the county, or she'd be here railing on him about his cholesterol.

Or she'd be sitting here holding my hand.

I'm wilting in a chair, my eyes raw. He hasn't pressed me for answers anymore, but some dynamic has shifted. I don't feel alone. I don't have to hide.

He tells me to get out sodas and plates for us, and his voice is gentle and even. Like it's any other day.

I do. And then he's sitting next to me.

All of a sudden, it's like he's dropped a blanket of expectation onto my shoulders. My hands fold against my stomach.

"Hey." He gives my shoulder a gentle shake. "We'll get through it. Okay? Whatever it is."

I hold my breath and nod until my lungs are screaming for oxygen. Even then, I only let a bit of air in.

Dad hasn't touched his grilled cheese. "This has nothing at all to do with Matthew, does it?"

I shake my head slowly.

"Eat your sandwich, Rev."

I clear my throat. My voice is low and rough, but not broken. "I need to show you something."

"Okay."

My father's letter has been between my mattress and box spring since last Thursday. It's not the most original hiding place, but I make my own bed, and I've never given Mom and Dad a reason to search my room.

I'm not afraid to give it to him now. Whatever happened in my bedroom has snapped the cords of tension that held me together for the last few days.

The envelope feels fragile and brittle, flakes drifting away from the burned edge. I drop it in front of Dad without ceremony, then drop myself into my chair.

I cross my arms against my abdomen again. I can't watch his expression when he reads it.

No. I'm lying. I have to watch his expression. My eyes are locked on his face. I'm not breathing again.

He puts his reading glasses on, then slides the letter out of the envelope carefully.

His expression goes still almost immediately. His eyes look up over the edge of his glasses. "Where did you get this?"

"It was in the mail."

"When?"

"Thursday."

His eyebrows shoot up. "Thursday!"

I jump, a little. He looks back at the letter. Reads it again.

His eyes flick up to meet mine. "When I found you in the backyard. When you were upset."

My breathing goes shallow again. My knee bounces under the table. I nod, almost imperceptibly.

He removes his reading glasses and sets them on the table. "Rev." His voice is grave. "Did I say something that made you think you couldn't tell me about this?"

That's not a question I expected him to ask. "No." My mouth goes dry, and I have to clear my throat again. "I don't—I didn't know what to do."

"Is this the only letter?"

I nod. "The only written one. Yes."

"The only written one?" His glasses go back on, and he scans the letter again. "What else is there?"

I rub my palms against my knees. "I e-mailed him. He's been writing back."

Geoff looks incredulous. "You've been e-mailing with him?"

I look away. "I'm sorry." My eyes are hot again. I rub my face. "I'm sorry. I didn't want to upset you. I know I screwed up."

"Rev." Dad scoots his chair closer to me. He puts a hand over mine. "You didn't screw up. I wish—I wish I'd known—"

I flinch. "I know. I'm sorry."

"No. That's not what I mean. I wish I'd known so I could have helped you."

He's so calm about all of this. I expected a flurry of activity. Calls to lawyers or the police for some reason. I've been so anxious about my father showing up at the front door, armed with a crucifix and a shotgun, that having someone sit here and talk allows me to take the first deep breath I've had in days.

"I just—I felt—" I have to force my breathing to slow so I can talk like a normal human being. "Like I was betraying you. By talking to him."

"You aren't betraying us, Rev. I don't want to see you get hurt, but talking to your father isn't a betrayal to me. Or to Mom. No matter what, we love you. Everything about you."

His words warm me from within, but I snort and push hair back off my face. "Even when I'm screaming at you to get out of my room?"

"Even then. We all push sometimes, just to make sure someone is on the other side, pushing back."

It makes me think of Emma, her aggressive words in the car. I have to shove the thoughts out of my head. "What if I push too hard?"

"Not possible."

The words should be reassuring, but anxiety still winds lazy figure eights through my rib cage. "I think I almost did."

"Oh, Rev." He pulls me forward, into a hug, then kisses the side of my forehead. "Not even close."

• • •

We eat our sandwiches. I clean up, while Geoff reads the e-mails on my phone. He's been making notes on a legal pad.

"Other than the first," he says, his voice analytical now, "have you sent him anything?"

"No."

He looks at me over the rim of his glasses again. "Do you want to?"

Answer me.

I shrug and look away.

"Do you want him to stop?" Dad says.

Yes. No. I don't know.

I'm frozen against the edge of the sink. I can't move.

"That's an important question," Dad says. "I'm asking if you want me to file for a restraining order."

"If you do that, he's not allowed to contact me at all, right?"

"Right."

"Was there one before? Is that why he waited until now?" It's such a relief to be able to talk to someone about this. Someone who can give me answers. Someone who can tell me what to do. I didn't realize how much I needed this support until I had it. I want to collapse on the floor.

"In a way. His rights as a parent were revoked. He was not allowed to contact you while you were a minor."

"How do you think he found me?"

"I don't know, but I plan to ask our attorney." Dad pauses. "Do you want me to look into the restraining order?"

"I think—I think that would be worse. Knowing he's out there, but not knowing—" I break off and swallow.

Dad takes off his reading glasses. "May I give you my thoughts?"

"Yes." My fingers grip the counter behind me.

"You're eighteen. You can make your own decision about this. Mom and I will give you whatever support you need." He pauses. "But these messages aren't positive, Rev. This is not a reformed man looking to make amends. This is a disturbed man who tortured you for years."

The words make me curl in on myself, just a little. "Sometimes . . ." My voice is very soft, and I can't manage more than that. "I keep wondering if this is a test. If it's all a test."

"A test from God?" Dad has always been very open about discussing religion. He enjoys debating theology. He and Mom aren't religious, but he finds the whole concept fascinating. When I was a child, Mom took me to a local church because she thought it would be something comforting and familiar, but being in a church was too reminiscent of my father. I would sit next to Mom on the pew and shake.

I've tried going back, but it never lasts.

"Yes," I say. "A test from God."

"We all have free will, Rev. If it's a test for you, it's a test for me, for Mom, and even a test for your father. He's choosing to send you these messages. You could look at all of life as a test. No one lives in a vacuum. Our actions have an impact on everyone around us. Sometimes without us even realizing it."

It makes me think of Emma again. She was in real pain this morning.

And Matthew. Something happened at lunch. I don't know if I made things better, or if I made things worse.

And Declan. When I pulled out my phone to show Dad the messages from my father, I could see a text message waiting.

I didn't click on it. I'm such a coward.

"A test implies that you alone are being challenged," Dad says. "But that's impossible when you're surrounded by others whose actions affect your decisions. And do you really believe that there's a God who specifically chooses people and assigns them with challenges? Based on what?"

I'm not sure how to respond to that.

He leans back in his chair. "Sometimes events are set in motion from so far away that it's almost impossible to draw connections until well after the fact—and then, where was the test? At the beginning? In the middle? All along? Then we're back to thinking all of life is a test. And maybe it is. But if someone is raised with a different belief system, can they be judged by ours? How is that a fair test? We can only do the best we can with what we're given."

"I know."

"Do you? Because I wonder if there's a part of you that's still seeking your father's approval, even after all these years. I wonder if you've been seeking it all along, with the way you've practically memorized the Bible. I wonder if it isn't curiosity that made you send him that e-mail, but obligation. I wonder if it's easier to think God is testing you instead of admitting that your father truly hurt you, Rev. If there's any test here, it's one you've created for yourself."

His voice is so gentle, so kind. My fingers are gripping the counter so hard that I'm worried I'll crack the granite. "What's the test?"

But I know.

"Do you want your father in your life?"

My voice is a whisper. "I don't know."

"I think you do know, Rev."

Steps thump on the back porch steps, and I glance at the clock above the microwave. Cabinets block the view of the sliding door from here, but it's the middle of the afternoon. Matthew must be home from school.

He could have run. He didn't.

Dad stands to open the door for him. Matthew all but pushes past him without a word. He doesn't spare me a glance. Just blows through the kitchen and makes the turn for his bedroom.

So I guess the rest of the day didn't go well.

Then another set of feet stomps across the porch.

It's Declan. I know it's Declan.

Shame lights me up inside. I wish I could hide in my room, too.

He blows into the kitchen like a hurricane. I edge toward the sink, before I realize what I'm doing and force myself to stand my ground.

"Hi, Declan," says Dad, like nothing is going on, and it's any other afternoon.

"Hey." Dec blows past him, too, and comes around the row of cabinets to face me. His expression is fierce. His jaw is swollen and bruised. I clocked him good.

I wince. I have no idea what to say. "Do you want to hit me back? You can."

"No, I don't want to hit you back, you idiot. I've sent you like thirty texts. Are you okay?"

My eyebrows go up. "You're asking if *I'm* okay?"

"Yes."

It's like the moment I realized Dad wasn't going to let me chase him out of my room. I want to crumple on the floor. "No," I say. "I'm not."

"Then come on."

I don't move. My head is spinning. "Where are we going?"

"Downstairs. Get your gloves. If you need to throw punches, let's find something better than my face."

TWENTY-SIX

Emma

My parents are hammering out a separation agreement in the kitchen.

I'm on the couch, staring at an old movie on Netflix, listening to them bicker over things like who has the bigger car payment and who should pay how much for groceries. Neither of them has said a word to me since I got home from school. They're locked in a bubble of their own making.

I wish I could be locked in the bubble of my bedroom, but I can't stand the thought of not knowing what they're trading away.

When they're done, I'll be just another line item.

I can't do this. I can't be here.

I whistle and grab the leash.

The rain has slowed to a trickle. It's become habit to head toward the church, and Texy makes the turn at the end of my street automatically.

I'm secretly hoping Rev will be there, waiting for me.

Yeah, whatever. We have no plans to meet, and after the way I snapped at him in the car, I can't imagine him waiting around for more.

But I'm still hoping.

I ate lunch in the library, hunched over a computer. Avoiding Cait. Avoiding Rev. Avoiding life. I wanted to skip another class, but without a car, I didn't know how to get off the school grounds quickly enough, and I really had no desire to walk in the rain.

Instead, I logged in to Battle Realms and played with Ethan. There's a pretty clear sticker at the top of every monitor that says NO GAMING DURING SCHOOL HOURS, but there's also a pretty clear part of my brain that ignores it.

The church benches are empty. The grassy stretch beside the building is empty.

Of course. No rom-com meet up tonight.

I let Texy do her thing, then whistle. She comes right to me, erasing any remaining hope that Rev is sitting somewhere with nuggets, just out of view.

I'm pathetic.

You have a nice reassuring Bible quote about divorce?

I should never have snapped at him like that. I wonder if Mom would like it if I told her I inherited her tendency to make snippy comments instead of her commitment to medicine.

Maybe I should walk to his house and apologize.

Before I know it, I'm doing exactly that. It's easy enough to find the house again. Lights shine in each window, beacons through the steamy drizzle. His parents seemed kind.

As soon as the thought enters my head, I know I'm not going to knock on his door. I can't be around a normal family. Not right now. Not with the mess waiting for me at home. It's the same reason I can't go to Cait's.

My phone chimes.

Ethan.

Ethan: How's it going tonight? I looked for you online.

Maybe this is a sign.

I turn away from Rev's house and head back toward the church, texting as I walk.

Emma: I'm walking the dog because they're hammering out a separation agreement.

Ethan: Not going well?

Emma: When I left they were screaming over who contributed what to the down payment on the house. Guess.

Ethan: Ouch.

Emma: Tell me about it.

Ethan: Is it a pain to have to walk the dog every night?

Emma: No, I don't mind it. Mom says it's the only way she can get me away from a computer, but it's quiet. And I have a phone.

Ethan: What's your dog's name?

Emma: Texas.

Ethan: Send me a picture.

I hold up the phone and click my tongue. Texas looks up at me over her shoulder, ears lopsided. I press the button to capture the image, then send it to him.

Ethan: She's pretty.
Emma: Thanks. She's a good dog.
Ethan: I wish I had a dog. I think it would help to have someone on my side.
Emma: She's good for that.

I bite at my lip, then add another line.

Emma: Are you lonely?
Ethan: What do you think?

I stare at his message. Before I can come up with a response, he adds another line.

Ethan: I'm sorry. I didn't mean to be a dick.
Emma: It's OK. You weren't.

He doesn't write back.

Great. Now I've ruined another friendship, without even trying.

But then a long message appears.

Ethan: Yes. I'm lonely. I spent a year locked in my bedroom. I'm online all night. The only people I really talk to are all in-game. During the day, everyone ignores me. It's not their fault—I ignore them back. But it doesn't exactly help you climb to the top of the social ladder.

I don't know what to say. There's something terribly sad about his experience.

I wonder if I should thank my mother for forcing me to get out of the house every day.

Ethan: I'm sorry. Overshare.
Emma: No, I'm sorry. Is there anything I can do?
Ethan: Lend me your dog?

Then he sends the smiling emoji with the sunglasses.

Emma: Ha-ha, anytime.
Ethan: I'll hold you to that.

Then he sends another smiling emoji.

Ethan: I don't suppose you'd send me a picture of you.
Emma: Why?
Ethan: I'm just curious. I keep seeing you as Azure M and I know that's not accurate.
Emma: I keep seeing you as the guy in OtherLANDS.

There's a long pause, and then a picture comes through. It's grainy and dark, but it's him. IT'S HIM. He's got short blond hair. Light eyes. A narrow face and broad shoulders. The light from his computer reflects off his face, making him look washed out, but I can tell he's got a nice smile. Shy, but nice. Soft cheeks.

And thank god he's fully clothed. Well, his upper body is fully clothed. That's all I can see. He could be naked from the waist down, for all I know.

WHY IS MY BRAIN SUPPLYING THOUGHTS LIKE THIS?

He's got a hand up, exactly the wave pose that he uses in the game. It makes me grin.

Another line of text appears immediately.

Ethan: I can't believe I sent you that. I think I'm going to have a heart attack.

My heart softens.

Emma: Don't die until I can return the favor. Here. Hold on.

I hold the phone out in front of me and try to take a picture.

Okay, I take seven. The flash washes me out in each one, so I finally choose one that doesn't look too silly, and I send that.

Ethan: You really do look like Azure M.
Emma: No, I do not.
Ethan: You do.

Emma: Azure M does not have glasses.

Ethan: Maybe this is your secret identity.

That makes me smile.

Emma: You kind of look like Ethan.

Ethan: Good thing. I am Ethan.

Emma: You know what I mean.

Ethan: I do.

Emma: It's nice to meet you, Ethan.

Ethan: It's nice to meet you, Emma.

Emma: I'm glad you texted me. I really needed a distraction.

Ethan: I'm glad I texted you, too.

Emma: I can go home and get on OtherLANDS if you want to play.

Ethan: I'd like that.

Emma: See you in ten.

I cluck my tongue to Texy. "Come on, Tex."

She pulls toward the church, toward Rev's, toward everything I don't want to think about.

I pull her in the opposite direction and we head toward home.

TWENTY-SEVEN

Rev

I thought I was exhausted before.

Now I'm a sweaty mess, and my muscles have turned to gelatin.

We took a break for dinner—an awkward, silent affair where Kristin tried to force conversation, Matthew ignored every word spoken to him, and Declan made jokes about how he needs to eat through a straw after what I did to him.

Now we're back in the basement. Every time I pause for breath, Declan says, "Do you want to stop?"

And then my head fills with thoughts about my father, about Emma, about this twisted, complicated mess, and I throw another punch.

It's after eight now. I break away from the bag, panting. He throws a water bottle at me, and I almost down the entire thing in one swallow. Even with the gloves, my knuckles are raw, my shoulders shaking from overexertion.

"Stop?" says Declan.

I want to say no, but my head is nodding without my consent.

He lets go of the bag and drops onto the yoga ball in the corner.

I straddle the weight bench and lean back against the mirror on the wall, then strip the gloves from my fingers.

He's relaxed. There's no tension in the air.

Even still, it's hard to look at him. "Are you mad I didn't tell you?"

"No." He pauses, and his voice turns thoughtful. "You were going to tell me Friday night, weren't you?"

There's a note of regret in his voice. I shrug.

"And then I went off about your father," he continues.

"It was okay," I say.

He leans back into the corner and looks at the ceiling. "Since we're sharing daddy secrets, I've got one, too."

That gets my attention. I straighten, pushing off the mirror. "Yeah?"

"I'm going to visit him."

Declan has never visited his father in prison. His mother never has either. "Really?"

"Yeah." He hesitates. "I couldn't tell Mom." Another pause. "I looked it up. They have visitation hours on weekdays. I could go after school. Mom and Alan are so focused on the baby coming that I don't think they'd notice."

He's given this a lot of thought.

I've been so wrapped up in my own drama that I haven't given a moment's consideration to what's going on with him.

"You want company?" I ask him.

"Nah. I'm all right."

I'm not sure what to say to that, and we lapse into silence. Mom and Dad are watching some superhero drama upstairs, and that's not their usual thing at all. I wonder if they're trying to coax Matthew out of his room somehow.

Declan speaks into the silence. "Yeah. I want company."

I knew that five minutes ago, but it's a relief to hear him say it. We're okay. "When do you want to go?"

"Tomorrow?"

I nod. "Okay."

Motion flickers at the corner of my eye, and I freeze. It's like the other night, when I knew I was being watched.

But it's *not* like the other night. The demons in my head are quiet. Or maybe they've been tamed by the people in this house.

I look at Declan. "I think Matthew is down here," I whisper, so quietly I'm almost mouthing it.

He's not quiet at all. "Where?"

I glance at the far corner, where the basement dips into darkness, and a door leads to the laundry and the spare bathroom.

Declan rolls off the yoga ball and heads for the corner. "Hey. Matthew."

I don't see this going well. I push myself off the weight bench and head forward to stop whatever is about to happen.

But Declan just gestures over to where we're sitting. "You want to hang out down here, just do it."

For a moment, there's an expectant pause in the air.

And then Matthew slides out of the darkness. He's good at sneaking, because I never saw him slip down here. I drop back onto the weight bench.

Declan drags an ottoman away from the couch in the opposite corner and abandons it beside Matthew. "Here. Sit down." Then he reclaims the yoga ball.

Matthew looks at me, and then he looks at Declan, and I think he's going to bolt up the stairs.

He doesn't. He sits down.

This *definitely* feels like a test.

"You can't hang out in the shadows like a creeper," says Declan. "You'll freak Rev out."

"Thanks," I say.

"What? It's true."

He's right, so I can't argue the point. But I like how he just put it out there. I sat on the bench whispering about it. Declan solved the problem.

I do spend too much time in my own head.

"Don't sneak up on him either." Declan rubs his jaw. "Because Rev can punch like a mother—"

"Dec." I roll my eyes.

"I'm glad you hit me, though. You think those douchebags are going to hassle Matt after seeing you do *that*?"

"Dude. Shut up."

"I'm serious." He looks at Matthew. "You wait. You said they didn't even talk to you this afternoon. I guarantee they won't even *look* at you."

"When did this conversation happen?" I ask.

"When I drove him home."

"You—what—?"

Declan looks at me like I'm not following a simple conversation, which is pretty much on point. "How else do you think we got here at the same time?"

"I hadn't really thought about it." Again, I'm amazed at Declan's ability to *do* that. I wish I had whatever it is that gives him this confidence. I sat at a dinner table with Matthew and he insisted on riding the bus. Declan gets punched in the face and he drives the kid home on his first day.

Declan glances at Matthew, who hasn't said a word since sitting down. "And calling it a 'conversation' is a bit of a stretch."

Matthew shrugs.

"Why were they hassling you?" I say.

He shrugs again, but this time it's less committal. He knows why.

"Do they know you?" I ask.

He doesn't answer.

"They seemed to know you," says Declan.

He said he's gone to Hamilton before. I wonder if he's been in trouble there. I wonder if Mom and Dad know, or if there's some weird student privacy thing that would prevent Mr. Diviglio from telling them.

"Who's Neil?" I say.

A kind of frozen fury takes over Matthew's expression. "No one."

"Doesn't sound like no one."

"I said, he's *no one.*"

"All right, all right." Declan's tone is almost lazy, but it takes the edge out of the air. "He's no one." He pauses. "Does this *no one* go to Hamilton?"

I don't think Matthew is going to answer, but he does. "Not anymore."

I don't know anyone named Neil, but that doesn't mean anything. Hamilton has over two thousand students, with kids from all over the county, thanks to the way waterways cut through towns. There are almost six hundred seniors this year, and I couldn't name everyone in my own class, much less any others.

"Was he your boyfriend?" I ask carefully.

"No." Matthew's voice is tight. "I'm not gay."

"It's okay if you are," I say. "Mom and Dad don't care. I don't care."

"I don't care," says Declan.

Matthew's expression is fierce. "I don't care either. But I'm not."

I have no idea whether he's telling the truth, but I'm not going to push the point. I shrug. "All right."

"Declan?" Kristin calls down from upstairs. "Your mom wants to know if you're coming home soon. She needs to move some furniture."

"Okay," he calls back. He sighs and rolls off the yoga ball again, muttering under his breath. "This is killing me."

"Is this happening a lot?"

"Every day, Rev. Every day. If she has me rearranging the living room again, I'm going to move in with you."

He goes, and we both know he'll move the furniture a dozen more times if his mother asks him to do it.

I expect Matthew to bolt up the stairs after Declan, but he doesn't.

I need a shower in the worst way, but this is the first time he's voluntarily put himself in my presence, and I don't want to wreck it.

The quiet settles in around us, broken only by the sounds of explosions on the television upstairs.

"I didn't know that," he says finally. "That I was freaking you out."

"It's my problem. Not yours."

He shakes his head and looks around the room. "I forget that we're all screwed up."

"Who's *we*?"

"Kids like us. Foster kids." He pauses. "Declan told me about—about what happened to you."

I shift and rub a hand across the back of my neck. I want to be irritated—but I'm not. What happened to me isn't a secret, and Declan is the last person who would gossip about it.

I let my tone match his, even and careful and quiet. "Did the same kind of thing happen to you? With your father?"

"No." Matthew doesn't look away. "I have no idea who my father is. I haven't seen my mother since . . . forever." He grimaces, then scrubs his face with his hands. "I don't even remember what she looks like."

I want to say *I'm sorry*. It's such an automatic response. At the same time, it's a worthless one.

"I've been in eleven foster homes," he says. "How many have you been in?"

"One." I circle my finger to indicate the room we're sitting in. "I came here when I was seven. They adopted me when I was twelve."

He snorts, as if that disappoints him somehow. "You're lucky."

Lucky. I could take off my shirt and we could debate *luck* until the end of time, but for what it's worth, I agree with him. I nod. "I know I am."

He falls into silence for a while. Then he looks up. "Neil was my foster brother."

I study the fading bruises on his face and wonder if Neil had something to do with them. "At the last house?"

"No, the one before. Neil goes to a private school now, but he used to go to Hamilton. They made him transfer. He's a junior. Those guys from the cafeteria are friends of his. That's how they know me."

Matthew's voice is unwaveringly even, but everything I know about him could fit in a tiny box with room left over. I have no idea where this conversation is going.

"At the house with Neil," he says, "they used to padlock the bedrooms at night. Lock us inside. They're not supposed to— it's a fire hazard or something. But people do it anyway. If kids run away, they lose that monthly check, you know."

I hold absolutely still.

Matthew shrugs, but his body is completely rigid. He looks at the opposite wall. "They used to lock me in with Neil." He gives a strangled laugh. "Like I said, juvie would have been better. I've heard stories of prison, and *that* probably would have been better."

"Why didn't you tell someone?"

He glares at me. "I *did*. But it was my third home this *year*, and it was my word against his. They lock kids in their bedrooms. You think anyone gives a crap about what happens inside?" Another strangled laugh. "They probably knew. He wasn't quiet."

"What did he do?"

The look in his eyes is brutal. "Guess."

I don't want to guess. I don't have to guess. "How long did this go on?"

"Forever. I don't know. Four months. But then he got in trouble at Hamilton for assaulting another student, and my social worker finally took me seriously. Neil was transferred to a new school. I was transferred to a new house."

My breathing has gone shallow. "Your last house."

"Yeah." His eyes are shining, but there are no tears in his voice. Not even a tremor. This is a kid who's learned how to hide emotion. "I was the only foster kid. For like a *day*, I was relieved. You ever hold your breath so long that it starts to feel like you can't remember how to breathe? That's what getting away from Neil was like. But then the man started getting too friendly."

"Your foster father?"

"Yeah. But nothing about him was a *father*. Or should be a father." Matthew shakes his head, almost with self-disgust. "I was so screwed up. I didn't know what was going on until he started coming into my room at night. At first he told me I was having nightmares and he wanted to make sure I was okay. But then he started rubbing my back—" He shudders, and the motion seems involuntary. "When he finally came after me, I fought like hell. He pinned me down, but his wife came home and found us before he could do anything. He said I attacked him." Matthew gives me a level look. "And now I'm here."

That explains the marks on his neck. The fight he "started."

"Matthew. We can tell Mom and Dad. They'll report him. They'll—"

"No!" He shouts it at me. He swallows, but his voice is so fierce. "I told you because—because of what Declan told me. But I am not telling someone else. I got away. It's over."

"But he could be doing that to someone else! Don't you—"

"NO!"

"But—"

"He will find me and kill me." For the first time, his voice shakes. Matthew's eyes glitter in the shadowed basement. "Why do you think I took the knife?"

"Boys?" Mom calls down from upstairs, then descends a few steps to peer around the corner. "What's going on?"

I don't know what to say.

Matthew shoves off the ottoman and charges up the stairs. Mom puts a hand on his arm. "Matthew, honey. Stop. Let's talk—"

He brushes her hand off and flies toward his room. The door doesn't slam.

Mom studies me. "Rev?"

I still don't know what to say. "It's okay. We're okay." It's not. And we're not. And my tone makes that so obvious.

He will find me and kill me.

I still don't know what to say.

As usual, Mom rescues me. "Should I go talk to him?"

"Yes."

She doesn't even hesitate. She turns around and heads up the stairs.

TWENTY-EIGHT

Emma

My father has finally convinced me to have breakfast with him.

Unfortunately, it's Tuesday, I have school and he has work, and this breakfast is taking place at 6:00 a.m.

The Double T Diner is packed, which I didn't expect, and louder than necessary for this time of the morning. There's a tiny jukebox on every table, and half of them are playing. The waitstaff bustle around, pouring coffee and slinging plates at high speed.

I'm half asleep in the corner of a booth, wishing I had a pair of sunglasses. Don't these people need to sleep?

It was weird for Dad to pick me up, too. I sat in the foyer, waiting for his headlights to cruise up the street. I wonder if this is what it's going to be like when they stop arguing about visitation rights.

My throat closes up, and I take a gulp of coffee. It's hot and I almost cough it all over the table.

"Careful," my father says. "She just poured that."

It's the first words he's spoken to me since we sat down.

This whole breakfast feels remarkably awkward. I just need to get through the next ninety minutes, and then he can drop me off at school.

Where I can be remarkably awkward around Cait and Rev. And everyone else.

Dad is texting someone. I'm super glad he wanted to go out for breakfast. I could have been ignored in my pajamas.

I can't believe I was so excited to show him OtherLANDS.

My phone pings with a message. It's way too early for Ethan, or even Cait, so it's probably spam.

No. It's a different kind of nightmare.

Tuesday, March 20   6:42 a.m.

From: N1ghtm@re5

To: Azure M

Is it your birthday? Because I have a little surprise for you.

I freeze. There's no attachment to his message.

My heart rate has tripled. I haven't heard from him in days. I had actually started to hope he'd grown bored with this.

"Were you up late?" Dad says.

His voice interrupts my thoughts, though he's still looking

at his phone. For a minute, it makes me wonder if he's talking to me at all.

I swallow and jerk my attention up. "Yeah," I say. "I have a new friend I'm gaming with."

"Oh yeah? Someone from school?"

"No, just a guy I met online." I can't stop staring at my phone.

What kind of surprise?

I want to write back.

At the same time, I don't.

And I can't block him from here.

I can't stop thinking about his comment about my profile picture, how the Hamilton High sweatshirt is visible.

"What guy?" My father's eyes snap up briefly, before returning to his phone.

I wave a hand. "I don't know him in person. We just game together sometimes."

"Are you being safe?"

For the first time, my father's words get my full attention. He's worried about Ethan when I have some guy promising a surprise. I glare at him. "I don't know, is it safe to send him naked pictures? Or could that go badly?"

"Emma." I *almost* have his full attention now. He actually makes eye contact.

"I'm sixteen years old, Dad. I'm not an idiot."

"You never know who's on the other side of the screen, Emma."

"I know that." I am literally living with that *right this very second.*

I should tell him about Nightmare. But right now I don't want to tell him about anything. Fear and irritation and anger are having a cage match in my belly.

Our waitress appears beside the table. "Are y'all ready to order?"

"Go ahead," my dad says, attention back on his phone. "I'm just having coffee."

Irritation wins the match. "You asked me to breakfast and you're only going to drink coffee?"

His eyes flash up again. "Emma."

"I'll have the Chesapeake Benedict," I say, just to irritate him further. It's the most expensive thing on the menu: eggs Benedict with a crab cake on top.

My dad doesn't even flinch.

"You got it," says the waitress, scribbling on her pad.

Guilt socks me in the face as I remember Mom talking about putting the house on the market because of money.

"Actually," I say, "I'll have the pancake short stack."

She scribbles out whatever she wrote first. "Sure thing."

Then she takes our menus and she disappears.

My dad keeps texting.

I take a slower sip of my coffee. "What's going on?" I say to him.

"Oh, you know how these things get. Last-minute fixes before release."

"They must be really missing you this morning."

He snorts. "You have no idea."

HE DOESN'T EVEN GET THE IRONY.

Another sip of coffee. Maybe I need to hammer it home. "It's a shame you had to waste your time with me."

"It's not a waste of time," he says, tap-tap-tapping at the screen. "I can do both."

My expression turns into a line-face emoji.

Whatever. I pull out my own phone. Nightmare's message is still sitting on top. I close it before I start hyperventilating again.

Besides, what's the worst thing he can do? Show up at school? It's not like he can find me from an image of my *back*. He might have a hard time if the only identifying mark is a girl with a dark ponytail. He's already sent me an image of my avatar—not like I haven't been down that road before.

I take a deep breath. This will be okay.

I want to text Cait but I've burned that bridge.

I've burned the bridge with Rev, too.

I'm stranded on this island all alone.

Maybe I could write Rev a note. He said his best friend used to exchange notes with his girlfriend before they met in person.

I pull up a browser on my phone and look for a Bible verse about divorce.

Anyone who divorces his wife and marries another woman commits adultery.

Nope, not that one.

A woman is bound to her husband as long as he lives. But if her husband dies—

Okay, *definitely* not that one.

However, each one of you must also love his wife as he loves himself, and the wife must respect her husband.

According to that one, my dad is married to his iPhone.

A lot of these are about sex—and exactly *zero* of them are reassuring. I wrinkle my nose.

"What are you frowning about?" says Dad.

"I'm reading the Bible."

"You're—*what?*"

"You heard me." I wave my hand, making no effort to hide my irritation. "Go back to your game stuff."

"Emma . . ." He sounds like he's not sure how to proceed from here.

I can't help him. I personally have no idea how to proceed. Burying my face in electronics has worked in the past. At least computers do what I want. I don't glance up.

I don't understand how Rev can find any of this reassuring at *all*. Honestly, I'm tired of reading about how divorce is seventeen kinds of forbidden unless someone dies.

I change my search query to *Bible verses about forgiveness*.

Now they're all about asking God for forgiveness. Also not what I want.

The sad thing is that I could probably walk up to Rev and say, "Is there a good Bible quote for asking someone to forgive you? I need it."

Actually, that would make a pretty good opener for an apology, now that I think of it.

No, it might sound like I'm mocking him.

I need to keep looking.

The waitress returns to our table and unloads a plate of pancakes. The cup of butter is melted, which is *awesome*. I pour it all out, then add a gallon of syrup.

"Do you want to talk," says Dad, "or are you going to have your face in your phone the whole time?"

I slam my phone down on the table. "Are you kidding? Tell me you're kidding."

We draw the attention of everyone around us.

"M&M," my dad says, his voice low. "I don't understand what you're so—"

"You don't understand what?" I snap. "You don't understand why I'm upset? How about the fact that I had to get up at 5:00 a.m. to go to breakfast with you, but—"

"I'm sorry it's such a hardship." His eyes flash.

"—but you won't look away from your phone to have a conversation with *me*. So when I start looking at *my* phone because I'm bored and you're not even eating—"

"I have a *job*, Emma."

"—you get on my case about ignoring you, when that's all you've been doing since you picked me up."

"First of all," he says, punctuating his words with his finger against the table, "I am not goofing off on my phone. You know this is already a tense time for me, without everything else going on. Second of all—"

I snort. "Gee, then maybe you shouldn't have asked for a divorce."

"—I asked you to breakfast because I *miss* you, and I don't deserve this attitude right now."

"You're right," I say sweetly, my voice dripping with sarcasm. "You don't deserve this at all. Maybe I should go outside and have a glass of wine, you can roll your eyes over a bottle of beer, and we can have a discussion like grown-ups."

"What?" he snaps. "What do you want from me, Emma?"

Attention.

I almost say the word. The weight of it is right there in my mouth, like something I need to spit out or I can't breathe.

I have all of Mom's attention, and I don't want it.

I have none of his, and I *crave* it.

How can they both be so blind?

"Nothing," I whisper. That dagger of shame buries itself a little more deeply. I clear my throat. "I think you need to take me home."

He sighs. "Emma."

"I don't want to be here. I need to go home."

"Eat your pancakes. We can talk about school, or whatever game you're playing—"

"Home." I shove the plate away. "I want to go home."

"You're being ridiculous," he snaps. "I don't know what your mother is telling you, but I'm not going to have you behave like this every time I see you."

My throat tightens again. "She's not telling me anything." I slide out of the booth. "You don't have to worry."

His phone rings, and he glances at the screen. "Stop. Emma, stop. I want to talk to you about this." He doesn't even wait for a response. He answers the phone. "Yeah, Doug, give me thirty seconds, okay?"

Thirty seconds. He thinks we're going to resolve this in thirty seconds.

"Take your call," I say. I toss my bag over my shoulder.

"Where are you going?"

"I need some air. Take your call. I'll wait outside."

For some reason I expect him to disconnect the call and chase me out of the restaurant. He doesn't. I hear him behind me saying, "Thanks, Doug. I'm just here with my daughter . . ."

Hilarious. He makes it sound like Doug is interrupting a nice time.

I find a spot on a bench in front of the restaurant. The air is brisk and stings my ears, but the rain has finally left the area. Cars fly by on Ritchie Highway. I can see Dad through the window, chatting away.

I wish I could just leave. A bus stops just down the road, and I wonder if I have the guts to run and catch it, and just ride forever.

No, I don't.

Also, that would take some serious cardio.

Without warning, tears form in my eyes. I've never felt so alone.

I dial Cait.

Her mom answers. "Hello?"

I sniff and try to hide the tears in my voice. "Hi, Mrs. Cameron. It's Emma. Is Cait awake yet?"

"She's in the shower. It's very early, dear."

"I know." I sniff again, and then it's like my eyes refuse to keep up this fight. I start crying full out. "I'm sorry. I'm sorry. Can you just tell her I'll see her at school?"

"Emma? What's wrong?"

Her voice is so warm. It's at such odds with my parents, who speak with nothing but vitriol. "It's nothing." My voice cracks. "It's nothing."

"Oh, sweetheart. You're crying. It's not nothing. Are you okay?"

"No." All this emotion is fighting its way out of me. My sobs make it almost impossible to speak. "My parents are getting a divorce." A diesel truck revs to life nearby.

"Emma. I'm so sorry. Where are you?"

"I'm sitting outside the Double T Diner. I was supposed to have breakfast with my dad but he's too busy."

"Oh, Emma. Do you need me to come get you?"

"Yes," I say. "Yes. Please."

"I'll be there in ten minutes. You stay right there, do you hear me?"

I spend the entire ten minutes wringing my hands and wondering if I should call her back and tell her not to come. Wondering what I'm going to say to Cait when I see her.

Wondering if my dad is going to notice the passage of time, or see that I'm sitting out here sobbing into my hands.

He doesn't.

I spot Mrs. Cameron's shiny maroon minivan as it pulls into the lot, and I send my dad a quick text.

Emma: Going to be late for school. Getting a ride with Cait.

Maybe that'll wake him up.

He glances at his phone, then looks out the window just as the minivan stops in front of me.

He gives me a thumbs-up. A frigging thumbs-up.

I turn back to the minivan. Cait is opening the door.

"I'm sorry," I say, and I burst into tears *again*. "Cait, I'm so sorry—"

She launches herself at me and wraps me up in a hug. "Oh, Emma. You should have told me."

"Come on, girls," calls Mrs. Cameron. "I need to get the boys to school, too."

We climb into the van. The door slides closed.

And I remember what it feels like to be wanted.

TWENTY-NINE

Rev

Rev,

For I know my transgressions, and my sin is ever before me.
Psalm 51:3.

In other words, I'm sorry.

Emma

The note was shoved through the slats on my locker, and I
don't find it until I'm swapping books before lunch. I read it
three times.

I'm not sure how to respond. My head is still full of anxiety
about my father. About Matthew, who told Mom nothing, and
now his life secrets carry equal weight with mine. I don't know

if Emma's apology is a brush-off, or an invitation for more discussion, or if she's so lost in her own issues that we should just
let it drop here.

I don't know. I don't know. I don't know.

I shove the note in my backpack. I need to eat.

Declan is waiting at our table.

To my surprise, so is Matthew. A brown paper bag sits on the
table in front of him, but he hasn't pulled anything free. I wonder if he's waiting to see if I'm going to chase him away. The ride
to school this morning was filled with his usual silent rebellion.

I wonder if *he's* wondering when I'm going to reveal his
secrets.

Maybe I should. Telling Dad everything was such an unexpected relief. I'd been so worried that he would condemn me—
and instead, he reminded me I'm not so alone.

This isn't my secret to tell, though.

I throw my bag under the table and fish out my own lunch.
"Hey," I say.

Matthew waits for a moment, then opens his bag.

Juliet arrives at the table with a tray, trailed by her friend
Rowan, and Rowan's boyfriend, Brandon Cho. They're all laughing. Declan and Brandon don't have anything in common, but
they tolerate each other for the sake of the girls. Usually I have
to kick him under the table when his muttered comments get a
little too edged. I'm pretty sure Juliet kicks him from the other
side.

Matthew watches them all crowd onto the benches. His hand
stops on one of the containers Kristin packed.

The girls and Brandon give him a little wave and introduce themselves.

He mutters, "Hey," and turns his attention back to his food, though he still hasn't opened anything yet. A moment passes, but they let it go, and return to their conversation. I wonder how much Declan told Juliet about him.

I lean in against the table. "You all right?" I say to Matthew.

His fingers fiddle with the lid to a container. "I'm fine."

"We can go to another table."

"I said, I'm fine." He's not belligerent about it. His voice is low. It sounds like he's trying to convince himself.

A camera shutter snaps, and I jump. So does Matthew.

"Sorry," says Juliet. "I'm sorry. I should have asked. It was just—it was a good shot."

"It's fine." I tell my nerves to back off.

Matthew says nothing. He looks back at his food.

Juliet is pressing buttons on her camera, staring at the screen on the back. Brandon is on her other side, and he leans over to see. "It is a good shot."

She turns the camera around so I can see. Matthew and I are very still, facing off across the table, our expressions intense. The other students merge into a colorful, active blur behind us.

Rowan leans over to look, too. She's not a photographer like they are, but she says, "I like it. You should call it *The Final Showdown*."

"We're not fighting," I say.

Matthew still hasn't said anything.

Declan is quiet, too. I wonder if he's thinking about his

father. I wonder if he's told Juliet what he's doing. When he picked us up this morning, he said, "You still good for this afternoon?"

When I said yes, he changed the subject.

Juliet studies Matthew. "I should have asked you, too. I know Rev doesn't like—" Her voice falters. "I didn't mean to be insensitive."

"It's fine. I don't care." Matthew's voice is low and quiet. He's finally cracked open his Tupperware, but he's eating like an animal that's scared you're going to steal its food.

Declan said those boys from yesterday probably wouldn't bother him now, after what I did, but maybe he's wrong. Maybe Matthew is hiding here, with us.

It should be reassuring after our rocky start. It's not. It's depressing.

But then he looks over at me. "You don't like having your picture taken?"

I freeze. At the end of the table, Juliet winces. *I'm sorry*, she mouths to me.

And of course now I have everyone's attention.

"Leave it," says Declan. "They don't need to know."

Even here, my father has power over me. I set down my food and look at Matthew. "When I was a kid, my father used to take pictures. So I'd have reminders."

"Reminders of what?" says Rowan, before Juliet hushes her.

Matthew stares back at me. "Your father sounds like a real prick."

That shocks a laugh out of me. Matthew looks back at his food and doesn't say anything else.

I'm encouraged that he said anything, though, even something about this. I realize that I know the worst parts of his life, but otherwise, I know next to nothing about him.

"What's your schedule like?" I ask him.

His eyes flick up, like he's surprised by the question. That surprise might be the only reason I'm getting a response at all. "It's all right. They put me back in the same classes I had before."

I wonder what it would be like to constantly change schools, even if it's within the same county. To meet new teachers in the middle of a semester, to have to learn a new routine. Dad's words are loud in my head, about how the unknown can be especially frightening when you don't trust *anyone*. "Are you in class with those boys from yesterday?"

"Yeah."

"Are they still hassling you?"

He shrugs. "Whatever."

"Not whatever. You can switch classes, you know."

"Yeah, whatever. You think I'm going to be here all that long anyway?"

That takes me by surprise. "You can't keep running."

He snorts. "I'm not even talking about running."

I blink. "But—"

"I don't really want to talk about this, okay?" His shoulders are tight, and his eyes are on his food.

"Sure." I glance at Declan, to get his read, but he's locked in his own head again, trapped with his own thoughts.

Great. We can all sit here and be quiet.

I'm not even talking about running.

He must be talking about Mom and Dad. I want to tell him that they have never—not *ever*—given up on a child. They have never needed to find an alternate arrangement for anyone.

Then again, they've never housed another teenager before. And Dad asked me if he needed to find another arrangement for Matthew. If it was too much for *me* to handle. I said no. And even without knowing Matthew's history, I wouldn't have said yes. I wonder if Matthew knows that.

I look at his hunched shoulders, at the way he's tearing through his food, and wonder if it matters.

"Was that girl your girlfriend?" Matthew says, out of the blue.

"What girl?"

"The one with the dog."

"Emma. No." I have no idea how to classify her.

I glance at Juliet and Rowan, who've stopped focusing on me, and are now talking about Spring Fling. I don't even know when it is. It's some kind of miracle I even know it's a dance.

I assume Declan is going. I have gone to exactly one dance throughout all of high school, and that was Homecoming last fall. I went solely to play wingman for Dec.

Matthew continues, "That night I saw you in the rain, I thought you were making out."

The words hit me with a jolt. "No."

His eyes narrow just a little. "You sure?"

He sounds like he's a breath away from mocking me. I narrow my eyes back at him. Maybe Juliet can get another intense picture. "I'm pretty sure I'd remember making out."

"I think she has a class across the hall from me. In the computer lab. I saw her yesterday and again today."

"She's into coding." I pause, thinking of her letter. She was crying in Declan's car yesterday, and I had to go off on a rant. "How did she look?"

"Like a girl who's into coding." Matthew begins snapping containers back together.

I frown. "Where are you going?"

Matthew shoves the containers into his backpack. "I'm going to class."

"Lunch isn't over yet."

"Like it matters." Then he weaves through the other students.

I don't know what just happened.

My phone chimes. I yank it out of my pocket, glad for a distraction. Any distraction.

Any distraction except this one. It's an e-mail from my father.

Tuesday, March 20   12:06:16 p.m.

FROM: Robert Ellis <robert.ellis@speedmail.com>

TO: Rev Fletcher <rev.fletcher@freemail.com>

SUBJECT: Obedience

If a man have a stubborn and rebellious son, which will not obey the voice of his father, and who, when his father has chastened him, will not hearken unto him:

Then shall his father lay hold on him, and bring him out unto the elders of his city, and unto the gate of his place, and he shall say unto the elders of his city, "This, my son, is stubborn and rebellious, he will not obey my voice. He is a glutton and a drunkard."

And all the men of his city shall stone him with stones, that he die: so shalt thou put evil away from among you.

"Rcv. Hcy. Rev." Declan's voice.

I blink. Look up. Half the cafeteria has emptied. Rowan and Brandon are gone, but Declan and Juliet are watching me.

How long have I been staring at my phone?

Too long, if lunch is over.

I know the verses well. Too well. Better than any other verses in the Bible.

The lines are from Deuteronomy. The Old Testament, which is full of vicious stories like this one. The verses actually include a mother, too, but my father has clearly altered them to suit his needs. He did it once before. I'm not surprised he remembers the exact wording.

"Rev?" Declan says again.

The e-mail has the potential to crush me. I think it *was* crushing me, until Declan pulled me free.

The bell rings. We have three minutes to get to class. Declan glances at Juliet. "Go," he says. "You don't need to get in trouble."

She doesn't move. "You don't either."

"I'm okay," I say. "Go ahead." But I don't move.

Declan looks at Juliet. Something unspoken passes between them. She goes.

"Your father?" he says quietly.

I hand him my phone. He reads.

"Boys!" Mrs. James, my new favorite teacher, is rapidly approaching the table. "The first bell has rung."

"Come on," says Declan. He carries my phone with him.

I follow him.

"Do you want me to write back to him?" Declan says. "Because it's taking everything I have not to."

"No." I snatch my phone back from him.

The men of his city shall stone him with stones, that he die.

I cannot let this unravel me again.

I keep thinking about Emma's note. *For I know my transgressions, and my sin is ever before me.*

She was apologizing. Is this a sign that I should apologize to my father?

My phone *pings.* A text message slides down from the top. It's Dad.

Dad: Just checking on you.

I want to burst into tears right there in the hallway. I'm not alone. I'm not.

And maybe *this* is the sign I should be listening to.

I take a screenshot of my father's e-mail. I send it back to Dad.

"Come on," I say to Declan. I have to sniff back tears. He'll think it's allergies. Which is fine.

My phone *pings* again. Dad again.

Dad: You are not stubborn and rebellious.

You are kind.

You are thoughtful.

You are the best son we could have ever hoped for.

We love you. And we are proud of you.

The phone *pings* and *pings* and *pings* as his messages come through, and the words should be corny, but right now, each one is like an injection of reassurance into my heart.

We come to the intersection where Declan needs to go left and I need to go right. The hallways are almost deserted, and we have less than a minute until the bell, when we're supposed to be in our classrooms.

"Do you want to skip out of here?" says Declan.

"No." I scrub my face. My voice thickens. "No. I'm okay. I sent it to Dad."

"Good."

We part ways, and somehow I find my way to my seat in Pre-calculus. Students rustle around me, getting situated, ignoring me. For once, I'm glad for it.

My phone *pings* one last time.

Dad: Let me know if you want Kristin to come get you. It's OK if you need a break.

I smile and write back.

Rev: No. I'm OK.

After a moment, I pull my phone back out of my backpack and add another line.

Rev: Thanks, Dad

Then I lock the screen, shove it into my backpack, and pay attention to the class.

THIRTY

Emma

As iron sharpens iron, so one person sharpens another.
Proverbs 27:17

I'm going somewhere with Dec after school, but I can meet
at the church at 8 if you want to talk again.

Rev

Cait brings me the note at the end of the day.

I love that he wrote me a note back. I love his handwriting, neat and even, every stroke and slope controlled. It's very much *him*. I want to press the paper to my chest and spin around with it. I want to trace his name with my fingers.

I'm practically skipping to the bus beside Cait.

"So you really like him," she says.

Her voice is mellow. We spent lunch in the library, and I dumped my entire life in her lap. She knows about everything, from Mom and Dad and the divorce to Nightmare and his trolling. She knows about Rev and our secret meetings behind the church.

She knows what a screwed-up mess I am.

I stop skipping. "Am I being ridiculous? I am. You can tell me."

"You're not being ridiculous." She pauses, and a small, secret smile finds her mouth. "He's got a sexy voice. I never realized."

"You *talked* to him?" I stop short and almost round on her. "What did he say?"

"He didn't fling the note at me and walk away. Of course I talked to him."

I want to shake her. *"What did he say?"*

"Let me think if I can remember it right . . . he said so much . . ." She puts a finger to her purple lips and gazes at the sky. "Oh, right. He said, 'Would you mind giving this to Emma?'"

She says it in this low baritone impression of a guy's voice that sounds *nothing* like Rev, but once I have the words, I can hear him saying it.

I want to spin in circles again.

I keep thinking about his back against mine, that day we sat in the rain. Our fingers wound together. The long slope of his jaw, the way his eyes are dark under the hood of his sweatshirt. His mouth.

I spend entirely too much time thinking about his mouth.

The bus pulls up in front of the school, and Cait and I climb on. We flop into the olive-green seats.

"Want to come over?" she says.

The words are casual, but there's weight behind it.

Especially when she quickly adds, "If you want to go home and work on your game, it's fine. I was just asking."

"No," I say, and her face falls, just the tiniest bit. I shake my head quickly. "I mean, no, I don't need to work on my game. I want to come over."

"Really?" Her eyes go wide.

"Yeah." I shove my phone into the front of my backpack and zip it up tight. "I need a break from technology." I pause, wanting to offer something, since she's been so patient with me. "And since I have a date, maybe you could show me how to make my eyes look like that?"

Her face softens. "Yeah, Em. I can."

I think about Rev's note, the line about one person sharpening another. It seems that can work both ways, how you can turn someone against you as easily as you can build a friendship.

Or save one, I guess.

The bus doors close and the air brakes give way, and we rumble out of the school parking lot.

"I'm sorry for all the things I said," I say quietly. "I didn't realize what I was doing."

"It's okay," she says quickly.

"It's not." I study her, noticing for the first time that she's glued tiny green jewels along her hairline just below her ear, matched by a few green extensions that make her look just the tiniest bit punk. "You're really good at what you do."

She blushes. "Thanks, Em."

"No, I mean *really* good." I reach out and touch the jewels on her neck. "Like, who would think of this?"

She rolls her eyes. "I've already forgiven you. You don't need to kiss my ass."

"I just—" I hesitate. "I never thought it was a waste of time. I think . . . I think I might have been jealous."

"Jealous?"

I swallow. "Because your mom supports you."

Cait studies me. "Em . . ."

"What?"

She sighs. "Maybe your mom would support you if you gave her a chance."

My back stiffens—but then I think about breakfast with my father. I think about how distracted and distanced he was.

And much like my judgment of Cait reminded me of my mother, my avoidance of Mom reminds me of my father.

I look away. "You're right."

"Wait. What did you just say?"

I blush and give her a good-natured shove. "I said you're right."

"I'm right *and* I get to do your makeup? I think someone might need to pinch me." She feigns a gasp. "Do you want to stay for dinner, too?"

"Sure."

She puts her hands on my cheeks and stares into my eyes. "Who *are* you? What have you done with Emma?"

I laugh. "I'm your best friend." My voice catches. "I think I just forgot for a little while."

"Oh, Em." She throws her arm around my shoulders and leans into me. "You're going to make me cry."

I hug her back.

Then she says, "Does this mean I can do your makeup like Harley Quinn?"

I snort. "Don't push your luck."

"Black Widow?"

That makes me smile. "Deal."

THIRTY-ONE

Rev

It's harder to get into prison than I thought.

Maybe that's a good joke. Maybe I should say it to Declan.

Maybe not. He's sitting beside me in the waiting room, his knee bouncing. The room is more cordial than I expected, with green-striped carpeting and yellow walls. The only thing that signifies we're in a prison is the thick glass wall between us and the guards. And the heavy metal doors. The signs warning against smuggling contraband, stating that visitors may be required to submit to a strip-search before admittance.

Okay, it's obvious we're in a prison.

We've been sitting for half an hour, and that's after the hour-long drive to get here. We each had to fill out an application and consent to be fingerprinted. The guard behind the glass still has our driver's licenses, and we won't get them back until we leave.

Right now, we're waiting for our background check to go through. Then we have to go through a pat down, and *then* we'll be allowed back to visit his father.

If his father consents to a visitation.

I don't think Declan was prepared for this torture. I think he assumed it would be like a TV show: we could show up, ask to meet him, and we'd sit on the other side of a pane of glass while his father walks out and has a moment of surprise as he tries to figure out who we are.

No, his father is going to be told that we're here. And he's going to have to agree to meet with us.

So now we sit. We wait.

Other people wait, too, but no one as long as us. I guess they all have background checks on file already. The waiting room isn't crowded, though. Tuesday afternoons must not be a hotbed of activity at the Maryland State Penitentiary.

With a loud buzz, the metal door unlocks. Declan jerks like he's been prodded with a red-hot poker. He's done this every time the door opens.

This time, a guard does call us. The man's voice is bored as he announces, "Declan Murphy and Rev Fletcher."

Declan shoots to his feet. I'm right behind him.

"Are you sure you want me to come with you?" I say, my voice low.

"Yeah." His voice is tight. No emotion. He's afraid.

Declan is *never* afraid.

We have to go through three locked doors and down a small

hallway, until we're admitted to a small white room with no furniture. Declan's face has paled two shades, making the freckles splashed across his nose stand out.

"Is this where we're meeting him?" His voice is rough and quiet, yet steady.

"No," says the guard. His name tag reads MARSHALL, and his voice is still bored. "Spread your arms. Are you carrying any weapons?"

Declan shakes his head.

The guard glances at him. "I need a verbal answer."

"No."

The guard begins a pat down. Despite the boredom in his voice, he seems to be thorough, going all the way to Declan's ankles, and even running a hand through his hair. "Any drugs or paraphernalia?"

Declan shakes his head again, then clears his throat. "No."

"You're clear." He turns to me, and his expression is dispassionate. "That sweatshirt is too baggy. They should have told you to leave it at the front."

I freeze. Of course this is the one day I'm wearing short sleeves under the hoodie.

I've been standing here psyching myself up for the pat down, which will be bad enough. This is a new level. One I'm not prepared for.

The guard gestures with his hand. He thinks I'm hesitating because I don't know what to do. "I can leave it at the desk for you."

Declan looks at me. "It's okay," he says. "I can go alone."

But I'm already pulling it over my head, and I spread my arms. The air feels cool and foreign on my bare skin. I can't remember the last time I wore short sleeves without anything over them.

Declan knows every mark on me, and we have no secrets, but I brace myself for a comment from the guard.

He gives none. He doesn't even stare. He pats me down, which is surprisingly clinical despite what it looked like, and asks me the same questions he asked Declan.

Then he says, "You're clear," and just like that, he walks to the door on the opposite side of the room.

Declan looks at me. "Thanks," he whispers.

I shrug, like it's not a big deal.

Inside, I'm flailing.

But—maybe not flailing as wildly as I would have thought. The guard's disinterested manner helped. Maybe he's seen so many people come through here that nothing would surprise him.

The door opens with a loud buzz, and we're led into a room that looks a lot like a cafeteria. Fluorescent lights blaze overhead, but small windows sit at measured intervals along the ceiling. A dozen round tables are arranged throughout the room. Most of them are occupied. It's easy to spot the inmates—they wear faded orange jumpsuits. A low hum of conversation fills the room. A very pregnant woman is crying at one table. Five guards line the wall.

I expected glass partitions and telephones.

I think Declan did, too, because his breathing quickens.

Then I realize he's staring at a table two-thirds of the way across the room. A lone man has spotted us, and he stands up. He looks familiar, but there's no way it can be Declan's father, because this man appears smaller than I remember. Jim Murphy always seemed to tower, his personality bigger than life.

This man is tall, but no taller than we are. His hair is reddish brown and threaded with gray, and he wears a full beard. But his steely gray eyes are the same as the ones looking out of Declan's face. His shocked expression is virtually identical to the one Declan wears.

Of course he doesn't seem as tall. We haven't seen him since we were thirteen.

We're all frozen. No one moves.

Guard Marshall speaks behind us. "Your inmate can't leave the table. Any contact is limited to three seconds. Keep your hands above the table. You can take a seat when you're ready."

Your inmate. It sounds so intimate—and so alienating.

But the words spur Declan into motion. He strides forward, and I follow. We weave through the other visitors, then stop across the table from his father.

I hang back, just a bit, because I don't know what Declan wants to do. Is he going to hug him? Shake his hand? Yell at him?

Declan might not know, either. He said as much in the car.

For now they just stand there staring at each other.

"Murphy!" a guard barks from the wall.

Both Declan and his father jump and turn. Which would be almost comical at any other time.

"You and your party need to be seated," the guard says.

We all drop onto seats. The table is cold and steel and built into the floor.

Declan's father can't seem to stop staring. He and Declan

have that in common, too. I can't stop staring either, if I'm being strictly honest.

This whole moment is so . . . surreal. I thought I'd feel some familiarity, but this man is a stranger. He's thinner than I remember, his expression more guarded. Declan and I have been best friends since we were seven, and my memories of his father are clear. Camping in the backyard, telling ghost stories with flashlights, and making s'mores around the fire pit. Eating dry Froot Loops on the couch and playing Xbox past midnight, until his mom would come down and shake her head at all of us. Backyard cookouts with our families, our dads shooting the breeze as they stood around the grill with a few beers.

I remember when Declan's father had more than a few.

Declan's memories must be twice as clear, twisted with many that aren't so happy. He partly blames himself for his sister's death. He always has. I wish I knew what he was after—an ending or a beginning.

"Hi," he finally says. His voice is gravelly and quiet, as if he's not sure he's ready to speak. "Dad."

His father puts a fist to his mouth, then lowers his hands to rub his palms against the orange pants, before bringing them back on top of the table. Until now, I hadn't noticed that his hands are shaking. "Hi. Declan." His voice carries the faintest tremor. "I wasn't ready for—" He has to clear his throat. "You sound like a man."

Declan seems surprised by that. "I'm eighteen."

"I know. I know you are." His gaze shifts to me. "And . . . Rev?"

I nod.

Mr. Murphy's breath shakes. "I'm so . . . I'm so glad you boys are still friends."

"Of course," says Declan, his voice uncertain.

They fall into silence, just staring at each other. The air is full of nervous energy, on both sides. I want to leave the table, to give them some space, but I don't want to leave Dec here when it all still feels so unpredictable.

His father takes a long, shaking breath. "When they—when they told me you were here—" His face almost crumples, and he presses a hand to his eyes. "I thought it was a joke."

Declan's eyes are wet, too, but he snorts. "That would be a shitty joke."

His father laughs through his tears. "You're right. It would be." He reaches out a hand and places it over his son's. "I'm so glad you're here. I have missed you—" His voice breaks. "I have missed you so much."

Declan's breath catches, but he turns his hand to clasp his father's. "I missed you, too."

"Murphy!" the guard barks. "Three seconds."

They let go. Draw back. A reminder that this is not a normal father-son reunion.

But the interruption seems to help them move past the tears. "Does your mom know you're here?"

Declan shakes his head. "I thought—" He hesitates as if unprepared for this question. "I thought it might upset her."

His father nods, and a wave of emotion washes over his face. "She's doing okay, though?"

"She—" Declan takes a breath, and his hesitation is full of things he's not sure he wants to talk about. Her marriage to Alan. Her pregnancy. I know this because he talked about all of it in the car. "Yeah. She's okay."

His shoulders are tense. He's worried his father is going to press for more information, and this visit is going to go south.

But his father doesn't. He reaches out a hand to touch Declan again, almost as if he can't help it. "I need—I need to tell you how sorry I am. How sorry I am for what I put you through. How sorry I am for poor Kerry." A tear snakes down his face.

Declan nods. "I'm sorry, too." He pulls his hand back, then glances at the guards. "I don't want them to yell at me again."

His father smiles through the tears, then swipes at his face again. "They're yelling at *me*."

"Oh." Declan looks abashed.

"Tell me about you. Tell me what I've missed."

Declan takes another breath and lets it out. "I don't know how to put five years into thirty minutes."

His father's eyes mist over again, and he quite visibly shakes it off. "Try. Please."

Declan's face changes as he sifts through memories. I wonder what he's looking for. His mom isn't a safe target. He may not feel comfortable talking about Juliet, given the way they met, and how so much of their relationship is woven through grief and healing.

It's strange, to sit here with them and know I was a part of Declan's life for so long, and his father knows none of it.

With a start, I realize the opposite is also true.

Declan finally says, "I still have the Charger."

"You do!" His father lights up.

Declan nods. Some of the tension drains from his posture. He can talk about cars with anyone, anywhere, until the end of time. So can his dad.

Declan says, "I finished rebuilding it after—" His voice stops. "*After*. I'd show you a picture but they wouldn't let us bring our phones in."

"That's okay. That's okay. I'd kill to get my hands on an engine again."

His words hang in the air for a moment. It's like they both realize what he's said.

Declan lets it go. "I've been doing some work with this auto club. All custom stuff. It's been fun. I'm putting away some money for school."

"School! That's right, you're graduating this year. Where are you going?"

"Hey," I say, and it's almost as if they've forgotten I'm there. Which is fine. Which is good, actually. "I'm going to go wait by the door so you can have some privacy." I glance at Dec. "Okay?"

"Yeah," he says. "Thanks, Rev."

I'm worried the guards are going to give me a hard time for not sitting "with my party," but I walk over to the door, and the guard standing closest asks me if I'm ready for an escort out. I say that I'd rather wait, if that's okay, and he gestures to an empty table.

"Rules still apply," he says.

I can't exactly touch anyone from here, but I guess he means I need to keep my hands visible. I can do that.

It feels odd, though, to be sitting at a table, my bare forearms right *there*. I take off clothes to shower and change, obviously, but I don't really *look* at myself. The scars are many and varied. The arcs from the stove. The thick white lines from the knife wounds that probably needed stitches, but never got them. Small pink patches where I was burned with a match or a lighter. The embedded ink where my father wanted to make sure a message *really* stuck with me.

Like seeing Jim Murphy, these marks are familiar, but they feel foreign, too. I stare at them so long, I begin to think I'm staring at someone else.

"Rev. We're done."

I look up at Declan—and he looks . . . *raw*. My eyes flick to the table where they were sitting, but his father is gone.

"You okay?" I say.

"Yeah." And then he just turns for the door.

He doesn't say much as we sign out, get our things, and leave the facility. The sun has begun to set, bringing a bite to the breeze. When the air hits my arms, I don't want to put the sweatshirt on. I want to stretch my arms out and feel it.

I feel like a fool, walking along beside my friend, who is so obviously Going Through Something. When we're in the parking lot, he pulls the keys out of his pocket and holds them out.

"Can you drive?"

I don't question this; just close my fingers around the steel. "Sure."

It's not until we're climbing into the car that he finally seems to look at me. "You didn't put your sweatshirt back on."

"I know." I start the ignition and put the car in gear. "Are you hungry? I told Mom we might not be back for dinner." She knows where we are. I can't lie to them anymore, and I know she won't tell Declan's mom.

"No." He stares out at the sinking sun. But then he glances over. "If you want to stop, go ahead."

"I'm fine."

When we're on the highway, the road humming below us, he finally speaks. "I don't know what I expected. I think I turned him into this monster in my head. If that makes any sense." He glances at me and doesn't wait for a response. "Of course it makes sense. But I was so worried he wouldn't want to see me, that he's blamed me all this time. But he doesn't. He blames himself. And he's so sad. I didn't expect him to be so sad."

Declan rubs his hands across his face. "He's just a man who screwed up, Rev. He's just—he's just a *man*. I don't think I ever realized that. Isn't that stupid?"

"No," I say.

He doesn't say anything else. The car gradually darkens as the sun sets, and we're trapped in the safety of this little cocoon. He's so intensely quiet for so long that I glance over.

He's sound asleep.

Wow. At least he asked me to drive.

I glance at the clock on the dash. We're almost home, but it's only half past six. I don't have to meet Emma for another ninety minutes.

So I skip our exit. I drive. And Declan sleeps.

THIRTY-TWO

Emma

There's a meeting at the church tonight, so the lights are on, the parking lot crowded. A few people mill around by the front entrance. I wasn't sure if Rev wanted to meet on the benches again, but we don't have that option unless we want to share with a man wrangling two toddlers.

I go around the other side, Texy trotting along dutifully beside me. I can't let her off the leash with this many people here, and I want to prevent some do-gooder from yelling about how I can't let my dog crap on the lawn.

Then I drop in the grass, fish out my phone, and wait.

I have a little surprise for you.

So far, nothing more from Nightmare. And every passing minute feeds tension into my muscles. Outside of the game, his messages are full of subtext, but they contain nothing directly threatening. I don't even have a way to prove they're coming from the same person.

I wish I could turn my thoughts off.

Rev must have Declan's car, because I recognize the vehicle that slows and parks along the curb.

When he gets out of the driver's side, I watch him pull on a sweatshirt, then muss up his hair to shake the static out of it.

He wasn't wearing a sweatshirt. Interesting.

Texy is excited to see him, and I drop the leash so she can greet him properly. She practically tackles him.

He rubs her face and neck, wrestling her a little. I can see his grin from here. It lights up his whole face. I don't think I've seen him smile like that before. He looks more . . . relaxed than he's been. I wonder what's changed.

Also, I'm jealous.

"Hey," Rev says. "I didn't know this place would be busy."

"Me either."

"Do you want to go somewhere?"

Allow me to fall over. I glance behind him at the car. "Your friend wouldn't mind dog hair in the car? And where could we go with Texy?"

He shrugs. "I meant we could walk for a bit. Dec is asleep in the passenger seat."

"Really? It's eight o'clock."

"He's had . . . a long day."

"We can walk. Is it okay to leave him?"

"We're not really *leaving* him." He points. "We can walk up to the dead end."

"Okay."

So we walk. The grass surrounding the church has been mowed recently, and the scents of cut grass and pollen are thick in the air. The few days of rain have brought colder temperatures, and the breeze bites at my cheeks.

I have no idea what to say.

He must not either, because he walks in silence. Texy's dog tags jingle as she jogs along.

"I'm sorry," Rev says. "I shouldn't have snapped at you in the car when you were asking about my parents."

"You don't have to apologize."

"No. I do. It's okay to ask. You know that saying about how there are no bad questions, only bad answers? Dad says that all the time. He loves that people ask questions. He loves *when* people ask questions, especially about race or politics or religion. He says the Internet makes too many people loud, and too many people silent, but the loud people are all we hear. We have to ask questions to hear the silent people."

"I think I'd like your dad," I say.

Rev smiles, and there's genuine warmth there. "I didn't mean to get too serious. But you apologized, and I felt like I needed to."

He didn't need to. Or maybe he did, because he's removed the wedge between us so simply, with just a few words. "I liked the quote in your note. About one person sharpening another."

He nods. "It's one of my favorites."

A car slides down the street, and Rev glances behind us, to make sure it goes past his friend, and then he turns his gaze forward again.

"I actually looked for a lot of quotes about divorce first," I say. I frown and push a strand of hair out of my face. "They were all . . . terrible."

"Sometimes I have to remind myself that the world was different when those words were written down. And even though they're supposedly inspired by God, they're still being inter-preted by humans—and humans can be wrong. When you zoom out and look at everything, any belief system can seem a little crazy. Especially when you look at what people do in the name of religion."

"Are you talking about wars?"

"I could be, but no. I'm talking about people."

"What kind of people?"

We've reached the end of the road, where there's a guardrail backed by woods. Road grit and debris sits thick in the street, because we're half a block from the intersection, and the only house here has a For Sale sign, and looks deserted. The overhead light has burned out.

Rev turns and sits on the guardrail. We can see the church from here, Declan's car sitting quietly in the street. The stained glass windows of the church are stunning with the light from within, the crucifixion images blurred into masses of color that don't depict suffering from here, only beauty.

"All kinds of people," Rev says quietly.

And then I realize he's talking about his father.

I sit down on the guardrail beside him, then drop Texy's leash to let her nose around.

"You weren't wearing your sweatshirt in the car," I say.

He's quiet for a moment. "We went to visit Declan's father. They wouldn't let me wear it inside."

My eyebrows go up. "Jeez. Where's his father? In prison?"

I'm joking, but Rev nods. "Dec hasn't seen him in five years. Like I said. Long day. I think he's wiped out."

Five years. I try to imagine going five years without seeing my father.

Right now, I welcome the idea.

I glance over at Rev. Every time I'm with him, I want to stare. Some of that is because he keeps so much hidden. All I ever see is the edge of his jaw, the sculpted arch of his lips, the line of his nose. His eyes, always in shadow.

I think of gaming, where I'm in control and no one sees the real me. I wonder if the computer is my version of the hoodie.

Our hands are side by side on the guardrail, but tonight is different from Saturday. I don't have the nerve to take his hand.

"Why'd you put it back on?" I ask him.

"I don't know."

"Liar. You do know."

He goes still, but then he shakes his head and gives a little laugh. "You're fearless."

I must be dreaming this conversation. "I'm *what*? No, I'm not."

"Yes. You are. You never hesitate." He turns his head to look at me fully. "I think it's what I like best about you. It's why I thought of the verse about iron sharpening iron. Every time I'm around you, I want to be braver."

My head spins. And here I thought that Ethan calling me a *badass* couldn't be improved.

Rev turns and looks back at the road. His foot kicks at the grit there. "I put the sweatshirt back on because I didn't want you to think less of me."

"Rev." I'm shaking my head. "I could never—"

He takes his sweatshirt off.

All the breath leaves my lungs in a rush. I was wrong before. *Now* I'm dreaming.

He drapes the sweatshirt beside him. He's not looking at me. "If I have a stroke, call my parents," he says.

I can't help staring. The black T-shirt clings to his frame, and we're sitting at the dark end of the street, but the scars on white skin are obvious. So is the black, spidery writing that stretches down each arm from wrist to sleeve, making for unusual tattoos.

Though honestly, I can't look away from his biceps. "Okay. If I have one, you call mine."

He laughs, softly, and glances at me. "That's the second time I've done that today. Each time, I expect it to be horrible—and then it's not."

"Horrible how?"

"I don't know. I don't know what I think is going to happen. Isn't that strange?"

"No."

"Before this afternoon, I would have said there are only a handful of people who've seen me in short sleeves."

"I can't believe you're sitting here like this, but you called *me* fearless." I pause. "And you've never gone to school like this?"

"No." He pauses. "Don't you know? They call me the Grim Reaper."

"I do know. I didn't know that *you* did."

He gives me a look. "Come on. I'm weird, but I'm not stupid."

I think it's funny that he calls himself weird. He's the most self-aware teenager I've ever met. "Does it bother you?"

"In middle school, it used to bother me a lot."

"What happened?"

"Nothing happened. I sat in the back of the classroom and ignored it, and eventually they got bored and found a new target." He shrugs, like this is nothing. "This is so strange," he says. "I forgot what air felt like." He stretches his hands out over his head, then lets them fall into his lap. "I feel like a little kid."

If he doesn't stop stretching his arms around, I'm going to start swooning. I lean closer. "What does your tattoo say?"

"It's not a tattoo." He pauses. "I mean, it *is*, but—my father did it himself. It goes all the way across my shoulders. From one arm down the other."

Every time he tells me something about his father, I don't think it can get worse, and then it *does*. I swallow. "He did it *himself*?" I stop myself before asking if it hurt. Of course it hurt.

"Yes."

I begin to make out the words. "'. . . so shalt thou put evil away from among you—'"

He slaps a hand over his forearm. "Don't read it out loud."

I jerk back and straighten, horrified. "I'm sorry."

"No." His voice is tight. After a moment he very deliberately pulls his hand away, then braces both hands on the guardrail. "I'm sorry. It's a verse about how a disobedient child should be put to death." He pauses. "He sent it to me in an e-mail this afternoon, too."

Wow. I don't know what to say.

"I hate it," he says, and I think it's the first time I've ever heard venom in his voice.

"Do you want to put your sweatshirt back on?" I whisper.

"Yes. And no." He makes no move to grab it.

"Do you want to hold my hand?" I hold mine out.

He looks over in surprise.

Then he takes a slow breath and laces his fingers through mine.

His palm is warm against my own, his fingers sure and strong. This is what's missing from my online friendship. The warmth of a human connection. The sound of his breath and the feel of his skin. For a moment, I want to close my eyes and revel in it.

"Are you going to leave the sweatshirt off for school tomorrow?" I eventually ask him.

"I don't know. I don't think so. I don't want—I'm not ready."

I glance over and let my gaze travel over his arms again, the muscled planes of his chest. My cheeks are going to catch on fire, but I'm also honored he trusts me this much. "I guarantee you, no one would be looking at your scars."

Now *he's* blushing. He looks away. "You're funny."

"I'm not even kidding. If I punch you, would you even feel it?"

His eyebrow goes up. "You think you could make contact?"

It's the closest thing to flirting that he's ever done. It makes me *want* to punch him, just to see what he'd do. I look into his eyes and see stars there. "Want to find out?"

He laughs. "See? Fearless." Then he sobers. "Go ahead. Give it your best shot."

"What if I knock you over the guardrail?"

"I'll ask you to show me how you did it."

I love how there's no arrogance in his voice. Especially since he could probably knock *me* over the guardrail with one finger.

Maybe that's what gives me the courage to make a fist, draw back an arm, and swing.

He moves like *lightning*. I expect him to knock my arm away, but he doesn't. Not really. He moves inside the circle of my motion, and suddenly I'm wrapped up in his arms, his face against my shoulder.

He's so warm against me. I'm breathless and giddy. "I should have tried to hit you a long time ago."

"You weren't really trying to hit me." He lets me go, and honestly, that's a real shame.

He's standing now, and I stare up at him. "You stop a punch with a hug? I totally pegged jiu-jitsu wrong."

He laughs, full out. "The point is to stay close." He pauses. "Distance gives someone room to hurt you."

"Can you do it again?"

"Sure."

I swing again. He catches me again.

"I think I'm going to need about a hundred more demonstrations," I say.

He laughs again, and I can feel it through his body. Saturday night I was ramped up over the feel of his back against mine. This is a billion times better.

He's slower to let me go this time.

"So that's really how to stop a punch?" I say to him. "I feel like TV has lied to me."

"Technically I should bring you to the ground, but—"

"That sounds promising."

Clearly my brain has disconnected from my mouth. My face catches on fire.

His eyebrows go up. Way up. He gives a choked laugh. ". . . but I didn't think you'd appreciate that on the pavement."

I take his hand. "Okay. Come on."

He follows readily, and I lead him into the yard of the vacant house. My heart skips along in my chest. The grass is lush, and the ground is soft from the recent rain. Texy trots around the yard, dragging her leash behind her.

"Show me for real," I say.

Rev hesitates. He looks like he's deliberating.

"Scared?" I tease, but my voice is breathy.

"No." He pauses, and a blush finds his cheeks again. "Maybe. Are you?"

"I'm fearless, remember?" I close my fist and swing.

He catches my upper body, but I'm not ready for the foot that hooks my leg. I'm on my back in the grass before I even realize I'm going down.

His weight is heavy against me, his face close to mine. I can feel his breath against my neck.

I would totally be okay with staying *right here* for the next hour.

Texy chooses this moment to start licking my forehead. I giggle. "Texy—go away. Go, dog!"

She licks my forehead again and trots off.

Rev has drawn back. He's looking down at me, his hands braced on the ground beside my shoulders. It's doing amazing things to his biceps. "Was it everything you thought it would be?"

I laugh. "All that and more." I pause. "What happens next?"

His eyes glitter in the darkness. "You tell me."

"You're the jiu-jitsu expert."

"Well." His voice is rough. "In jiu-jitsu, you wouldn't let me get this distance."

"Distance is bad?"

He nods. "Distance is bad."

My hands find his shoulders, just the bare brush of fingertips against his warmth, tracing down the length of his sleeve until I find bare skin.

He goes completely still. The smile is gone.

I let my fingers go still, too. "Is this okay?" I whisper.

He nods—the movement small and barely perceptible, like he doesn't trust his voice.

I trace a few more inches of skin with my fingers, and he shivers.

"Still okay?" I whisper.

He nods again. One arm goes down to an elbow, and he's closer now, a bit of his weight against me. His chest expands against mine as he breathes.

"Okay?" he whispers.

Now it's my turn to nod.

His fingers trace the line of my face, lingering like he wants to memorize the feel. The arch of my eyebrow, the slope of my cheek, the curve of my jaw.

My hands have gone still on his arms. Every brush of his fingers fills me with warm honey. I reach up to find his face, his jaw just a little rough under my palm. I want him closer, all at once.

Distance is bad, indeed.

His eyes fall closed, and he turns his face to kiss the inside of my wrist. I exhale.

"Okay?" he says softly.

I nod vigorously, and he smiles.

Then his lips brush mine, and I gasp. My fingers lace through his hair.

Another brush of his lips, but this time he lingers a bit longer. His mouth moves against mine, and my lips part in response. He tastes like cinnamon and smells like vanilla and I am drowning in the moment.

His hand finds my waist, the sliver of skin where rolling in the grass has pulled my shirt away from my jeans. My own fingers have slipped under his sleeve, and I'm gripping his shoulder, holding him against me.

Then his tongue brushes mine, and it draws a low sound from my throat. His hand slides below the hem of my shirt, his palm hot against the skin of my waist. My world zeroes in on this moment, the warmth and the sweetness and the feel of his body against mine.

Then Rev draws back. His breathing is a little quick, his eyes dark and intense. "I have no idea what I'm doing, but I feel like I should slow down."

I'm almost panting. "I have no idea what you're doing either, but I feel like you're really good at it."

He smiles and draws back farther.

"No," I say. "Distance is *bad.*"

His smile turns into a grin—but he rolls to the side to lie next to me. "Hold on. I'm having an existential moment." His fingers wind through mine.

"Is that a euphemism for something else?"

He laughs. "No comment."

I cannot *believe* what's coming out of my mouth.

God, I've played online too long. Now *that* feels like a euphemism. Thank god I didn't say it out loud.

I roll up on my side and look down at him. The shadows almost hide his scars, and the moonlight makes his eyes sparkle. His face is open, his expression unguarded. This is the most relaxed I've ever seen him.

"Wherever you take jiu-jitsu," I say, "they should put this in the brochures. I feel like more people would do it."

He picks up our joined hands and draws my knuckles to

his mouth, dropping a kiss there. "I'll put it in the suggestion box."

I shift closer to him, putting a hand against his chest to support my weight. "What else can you teach me?"

He grins. I love how it lights up his whole face. This is a Rev no one sees. "I'm sure I can come up with something."

THIRTY-THREE

Emma

My imagined scenarios of making out with a guy never involved jiu-jitsu.

Not that my imagined scenarios ever went very far.

Now they are. Going that far, I mean. Kind of. I don't have any experience to speak of. But I've seen *Game of Thrones*.

Great. Now I'm blushing in the grass. I want to hide my face. Thank god Rev's gaze is trained straight up, at the stars scattered in the sky above us.

Our fingers are laced together again, his palm warm against mine. Texy is flopped out in the yard somewhere nearby. My lips are swollen, my hair is a mess, and grass prickles my arm, but I don't care. I'm thinking about the feel of his arms wrapped around me, of those brief moments when he would go still, and my world tunneled down to touch and breath and my heart beating so hard.

I will never stop blushing.

He rolls up on one elbow, eliminating half the distance between us. Looking down at me, he blocks the moonlight, and his face is in shadow, his eyes catching nothing but starlight. Our faces are less than six inches apart. "What are you thinking?"

I bite my lip. I'm thinking my cheeks are going to burn right off my face.

"Come on, Fearless," he whispers. His eyes are so intense, dark and shining. His hand lifts, his fingers brushing a piece of hair out of my face. His touch is featherlight, but hits me like a bolt of lightning. Every time we break to breathe, I think it's a good thing, but then he touches me, and I want more of it, all at once.

His thumb brushes across my cheek. My whole body warms again, just from that one touch. My lips part, almost of their own accord.

Texas barks.

I jump a mile. I sit up like a shot. Our heads knock into each other.

Ow. Hello, awkward.

Somehow I manage to catch Texy's leash, but she drags me through the grass before I get her under control. She was ready to bolt after an elderly man walking a tiny Yorkie. The man glares at us but continues walking.

I rub my forehead and look at Rev. He's doing the same thing.

"Do you believe everything happens for a reason?" I say.

He smiles. "'Now faith is the assurance of things hoped for, the conviction of things not seen.'"

"I might need that one translated."

He shifts closer and leans in, as if to whisper in my ear. I shiver at his closeness. "It means," he says softly, "things happen when they're meant to happen."

His cell phone chimes. Twice.

He straightens and sighs. "Like that."

When he looks at his phone, he laughs. "Dec wants to know if I left him in front of a church on purpose." He slides his fingers across the phone to reply. "I should mess with him and say I don't know what he's talking about."

I smile, then pull out my own phone to check it, too. The ringer has been off, but I don't expect much. Mom probably didn't even notice I was gone, and even if she did, she never worries when I have the dog with me.

To my surprise, I've missed twelve messages. All from Ethan. He started at 8:30 p.m.

Ethan: Have you logged on to OtherLANDS lately? Something is going on. You need to get to a computer.

Five minutes later.

Ethan: OK, there's definitely something going on.

Four minutes later.

Ethan: There are signposts in all of your lands. I'm looking at one right now that says Azure M is a cunt.

Every ounce of warmth generated by Rev has been replaced with ice. I can't breathe.

Ten minutes later.

Ethan: Emma, please check your messages.

Do you have any info on the guy who was sending you those e-mails?

I looked for his earlier accounts but they don't exist.

Was he on 5Core? I know people who can track him down.

I'm shaking.

Eight minutes later.

Ethan: It's worse.

Look.

There's a picture of what must be his computer screen. Right in the middle of my tavern, the gathering place for new characters, is a huge pornographic image. It's blurry on the phone, but I can make out a woman on her knees.

A small sound escapes my mouth.

Ten minutes later.

Ethan: Emma. I'm so sorry.

The last message was sent fifteen minutes ago.

"Hey."

I look up. My fingers are shaking on my phone. Rev is studying me.

"Are you okay?" he says.

"I don't—I don't know." I read Ethan's messages again. He's
going to get a read receipt on all of them at the same time. He
must be sitting there staring at his phone, because I see him
begin to type another message.

"Is it your parents?" says Rev.

"No—it's just—it's a guy I game with sometimes."

"Nightmare?"

I swallow. "No. Ethan is a friend. But something happened.
He—I don't know what to make of these messages."

"Can I see?"

I hesitate, then hand over my phone, just as a new message
from Ethan appears. I can't see what it says.

I almost don't want to see what it says. The first screenshot
is enough.

Rev reads for a moment, then looks up at me. "Emma. You
need to—to call the cops or something. This has to be illegal."

"I need to go home. I need to shut down the game. I can
block him—"

"Don't you think this has gone beyond blocking someone?"
He scrolls through the messages again. "Does this Ethan guy
know who's doing this?"

My cheeks redden. I grab my phone back. "No."

"He says he knows people who can track him down. Do you
think this is someone at school?"

"No—Ethan doesn't go to Hamilton. I don't—he's just a friend in-game. I don't know him in real life."

Rev frowns. "But he has your cell number?"

"Yes!" I snap. "And thank god, because otherwise I wouldn't know this was going on at all." This is terrible. I need to get home. I need to shut down OtherLANDS.

I'm a breath away from crying.

Texy shoves her nose under my hand, and I rub her ears absently.

"Can you fix it?" says Rev. "What can I do?"

I look down at my phone.

Ethan: Can you get home? I can help you find him.

"Nothing," I say. I look up at Rev. "I need to go home."

"Okay. Let me just take Dec his keys—"

"No. I need to go fix this." I swallow. That filthy image is burned into my eyeballs. I want to cry. I want to punch someone. I want to scream.

He takes my hand. "Emma—it's okay. I'll go with you."

I jerk away and glare at him. "Are you kidding?" I demand. "Did you see what he did?"

"Yes. I did."

I'm wasting time. I start walking. "I need to go home," I say. My voice breaks. "Okay? Just let me go."

Rev frowns. "Emma. You need to tell your parents. Please, I'll go with you—"

"You think I can tell my *parents*? Are you *kidding*?"

"This is not just some Internet troll," he says, his voice fierce. "Why won't you let anyone help you?"

"Because I can handle this, Rev. You don't understand."

"Emma." He's still following me. "I trusted you to help me. When I needed to tell my parents about my father's letters—"

"No." I round on him. "You told me to go away. And I did."

He stops short. He knows I'm right.

"I can handle this," I say. "You told me that if someone didn't want your help on the mats, that you wouldn't help. That you wouldn't interfere. This is me telling you. It's my turn to tell *you* to go away."

Those words stop him in his tracks. I regret them immediately. It's like I can't control what comes out of my mouth.

"Okay," he says quietly.

I wish he would follow me. He doesn't.

I slip into the darkened shadows along the road.

THIRTY-FOUR

Rev

Tuesday, March 20   10:05:44 p.m.

FROM: Robert Ellis <robert.ellis@speedmail.com>

TO: Rev Fletcher <rev.fletcher@freemail.com>

SUBJECT: Proverbs

He who sires a fool does so to his sorrow, And the father of a fool has no joy.

My phone chimes with the e-mail as I'm walking up the steps to go in through my back door. The kitchen is dark, and I slide the glass door carefully. Heavy silence greets me, and I tiptoe across the tile floor. I never ate dinner, and I'm starving. I grab a box of cereal and a Gatorade from the fridge, then prepare to sneak down the hallway.

"Rev." Mom's soft voice catches me when I step into the hallway.

I turn and find her sitting with a book in the corner of the family room.

"I thought everyone was asleep," I whisper.

"They are. I was waiting up."

"For me?"

She nods. "How did it go?"

It takes me a moment to realize she's asking about Declan. Our trip to the prison feels like it happened days ago. I don't want to talk about Declan and his father any more than I want to talk about what happened with Emma. Her parting words won't get out of my head.

It's my turn to tell you *to go away.*

I don't know if I deserved that. Maybe I did.

I wish I could redo it. I wish I could fix this for her. I wish I could protect her somehow.

I drop onto the couch across from Kristin and thrust my hand into the cereal box. "It was fine. It was good for him, I think."

"You were gone a lot later than I expected."

"Dec fell asleep in the car. I drove around for a while." I pause. "Then I went for a walk with Emma."

"Emma." Mom's expression warms. "I've been hoping to hear more about Emma."

My own expression darkens. "You have?"

"Of course." She pauses. "It's nice to see you coming out of your shell a little bit."

Interesting. That pushes away some of my irritation. "You think I hide?"

"I wouldn't call it hiding. But I do think you keep your environment very tightly controlled. You and Declan both do." She hesitates. "Honestly, I wondered if him finding a girlfriend would open a little door for you, too."

That's a pretty frank assessment, and I'm not sure I was ready for it. I pick marshmallows out of the cereal in my palm. "Huh."

Mom waits.

My thoughts are such a tangled mess, and I need time to sort them out. "Would it be all right if we don't talk about Emma yet?"

Her eyebrows go up, just a bit, but she nods. "Of course."

I glance at the hallway. "How was Matthew tonight?"

"Good. He and Dad went for a walk after dinner."

That's shocking. I'm sure my expression shows it.

Mom smiles. "He was offered the choice of going for a walk or doing dishes."

If we were laying bets, my money would be on Matthew standing in the kitchen with a dish towel, his thoughts locked securely in his head.

But then I think about how he sat at the cafeteria table with me and Declan, after dropping such a bomb the night before. Dad said that sometimes we push to see if anyone is pushing back.

I wonder if I pushed back in the right way.

Mom is still watching me.

"Don't stop reading," I say. "I don't think I want to talk."

She gives me a long look, then opens her book. I pick at cereal and listen to the quiet flipping of the pages. The sound is embedded in my memories. She'd read by my bedside when I was young, straining her eyes beside the night-light, waiting for me to fall asleep. She does it with every child who comes into this house. She wants them to know she's there.

"Why did you adopt me?" I ask.

She closes her book gently. "Because we love you, and we wanted you to be our son."

She genuinely means that, but I don't want platitudes. "No. Why *me*?"

"I don't think I understand what you're asking me, Rev."

"You've had dozens of foster kids. Why *me*?"

She's quiet for a long time, until I wonder if this was the wrong question to ask.

"You know we love children," she says. "When we got married, we didn't even wait. We wanted children so badly. But then . . . I had a miscarriage. That's common, especially the first time, but it was still devastating. But then it happened again. And again. And then a fourth time. I remember sitting in the doctor's office, reading some silly magazine, and it flipped open to this article about a woman with eight children, and she joked that she'd been pregnant for a decade. I remember reading that and hating her. I walked out. I cried all night." She pauses. "We talked about adoption. Another family from the neighborhood had adopted a baby, and we talked to an attorney about our options. Geoff was ready to write a check to an adoption agency, but it just . . . it didn't feel right to me. I was so depressed about losing so many babies, though, and I didn't want to let him down, so we went out for coffee and I agreed to do whatever he wanted to do."

She pauses again. I know there must be more, so I wait. My adoption was not traditional in any sense.

"When we walked out of the coffee shop, there was a woman there with a flat tire. She asked if we could call her a tow truck. Geoff offered to change her tire, and she agreed. She was late to pick up a child."

"Bonnie," I say in surprise. Mom's friend. I know how they met. I never knew the circumstances surrounding it.

Mom smiles. "Bonnie. Yes. While Geoff changed her tire, she and I got to talking. She's the first person who mentioned foster parenting. I had her over for lunch the next day. We hit it off immediately. It was meant to be. I know it was. It took me longer to convince Geoff. I know now that he was more worried about me. He'd seen me lose so many babies; he was worried about how I would deal with having to give a child back.

"So we went through the steps. The interviews, the home visits, all of it. We got the room ready. And then we waited for the call. I thought it would be something immediate. It wasn't. After a few days, I began to doubt. Geoff was so anxious. The room was so empty. I began to wonder if I'd made the wrong choice. One night, I went to bed, but I couldn't sleep. I still remember looking at the clock every hour. I was so exhausted. By five a.m., I hadn't slept all night. I remember thinking, 'Please. I know there is a child who needs me. Please.'"

She swipes at her eyes, then reaches for the tissues on the end table. "Oh my goodness. I wasn't prepared for this conversation.

I thought we were going to talk about Declan." She blots her face, then smiles at me through the tears. "But that very instant— Rev, the *very instant* I had that thought—the phone rang. And it was Bonnie. About you."

I obviously don't remember this from her side, but I remember it from mine. After the police took me away from my father, I was sent to the hospital. Many of those moments are carved into my brain—though some of it is blank. I sometimes wonder if I just couldn't process it all. I had never seen a doctor. No shots, no physical exams, *nothing*. If I'd been healthy, maybe they would have given me a day or two to get used to the idea, but the ER staff couldn't ignore a broken arm. They couldn't ignore the scars and the marks. I was so desperate to get out of the hospital that I would have gone anywhere, with anyone.

And when Bonnie brought me here, I thought I was dead. I thought I was in hell. I thought I was being punished.

"You were so afraid," Mom says softly. "I had read so many stories about foster children. I had imagined so many different scenarios, but nothing like you. I thought our biggest challenge would be an infant going through withdrawal, or maybe a toddler with a developmental disorder. But you—you wouldn't speak. You wouldn't let anyone touch you. Bonnie told me later—much later—that the hospital's social worker was pushing for you to be sent to an institution. She actually threatened to get a court order, and Bonnie got in her face and told her to try."

I'm so still. I didn't know any of that.

I mentally erase everything I know of my life and try to imagine myself growing up in an institution.

I fail. All I can see is the prison where we left Jim Murphy, and I think that might not be too far off the mark.

I swallow. "I'm sorry."

"Why are you apologizing?" She uncurls from the chair and moves to sit beside me on the couch. She takes my hand and holds it between both of hers. "When you ran to Declan's that first day—oh, we were so worried. Geoff thought we'd made a mistake. I was so afraid to call Bonnie, because I was sure they'd take you away and send you somewhere. And when we found you with Declan, when we found you playing with Legos . . ."

Her voice trails off. One hand presses to her chest and her eyes close.

"What?" I say softly.

Her voice is so quiet. "I'll never forget the look on your face. The way you dropped the Legos and backed away from them. I've never seen that look in another child, and I hope I never do."

I remember those moments. That first day, when my world turned upside down, when the burns from the stove coil were still hot and pink under the bandages. I dropped those Legos because I worried they'd do something worse than my father, like cut my hands off. I knew nothing of play, but quite a bit about consequences.

They didn't punish me. They didn't even make me leave Declan's room right away. She sat down with us and started building, too.

I think of Matthew and his story about Neil, about his other foster father. I look at Mom. Her eyes are so kind. She wants the best for everyone. "You might."

"I know." She squeezes my hand. "I might. And I'll do my best to help them through it."

"You still haven't answered my question."

"Rev, I'm not sure I can. Why *not* you? The moment that phone rang, I knew you were meant to be here. I still remember the first moment you laughed." Her hand goes over her chest again, but then she lifts it to press a palm against my cheek. "Oh, it took so long. And you grew into such a generous, kind young man—"

I push her hand away, but not unkindly. "Okay, okay."

"Oh, Rev, but you are. I remember when you were ten, and you asked why we couldn't help another child, too, since we had another room. I couldn't believe it. Of any child, you deserved the peace and quiet of being here by yourself, but you wondered why we weren't helping more. So then we brought in sweet little Rose. You remember her, don't you?"

"Yes." Rose was the first foster child after me. She was two. She must be ten now. Mom would know. She's probably seen her. She does her best to stay in touch with all the children who have lived with us.

"Of course you do. Her poor mother worked so hard to get clean. I remember Geoff was so worried about how difficult it would be to give Rose back, and it was. It's always difficult. But I love helping other mothers." She pauses. "After Rose went home, you asked me—"

"I asked when I would have to go home." My voice is rough. I remember that.

"Yes." She pulls another tissue and presses it to her eyes.

"Your voice—I'll never forget your voice. You poor child. I told Geoff that night that I wanted to adopt you—and he had already talked to our attorney. It took forever. I was so worried that man would find some loophole, some way to take you away from us." Another tissue. "I've never been more relieved than when the judge finalized the order."

"Me too," I say honestly. The day is so clear in my memories. The new suit I'd worn for court. The attorney clapping me on the shoulder. The realization that my father could do nothing—*nothing*—to separate me from my new family.

Nothing except send me a letter after my eighteenth birthday.

I frown. "Did Dad find out anything about him?"

She hesitates. That is very much unlike her.

"Tell me," I say.

"He lives in Edgewater," she says. "That's all our attorney could find so far."

Edgewater. Southwest of Annapolis. Not far at all. We drove farther to visit Declan's father.

But then . . . I knew he had to be close. I saw the postmark on his first letter.

I wait for this news to strike me like a bullet, the way so many other things have hit me recently. It doesn't. This is a fact. He lives in Edgewater.

No, this is more than a fact. This is a gauntlet, tossed at my feet.

I think of Declan, sitting terrified in the prison waiting room. If he could do that, I can do this.

"I want to see him," I say.

Kristin sniffs and balls up the tissues in her fist. "I was worried you would say that."

I try to figure out her expression, the emotion in her voice. "You don't want me to."

"No, Rev. No. I don't." More tears follow the first, and she fishes more tissues from the box.

"Are you worried—do you think—" I don't know how to finish either of those statements.

"I'm worried about him hurting you. I'm worried about him causing you to doubt yourself. When Geoff told me what was going on, I felt so *stupid* for not realizing it earlier. I saw the e-mail he sent you earlier, about putting a disobedient child to death. What kind of *hateful, evil*—"

The floor creaks down the hallway, and she stops. I think Geoff is going to come out of their bedroom and stop her tirade, but no one appears.

"No," she says more quietly. "I don't want you to go."

I sit there and think about every moment over the last week, every e-mail from my father, every word I said to Emma, to Declan, to Matthew. I think about my conversations with Dad, about how everything may happen for a reason, but there are reasons behind reasons, and events we can't control, causing ripples we may never see.

When I speak, my voice is quiet. "After Declan saw his father, he said, 'He's just a man.' My father is, too. I don't think I ever realized that. He was always the head of his congregation. He was always bigger than life. But . . . he's not. And I think I need to see it for myself."

She says nothing for the longest time, and when she does, it's not the word I expect.

"Okay," she whispers.

Then she kisses me on the head, walks down the hall, and disappears into her room.

● ● ●

Matthew isn't sleeping.

Silent darkness pours from his room, but a nervous energy hangs in the air, letting me know he's still awake.

His door is mostly closed, but not latched, so I knock gently, a motion that eases the door open a few inches.

You'd think I barreled in with a shotgun. He sits straight up in bed.

"Sorry," I say.

He says nothing.

"I just wanted to say hi. I'm sorry we dropped you and ran this afternoon."

Still nothing.

"All right," I say, grabbing his doorknob and moving to pull the door back into its original position.

"I heard a little of your conversation with Kristin," he says.

I stop with my hand on the knob. I'm not sure what to make of that comment.

"I wasn't eavesdropping," he says quickly. "I just went to the bathroom."

"Yeah?" I wonder what he heard.

"Did your father teach you to fight, too?" he says.

The question takes me by surprise. "No. I learned after."

"I wondered."

He falls silent again. I let my hand fall off the doorknob.

My room is a welcome refuge. I drop on the bed and put an arm across my eyes to block the light.

Then I sit up and strip off the sweatshirt, leaving the T-shirt. I want the air against my skin again. I drop back onto my pillow and let my arm fall across my eyes.

My *arm* is against my eyes. I wish I could catalog this feeling. It's like seeing the ocean for the first time. Or feeling snow melt on your tongue.

Making out with Emma in the grass was like this, too. All of it, so completely strange and wonderful and unexpected. There were moments when my arms closed around her and I wanted to say, *Stop. Wait. Let me hold you just like this.*

And then it all fell apart.

I pick up my phone and send her a text.

Rev: Are you OK?

I wait forever, until I don't think she's going to write back at all.

A voice speaks from my doorway. "Holy *crap*."

Matthew. I feed my arms through the sleeves of my sweatshirt without even thinking about it.

No, I'm definitely not ready to face school like this.

The realization is depressing. I can't keep the emotion out of my voice. "What's up?"

He hasn't moved from the doorway. His dark eyes reveal nothing. "You don't have to put the sweatshirt back on for me. I don't care. I was just—surprised."

I fidget with the ribbed cuff on the sleeve, but I can't make myself take it back off. The ground between us is too uncertain.

I look over. "You want to come in?"

He does. He sits on the edge of the futon closest to the door and pulls his knees up to sit cross-legged. The bruises on his face have faded considerably, leaving mottled yellow and no swelling.

"Did Geoff teach you?" he says.

He's asking about fighting again. "No. I go to a school."

"Oh."

I can't identify the note in his voice. It's not disappointment, but it's close.

"You want to learn?" I say. "There's a fundamentals class on Thursdays. We could go."

He snorts, a sound full of derision. "They aren't going to pay for something like that for me."

"Well. They might. But, either way, you can try it for free for a few weeks." I pause. "I can show you, too."

"Maybe."

He doesn't say anything else. He doesn't move from the futon, either.

I glance at the clock, then back at him. "Do you want to talk about anything else?"

"No."

But he still doesn't move.

I wish I could see inside his head. I wish I could figure him out. I consider how he joined us at the lunch table, almost hiding at the end. I consider his past and wonder if an empty room is a source of anxiety instead of refuge. I know what it's like to fear the unknown.

I grab one of my extra pillows and fling it at the futon. Then I reach up and turn off the light. "Hang out if you want. But I'm going to sleep."

Then I roll over and turn my back to him.

But then my phone chimes. Emma.

Emma: I'm OK. This is such a mess.

I hesitate, unsure about how we left things. Slowly, I slide my fingers across the screen.

Rev: I'm here if you want to talk.
Emma: I shouldn't have said what I did. I'm sorry.

Some of the tightness surrounding my chest eases.

Rev: I shouldn't have pushed so hard.
Emma: I just want to solve this on my own. It's important to me.
Rev: I know. But you don't have to be alone, Emma.

Emma: Thanks, Rev.

Rev: Do you think you can fix your game? I wish I could help you.

Emma: I wish you could jiu-jitsu this Nightmare guy.

Rev: You want me to make out with him, too?

As soon as I type the words, I blush. Then I remember I'm not alone in my room.

I glance over at the futon. Matthew's head is on the pillow. His eyes are closed.

If he's not asleep, he's doing a good job faking it. I don't think he's ever closed his eyes in my presence.

Another message comes through.

Emma: No, you can save those jiu-jitsu lessons for me.

My heart jumps around until I feel like flying.

Then another message comes through.

Emma: I need to reboot my server and fix some code. Can I talk to you in the morning?

Rev: Sure

Emma: ♡

That kick-starts my heart. I'm blushing before I realize it.

It takes me forever to fall asleep.

But for the first time in a long while, I don't mind one bit.

THIRTY-FIVE

Emma

Ethan: I found him.

The text message wakes me up at 5:30 a.m. I sit up in bed, rubbing my eyes.

I don't want to remember anything, but I do.

What Nightmare did.

What Rev did.

What I did.

It takes me three reads before I realize what Ethan's saying.

Emma: You found him??

Ethan: It took me all night.

Emma: You've been working on this all night?

Ethan: Well, after you took down your game, I had nothing else to do . . .

I *had* to take down my game. It was the first thing I did. The damage was rampant. Everywhere. Nightmare must have spent all day digging through my code.

I have backup files, so it'll be easy enough to put it back the way it was, but I won't be able to shake the feeling of violation so easily.

Thank god I never told my father about this. I imagine his comments.

Great game, hon. Love the peep show in the tavern. Way to build security.

I wince and look back at my text messages.

Emma: HOW?
Ethan: I told you. I know people.
Emma: Who is he?

An image appears on my phone. It's a student ID. The kid's name is William Roll. I don't know him at all. I look at the graduation year.

Emma: He's a sophomore?? At South Arundel?
Ethan: Yeah. I sent his mom all the screenshots.

I choke on air and have to read that again.

Emma: You did WHAT?
Ethan: His principal, too. That crap is crazy.

I stare at his messages, torn between relief and disappointment.

The one major problem in my life, and I couldn't even solve it on my own.

Ethan: Don't worry. I fuzzed out your information.
Emma: Thanks.
Ethan: NP

I don't know what else to say.

Ethan: Sorry. I should have asked what you wanted to do. But I hate when these punks harass good people. You worked hard on that game.
Emma: No. Thank YOU. I never would have been able to find him.
Ethan: You're welcome. And now I need to figure out how to convince my mom I've been sick all night so I can crash today.
Emma: Go get some sleep. You're my hero.
Ethan: ☺ ♡

I stare at the heart for a full minute. It's just an emoji. It doesn't mean anything.

I should text Rev. My heart emoji to *him* did mean something.

Now I'm blushing. Maybe breakfast first.

Mom is in the kitchen when I come downstairs, which is a

huge surprise. No yoga, no country music. Instead, papers are spread across the kitchen table, and they look like bills or financial statements. A pen sits in her hand, suspended over a legal pad. A mug is steaming beside her, but she must have gone through a pot already, because the coffeemaker is chugging away on the counter.

My mother? An entire pot of coffee?

She looks up when I appear in the doorway. The skin below her eyes is baggy, but she doesn't look like she was crying. She looks tired.

"Hi," I say cautiously.

"Hi, Emma."

I can't read her voice. If anything, she seems subdued, and Mom is never subdued.

On any other morning, I would ignore her, grab a huge mug of coffee, and head back up to my bedroom. But I keep thinking about Dad at breakfast, how his attention was solely focused on his iPhone and the new game release.

For the first time, I wonder if Mom is lonely.

I sit down at the table. "What are you doing?"

She looks back at the notepad. "I'm trying to put together a picture of our financial situation for the attorney. I don't want to leave anything out."

"Oh."

She glances at the clock over the stove. "You're up early."

"I have to go to school."

"I know *that*, Emma. But the bus doesn't pick you up for another forty-five minutes."

A shadow of her usual attitude has slipped into her voice, and I have to force myself not to react to it. For the first time, I wonder if her agitation is a reaction to mine.

"I thought maybe I'd make breakfast." I pause. "For us. Do you want some?"

Silence hangs in the kitchen for a brief moment that somehow seems interminable. "Yes. Thank you."

So I make scrambled eggs. It's usually quiet at this hour, but the whisk in the bowl has never been so loud. My back is to her as I push the eggs around the pan, but it's not uncomfortable. I don't feel like she's watching me. I feel like she's adrift, like her chair is a rowboat without oars, and I'm standing on a distant shore.

I dump the eggs on a plate, pour some salsa on top, and place the dishes on the table. "More coffee?" I say.

"No, you made breakfast. I'll get the coffee."

Once we're seated, the scrape of forks on china is louder than the whisk was.

Midway through her food, she sets her fork down and looks at me. "I know you hate me for this, Emma. I'm sorry. I couldn't do it anymore."

I freeze, the fork suspended in midair. "I don't—" My voice cracks, and I have to clear my throat. "I don't hate you."

"I deserve to be happy, too."

"I didn't know you weren't."

But I did. As soon as the words are out of my mouth, I feel how untrue they sound. Mom does, too, because her eyes lift and lock on mine.

"I did," I say. Emotion forces its way into my chest, making everything tight. "I'm sorry."

"No," she says. "You don't need to be sorry. It's not your job to make me happy."

"It was Dad's."

She shakes her head. "No, not his either. It was mine." She looks around. "You know how they say money can't buy happiness? I sure tried."

I don't know what to say to that, so I scoop more eggs. So does she. We lapse into silence again.

Eventually, she sets her fork down again. "I'm sure breakfast with your father was more fun than this. I'm not much company right now, Emma."

"He was worse," I say.

Her eyebrows go up. "What?"

"He was worse." I pause. I can't look at her for this. "He wouldn't look away from his phone. I had to call Cait's mom to come pick me up so I could make it to school on time."

"Emma." She puts her hand over mine. "You could have called me."

I stare at her hand, the perfectly even fingernails, and realize I don't remember the last time my mother touched me. "I didn't— you were already so mad at him. I thought you were mad at me, too."

"I'm not mad at you, Emma." She pauses. "And I'm sorry breakfast was a disappointment. You've always idolized your father."

I have to swipe at my eyes, and I wish they would knock it off. "I never realized he was like that."

Because I was always buried in my own devices, my own projects. I wanted to be just like him. I never looked away from a screen to see what was going on around me.

"I'm sorry," I say.

"No," she says. "I'm sorry. I should never have let this go on so long." She looks around the kitchen again. "I don't even know what we're doing with this house. We don't need all this space. We don't need all these things. I remember when we were looking in this neighborhood, your father said, 'It'll be tight for a while. I don't want to have a big house and a miserable family.' And that's just how we ended up."

"I'm not miserable," I whisper.

"You're not?" She sniffs. "I am."

I flinch.

She looks around again. "I've always wanted the best for our family, Emma. I was raised to work hard. I worked hard in medical school, I work hard at my job. I thought your father was this free spirit, that he'd give me some balance. I didn't realize it meant I would always be the one working hard."

I tense. "Dad works hard, too."

She looks at me. "Do you really think so, Emma?"

"I—I know so, Mom. He's always working—"

"He's always gaming." Her voice is very quiet. "There's a difference—"

"I *know* there's a difference." I shove my chair back.

"Emma." Her voice is very quiet. "Let me tell you something."

I don't want to wait—but I don't want to bolt, either. I take a breath. "Fine. What."

Her eyes lift to find mine. "Your father has been laid off. Again."

The words hit me like two separate bullets, and I can't decide which hurts more.

"Again?" I whisper.

"He's always had trouble keeping a job long term. But when he completes the release of this game next week, his company is letting him go."

"But—but Dad's always had a job."

"No. Emma. He hasn't. He's always had a game to play, but he hasn't always had a job." She pauses. "Part of that is the nature of his job. He does a lot of contract work. But part of that is the nature of *him*. Which is why I try to pull you away sometimes." Another pause. "Why I want you to have a career that will give you some stability."

I swallow.

She puts her hand over mine. "We'll be okay. We're always okay."

I don't know what to say. We've grown so far apart that I'm not sure a map exists to bring us back together.

She gestures at the plates. "I mean, look at this. You made us breakfast."

"It's scrambled eggs."

"It's breakfast." She pauses. Her eyes lock on mine again,

and I'm struck by the fact that I can barely remember the last time I had her attention—or when I gave her mine. "I'm sorry, Emma. I'm sorry we're going through this."

I look back at her. "I'm sorry I haven't been a good daughter."

"Oh, Emma." Her voice breaks, and for the first time, I think it's genuine. "I'm sorry I ever made you think that. I love you so much."

The emotion in her voice brings my own to the surface. I have to put a hand to my eyes. "I love you, too."

"I only want the best for you."

"I can do better, Mom."

She smiles. "Me too."

● ● ●

I stake out Rev's locker. I put on eyeliner and a little blush this morning. When Cait saw me on the bus, her eyes almost bugged out of her head.

Then she offered me some lip gloss.

Rev's not hard to spot. The dark hoodie is back. He's hiding again. I think of the way I chased him away and wonder if I have something to do with that.

But then again, he texted me this morning to ask if I still wanted to meet before class.

Nervous energy explodes in my abdomen.

He stops in front of me and smiles, though it's tentative. "Emma."

I blush. I could roll around in the way he says my name. "Hey."

He reaches out to brush a piece of hair away from my eyes. His fingers brush along my cheek and I shiver.

I want to tackle him right here in the hallway.

Then he says, "Everything work out with your game?"

"Oh! Yeah. Yes." I can't stop thinking about kissing him, and I babble. "Ethan found the kid who was doing it. He sent screenshots to his principal."

He goes still. "He did?"

"Yes. He said he knows someone who can get into 5Core and—"

"I thought you said you wanted to solve it yourself."

"I tried. I don't know how to hack into the system to find someone's identity. I'm not *that* kind of computer geek."

"Oh." He's quiet for a heartbeat of time, but it feels like an hour. "Hey, I need to change out my books."

I move aside and watch him swap out whatever he needs. His movements are quick and efficient, and he doesn't look at me at all. With the hood obstructing most of his face, it's impossible to gauge his mood—though it feels like we've moved away from face stroking.

He pushes his locker closed gently, then shrugs his bag over a shoulder. "I have Pre-calc. Can we head that way?"

His voice has gone cool. I nod quickly. "Yeah. Sure."

It's weird to walk down the hall with him. People have never gotten out of my way, but they get out of his. And he's right— they do stare at him. Or maybe they're staring at us. I see plenty of eyes flicker over me. I wonder what they think.

I glance at him to see what he makes of the attention, but I still can't see his expression.

"Can you put the hood down?" I ask him. "Unless you don't want to . . . ?"

"It's fine." He shoves it back, then glances at me. "Better?"

He looks different in the bright lights of the hallway. This is the first time I've seen him with the hood down in decent lighting. His hair is a shade lighter than I thought, his skin not quite as pale as I imagined. "Yeah." I swallow. "Thanks."

I'm so off balance now.

"You're mad about the Ethan thing?" I guess.

"I'm not mad, Emma."

"You don't sound happy." I rush on. "I just told you I couldn't solve it myself—"

"I know." His jaw looks set. "And last night I told you that you didn't have to solve it yourself. And then you got in my face and said you didn't *want* help."

"I didn't!" I say. "And I didn't want it from *him* either."

"So you told him not to interfere, and he did anyway."

"No—he was helping—" I'm losing track of this conversation. This argument. I feel like one of us is wrong here, and a small part of me worries that it's me. "Ethan just fixed it because he could. He thought he was helping."

"Sounds great. You know a lot of really stellar people online."

"What is wrong with you? I don't even know Ethan! How can you be jealous of a guy I don't even know?"

He flinches, then frowns. "You think I'm *jealous*? Do you have any idea what it sounds like when you say, 'I told him not to and he did it anyway'?"

Now I feel like *I've* been punched.

The first bell rings, and he steps back. "I have to get to class."

"Wait." I don't understand how these threads of my life keep unraveling so quickly. "Please don't just walk away. We can meet at the church tonight. We can talk. Okay?"

He hesitates, and time zooms down to this breathless moment where I'm convinced life will keep kicking me in the teeth.

But then he nods. "Okay."

THIRTY-SIX

Rev

This shouldn't be so hard.

Maybe that's a sign. I keep trying to make things work with Emma, but maybe we're both too screwed up and broken.

I tell Declan everything. Matthew, too, because he sits at the lunch table with us like he's been doing it all his life.

He slept on the futon last night. He was sound asleep when I woke up, and I left him there. He hasn't said a word about it, so I haven't either.

The cafeteria isn't crowded today. The weather outside is beautiful, so most people have taken their trays out onto the quad.

I wish Juliet were here, because she could give a girl's point of view, but she's working on something for the yearbook.

"What do you think I should do?" I ask.

Declan spreads his hands. "What do you want? You said you're going to meet her tonight."

"I want you to tell me what I'm supposed to do."

"No." Declan shakes his head. "You spend so much time worrying about what you're supposed to do. This is about what you *want* to do."

"I don't know what I want to do." Just like everything else in my life, Emma isn't simple. She's complex.

I can't believe she thinks I'm jealous.

Then again, yes, I can. From her descriptions, everyone else in her life is selfish and controlling; why not me, too?

"Hey." Declan reaches out and taps me on the top of the head. "Get out of your head. Eat some lunch."

"This is so complicated."

"It's not complicated," Declan says. "This is a girl who wants to talk. You know how to do that. A girl thinking you're two different people is complicated."

"What?" says Matthew.

"Long story."

I shove my lunch sack across the table. This sucks. "I'm not hungry."

Declan's words rattle around in my head, though. *You spend so much time worrying about what you're supposed to do. This is about what you* want *to do.*

This feels like the conversation I had with Dad.

Do you want your father in your life?

I don't know.

I think you do know, Rev.

Declan wanted to confront his father, so he did it.

Even Matthew wanted to take action. He picked up a knife and was ready to walk out the front door.

Not a *wise* course of action, but he was *doing something.*

Emma wants to talk.

And here I sit, frozen with indecision.

Across the table, Matthew has gone still, too. He's doing that looking-without-looking thing, the way he did the first few nights he lived with us.

"What's wrong?" I say.

"It's nothing."

"The way Neil was 'no one'?"

His eyes flash to mine, but he sinks into himself. "Don't talk about that."

I scan the people in the cafeteria, but then I spot them—the boys who were hassling him the other day. "Are they still bothering you?"

"Leave it."

"Dude. They can't—"

"*Leave it.*"

Declan turns to follow my gaze, then looks back at me. "Friendly reminder, but if you get into it, hit *them*. Not me."

"I'm not getting into it with anyone."

Matthew has stopped eating entirely. His shoulders are tight, and his fingers fidget with the lid of a container.

"You should tell Mom and Dad," I tell him.

He snorts. "Sure."

"You don't think you can?"

"Don't you understand that I'm trying not to cause a problem?" His voice is low and derisive, but he glances across the cafeteria.

Those boys are paying at the register. One of them spots us, then pokes his friend to indicate where we're sitting.

Matthew shoves his food back into his lunch sack. His motions are tightly controlled.

"Where are you going?" I say to him.

"Nowhere." His backpack goes over one shoulder, and he strides away from the table.

I want to let him go. I don't like confrontation. But maybe that's the whole problem.

"Watch my stuff," I say to Declan.

Matthew beat me through the door to the hallway, but I catch up to him fairly easily. He's heading toward the south side of the school, which surprises me. All that's down this way is the fine arts wing. Juliet is probably down here in the photo lab.

He doesn't stop walking. He doesn't even look at me.

Without warning, he ducks into a classroom.

It's so unexpected that I almost walk right past it. This is the art studio, a room where I've never had class. A fine arts elective is required to graduate, but I took Music Appreciation freshman year, just to get it out of the way.

The art studio is a huge room, but it somehow seems cramped. Color is everywhere, from the paintings and drawings strung along the walls to the reams of paper, jars of tempera paint, and rolls of newsprint lining the back half of the room. Half the room has six long tables, with stools pushed underneath. The other half has a dozen easels. The lighting in here comes from overhead track lights instead of the fluorescents everywhere else. It's a quiet room. A peaceful room.

I wonder if he has class here or if this is just a convenient place to hide. "Do you take art?"

He hesitates, then shrugs. "Yeah. It's just an elective." He drops his bag under the whiteboard at the front of the room, then moves to the narrow shelves under the window. A dark canvas slides free, and he carries it to an easel.

Once the canvas is in the light, I realize it isn't dark. The painting is. Most of the canvas has been painted in wide swaths of red, with black streaks and jagged, broken curves throughout. The uppermost part of the canvas is still untouched. It's very abstract, but the painting radiates with anger.

Matthew sets it on an easel. He hasn't looked at me since we've walked in here. The air is uncomfortable suddenly, as if I've walked in on something very private.

"This is more than an elective, isn't it?" I say.

He doesn't answer that question, but he doesn't have to. "I started it a few months ago. Mrs. Prater still had it. At first I was glad, because it always sucks to leave something unfinished. But I keep messing with it and I can't get it right. I might trash it and start over."

The more I look at his painting, the less I want to look away. My eyes keep finding tiny details. Small streaks of purple and orange almost hidden by the twists of red and black.

"How did you learn how to do that?" I say.

"I don't know." He shrugs. "One place where I lived, the woman was an illustrator—like for kids' books? She used to let me paint." He pauses. "And it's something you can do at pretty much any school."

A wistful note has entered his voice, and I wonder what happened to this illustrator. It's the first time he's mentioned a foster home without any resentment in his voice.

He glances at me, as if reading my thoughts. "Her husband's job got transferred, and they weren't interested in adoption. You can't leave the state with a foster kid, so . . ." He shrugs again.

"You're really good."

He gives me a cynical smile. "You don't even know what you're looking at." But he looks pleased.

"Do you have anything else here?" I say.

He nods, and his eyes lift to the wall. "Up there. The woods?"

I find the painting he's indicating. It's primarily black and gray, dark trees on a night sky. Stars peek between barren branches. There's nothing to indicate winter, but somehow the painting makes me think of cold weather. At the base of one tree is a small dark form, like someone crouched, and a burst of color, yellows and oranges, like a fire.

I think about what he just said. *It always sucks to leave something unfinished.* I wonder how many paintings of his are stashed in art rooms around the county, works that he began and then abandoned.

This feels like more of a secret than what he told me about

his prior foster homes. There's nothing to indicate an affinity for art among his things. It softens him somehow.

"You should tell Mom and Dad," I say. "Tear down that alphabet border in your room and paint something of your own."

He smiles. "That would be cool." But again, the smile vanishes. "They wouldn't let me do that."

"Why not? It's just paint."

"Because it's not my house."

I don't know what to say to that. But I do know I can't force it. I shrug. "Well, you should tell them about the artwork. They'd get you some supplies. Paint or whatever."

For the briefest instant, he looks like he's considering it, but then his expression closes down. "They already spent money on the bed and things."

It's the second time he's mentioned money. What did he just say in the cafeteria? *Don't you understand that I'm trying not to cause a problem?* I've thought about all the things he's done since he moved in with us. The running. The knife. The hiding in the dark. I haven't really thought about the things he *hasn't* done. He hasn't given Mom or Dad a hard time. He hasn't gotten in trouble at school. He hasn't dodged chores or started fights or even raised his voice.

He hasn't fought back against the kids who've been tormenting him.

It reminds me of Dad's comment about how we have to ask questions to hear the quiet people.

For all Matthew's bravado about jumping from foster home

to foster home, and for all his certainty that his time with us is limited, I hadn't realized how much that must weigh on him. It reminds me of being with my father, the span of time between action and discipline, when I knew something terrible was coming, but I didn't know when, and I didn't know how.

The uncertainty, the waiting, must be awful.

My phone chimes, and I pull it out of my pocket.

Wednesday, March 21   12:05:34 p.m.

FROM: Robert Ellis <robert.ellis@speedmail.com>

TO: Rev Fletcher <rev.fletcher@freemail.com>

SUBJECT: Answer me

"My days are swifter than a weaver's shuttle, And come to an end without hope."

Perhaps that is too subtle. Perhaps you've forgotten your lessons.

I demand a response.

Maybe it's the demand. Maybe it's the time I've spent with Mom and Dad. Maybe it's everything going on with Emma, or with Matthew, or with Declan.

But this time, his e-mail doesn't upset me. It pisses me off.

The lunch bell rings. I need to get back to the cafeteria to get my stuff.

Matthew is sitting on a stool in front of his easel. "I think you know what you want to do."

I snap my head up. "What?"

"She likes you. I think you know what you want to do. You just have to get your nerve up and *do it*."

He's talking about Emma.

I'm thinking about my father.

Students begin filing into the room. Matthew glances at the clock on the wall. "Don't you need to get to class?"

He's right. I do.

I shove the phone in my pocket and turn for the doorway.

But then I stop and turn back. "Hey," I say, keeping my voice low. "You don't need to keep running from them. I've got your back. Dec does, too."

He looks startled, but he covers it quickly. He looks back at his painting. I don't think he's going to say anything.

And I really *am* going to be late to class.

"Hey," he calls after me. I barely hear him over the rush of students fighting to get into the classroom.

I turn back. "Yeah?"

"Thanks."

● ● ●

Declan is waiting in the hallway with my backpack. He's got a free period after lunch, so I know he doesn't need to be anywhere.

"All okay?" he says.

"Yeah. Hold on."

I pull up my father's e-mail, and before I can think about it, I hit Reply.

Wednesday, March 21   12:09:14 p.m.

FROM: Rev Fletcher <rev.fletcher@freemail.com>

TO: Robert Ellis <robert.ellis@speedmail.com>

SUBJECT: RE: Answer me

I'm not doing this over e-mail. If you want to talk, we're doing this face-to-face. Tell me when and where.

I hit Send before I can think better of it.

Then I grab my backpack and start walking.

Dec hustles to catch up with me. "What just happened?"

I hold out my phone so he can see. He reads quickly.

"Holy shit, Rev."

Normally, I'd give him a look, but right now, I don't even care about profanity.

Dec glances at me and misreads my silence. "Sorry. But you doing *that* deserved a 'Holy—' "

"I got it."

"Here. He wrote back." Declan thrusts the phone at me.

Another e-mail. An address—his apartment, judging by the fact that he includes a unit number. Or *an* apartment, but the city is Edgewater, so I'm guessing it's his.

A time. 4:00 p.m.

Holy shit.

Declan is studying me. "What are you going to do?"

My breathing has gone shallow, and my heart rate has tripled. Despite that, I feel surprisingly calm.

I look back at him. "I'm going to borrow your car."

THIRTY-SEVEN

Emma

He hasn't texted me.

I've checked my phone at least a thousand times today. Nothing. And now I'm on the bus, heading for home.

Emma. The way he breathed my name is locked in my ears, looping on repeat. *Emma. Emma. Emma.*

I need to fix this. My relationships with everyone are fractured and unstable.

"He'll text you," says Cait. She's been watching me open and close the iMessage app. "And even if he doesn't, he said he'd meet you tonight, didn't he? Didn't you say he has a lot going on?"

"Yeah." And he does. I know he does.

But so do I.

I bite at my lip. "I'm so worried that I broke our . . . whatever."

"You didn't break anything."

"I might have. I don't know what's wrong with me."

Cait is quiet for a little while. "Emma, I don't think there's anything wrong with you. You speak your mind. That's a good thing." She pauses.

"Is that your way of telling me to stop being such a bitch?"

"You're not a bitch. I think you're just trained to protect yourself."

It makes me think of Rev, how he's trained to do the same thing, just in a different way. For different reasons.

"Maybe you'll need to approach him differently," says Cait. "When you fix things."

I give her a watery smile. "Thanks for saying *when*, not *if*."

The bus pulls up to the end of my street. Cait reaches out and gives me another hug. "Call me if you need to come over, okay? Mom will come get you."

The air is cool when I climb out of the bus, but sunshine pours down. By all measures, a stunning day. It's half past three, and the afternoon is mine alone. I fill my lungs with fresh air.

Things with Mom are tense, but not unbearable. I'm sure I'll *eventually* work things out with my father.

I'm okay. Another deep breath. I'm okay.

Then I turn the corner and see the For Sale sign in front of my house.

She really did it. I didn't think she'd do it.

I'm light-headed. My vision fills with spots.

I need to breathe. I need to breathe.

My feet move me forward. The world zooms down to the

letters on the sign. F-O-R S-A-L-E. The white wooden post. The metal board, swinging in the breeze.

The strange cars in the driveway. One is a sleek sedan. The other is a larger SUV. Both are expensive and shiny.

As I get closer, I realize people are on our front porch. A woman in a sharp pin-striped suit is standing by the front door. A young couple with a baby in a carrier stands beside her.

"You said this just went on the market today?" the man is saying.

"Yes," says the woman in the suit. "It's unusual to find a Craftsman in Annapolis. The interior is impeccable. The family really took care of the property . . ."

She unlocks the door. They disappear inside.

She can't do this. She can't.

She hasn't even told me where we'll *go*. I thought this was a threat against Dad. Something to spur his sympathy. Something to try to save the marriage.

I had no idea she was serious.

And the house went on the market *today*? She didn't think to mention this over breakfast?

I can do better.

Me too.

What a crock.

I'm standing on the sidewalk in front of my house, hyper-ventilating. I need to get out of here before the happy couple looks outside and sees me lose my lunch on the lawn.

And Texy! Where is Texy? Why isn't she barking?

I burst through my front door. They haven't moved past the

dining room. All three people stare at me like I'm insane. The woman puts a hand over her baby's head, like maybe she doesn't want the infant to see such a train wreck.

Miss Pinstripe frowns at me. "Can I help you?"

"I—just—my dog—" My voice is shaking. I swallow. "I need to walk the dog."

"Oh! Are you Emma? Dr. Blue told me she would board the dog this week for showings. I'm sure she's having a good time at the kennel."

She put Texy in the kennel. She took my dog and she didn't tell me.

What a bitch.

"Are you feeling all right, dear?" The real estate agent moves toward me. Her voice is a little worried, a little irritated, like this isn't going to help her earn a commission.

I need to get out of here.

"No—I'm sorry." I swipe at my eyes before I start bawling in front of complete strangers. "I need—I need to go—"

And then I'm outside, and the pavement is below my feet, and I'm running.

● ● ●

Rev isn't beside the church. I have no idea why I thought he might be here. It's the middle of the afternoon. I'm panting and sweaty and I'm ready to collapse.

I pull out my phone and text him.

Emma: Rev. I need to talk to you.

I wait and wait and wait. He doesn't answer.

Emma: Please. I know you're mad. Please don't ignore me.

He ignores me.

Or maybe he doesn't see my messages. But the way fate's been treating me, I think he's ignoring me.

I dial Cait. It's only been fifteen minutes since I saw her last, so I know she's still on the bus, but her mom might be home.

She's not home. They have an answering machine, but I'm sobbing so hard by the time it gets to the beep that I just hang up.

I call my mother.

By some miracle, she answers. "Emma?"

"You put the house up for sale?" I yell.

A pause. "Emma, I told you that we can't afford to keep the house. When I called, the agent said she had a couple who wanted to come by today. I had to make a quick decision. I'm sorry."

"You didn't even tell me! Where are we going? What's going to—"

"Emma." Her voice drops. "I need you to get it together. I am not in a place to discuss this."

"You were supposed to do better." My voice breaks. "Do you think this is better?"

A sigh. "Emma—"

"Forget it." I can't believe I made her breakfast. I can't believe I felt any pity for her at *all*. I push the button to end the call.

Then I sit down in the grass and cry. I cry forever.

I try Cait again. No answer. I don't leave a message this time either.

Am I desperate enough to walk to Rev's house?

Apparently so, because I find myself on his front step, knocking on his door before I'm ready. I hear someone throwing dead bolts, and I hurriedly swipe at my face.

I'm a mess.

What am I doing?

If I'm lucky, they won't call the cops and say a maniac is on the front step.

The door opens, and Rev's foster brother stands there. I don't think Rev ever told me his name.

He takes one look at me and says, "Rev isn't here."

That brings on a fresh round of tears before I can stop them. I press my hands to my eyes. "Of course not. Okay." I turn away.

"Wait—do you want me to get Kristin? Or—"

"Matthew, honey?" A woman's voice calls down from the upstairs. "Who is it?"

"No. No." I wave my hand at him and choke on tears. "No."

"But—are you okay? She can call him—"

"No." I run down the steps. This was such a mistake. This is so humiliating. I'm such a fool.

I collapse in the grass beside the church again. The stained glass windows glitter in the sunlight.

I try Cait again. Still nothing. It's almost four, so she should be home by now. This time I leave a tearful message. "Call me? Okay? Call me."

I hang up.

Almost immediately, my phone *pings* with a text. My heart leaps. Is it Rev?

It's not Rev. It's Ethan.

Ethan: Hey. I haven't heard from you all day. All OK?
Emma: No. Not OK.
Ethan: What's wrong?
Emma: Everything.

My phone lights up with an incoming call. It's Ethan.

I don't even hesitate. I swipe to answer.

"Hello," I say, my voice thick with tears.

"Emma. What's wrong?"

His voice sounds exactly the same as it does in-game, which is surprising for some reason.

My breath hitches. "My mom is selling the house. She took my dog away. There were people there looking at it. I've been trying to call my friend—"

"Whoa. Slow down. She took your dog?"

"She took her to a kennel so people could look at the house." My voice breaks and I start crying again. "I don't know where we're going to live."

"Oh, Emma. I'm so sorry."

"I don't know where to go. My friend won't answer her phone. I can't go home because those people are there."

"Do you want me to come get you?"

His voice is so kind. I sniff and swipe at my eyes. "You don't even know me."

He gives a short, self-deprecating laugh. "I do know you. Kind of." He pauses. "We can go for coffee or something. Where are you?"

"I'm in the grass beside Saint Patrick's. In Annapolis."

"Funny."

"Why funny?"

"Because that's where we go to church. I'm fifteen minutes away. Are you going to be okay?"

"Yeah." I take a long, shuddering breath. "Thanks."

"See you soon."

THIRTY-EIGHT

Rev

The drive to Edgewater takes forever. The farther I drive, the more I regret forcing Declan to stay home. He wasn't happy about it, either. I thought I was going to have to steal his car.

But this, I need to do alone. This visit is nothing like his journey to find his father.

There is nothing positive here. Not even memories.

"What if he tries to hurt you?" Declan asked.

"I won't let him." This much I know. He will not touch me. My muscles are tense already.

"What if he has a gun? You can't ninja a bullet."

That question almost got me. But then I said, "You can't either. I'm going."

Somehow I find my father's street early, and it's not what I expected. The neighborhood is peaceful and quiet, with large single-family homes set back from the street. I don't see any apartment buildings, and one would be very out of place on this road. I wonder if I have the wrong street. Road names are reused all over the county. But when I pull over to reset the map on my phone, it puts me right back here.

Maybe it's a home that's been converted to apartments?

That must be the case, because the address leads to a large yellow house with white trim. Gray stones edge the garden, surrounding huge bushes set at regular intervals. The driveway leads to a small parking lot. A handicapped ramp has been installed alongside the porch stairs.

I back into a parking place, then sit and study the building. Six other cars are parked here, though the building doesn't seem large enough to support that many families. And I know I was taken from my father ten years ago, so I don't have a clear idea of his tastes, but this doesn't look anything like a place I could imagine him living.

Now that I'm here, I can't force myself out of the car.

This hold he has on me seems impenetrable. I remind myself that I'm not a child. I drove myself here. I'm almost six feet tall. I know how to defend myself.

I keep hearing Jim Murphy's voice when he first heard Declan speak. *You sound like a man.*

What will my father expect? What will he say?

My phone chimes and I jump a mile.

It's a message from Kristin.

Mom: Matthew says Emma was here, and she seemed upset. I thought you might want to know. XOXO

My eyes flick to the clock. It's 3:57 p.m.

Upset? Upset how? I wish Matthew had a phone.

Upset enough that she came looking for me.

But then I notice I've missed two messages from someone else. They came through while I was driving.

Emma: Rev. I need to talk to you.
Please. I know you're mad. Please don't ignore me.

I type quickly on the face of my phone.

Rev: Not mad. I was driving. You OK?

I wait, but no response comes back. And now I've been sitting here long enough to be conspicuous. It's 4:02 p.m.

I wonder if my father can see me.

Dec's comment about the gun is *so* unwelcome right now. I try to imagine my father with a sniper rifle and fail. It wouldn't be his style.

I need to get out of this car.

It's nice to see you coming out of your shell a little bit.

I don't think this is what Mom meant.

Her words do the trick, though. I climb out of Declan's Charger. My feet shift in the grit of the parking lot and I study each window in turn. My heart pounds. I examine each pane of glass, watching for a face to be looking back at me.

Nothing. All the windows are covered by blinds or drapes.

I should push the hood back, I know. I should try to look

normal. This hoodie is like a security blanket right now. For a weird moment, I'm glad my father isn't in prison.

Then I shove the hood back. Mom and Dad have drilled manners into me for years. I won't walk into someone's home looking like the Grim Reaper.

As I climb the steps, the front door opens. I flinch at the sound, but it's only a young woman in nursing scrubs heading out. She must be another tenant heading to work.

But she spots me and stops. Her eyes are tired, but kind. "Oh. Hello! Are you here to see a guest?"

I'm thrown. To see a guest? Would that make this a hotel? "I—I don't know."

The tiniest frown line appears between her eyes, but otherwise, her expression doesn't shift. "Who are you here to see?"

I don't want to say "my father" out loud. I also don't know what business this is of hers. Her expression is so expectant that I can't ignore her, though. "I'm going to unit one oh five."

"Oh! Mr. Ellis?"

I swallow. "Yes. You know him?"

The frown line appears again. "Of course. I'm Josie. Come with me." She turns and heads back through the door she just left.

Now I'm doubly confused. Does my father have a roommate?

Once through the door, I find myself looking at a large counter that runs the length of what must have been the living room of the house. A few sofas sit at angles to the walls, with a TV mounted overhead. Magazines are strewn across a coffee table between the sofas.

Behind the counter, two other women and one man sit at

monitors. They're all wearing scrubs, just like Josie. On the wall behind them, in large, scripty blue letters, is a sign that reads Chesapeake Hospice.

My mouth goes dry.

This can't be right. I stop there in the hallway. "Wait."

Josie stops and peers at me again. This close, I realize she's not as young as I originally thought. Gray winds through her hair at the temples, and more lines crowd around her eyes as she becomes concerned. "Are you all right?" She pauses. "Is this your first time here? It doesn't need to be frightening."

Her voice is so kind. She reminds me of Mom.

I swallow. "Wait." My voice is barely audible. "Wait."

Now they're all looking at me.

Another nurse steps away from her monitor, fills a small paper cup with water, and brings it to me. She's older, and she pats my hand as she gives it to me.

Now I'm embarrassed. I take the cup sheepishly. "Sorry. I didn't—I wasn't sure what this place was. He just gave me a unit number. I thought it was—" I swallow. "An apartment. Not . . ."

Not a hospice facility.

Not a place where people go to die.

"So Mr. Ellis is expecting you?"

"Yes," I say.

"Wonderful," says Josie. "I can take you back when you're ready."

I'm not ready.

I'm not ready.

I'm not ready.

This doesn't seem fair. I can't confront my father on his deathbed. I try to reconsider all his e-mails with this knowledge. Did I misread everything? Was he reaching out for some kind of connection?

I'm frozen in this space between the desk and the door, and I want a do-over. I want to enter this building with full knowledge.

I should have brought Declan.

No. The thought makes my spinning thoughts go still.

I can do this.

"Sorry." My voice is husky. "I'm ready."

Josie leads me down the hallway, and around a turn. Our feet are soft on the carpeting. I would give anything for guards and bars right now.

Then she stops in front of 105 and gives a gentle tap. We're on the back side of the building; none of the windows here face the parking lot. He hasn't seen me yet.

"Come in," calls the voice from inside.

His voice. I remember his voice.

I take a step back without meaning to.

But then I steel my nerve, find my backbone, and walk through his door.

THIRTY-NINE

Emma

Ethan drives a silver Toyota Corolla. Completely boring car. When he pulls up, I'm surprised. For some reason, my brain keeps superimposing his in-game presence over the real guy. I thought he'd have something wild and crazy.

The window rolls down when he pulls up, and he frowns and says, "Azure M can't cry."

That makes me smile, and I swipe the last of the tears off my cheeks.

He looks exactly like the picture he sent me, which is a relief. He's bigger than I expected. Not fat. Just . . . husky.

I pull open the passenger-side door and climb into the front seat. "Hi. Thanks for doing this."

"An excuse to get coffee with a badass gamer girl? There are legends on Reddit about this."

"You're hilarious."

My door closes, and he clicks the Lock button, then shifts into drive.

This is so different from driving with Rev. That car was loud and aggressive. This is small and quiet. There's a name badge on a lanyard hanging from his gearshift. AACS is written in huge red letters at the top—Anne Arundel County Schools. Below that, in black print, is the name E NASH, followed by a smaller line that says INFORMATION TECHNOLOGY.

He sees me looking. "My mom's. She works in IT. I told you I know people."

"So she found him."

"No, I found him." He sounds a little irked. "I just used her system."

"Oh—no, it's awesome. I'm glad you did." I keep hearing Rev's voice, about how I wanted to handle it myself, and then Ethan took care of it for me. His words prick at my thoughts, refusing to leave me alone. "I was going to restore the game this afternoon, but then—well, you know." I blot my eyes again.

"That really sucks about your house," Ethan says.

"I can't believe she did that without telling me." I pause. "This morning, we talked. I thought things were getting better. She didn't even mention calling a real estate agent." I glare out the window and distantly hear him hit his turn signal. "She had to know I'd see the sign when I got home. What did she expect, that I'd be completely oblivious and just—"

I see where he's turning, and stop short. "Why are we getting on the highway?"

"Starbucks? Coffee?"

Oh. "There's one by the mall."

"I just know the one on Solomons Island Road. They have a drive-through."

That's on the other side of Annapolis. But what's the difference, really? It's only a few miles down the highway.

"You're going to bring the game back up?" Ethan says.

"I want to," I say. "Especially since Nightmare is gone."

"I'm glad I found him for you," he says.

My phone rings, vibrating against my leg. I slide it out of my pocket.

Cait.

"Hey," I say.

"Em? Are you okay?"

Beside me, Ethan sighs and mutters something under his breath.

I frown at him. But then, I'm awkward all the time. Maybe he suffers from the same curse. "Sorry," I whisper, moving the phone away from my face. "I left her like a hundred messages." I put the phone back. "Cait. Yeah. I'm okay."

"Mom says we can come get you. Where are you?"

"Oh." I glance at Ethan. "I'm okay now. We're going to Starbucks."

"We?"

"Yeah. Me and a—a friend."

Her voice warms. "Oh, did Rev finally call? I told you he would."

I'm very aware of Ethan's attention right now. I'm pretty sure he can hear every word.

"No, it's—Cait, can I call you back?"

"Sure. Take your time." She clicks off. My phone goes back to the Home screen.

There's a text message waiting. How did I miss a text message?

Rev: Not mad. I was driving. You OK?

My heart flutters before I'm ready for it.

"Who's Rev?"

For half a second, I forgot I was in a car with Ethan. "What?"

"Who's Rev?"

I don't know if he can see the screen or if he eavesdropped on the phone call, but either way, it feels unfairly intrusive.

"Just a friend."

"Oh." His voice sounds irritated.

The air in the car has shifted. "Are you mad about something?"

"I don't know, Emma." He gives a little laugh. "I don't know what to think."

I swallow. "He's just a guy from school."

"You just said he was a friend."

"He is!"

"Is he the same friend you were out with the other night?"

I hesitate without meaning to. That's all he needs.

Ethan looks away from the road to glare at me. "Who do you think you are? What kind of game are you playing?"

"I'm not playing a game!"

"When I called you, you were acting like you had no one to care about you, and since you got in the car, you've had two people reach out."

"But . . ." I stop. He does have a point.

Wait. Does he?

He runs a hand through his short hair. "You know how much this means to me."

Every time he says something, my brain has to process it twice. He speaks as if he's talking more to himself than to me. "How much what means to you?"

"This!" He glances at me. "You and me."

And then I realize we've passed the exit for Solomons Island Road.

My heart turns into a brick in my chest. "Where are we going?" I say.

"Sorry," he says. "You made me upset. I missed the exit."

But he doesn't slow down. He doesn't even change lanes.

"Just take the next one. Just take me home."

"I will," he snaps. "Just give me a minute, okay?"

I give him a minute. The car does not change lanes. We fly past the exit for Jennifer Road. Then for Riva Road. My heart pounds in my chest.

I slide my fingers across the phone to reply.

Emma: No. Not OK.

"You're texting him right now?" Ethan explodes. "In my car? What kind of girl *does* that, Emma?"

The kind of girl who would give anything to be anywhere else right this moment.

I feel very small and alone in the passenger seat. I pray for the little gray dots to indicate Rev is writing back.

They don't appear.

Ethan's driving in the left lane, flying past other vehicles. He doesn't look ready to exit the highway anytime soon. I glance at the odometer. He's going almost ninety miles an hour.

My heart rate triples. Maybe a cop will see us and stop him.

I have never wished so hard for a speed trap in all my life.

I swallow. "I'm sorry. Can you please take the next exit?"

He says nothing. He keeps driving. The car continues flying along the pavement. His jaw is set, his fists tight on the steering wheel. Fear wraps around that icy brick in my chest.

"Ethan?" My voice trembles. "Please just take the next exit."

I glance at my phone. Rev hasn't responded.

My fingers fly across the phone.

Emma: with ethan

The fist comes out of nowhere. My head hits the window. Pain explodes into my face from both sides. The phone goes flying and lands somewhere between the door and the seat.

I taste blood in my mouth.

This is bad. I am so stupid. I'm breathing so fast I'm going to hyperventilate. Black spots fill my vision.

NO NO NO. I need to stay conscious.

I need to stay conscious. I tell the black spots to back off.

It takes a moment, but they listen.

I'm gasping against the window. This hurts more than anything I can ever imagine hurting. My teeth feel loose somehow, and my jaw aches something fierce. I wish I'd paid more attention to Rev's words about self-defense and less attention to the feeling of his arms wrapped around me.

The worst part is the little sobbing sounds coming out of my throat.

"I didn't think you'd be like this," Ethan says. "I thought you were different."

No kidding.

I don't want to straighten. I don't want to answer. The speed of the car traps me more effectively than anything else. My phone is sitting right *there*, upright against the door. The messages between me and Rev. He still hasn't written back. I slide my hand to reach for it.

I bump it. It slips down.

NO.

Maybe I can still reach it. Maybe.

I can reach the screen, but I can't get my fingers around the case. I strain, and my middle finger brushes the little "I."

Great. Now I have Rev's contact information instead of a texting screen.

Not that I could have sent a text. The bottom half of the phone is too low. This is useless.

I need to think. I need to *think*. Ethan is breathing hard

beside me. He's stopped talking. I don't know if this is a good thing or a bad thing.

I try to reach the button to call Rev. It's too far to the right. I strain hard.

A long shot anyway. Who knows if he would have answered. And how would he have found me?

Wait. A link sits below his contact information. I've never used it before.

Share My Location.

I strain to tap it.

My head is suddenly jerked left. I cry out. Ethan's hand is wrapped in my braid. My head jams into his midsection. It's just his abdomen, but it's horrible. I can smell him, a combination of detergent and male musk that makes my stomach turn. I can see his feet. The grip on my hair is tight and painful. His forearm pins my face.

"What were you doing?" he snaps.

I don't know if I tapped the link. I don't know.

And even if I did, what will Rev do with that? He has no idea what's happening.

"Please," I gasp. "Please, Ethan. I'm sorry. Please just let me out of the car."

"No. I want you to think about what you've done."

"You're right," I babble. "You're right. I was really rude. I'm sorry." My hands are free, but if I grab the wheel, I'll wreck the car. We're going too fast.

We've gone so far past the exit that I don't know where we are. Now I'm more panicked that he *will* stop.

"Please," I whisper. "Please, Ethan. I'll do whatever you want. Just let me go."

"Whatever I want?" he says. He flicks the turn signal. "I like the sound of that."

FORTY

Rev

My father sits in one of two armchairs by the window, which takes me by surprise. After the hospice realization, I expected to find a bed-bound invalid. He's wearing a green sweater and a pair of jeans. An IV line disappears under his sleeve, and a bag of fluid hangs suspended behind the chair. A plastic tube wraps around his face to feed him oxygen, too. Otherwise, this could be a room anywhere.

He hasn't said anything. I haven't either.

Josie is between us, efficiently checking his arm, checking the IV monitor, checking the oxygen tank. Silent motions so she doesn't get in our way.

I want to beg her to stay in the room.

At the same time, I want to beg her to leave.

Everything about him is thin. Thin, graying hair. Thin skin. *Thin.* The clothes all but hang on his frame. His cheekbones jut out from his face, making his eyes look deeper than I remember. He should be in his late forties, but he looks ten years older. Maybe twenty. I could pick him up and break him.

I think of that moment in the kitchen, when I admitted that Matthew makes me nervous, how Declan said, *Rev. Seriously. You've got that kid by like forty pounds,* and I said Matthew didn't make me nervous that way.

That feeling is identical to what I'm feeling now.

No, not identical. What I'm feeling now is amplified times a billion.

I don't want to say hello. I don't want to be the first to speak.

I want to hold a pillow over his face and finish whatever his body has started.

Josie completes whatever she needed to do, and she slips out the door. It closes with a gentle click behind me.

"Ah," my father says. "Now I see."

His voice makes me want to cower, and I have to hold very still. "Now you see what?"

"I see the boy trying to be a man. Your e-mail amused me." He laughs softly. "Your demand to speak face-to-face. As if you were taking something I did not want to give."

My phone *pings* with a text message. I ignore it. "How did you know where to find me?"

He shrugs. "Does it matter?"

"Yes."

I don't think he's going to answer me, but he glances at the door. "There was a woman here. A former judge. We became friends. I spoke of how I wanted to find my long-lost son. She pulled some strings for me."

There was a woman here. He convinced a dying woman to do him a favor. My father, a man who convinced an entire congregation of his benevolence. Of course.

"Why did you want to find me?"

" 'The rod and reproof give wisdom, but a child left to himself brings shame to his father.' Have you been left to yourself, Abraham?"

The name hits me like a bullet. I flinch. "That's not my name anymore."

"I gave you that name. It is yours whether you want it or not." He pauses. "Abraham."

I flinch again. The name dredges memories from somewhere deep inside me. I want to get down on my knees and beg forgiveness. The instinct is so powerful.

But then I think about what he said. *A child left to himself brings shame to his father.*

It's a verse from Proverbs. The words stick in my mind, poking at me, until I figure out why. I look at him. "The verse is that a child left to himself brings shame to his *mother.*" I pause, thinking of Mom's palm against my cheek last night. *You grew into such a generous, kind young man.*

I focus on that feeling. It's almost enough to chase my father's influence out of my head.

He looks surprised that I've corrected him. "I believe it's open to interpretation."

Of course he does. "Fine. Interpret however you want. I haven't brought shame to my father or my mother."

"Perhaps I should be the judge of that."

"You're not my father anymore."

"Abraham, I am still your father. You are still my son. Nothing can change that."

I grit my teeth. Another verse comes to mind, stopping fury before it comes out of my mouth. *A soft answer turns away wrath; a harsh word stirs up anger.* "Stop," I say, but my voice sounds weak instead of soft. "Stop calling me that."

"You've been gone away too long, Abraham." His voice is gentle. "I can see how the world weighs on you. Come sit by me."

My heart slows, just by virtue of that tone in his voice. When I was a child, I learned to *crave* it. A gentle voice meant I had a chance to get things right.

I can't say anything. I'm worried that my mouth will open and I'll promise him everything he wants.

"Come," he says again. He doesn't say my name. "Let me see how you've grown. You've obviously kept up your lessons. I'm proud of you."

His words hit their target. I sit in the other chair.

He reaches out and puts his hand over my own. My hand shakes, but I don't pull it back.

"Do you know why I chose that name?" he says. "After your mother lost her battle with evil, I knew you would have to be strong to overcome those forces. I knew you would be tested again and again. So I named you Abraham."

Of course I know this. He used to tell me all the time.

I've read the whole story. The ultimate test was when God asked Abraham to kill his own son, and he actually went to do it, hoping God would intercede.

Every time I read that passage, I wonder about that level of faith.

My father keeps talking. "I knew you would be tested again and again. When they took you from me, I knew that would be your biggest test of all. I knew you would come back to me. And you have."

I haven't.

But I can't say the words. Because I have. I'm here.

I want to close my eyes and think of Geoff and Kristin.

Mom and Dad.

Not Geoff and Kristin. Mom and Dad.

I take a long, shuddering breath. Mom was right. I should never have come here.

He's more than a man. He always has been.

"What do you want?" I say.

"I want to die," he says simply.

I stare at him. "I don't understand."

"Don't you?" He lifts his hands. "Do you not see? Do you not see what has become of me?"

I still don't understand.

"This pain. This is my test, Abraham. The agony. This is my punishment for letting you go. And now you have returned." His arms drop, and he rests his hand on my forearm. He gives it a squeeze.

I wonder if he knows his hand is directly over the burn from the stove.

Maybe he does. My father does nothing that isn't deliberate.

If it's deliberate, it's a mistake. It's a reminder. A needed reminder.

You were so afraid.

My arm turns to steel.

My father is still looking at me, his eyes almost haunted. "You have returned. My boy. This is a sign. A gift. You are here to end my suffering."

It takes me a moment to realize what he just said. Shock freezes me in place. My breathing goes shallow.

"What?" I whisper.

"Your purpose here. You have come to end my suffering."

A moment ago, I literally considered putting a pillow over his face.

Now the thought makes me sick.

"My lungs are filled with cancer," he says. "It would take nothing. Your hand. For just a moment."

I don't know if he wants me to suffocate him or break his neck or something else I can't even consider, but I fly out of the chair and back away from him. "No."

"Yes. 'It was by faith that Abraham obeyed.' Do you not see?"

I see nothing. I see everything. I shake my head fiercely. "No."

"I am in such pain." His voice breaks. "How can you bear to witness such suffering?"

Time stops. The words hit me like a thousand knives. A hundred fists. A strike of lightning. A burst of flame.

"How could *you*?" I yell. "How could *you* witness such suffering? Do you know what you did to me? Do you have any idea?"

"I raised you," he says gently, but now his voice has no power.

"You *failed* me."

"I created you."

"I don't care." I'm still yelling. I wish Dad were here to catch me now. "You are not my father."

"I am. I suffer now because of *your* failings. You will do this for me."

The door clicks. Josie pokes her head in. "Is everything okay in here?"

"No," I say.

"We're fine, Josie," my father says kindly. "My son is upset. You understand."

"Of course," she whispers. She ducks away. The door clicks shut.

Everyone always does what he wants.

"Do it yourself," I say, my voice a whispered rasp. "Do it yourself."

"You know I cannot. I want to enter the kingdom with purity of—"

I slam my hand into the wall. "I AM NOT DOING THIS!"

Pain rockets up from my wrist. It's good. I welcome the pain. It centers me.

I don't know what I'm doing here. I don't know what I expected. There's no closure in this room.

I grab the door handle.

"Please," my father says. His voice breaks again, and in it, I hear the pain he must feel. Despite everything, his pain tugs at something inside of me.

Some of it is empathy. Some of it is not.

I know pain like that.

"Please," he says again, and his words have dissolved into a sob. "My son. Please. I am dying."

"Good."

Then I slam the door behind me and walk out.

● ● ●

I fly out of the parking lot. I need to get away from this place. My foot can't step on the accelerator hard enough. Declan will have a fun project tomorrow, because I'm beating the hell out of his transmission.

When I reach the stop sign at the end of the street, I'm panting. The car feels insufferably hot.

I pull against the curb and turn on the hazard lights. I need to get it together.

I yank the sweatshirt over my head. Rub my face.

It would take nothing.

Your hand.

For just a moment.

I can't breathe. I'm the one suffocating.

But then I can. Air flows into my lungs.

I said no. I said *no*.

He *was* just a man. A terrible man.

And he could not bend me to his will.

My wrist still aches from hitting the wall. I flex my hand, then stare at my fingers in wonder.

It would take nothing.

Your hand.

He wanted me to kill him.

After everything he did to me, it shouldn't be shocking—but it is. He wanted me to *kill* him. Did he think I would do it because of my childhood? Because we're strangers now?

Or did he think I would do it simply because he told me to? Maybe all three.

I press my hands to my temples. Declan and I had a conversation in the car about violent thoughts. I've been so sure I would one day act on them.

I said no. I said no to my father. The one man deserving of my rage and violence.

I said NO to my FATHER. For the first time in . . . ever, I feel in control.

I'm giddy now. Breathless. Shaking.

I need to call Declan. He's probably been staring at his phone for the last half hour. I run a hand through my hair to push it off my face, then dig through my pile of sweatshirt to find my phone.

Messages wait on the screen. Declan couldn't even wait.

But then my eyes focus. Not Declan.

Emma.

Emma: No. Not OK.

with ethan

Emma Blue has shared her location with you.

My heart stops beating. When did she send these messages? I look.

Twenty minutes ago.

Twenty minutes.

with ethan.

How? How did that happen?

She shared her location. Dad has done that by accident before, when he gets frustrated and starts pushing buttons he doesn't know how to use. But Emma is technologically savvy. If she shared her location, she needed me to know it.

No. Not OK.

Oh, Emma.

I stop thinking and call her. The line rings and rings and goes to voice mail.

I know nothing about Ethan except a name. I know he plays computer games. I have no idea where he lives. From my conversations with Emma, I don't think she knows much more than that herself.

Guilt eats at me. I should have messaged her earlier. I was too twisted up with thoughts about my father.

Stop. Guilt later. Back to the messages.

A tiny map appears below the line about sharing her location. I tap it. She's on the other side of South River. Maybe ten minutes away.

She's also moving. Heading east. Away from me.

She's in a car.

EMMA. WHAT DID YOU DO?

I shift into gear.

Wait. I switch to my messages with Declan. I send him *my* location. Then I send him a text to call me.

Then I go back to her map and snap the phone into the clip on his dashboard.

I need to get back to the highway. I floor the accelerator.

Declan calls me immediately. I push the button for speaker.

"I need you to call nine one one," I say.

He must hear the urgency in my voice. There's alarm in his. "What happened? Are you hurt?"

"It's not me. It's Emma. She's with a guy. Something's wrong."

"Wait. What?" His voice is incredulous. "Rev. What about your dad—"

"Later, Dec. Later. Help me."

"Okay." I hear rustling. "I need more information. What guy? Where is she?"

"I don't know. His name is Ethan. She's been talking to him on the Internet."

"Where is she?"

"*I don't know.* She sent me her location. I'm trying to go to her."

"You're—Rev, what are you doing?"

"I don't know! But I don't know what else to do!" I blaze through a yellow light just as it turns red. I'm a mile from the highway. Emma's dot continues moving.

"Okay. Chill out. Hold on." He's breathing hard. "Damn it, Rev. I should have come with you."

"What are you doing?"

"Mom and Alan aren't home. I don't have another phone. I'm running to your house."

I hear the sliding door. I want to tell him we're wasting time, and he needs to call the cops.

At the same time, I know that's impossible. We have no information. I don't even know what kind of car he's driving. What is Declan going to say? *Tell the cops to look for a car with a girl wearing glasses.*

"Rev. I'm in your kitchen. I'm putting you on speaker. Tell Kristin everything you know."

I do.

All the while, I watch that dot move along the highway. I'm on Route 50 now, going way too fast. He must be speeding, too, but I feel like I'm gaining ground.

Kristin has dozens of questions, none of which I can answer. Do I know Emma's mom's name? What about her dad's? Do I know anything at all about Ethan, like where he lives or goes to school? Do I know where Emma lives?

No. No. No. No.

Fear began as a tiny twisting tendril in my stomach, but it's grown into something more invasive.

"Rev," says Kristin. "Do you think there's any chance she's being dramatic?"

I think of Emma, with her walls built every bit as thick as my own. She would not send a text like that if she didn't mean it. She would not send her location without cause.

"No," I say.

The dot leaves the highway. "They're on the other side of the Severn River," I say. "They just went north on Ritchie Highway."

They're at least eight miles ahead of me, but I'm still catching up. We're heading toward Arnold and Severna Park now. Ritchie Highway is full of traffic lights, and it's nearing rush hour, so I'll be able to catch up a little bit. Hopefully.

I realize the line has been quiet for a while. They're letting me drive. I'm letting them think.

Then Kristin says, "Rev, what were you doing all the way down there?"

Her voice is so quiet, so careful, and I know she knows.

Emotion hits me so hard and fast, and I almost lose it.

It would take nothing.

Your hand.

For just a moment.

I need to tell her everything.

"Later," I say, and my voice breaks. I take a breath and hold myself together. "Later, Mom. Okay?"

"Okay," she says. "But Rev. Please tell me you're okay."

"I'm okay," I say. "Mom. I'm okay." I pause. I need to focus. "I'm at the exit. I'm getting on Ritchie. They're still heading north."

"When they stop," she says, "tell me the address." Her voice is firm. "Park far away. Wait for the police. Do you understand me?"

Her voice is so serious. "Yes."

"You don't know the situation, Rev. All you have is one text message. Do you—"

"I know. I know."

The dot turns left. "They've turned!"

"What road?"

"Arnold Road." I can see it, several blocks ahead. "There's a CVS."

"I know where it is." She's quiet for a moment. "There's an old park-and-ride lot back there."

An old parking lot. Fear expands into my chest.

"Hey." Declan's voice. "She's on the phone with the police. I'm watching you on the map. You okay?"

"Yeah."

The dot stops. I'm stuck at the light for Arnold Road.

"They stopped," I say. I swallow. "Half a mile down. On the right."

He repeats that for Kristin.

This light is taking forever.

Declan must take me off speaker, because his voice is suddenly low and clear. "Rev. You don't know anything about this guy. I was kind of kidding about your dad having a gun, but—"

"I know, Dec. I know. I'll wait."

"Promise, Rev."

"I promise."

Then the light changes, and I make the turn to follow.

FORTY-ONE

Emma

We've been driving forever.

Ethan's hand hasn't let go of my braid. He grips the hair so tightly that I know pieces are pulling free from my scalp, bit by bit.

It hurts. A lot.

I've been crying into his shirt. I keep trying not to, but it's impossible.

Freeway changed to surface streets miles ago, but my face is shoved down, almost into Ethan's lap, and I have no idea where we are. Between his fist in my hair and his arm pinning me against him, Ethan has such a tight grip on my head that I can barely breathe. At the first traffic light, I struggled and tried to press on the horn, fighting his hold, trying to gain some attention from nearby vehicles.

Ethan slammed my head into the center console. Blood runs into my eye from somewhere.

Now he's pressing down on my shoulder blades, keeping my head low. At first I think he's pushing me toward his crotch, but then I realize he's just trying to keep me out of sight now that we're in heavier traffic. Sunlight streams through the windows. A beautiful day out there. A complete nightmare in here.

"I can't believe you're doing this to me," he keeps saying. "I can't believe you did this, Emma."

"I'm not doing anything to you," I say.

"You are. You asked me out, and then you started playing games."

"Please, Ethan. Please just let me out of the—"

"NO." He jerks my braid so hard that my neck is wrenched sideways. Stars flicker in my vision. The car turns sharply, and I'm completely off balance. My face is rocked into his lap. I almost throw up on him.

Then another turn. And another. The car rocks as we go over several small bumps.

And then we come to a stop. He kills the engine.

I shouldn't think about killing things.

We're in the shade. Somewhere under a canopy of trees. The lacy pattern of shadows throws Rorschach images across the upholstery. I can hear traffic, but it's distant.

My breathing is suddenly loud.

So is his.

And then I realize he's crying. "I don't know what I'm doing," he says softly. "I don't know what I'm doing."

"It's okay." I swallow back my own tears. My voice wavers. "It's okay. Ethan, just let me out."

He hasn't let me go. If anything, he's clutching my hair more tightly. "I liked you so much."

I want to punch him in the crotch, but I have no leverage. I don't want him to hit me again. But if he's talking, he's not hurting me. I need time to think. "I like you, too. You're my favorite game partner."

"But that's all I am to you. A game partner."

"No," I say. My voice sounds thick. "We're friends."

"I found Nightmare for you. I did that for *you*. Doesn't that mean anything?"

A siren kicks up in the distance.

Oh, please be for me.

I know there's no way.

Another siren joins it.

Oh, please. Oh, please.

They seem to be growing louder. Closer.

Maybe someone saw us. Maybe my location went through to Rev after all.

Maybe. Maybe. Maybe.

Ethan freezes.

The sirens grow loud—then rocket past. They don't stop.

NO. Oh, god. No.

But he's quieter now. More mellow.

"Can you let me go?" My voice shakes. "We can talk. We haven't gotten a chance to talk yet."

For an eternal moment, he doesn't move. I worry I've said the wrong thing.

"Okay," he says. "Okay. Yeah." He lets go of my hair. I straighten in the seat.

We're in an old parking lot, facing the woods. I can't see anything else. I hold very still. I think about my position. I think about his.

And then I grab the lock with one hand, seize the door handle with another, and burst out of the car.

"Help!" I scream. "Help me!"

It's an abandoned parking lot. We're surrounded by woods. Ritchie Highway is five hundred feet away, cars racing by on the other side of a line of trees.

There's no one here.

No one except Ethan, who moves fast for someone his size. I expected him to be slow and lazy, but maybe hiding in his mom's house gives him a lot of time to work out.

He brings me to the ground. He's so heavy. I crash into the pavement. I fight to roll away, but he traps me on my back. Asphalt tears into my skin.

And then—*and then*—I do remember something Rev said. It's like his voice is in my head. *Stay close. Distance gives someone room to hurt you.*

When Ethan draws back, I hook an arm around his neck. Another under his arm. I cling to him.

I can feel his surprise. He tries to shake me free, but I dig in with my nails. I press my face against his. I hold on for dear life.

Sirens again. Coming closer again.

I'm underneath him, but suddenly I feel like I have an advantage. I can't breathe with his weight on me, but he can't hit me when I'm up against him. I'm heavy enough that he can't get leverage to get himself off the ground. I refuse to give him my grip on his neck.

Then he tries another tactic. He rears back and slams me into the ground.

The back of my skull hits the pavement. I can't hold on. I can't see. I'm going to be sick.

He grabs my shoulders. Lifts me.

He's going to slam me again. My head won't be able to take it. The last thing I'm going to see will be his horrible face, crying about how we were friends, as he crushes my brain into the pavement.

And then his weight is just . . . gone. He's lifted away.

No, he's dragged away.

And then Rev draws back a fist and hits Ethan square in the face.

FORTY-TWO

Rev

Sirens are everywhere now, but they're too late.

I was almost too late. I tried to wait, but I couldn't.

He would have killed her. I could see it when he tackled her. He would have killed her.

My first punch almost sent Ethan to the ground. I wish I'd had the momentum to knock him flat, but I was off balance from dragging him off her. I hurt him, but I didn't knock him unconscious.

He's quick, and he tackles my midsection.

Ethan is not like Matthew. He's got some solid mass, and fury is a good motivator. He gets me off my feet. The pavement hurts when I land, especially since he's on top of me.

But then he draws back to hit me. He leaves himself wide open.

Every movement is so clear, almost happening in slow motion. My thoughts aren't clouded with self-doubt. Just crystal clarity.

I can't hit him from the ground. He's got the advantage. I lunge inside his movement and take control of his midsection. I duck my head into his shoulder. I brace one foot and flip him over.

Now I'm on top. I'm in control.

I've never hit someone from this position. I wait for my brain to imagine it, going too far, hitting him too hard, splintering bone and shattering his face. I wait for fear and hesitation to kick in.

While I'm waiting, training has already taken over. I've hit him twice. He's still. Blood is on his face, on my hands, on the pavement.

Oh. Oh no.

I think of my father.

It would take nothing.

Your hand.

For just a moment.

But Ethan's chest rises. He's breathing. He's alive.

My wrist didn't like me before. Now it hates me. Pain like fire lives in my forearm.

I look at Emma. Tears have made streaks of her makeup. A bruise has formed along the side of her face. She's hurt, but she's staring up at me.

"Are you okay?" I say. I want to go to her, but I don't want to leave him in case he wakes up.

She nods quickly. Her eyes stare up at me with some kind of wonder. "You found me."

"Yes," I say. "I found you."

She chokes on a sob and swipes at her face with both hands. "I did what you said. I tried to hold on to him."

"I know. Like I said, fearless."

She chokes on a laugh. "I'm so not fearless."

Police cars fly into the parking lot. The sirens are deafening. There's an ambulance, too, and Emma is quickly hidden by EMTs and paramedics.

The police arrest Ethan.

They arrest me, too.

Declan was right. It is terrifying.

FORTY-THREE

Emma

During the ambulance ride, there's this stupid little part of me that hopes my parents will reunite in the hospital and realize how much they need each other. I keep hearing Rev's voice saying *Things happen when they're meant to happen* and wondering if that means I had to endure everything with Ethan so my parents wouldn't get a divorce.

I must be delusional—which is possible, considering the situation I got myself into.

My fantasy does not happen. My father does not come to the hospital.

I talk to him on the phone, and he tells me he's trying to hang on to his job, and the worst thing he can do is step away right now.

He says, "Your mom is there for you, right?"

And yes. She is.

She sits beside my gurney in the ER. She has not let go of my hand except for when they took me for a CT scan. We've been here for hours, but she keeps asking me the same questions. Saying the same things.

She knows everything. About Nightmare. About Ethan.

About how I saw one threat so clearly that I didn't bother to pay attention to the other.

After she's heard everything twice, she gets very quiet.

"I need to understand something," she finally says.

I feel raw, cracked open. Only some of that is because of the head injury. "What?"

"Why wouldn't you tell me you were getting those messages? From that Nightmare person?" She pauses. "Or—at the very least, your *father*—"

"I tried." I swallow. "I started telling Dad, but he was so busy—"

She sighs, a sound full of disappointment. "Emma. I'm so sorry."

"I wanted to fix it myself. It's a very *male* industry." I look away. "I just—it happens to everyone. I didn't want to be all like I couldn't take the heat."

Mom sighs.

"And clearly I couldn't," I say disgustedly. "Since Ethan had to fix it for me."

Now she straightens up, and her face looks fierce. "He didn't fix anything, Emma. He could have killed you. You don't even *know* that he fixed anything. He just *told you* he did."

She's right.

She's so right. I'm such a fool.

She sighs again. "Let me tell you something about medical school."

My eyes have filled, and I'm still stuck on the fact that I fell for Ethan so easily. This doesn't sound like a prelude to a lecture, and I'm confused. "You want . . . to talk about medical school?"

"Yes." She pauses. "I used to go through the same thing."

"What same thing?"

"The sexism. The misogyny. The man's world."

"I don't think medical school is like a computer game."

She charges forward as if I haven't spoken. "This one time, when I was a resident, there were these two male doctors who would turn on pornography right in front of me. When I asked them to turn it off, they mocked me for being unable to look at a human body. I felt like an idiot. I put up with it for far too long, because I believed it was just part of what women had to go through."

I stare at her. I don't know what to say.

"That's all in your head, Emma." Another pause. "You're allowed to play a game without having to go through this. You're allowed to design a computer game without being harassed. You're allowed to go through life without having to put up with this, regardless of what kind of field it is. You are not *weak* for not wanting to look at pornography or not wanting to be called a—that disgusting word he used. I'm horrified that you thought you had to put up with any of it."

I swipe at new tears. "I'm sorry, Mom."

"No, I'm sorry. I'm sorry your father ever made you think that was acceptable."

"He didn't—"

"Emma, I think we need to come to an agreement."

"What?"

"I'll back off about the gaming," she says.

"You'll *what*?" Maybe I'm hopped up on painkillers because that does not sound like my mother.

"But I'm going to need to know what you're doing. And I'm going to need to know who you're doing it with."

"Mom—"

"You must agree." Her eyes fill now. "Emma, I need you to agree to this. I can't lose you, too."

Then I start crying. "Okay, Mom. Deal."

A police officer knocks on the wall, then tentatively pokes her head around the curtain. She looks to be around thirty, with hair pulled back into a severe ponytail. "Emma? I'm Jennifer Stone. I'm an officer with the Anne Arundel County Police Department. Do you feel up to answering a few questions?"

I hastily swipe at my face. "Yes. Yes. I'm okay."

She comes in and shakes hands with my mother, and then with me. Mom offers her the chair, which Officer Stone waves away. She leans against the wall between us, and pulls out a notepad.

"Would you mind telling me how you met Mr. Nash?"

It takes me a moment to realize she's talking about Ethan. Calling him Mr. Nash makes all of this sound more serious.

But of course it's serious.

I go through everything again. OtherLANDS. Battle Realms. The e-mails from Nightmare, and the way Ethan helped find him. As I'm talking, I realize again that I don't even know if Ethan really found Nightmare, or if he's still out there, waiting to do more damage. The officer promises to look into it.

My voice falters when I talk about the divorce and exchanging phone numbers, especially when Mom makes *tsk*ing noises.

"He said his mom and dad went through a divorce, too," I say. "He said he lived with his mom. We talked about how difficult it was. I thought we were friends."

Officer Stone makes a note on her pad. "And how old is Mr. Nash? Did he tell you?"

"He said he was a student at Old Mill."

"So he said he was in high school?"

"It—it was on his 5Core profile." I swallow. "I thought he was a senior."

She makes another note. "Do you mind if we keep your phone to pull any messages?"

"But—but I need—"

"Emma," my mother hisses. "Of course they can take it. Whatever they need to do to lock that man up."

I swallow. "Okay. It was in Ethan's car. It fell under the seat."

Another note on her pad. A lot of notes.

"Can I ask a question?" I say.

She stops writing and looks at me. Her eyes are cool and analytical, but there's compassion there, too. "Of course."

"How old is he really? Are you allowed to tell me?"

She flips her notepad back a few pages. "He's twenty-nine."

My heart flutters. I have to put a hand to my chest. Beside me, my mother is doing the same thing.

Officer Stone glances back at her notes, then meets my gaze. "He lives alone, in an apartment. No mother." A pause. "He works in IT for Anne Arundel County. That's how he had access to their servers."

E Nash. Information Technology.

It was literally hanging right in front of me. And I was stupid enough to believe it was his mother's.

"He has some charges of harassment and stalking on his record," says the officer.

"Emma." My mother starts crying again.

I'm not crying. I'm too shocked. "But—but—"

I almost say, *He was so kind. He was my friend.*

He was not kind. He was not my friend.

"This happens a lot," says Officer Stone. "These guys are smart. They take something you say and spin it in a way that you feel you have a connection. It doesn't take much to build from there." She hesitates. "You're very lucky this didn't end differently."

"He said he and his mother went to Saint Patrick's," I whisper. "He said she was controlling and mean to him."

Mom chokes on a sob. "And what did you tell him about me?"

I told him so much. The more I think back on our conversations, I realize I fed him everything he needed.

I want to curl in on myself. I feel so stupid. So foolish. They should put *me* in prison.

Officer Stone puts a hand on my shoulder. "Don't be too hard on yourself. Like I said, they're savvy. This wasn't his first time. And you're lucky. I heard what you did about sharing your location. I wish more people knew about that."

Rev. "Is Rev okay?"

"He was arrested—"

"What?" I demand. "Why?"

She puts a hand up. "This is a pretty clear case of self-defense, and the MTA has surveillance cameras on that lot. If your friend hasn't been processed and released yet, it'll be soon."

FORTY-FOUR

Rev

By the time they release me from the police station, night has fallen, and the pain in my wrist has gone from fire to inferno. The skin is swollen and purple under my sleeve. I've been gritting my teeth for the last hour, but I've been terrified they would charge me with assault, so I've kept my mouth shut and tried to be invisible.

I wonder if I'm going to have to call Mom and Dad, but an officer leads me out to the front lobby, and they're both there, waiting. Matthew isn't with them.

Dad doesn't even wait for me to clear the desk. He grabs me in a hug.

Mom piles on, too.

"I told you to wait," she says. Her voice is full of emotion. "Rev, I told you to wait."

I want to hug them back, but all this motion is jostling my

arm, and the pain is so intense that I'm worried I'm going to throw up on them instead.

"I love you, too." My voice is strained. "But Mom? I really think I need an X-ray."

• • •

My wrist is broken. Again.

I don't know why, but it seems fitting. A symbol of breaking away from my father.

This time, for good.

I'm sitting in the orthopedic waiting room with Mom and Dad. I've told them everything he said. They aren't mad that I went to see him.

They're mad that I didn't tell them where I was going.

I've heard a litany of what-ifs that could fill a book.

But I listen to all of them. I listen and let their love and concern fill me up.

They take me home.

I sleep like the dead.

FORTY-FIVE

Rev

Matthew is in my room when I wake up. He's sitting on the futon, reading a book. Sunlight pours through the windows, filling the room with light.

Light? I squint and peer at the clock on my bedside stand. It's after ten o'clock in the morning.

"Hey," says Matthew. "Look who's up."

I go to sit up—and my wrist reminds me of everything that happened. The cast is like a brick running from fingers to elbow. The whole thing aches.

I flop back down. "We're skipping school?" I say to Matthew.

"Kristin said you didn't have to go."

"You, too?"

He shrugs and glances at the closet doors. "I said I wanted to see you when you woke up."

Mom probably loved that, but I don't believe him for a minute. "You didn't want to see those guys who've been bugging you." I pause. "Declan would have looked out for you. I told you that."

"Not today." Another shrug. "His mom had the baby early this morning. He left around four."

"A.M.? Was he here?"

Matthew nods.

I rub my eyes with my good hand, then try to sit up again. "I need a few minutes. Do you know if there's coffee?"

He folds a page and sets the book down. "I can make some."

There's a text message waiting on my phone. Actually, there are three of them.

Emma: Please tell me you're OK.

I'm going to have my mom drive over to your house to make sure you're okay if you don't answer this.

Apparently my mom met your mom. They exchanged numbers. Awkward. But at least I know you're okay. Text me when you wake up.

I smile.

Rev: I'm awake.

But she must not be. No answer comes back.

I lock myself in the bathroom. I can't remember what the doctor said about taking a shower, and I have no desire to get a new cast, so that can wait. Brushing my teeth left-handed is enough of a challenge that I skip shaving entirely.

Getting dressed takes twice as long as it should. The short-sleeved T-shirt has been washed and folded and is sitting on top of my laundry pile. I don't even hesitate.

And I don't bother with a sweatshirt.

Matthew is waiting in the kitchen, eating Lucky Charms out of a box. His eyes widen fractionally when he sees my bare arms, but he doesn't say anything. He rattles the box. "Want some?"

I shake my head. "I only eat cereal at night."

He doesn't act like that's odd, but he does say, "Why?"

I pull a mug down from a cabinet. A memory comes to me, but this one isn't too terrible. "When I was five years old, a woman from church gave me a box of Froot Loops. I knew my father wouldn't let me have them, so I hid them under my bed. I sat and ate them in the dark after he was asleep." I pause. "I was so scared he would catch me, but the cereal was like crack. I couldn't stop. I kept the box for months. I remember praying God would make more. He didn't. I mean—obviously. So then I thought I was being punished. For my great cereal sins."

Matthew stares at me. He's not eating now.

"Sorry." I grimace and pour some coffee. "I didn't mean to say all that."

He sets down the box. Gets a bowl and pours some cereal into it. Adds milk and a spoon.

Then he plunks the whole thing down on the counter in front of me. "The hell with your father. Eat some cereal."

I stare at him, kind of shocked. Kind of touched.

Then I sit down and eat the cereal. I have to do it left-handed, so I'm clumsy, but I eat it. It's silly, but liberating.

Matthew continues to eat his out of the box.

We're quiet, but there's no strain to it.

After a while, he speaks into the silence. "I told Kristin."

There's no question what he's talking about. His voice is completely even. He's picking through the pieces of marshmallow on his palm. I force myself to keep eating.

"Yeah?"

"Yeah. Yesterday. After school. It was just me and her. I couldn't—I kept thinking about what you said. How he could have a new kid there." He finds a marshmallow in his palm and crushes it to dust.

"What did she say?"

"She asked me if I wanted to try to press charges." He shudders. "I don't—I can't do that. After everything with Neil." He crushes another marshmallow.

"You're destroying the good parts," I say.

He looks down at the colored dust in his palm. "Oh. Sorry." He swipes his hand on his jeans. "She asked if I would mind her filing a complaint with DFS." A pause. "I said that would be okay. I think."

He's not sure about that. I can hear it in his voice.

"It'll be okay," I say. "Mom will make sure."

He falls into silence again. We crunch on Lucky Charms. I think about Declan, who's at the hospital meeting his new baby brother. I think about how much our lives have changed in the last twenty-four hours.

"Can I ask you a favor?" Matthew says.

"Anything."

That throws him, but only for a moment. "If I do something that might screw this up, would you tell me?"

I set my spoon down. The cereal has gone soggy and I'm beginning to make a mess anyway. "You won't screw this up, Matthew. Mom and Dad aren't like that."

"But—just in case."

"Okay." I carry my bowl to the sink. "Anything else?"

"No." He hesitates. "Maybe."

"What's up?"

"Do you think you could just call me Matt?"

FORTY-SIX

Emma

Today is as stunning as yesterday: warm and full of sunlight. I sleep until noon.

When I wake up, Texy is in my room, curled up beside my bed.

Mom went to get her. She went to get her. Just for me.

I sit on the floor and cry into Texy's fur. My face aches, and I'm sure I have some spectacular bruises. Shame coats me on the inside. I can't escape it.

I was so foolish. So stupid.

Mom has left me a note.

I'm looking at some condos. Let me know if you want me to come back and get you. We should make the decision together.

Maybe tonight you can show me this game you designed.
I'd love to see what you created.

Love,

Mom

It brings on a fresh round of tears.

Eventually I need to shower and brush my teeth. The bruising isn't as bad as I expect. Most of it is along the side of my face. I leave my hair down, and you wouldn't know a guy backhanded me at all.

I turn away from the mirror before a new round of tears can get moving.

Mom gave all of my computer equipment to the police last night. At the time, I wanted them to have it. Everything felt tainted.

But now I wish I could go online.

And then I realize that again, I'm trying to hide.

I whistle. "Come on, Texy. Let's go for a walk."

● ● ●

He might not be home from school yet, but maybe his mom will let me wait inside. Texy and I climb his front porch steps, and I knock softly.

Rev answers the door.

In short sleeves.

With a cast on his arm.

"Emma." His tone is rich and warm, and I want him to say my name over and over again. He looks as surprised as I feel.

Shock knocks me back a step. Mom didn't mention this detail after she talked to Rev's mom. "You—you broke your arm?"

He grimaces. "Wrist, actually." He peers at me. "Are you okay? Should you be out walking?"

"They did a CT scan. No concussion. Just bruises. I took an Advil."

"Oh. Good." He lifts the cast. "It's a tiny fracture. It's not too bad."

"So we're both just a little broken."

His arm falls back to his side. "I think we were before."

I swallow. "Yeah."

Then we stand there so long that I begin to feel foolish. Texy moves forward and nudges Rev's hands. He rubs her ears while she wags her tail and looks at me, her tongue hanging out of her mouth. Rev still says nothing.

Maybe I should go.

"Do you want to come in?" he says.

"With the dog?"

"Of course." He pulls the door wide. Texy trots right in, her nails clicking on the tile entryway.

His foster brother appears at the top of the stairs. "Oh, sweet. A dog."

Texy woofs at him, but he jogs down the steps to pet her, and she immediately becomes his best friend.

"Come on," says Rev. He takes my hand.

His fingers are warm and secure on mine as he leads me up the steps.

"Hey, Matt, keep her dog company, will you?"

Texy is currently trying to shove her massive self into Matt's lap. "Sure," he says.

I'm surprised when he leads me to his bedroom. He leaves the door open though, and tugs me toward the futon.

"Should we sit back-to-back?" I say. I'm suddenly nervous, jittery about how this is going to go.

"No. Face-to-face." He sits down cross-legged, much the same way he sat on the bench in front of the church. His cast falls into his lap, a stark white reminder of how much went wrong yesterday.

I sit more gingerly. Most of my muscles hurt. "Rev." I hesitate. "I wanted to thank you—for—for what you did—"

"You don't need to thank me." His voice is hushed. Raw. "I feel guilty that I didn't text you earlier. If I'd called—" He pauses. "It's not an excuse, but I had a lot going on."

"I shouldn't have snapped at you when you were asking me about Ethan." I swallow. "It's not an excuse, but I had a lot going on, too."

His eyes are clear, unflinchingly holding mine. "I know, Emma."

Every time he says my name, it makes me shiver. "You're the only person in my life who isn't constantly disappointing me. I wasn't—I didn't know how to handle that. So . . . I'm sorry."

"Don't be sorry." He reaches up to brush hair away from my

cheek. "I know what it's like when you don't think you have anyone you can trust."

I close my eyes and lean into his touch.

But Rev draws his hand back. "Emma—what you said to me about Ethan yesterday. When you asked if I was jealous—"

"I didn't mean that. I didn't. I'm sorry. There was never anything between me and Ethan. It was—it was all manufactured. I was just looking for someone I could lean on."

"I know."

"And I know you weren't jealous. I know you were worried."

"No—" His face twists. "No, I was worried. Very worried. Especially when I saw how creepy his text messages were." He pauses. "But before that—maybe I was jealous. A little. And I didn't realize until yesterday that I kept talking about everything happening for a reason, and I was waiting for some kind of sign, when really what I needed to do was stop *worrying* about whether I was doing the right thing, and I should just ask you out."

I stare at him. "Rev . . ."

"Emma?"

"Yes?"

"Do you want to go to Spring Fling?"

I choke on my breath and almost burst out laughing. "You want our first date to be a school dance?"

Pink colors his cheeks. "Well. I *was* going to ask if you wanted to eat chicken nuggets beside a church, but that seems so last week—"

I giggle. "Yes. To both."

He strokes my cheek again. I reach up to cover his hand with my own, and I remember the cast.

I pull his hand down and trace my fingers over the backs of his. "I can't believe you broke your wrist," I say. "You hit him that hard?"

"I wanted to hit him harder."

"Does it hurt?"

"Yesterday, I wanted to cut it off. Today it's better."

I look up at him. "Can I sign it?"

He smiles. "Sure. I think there are some Sharpies in the desk."

There are three. Red, blue, and black. I lean down over his arm. "Do you care what I write?"

"Nope. Write, draw, whatever."

I put the blue pen against the cast. He strokes my hair as I write, and it feels so good that I want to write a novel on his cast.

But then I stop and look up at him. "What *does* Rev mean? You started to tell me, but then you never finished."

"Oh." He blushes again, and looks away.

"Is it from the Bible?" I say. "Like . . . the Book of Revelation or something?"

"No." He smiles. "But that's a good guess."

His room is so quiet, and the air between us is so peaceful. Any tension that existed is gone. I never want to leave. "Is it short for Reverend? Like a religious person?"

"No."

"Is it short for—"

His mouth quirks up. "Do you want to keep guessing, or should I tell you?"

"Tell me."

"It's silly. I was seven."

"*Tell me.*"

"Okay." He holds out his arm. "You keep writing."

I do. He talks.

"It was something I heard Dad say. At dinner. He's a college professor, mostly political science, so he's always talking about *something*. When I first came here, I barely spoke at all, but I listened to *everything*. He repeated a quote. 'The revolution is not an apple that falls when it is ripe. You have to make it fall.'" He pauses. "I had just gotten away from my father. The only verses I knew were from the Bible. I held that quote in my head and said it to myself over and over again."

I stop writing and stare at him. "Revolution."

"Yes." He pauses, then gives me a teasing smile. "But you can call me Rev."

"I love that." I continue drawing on the cast, creating large block letters. "Who said it?"

"Che Guevara. He was big on radical change."

I sit back. "Look. What do you think?"

He looks down. The smile disappears, but the look that replaces it is not unhappy. "You wrote 'Fearless.'"

"Is it okay?"

He raps his fingertips against the cast. "Yes."

"Are you going to keep wearing short sleeves so people can see it?" My voice is gently teasing, but it's a genuine question.

He hesitates.

"You don't have to," I say.

"No. No, I want to." He runs an aggravated hand through his hair. "I think—for so long, I was ashamed of the scars. I saw them as a mark of all the ways I failed my father. I didn't want anyone else to know how terrible I really was."

I take his good hand in both of mine. "Rev."

"When I was in the hospital getting the cast, a nurse said to me, 'You look like you survived someone pretty terrible, son.'" He pauses. "And other people have said that to me before. But yesterday—after seeing my father—"

"You saw your father?" I almost fall off the couch.

"Yes—I don't want to talk about him. He doesn't deserve any more of my attention. But when that nurse said that, I realized she was right. He gave me these scars. I survived *him*."

"You did," I say.

He stretches out his arms. "The only thing I hate is the verse. People see it, and they start to read it, and then I have to—"

"Here. I'll fix that." I uncap the black Sharpie. I put the tip against his arm.

He holds very still. My eyes flick up. "Is this okay?"

His eyes are very close. He nods.

I write. Our breathing is loud in the space between us.

"What are you writing?" he whispers.

"I'm turning his marks into a line of barbed wire. And then above that, I'm writing, 'The revolution is not an apple that falls when it is ripe—'"

He catches my face. Presses his lips to mine. His kiss is slow and patient, just like him. A brush of lips, followed by more.

When he draws back, just a bit, I smile. "I wasn't done."

"Sorry." He offers his arm again.

"Oh, I can finish that later." I blush and cap the marker. "I meant I wasn't done kissing you."

Then I pull him back against me, and meet his lips with mine.

ACKNOWLEDGMENTS

When I introduced Rev Fletcher in *Letters to the Lost*, I knew Declan's best friend would need a past as dark and twisted as Declan's was. The more I wrote about Rev in *Letters*, the more I wanted to be able to tell his story—I just didn't think about how wrenching it would be to get inside his head. This book took a tremendous amount of support from so many people, and I'm going to do my very best to not leave anyone out.

My husband, as always, is my best friend, my confidant, my rock. He pushes me to keep writing when I really want to just curl up and binge on Netflix—or when I want to give up. He also keeps the Kemmerer boys in line when Mommy needs to hide in the back room to knock out some words. Thank you, honey, for everything.

You would not be holding this book in your hands if not for the constant encouragement my mother gave me when I was growing up. She still likes to talk about how she kept the first book I "wrote"—in third grade, about a dog. Thank you, Mom, for everything.

My agent, Mandy Hubbard, is fearless and amazing, and I am so lucky to be on this journey with her as my guide. We had the opportunity to finally meet in person, and I totally burst into tears and hugged her for like twenty minutes. (Side note: I cry at the drop of a hat.) Thank you, Mandy, for everything.

My editor, Mary Kate Castellani, is like a magician. Seriously. This book took a lot of work to get it into shape, and somehow she saw the true story through the drafts I kept sending her. Mary Kate, I consider myself lucky to be able to work with you, and I have grown so much as a writer thanks to your guidance. Thank you for your patience, your brilliance, and your insight.

The entire team at Bloomsbury has been phenomenal, from the artwork on the cover to the people who do my copy edits to the publicity team—I am going to have to buy you all pizza and roses and boxes of chocolate, because I seriously just can't believe how lucky I am to have you all in my corner. Thank you for all you do on my behalf.

My publicist, Julia Borcherts of Kaye Publicity, works tirelessly behind the scenes, and she's the most patient and encouraging woman I know. Thank you, Julia, for all you do.

My best friend Bobbie Goettler has been along for the ride since the very beginning of my writing journey, and I don't know how I would get through any of this without her. She reads every word I write and helps me figure out how to make them stronger. Bobbie, you're an inspiration as a woman and a wife and a mother, and I'm so lucky to have you in my life. Thank you for everything.

This book was read by many, many people, in many, many different forms, and I'm going to try to remember you all. If I leave you out, please grab me by the shoulders and shake me, and then demand I take you out for drinks. Alison Kemper Beard, Bobbie Goettler, Amy French, Nicole Choiniere-Kroeker, Nicole Mooney, Jim Hilderbrandt, Joy Hensley George, Lee Bross, Michelle MacWhirter, Sarah Fine, Helene Dunbar, Shyla Stokes, Darcy Jacobsen, and Lea Nolan, thank you.

This book also took a tremendous amount of research. Special thanks to Maegan Chaney-Bouis, MD, for insight into what it's like to be a pediatrician, and for some entertaining (and depressing) stories about sexism in medical school. Special thanks to Sarah Vargo Kellner and the team at Conquest for showing me that a woman can kick ass at Brazilian jiu-jitsu. Special thanks to David Ley, PhD, for some insight into the aftereffects of child abuse, as well as how Brazilian jiu-jitsu can help someone move past trauma. Finally, special thanks to Detective Sergeant L. Gary Yamin of the Baltimore Police Department for insight into online harassment and stalking, and for some truly terrifying stories about how easy it is for teenagers to get in over their head online.

Special thanks to the Kemmerer boys, Jonathan, Nick, Sam, and Zach, for being so patient when I have to hunker down to write—and for being such incredible kids to hang out with when I don't. I love you all so much.

Finally, thanks to you. Yeah, you. You're holding this book in your hands, which means you're a part of my dream. Thank you so much for taking the journey with me.

Read on for a sneak peek at
Brigid Kemmerer's next contemporary
novel—a captivating, heartfelt story
about two teens struggling in the
space between right and wrong.

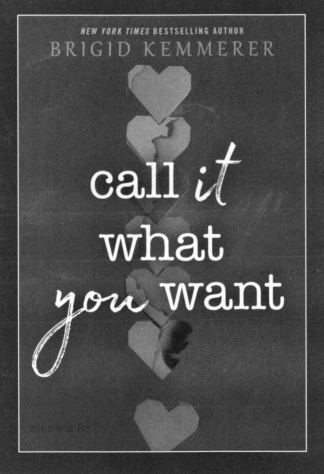

Rob

I eat breakfast with my father every morning.

Well, I eat. He sits in his wheelchair and stares in whichever direction Mom has pointed him. If I'm lucky, all his drool stays in his mouth. If he's lucky, the sunlight doesn't fall across his eyes.

Today, neither of us is very lucky.

I'm blasting alternative rock, the volume turned as loud as I can tolerate. He hated this music when he had the cognitive ability to care. I have no idea whether he can hear it now.

I like to imagine he can.

"Rob!" Mom bellows from upstairs, where she's getting ready for work. She never used to bellow.

She never used to have a job before, either.

It's been a great year.

"Rob!" she calls again.

I stare across the table at Robert Lachlan Sr. and shove a spoonful of cereal into my mouth. "You think she's talking to me or to you?"

A drop of saliva forms a circular mark on his shirt.

"What?" I yell back.

"Turn that down, please!"

"Okay."

I don't.

Until last spring, I never knew there was a right way and a wrong way to kill yourself. If you put a gun to your temple and pull the trigger, it's possible to survive.

It's also possible to miss and blow half your face off, but luckily Dad didn't do that. I'm not sure I could sit across the table from him if that had happened.

It's bad enough now. Especially knowing what he did *before* he tried to commit suicide. That's worse than all of it.

The suicide, I can kind of understand.

Mom says it's important for Dad to know I'm here. I'm not sure why. My presence isn't going to magically reconnect the neurons that will let him walk and talk and interact again.

If I could get my hands on a magic wand that would put him back together, I'd do it.

That sounds altruistic. I'm not. I'm selfish.

A year ago, we had everything.

Now we have nothing.

The living, breathing reason is sitting at the other end of the table.

I get up and turn off the music. "I'm leaving!" I call.

"Have a good day at school," Mom calls back.

Like that'll happen.

Maegan

My sister is throwing up in the bathroom. It's awesome.

I want to offer help, tissues or water or something, but I tried yesterday, and she snapped at me.

Mom says it's the hormones. Maybe she's right, though Samantha has never been someone people would call *nice*. If she's on your side, you're her best friend. If she's not, look out.

When Samantha left for college, half the cops at Dad's precinct threw her a party. It's not often that blue-collar kids go to an Ivy League school—on a full lacrosse scholarship, no less.

It's not often they come back pregnant, either.

There's a small, dark part of me that's glad I'm not the troublemaker, this time.

Another part of me squashes the thought and shoves it away. That's not fair to my sister. Unlike her, I've always been someone people call nice.

Well, until last spring, when people started calling me *cheater*.

The toilet flushes. Water runs. A minute later, Sam's door closes quietly.

Mom appears in my doorway. She's in a bathrobe, a towel wound high on her head. Her voice is soft. "Dad says he can drive you to school, if you're ready now."

"Almost."

"I'll let him know." She hesitates in the doorway. "Maegan . . . about your sister's condition—"

"You mean the baby?" I study my reflection in the mirror, wondering if the ponytail is a mistake. My fair skin looks pale and washed-out already. Besides, the first day of November has brought freezing temperatures, and my homeroom class has a cracked window.

She eases into the room and closes the door. "Yes. The baby."

I wonder if Samantha had hoped to keep the pregnancy a secret, even from our parents. She was already planning to come home this weekend, so her appearance wasn't unexpected. I just don't think she'd planned on walking in the door, hugging Mom, and then throwing up on her feet.

Even that might have been explainable, but then Sam burst into tears.

Mom's not an idiot.

Then again, Mom and Sam have always been close. Sam probably would have told her anyway. Just without the projectile vomiting. I reach for a colorful scarf. "What about it?"

"Your sister doesn't want anyone to know yet." Mom wrings her hands. "She's only ten weeks pregnant, so she's trying . . . she's trying to decide what to do." A pause. I wonder if my mother can't bring herself to say the word *abortion*. "I'm asking you to respect her wishes."

I pull on a denim jacket over my sweater. "I won't tell anyone."

"Maegan, your sister deserves your compassion."

"Mom. No one talks to me. Who would I tell?"

"Rachel?"

My best friend. I hesitate.

Mom's eyes almost fall out of her head. "*Maegan*. Did you tell her already?"

"No! No. Of course not."

"You know your father doesn't want gossip."

That makes me pause. I don't want to let Dad down. Well, I don't want to let him down *again*. "I won't say anything."

"Not to *anyone*, Maegan." Her gaze turns steely. "I need to know we can count on you."

I flinch. Dad honks the horn out front.

I grab my backpack. "I need to go."

"Be good!" she calls after me.

She says it every time I leave the house.

I used to say, "I always am," but that's not true anymore.

Instead, I say, "I'll try," and I let the door slam behind me.

READ ON FOR A GLIMPSE AT BRIGID KEMMERER'S *NEW YORK TIMES* BESTSELLING REIMAGINING OF "BEAUTY AND THE BEAST"!

"Has everything you'd want in a retelling of a classic fairy tale." —Jodi Picoult, *New York Times* bestselling author of *A Spark of Light* and *Small Great Things*

"Absolutely spellbinding." —Stephanie Garber, #1 *New York Times* bestselling author of *Caraval* and *Legendary*

RHEN

There is blood under my fingernails. I wonder how many of my people I've killed this time.

I thrust my hands into the barrel beside the stables. The ice-cold water bites at my skin, but the blood clings. I shouldn't bother, because it will all be gone in an hour anyway, but I hate this. The blood. The not knowing.

Hooves ring against the cobblestones somewhere behind me, followed by the jingle of a horse's bridle.

I don't need to look. My guard commander always follows at a safe distance until the transition is complete.

Guard commander. As if Grey has men left to command.

As if he didn't earn the title by default.

I swipe the water from my hands and turn. Grey stands a few yards back, holding the reins of Ironheart, the fastest horse in the stables. The animal is blowing hard, its chest and flanks damp with sweat despite the early-morning chill.

For as long as we've been trapped here, Grey's appearance is somehow a continual surprise. He looks as young as the day he earned a position in the elite Royal Guard, his dark hair slightly unkempt, his face unlined. His uniform still fits him well, every buckle and strap perfectly arranged, every weapon shining in the near darkness.

He once carried a gleam of eagerness in his eye, a spark for adventure. For challenge.

That gleam has long since gone dark, the only aspect of his appearance that is never remade by the curse.

I wonder if my unchanged appearance startles him, too.

"How many?" I say.

"None. All of your people are safe this time."

This time. I should be relieved. I am not. My people will be at risk again soon enough. "And the girl?"

"Gone. As always."

I look back at the blood staining my hands, and a familiar tightness wraps around my rib cage. I turn back to the barrel and bury my hands in the water. It's so cold it nearly steals my breath.

"I'm covered in blood, Commander." A lick of anger curls through my chest. "I killed *something.*"

As if sensing danger, his horse stomps and dances at the end of the reins. Grey puts out a hand to calm the animal.

Once there would have been a stablehand rushing to take his horse, especially upon hearing my tone. Once there was a castle full of courtiers and historians and advisers who would have turned over a coin for a bit of gossip about Prince Rhen, heir to the throne of Emberfall.

Once there was a royal family that would have frowned on my antics.

Now there is me, and there is Grey.

"I left a trail of human blood on the path out of the forest," he says, unaffected by my anger. He's used to this. "The horse led a good chase, until you fell on a herd of deer in the southernmost part of your lands. We stayed well away from the villages."

That explains the condition of the animal. We traveled far tonight.

"I'll take the horse," I say. "The sun will be up soon."

Grey hands over the reins. This final hour is always the hardest. Full of regret for my failure once again. As always, I just want to get this over with.

"Any special requests, my lord?"

In the beginning, I was frivolous enough to say yes. I'd specify blondes or brunettes. Big breasts, or long legs, or tiny waists. I'd wine them and woo them and when they did not love me, another was easily found. The first time, the curse had seemed like a game.

Find me one you *like, Grey,* I'd said, laughing, as if finding women for his prince was a privilege.

Then I changed, and the monster tore through the castle, leaving a bloodbath.

When the season began again, I had no family left. No servants. Only six guardsmen, two of whom were badly injured.

By the third season, I had one.

Grey is still waiting for a response. I meet his eyes. "No, Commander. Anyone is fine." I sigh and begin leading the horse toward the stables, but then stop and turn. "Whose blood made the trail?"

Grey raises an arm and draws his sleeve back. A long knife wound still bleeds down into his hand, a slow trickle of crimson.

I'd order him to bind it, but the wound will be gone in an hour, when the sun is fully up.

So will the blood on my hands and the sweat on the horse's flanks. The cobblestones will be warm with early-fall sunlight, and my breath will no longer fog in the morning air.

The girl will be gone, and the season will begin again.

I'll be newly eighteen.

For the three hundred twenty-seventh time.

Brigid Kemmerer is the *New York Times* bestselling author of *Letters to the Lost, More Than We Can Tell, A Curse So Dark and Lonely, Call It What You Want*, the YALSA-nominated Elementals series, and the paranormal mystery *Thicker Than Water*. She was born in Omaha, Nebraska, though her parents quickly moved her all over the United States, from the desert in Albuquerque, New Mexico, to the lakeside in Cleveland, Ohio, and several stops in between. Brigid is now settled near Annapolis, Maryland, with her husband and children.

www.brigidkemmerer.com

@BrigidKemmerer

These **real-life** stories will **remain** with you **long after** you've **turned the last page.**

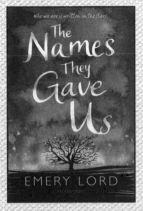

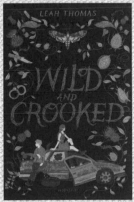

www.bloomsbury.com • Twitter: BloomsburyKids • Snapchat: BloomsburyYA

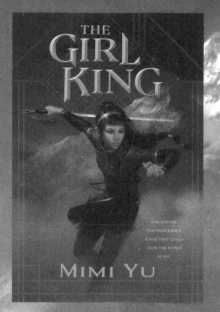
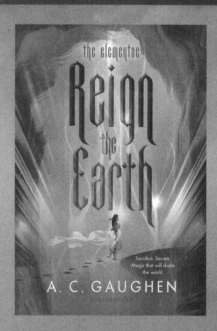
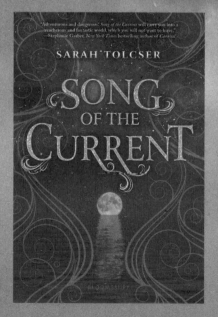